"Moving between England, Australia, and Malaysia, between the past and the present, between the old and the young, this is both a cracking story with compelling settings, and an absorbing and moving testimony to the complementary powers of romantic and familial love. It explores the meaning of a happy ending, and stresses the importance of seizing second chances, however late in the day they are presented to us, and however temporary the joy they bring."
ROSIE MILNE, AUTHOR, *CIRCUMSTANCE; TRUTH AND LIES IN THE MALAYAN JUNGLE*

"I found this book difficult to put down. Excellently written with memorable characters faced with the dangers of guerrilla warfare, interlaced with a once in a lifetime romance... in the hands of this master storyteller all the threads of the story come together in a wonderful climax.... at times Gidley's writing reminded me of Pearl S. Buck and Nevil Shute."
SALLY CRONIN, AUTHOR, *LIFE IS LIKE A MOSAIC*

"An absorbing story set in 1950s Malaya during the Emergency uprising. The backdrop and historical period are brilliantly evoked, from the dangers of jungle warfare to the bustle and glamour of Penang. At its heart is a poignant love story—the second half of the book follows up in more modern times—with strong, engaging characters about whom you come to really care. Based loosely on the author's own parents, this is an emotional and satisfying read."
JANET MACLEOD TROTTER, AUTHOR, *THE RAJ HOTEL SERIES*

"A gripping read that reminded me of the haunting sadness of classics such as *A Town Like Alice* and *Brief Encounter*, while becoming thoroughly absorbed in the authentic descriptions of post-war Malaya, rural Queensland, and sleepy Dorset, which the author describes with a pen dipped in affectionate familiarity."
DAVID FIELD, AUTHOR, *THE TUDOR SAGA SERIES*

"Gidley's vivid writing pulls you into the past and into the steamy, predator-ridden jungles of wartime Penang with adept story-telling that flows between 1948 and present day. The author creates a wraparound sensory experience for not only historical fiction buffs, but anyone drawn to intense, character-driven, drama-filled suspense."
ANNE O'CONNELL, AUTHOR, *DEEP DECEIT*

Praise

About the Author

A transient life has seen Anglo-Australian Apple Gidley live in countries as diverse as Trinidad and Thailand, Nigeria and the Netherlands, and another eight in between. St. Croix in the US Virgin Islands is home, for now.

Her roles have been varied—editor, intercultural trainer for multi-national corporations, British Honorary Consul to Equatorial Guinea, amongst others.

Gidley started writing in 2010 and is now working on a contemporary novel whilst researching for two more historical fiction books. She has short stories in anthologies, and also writes a regular blog, A Broad View.

www.applegidley.com

Have You Eaten Rice Today?

Apple Gidley

In memory of
Major John Girling, OBE
and
Major Jack St Aubyn
and
for all those who fought
for
Merdeka

Author's Note

This book has been bubbling for many years. It is a work of fiction based around actual events and people. I have taken liberties with some dates and have put words into real peoples' mouths—I hope in the vein in which they would have spoken. A few of those words are Malay and, in case their meaning is not clear, there is a glossary at the back.

A large portion of my childhood was spent in Malaysia and it is a country I love. I grew up with stories from my parents who met in the jungles of Pahang during the Emergency, and there they were back in Kuala Lumpur ten years later, with me in tow. But this is not their tale.

A note of explanation. The Federation of Malaya from 1948 comprised nine Malay states and two British Straits Settlements, Penang and Malacca, until independence in 1963, when the British colonies of Sarawak, Sabah, and Singapore joined the Federation and thereafter became known as Malaysia. Singapore left the Federation in 1965.

Have You Eaten Rice Today? is a story of endurance, honor, duty and love—with those four things the world can be conquered.

Prologue

THE REFLECTION, blurred around the edges in the mirror by steam from the hot shower, showed a slight man in a summer-weight tan suit, white shirt, ubiquitous tie and buffed shoes. His white hair, combed back, showed the barest of receding hairlines, and his brown eyes glowed behind rimless spectacles. The silver topped cane by his side gleamed.

Simon nodded, smiled, and made his way down the marble staircase of the E&O Hotel in Penang. Waiting at the foot of the stairs was his grandson.

The mâitre d' showed them to a low table surrounded by library chairs in the Planters Lounge. On the wall behind them hung a sepia map of Malaysia. Mirrored Peranakan cupboards stood guard either side and elegant brass lamps shed pockets of light. An oriental teak screen separated the area from the rest of the room, giving privacy but allowing air to circulate. Celadon jars lined a long sideboard, adding a subdued splash of color to the simple palette.

It was perfect. Straight out of Maugham. Max was itching to take notes.

"*Selamat petang, tuan,*" the waiter said in greeting, his smile taking in the old man's tie. He continued in English. "My father, he too Malay Regiment."

Max listened as his grandfather responded and rattled off an order, all in Malay.

"You're good, Fa. What have you ordered?"

"Champagne, to be followed by afternoon tea."

"Perfect. That's perfect." Max realized he'd have to come up with a different adjective. He looked around in silence and wondered at Fa's complete ease. "You're not in the least concerned, are you?"

"No. Strangely, I'm not."

Part One

Then

Chapter 1

Malaya, 1948

A PERSISTENT BUZZING brought Simon Frampton from the depths of sleep, rarely dreamless, and always jungle green. Dawn trickled through half-opened louvres and with it came mosquitoes. The little buggers could get through the most tightly tucked net, though closer inspection showed a number of tears in this particular one. A four-blade fan turned idly, shifting the once-white netting in a mesmerizing, grubby blur. Remnants of torn posters fluttered on otherwise bare, paint-peeling walls and gave glimpses of lurid scenes from Hindi-language films.

A speck of blood showed Simon had murdered one irritant and, rolling to the side of the low, slatted bed, he pushed his way out of the cocoon and padded, naked, to the window. Angling the louvres, he stood to the side and looked out over the corrugated iron lean-to at the back of the shophouse where Ah Tok had hidden his bicycle last night.

Ipoh, the capital of Perak, was slowly waking. Overnight rain made the streets sparkle in the watery morning glow and humidity would soon swamp the cool dawn air. The smell of coffee beans roasted in palm-oil margarine drifted up from kitchens, and he could hear mothers and grandmothers haranguing children, Mandarin and Malay filling the air. A hawker slip-slopped along the back street to market, a thin bamboo pole balanced across his shoulders with a basket at each end swaying in syncopated rhythm with his steps.

Simon looked around the room again. He hadn't stayed here before. Not quite the Club, but the sheets were clean and with Ah Tok on the ground floor and an escape route out the window onto the lean-to roof, Simon had been able to grab a few hours kip.

Three soft taps on the door, then a pause followed by a single rap, gave Simon time to tie a sarong around his waist. The old signal. Some things were never forgotten. He turned to face a plump, bald Chinaman sidling into the room with a cup of sweet steaming char, clean clothes draped over his arm.

"You are refreshed, *tuan?*" he asked in Malay, hurrying on before Simon could reply. "Drink. Then you go."

"I'm sorry, Ah Tok. Please thank Ah Moi. I won't show up again."

"*Ayaa, tuan.* Always can come. Bad time. Again. Like with Japs, nuh?"

***

Tucking his chin down, his shoulders dropping, Simon pushed the rusted bicycle out between the narrow shophouses, his feet scuffing the dusty lane. Funny how all the old tricks had come rushing back. Still, it had only been three years since his last foray into the murky world of covert operations. He had considered fore-going a wash before he left Ah Tok's place but the lure of ice-cold water from the Shanghai jar had been too great. He always had to shave. His thick stubble would tell the least observant person he was neither Chinese nor Malay, despite the tan. His wiry frame was an advantage and, though taller than the average Asian, as soon as he donned the clothes of a coolie, he managed to lose his added height. Ah Tok's baggy clothes were clean but unpressed, the trousers flapping above his ankles. He pulled his straw hat low and his feet, already dirty, slapped in worn sandals.

Missing Bob Thompson, the assistant commissioner of labor in Perak, the evening before had been a blow. Quite apart from looking forward to a *stengah* with his old friend, who had an unerring ability to gauge the mood of those around him, he had hoped to learn what the powers-that-be in Kuala Lumpur were planning.

Simon kept his head bent as he cycled out of town, but his eyes darted left and right, seeking any unexpected movement—the silence of an *amah* moments before bartering with a hawker, the sudden twist or lowered head, the reach of a hand inside clothing. What could be an attempt to kill him, or at least report him, could merely be the innocent day-to-day transactions of life. He shook his head. No one was trying to kill him. At least not yet. Although, if current events continued, that could change.

Within a matter of weeks Malaya had been plunged under a night-time curfew, with emergency laws of stop-and-search in an attempt to calm the mayhem of a concerted communist insurrection. An Englishman in coolie clothes with a Browning tucked tightly into his tied trousers would require an explanation he'd rather not give, and he needed to find out what he could through unofficial channels. For the time being he needed to be invisible. He sighed. He should've worn a sarong and *songkok*, Malays might be less likely to be stopped by nosy policemen. Everyone knew the Malay Communist Party was made up of mainly Chinese, but he had always found it easier to emulate the gait of a Chinese laborer rather than that of a Malay fisherman or farmer.

After the massacre of three British planters on rubber plantations near Sungai Siput it was hard to understand anyone having any empathy for the murdering bastards. Over the years Simon had shared stories and *stengahs* at the club with all three assassinated men. It was personal now, and the reason he had slipped away from the rubber plantation he managed, leaving only written instructions for his Indian assistant. He wondered if his masters in London had received his resignation yet. What a bloody mess Malaya was in danger of becoming, again.

Simon tightened his grip on the handlebars. The gap between his front teeth showed in a slight grin. He didn't know which was worse: bandits in the jungle, informers on the streets of Ipoh, or the security forces on edge. He pedaled south beside the sluggish waters of Sungai Kinta toward the tin-mining center of Batu Gajah, the action of an old man to anyone he happened upon, though his agile mind juggled all that was happening.

Chin Peng, so recently honored by the Queen for his bravery and support during the war against the Japanese, now put his considerable talents into causing havoc for the British and, at twenty-six, he'd risen quickly through the communist ranks. Simon found it incredible the man reportedly had a number of Japanese under his command. Expediency. And the irony was galling. Chin Peng and a few other members of the MCP were eligible for a British wartime pension.

Chin Peng's brutality, a man he had known, appalled him. The horror of the police station in Jerantut, in Pahang, being shot up and burned with policemen inside had struck a new low. Exacerbated by the summary execution of the first villager who dared show his face on the streets. The Communist Terrorist's determination to create terror in the hearts of villagers escalated when, at the lines of a rubber plantation near Kuala Lipis, they grabbed the wife and daughters of a man brave enough to attack and kill one of their own with a *parang* before being shot himself, prodded them at gunpoint into a hut and set fire to it. Simon's shudder at the savagery sent a wobble through his bicycle.

"*Selamat pagi.*" A man wearing a faded sarong and tattered shirt clambered up the bank of the river using a bamboo fishing rod as leverage. His face, partially obscured by a battered hat, was the color of weak tea. Simon returned the greeting and, keeping his head low, pumped his legs faster.

"*Saudara,* have you eaten rice today?" The man's voice calling him brother and enquiring as to his welfare, soft but insistent, followed him down the road.

This is what Simon hated. The uncertainty. He stopped. The man shuffled closer and as he neared his face broke into a broad grin.

"Fooled you!" The voice deepened, still quiet, still speaking Malay.

"Hobbs? Good God, you did."

"It took me a moment to realize it was you. You look so old."

"Thanks. I feel it," Simon replied in Malay.

Frank Hobbs nodded to a narrow path leading across paddy fields to one of the many small lakes in the area.

"Come on, there's a shack over there. We can talk."

Simon rolled the bicycle down the ditch and pushed it into the undergrowth. The men walked, unspeaking, along low berms to the hut. Nails protruded where planks had rotted and corrugated roofing hung in jagged strips. A gunnysack lay soggy in one corner, around it a few grains of scattered rice. Droppings littered the floor.

"Nice quarters," Simon said, reverting to English, his voice hushed.

"Indeed. But safe. And whilst we might be seen we can also see. Don't suppose you've got any cigarettes? Mine ended up in the river."

"Why the disguise?" Simon tugged a pack of Players from his pocket.

"I might ask you the same question. Thought it time to disappear. It's all right. I've got the blessing from on high. I was getting tired of being tied to a desk anyway." Frank grinned. "You too?"

"Enjoy it while you can," Simon said, nodding to the question and the cigarette. The men were silent as they watched smoke linger in wispy curls before wafting away on the light breeze that rippled across the shallow lake. "It'll be back to smoking any old leaves if we end up in the jungle again. A distinct possibility I'd say, if the last couple of weeks are anything to go by. Is the mine still dredging?"

"Of course. Got to keep the tin coming. It's a bit uneasy though. Suspicion threads its way through everything. At least with the Japanese we had a common enemy. Most of our people are Chinese which, I imagine, will bring its own problems. Who to trust, sort of thing."

"Where were you headed?" Simon asked.

"Ipoh," Frank replied. "Looking for Bob Thompson. He might have a job for me. Not many of us speak Malay, Mandarin, and Tamil."

"You're right there. But good luck finding Bob. I missed him last night."

"What do you think? Force 136 back in business?" Frank asked, referring to the cover name for a branch of the wartime Special Operations Executive in Southeast Asia.

"Distinct possibility, I'd say."

"Bloody business with Sir Arthur and the others at Sungai Siput," Frank said. "He was a good chap. They all were."

"That they were. However I can't help feeling the attacks weren't sanctioned by Chin Peng. In any event, the balloon's gone up and you can bet the MCP have scarpered into the *ulu*. I have no doubt they have caches of guns hidden. Arms we gave them, I might add."

"Different war, Frampton. Different time."

"Of course, but it does stick in one's craw somewhat."

They smoked silently. Simon looked over the shimmering green shoots of undulating young rice, his mind on Edward Gent. The man instrumental in forming the Malayan Union, and its first Governor, had refused to take the communist threat seriously.

"If that bloody man Gent had listened to us all, we might not be in this mess." Frank's tone was acerbic. "To promise the Chinese citizenship then rescind it. No wonder they're antsy. Can't blame them, they've been living on the fringes for years. And it's sending them to the MCP in droves. For Christ's sake, over 300 strikes last year."

"Destroy the rubber industry, the tin mining. Provoke mass unemployment and people will turn to communism. Or that's the theory." Simon scraped the stub of his cigarette on the bottom of his sandal, blew on it then put it back in the box. Old habits died hard.

"Did you see *The Straits Times* the day after the murders?" Frank asked. "Told Gent in no uncertain terms, 'Govern or Get Out.'"

"Well, he got out! At least he issued Stens to the police before he left. And to those planters able to handle them."

"While stocks last. I have a ghastly feeling this is not going to be a short-lived insurgency."

They talked a while longer then, each again donning their slouch, switched back to Malay as they neared the road and separated, arranging to meet in Ipoh at the end of the week. They agreed Frank would continue on in the hopes of catching up with Bob Thompson to speak to him on their behalf. Simon remained on the road to Batu Gajah, to see for himself the preparedness of tin mines in the area, and the mood of people in the town.

The short dusk switched to night and Simon kept to the deepening shadows of the Government Guest House gardens on Jalan Changkat, hoping to slip unseen up the outside stairs behind the kitchen. The cook raised his eyebrows before turning back to the pot, his wooden spoon spiraling an aromatic mustardy scent into the air that reminded Simon he hadn't eaten properly for three days. In a short few weeks Malaya had been thrust back into a time when it was better not to ask why a dirty Englishman was wandering around dressed like a coolie.

Simon nodded, then took the stairs two at a time to the room kept available for people like him. People in the shadows. He sighed. It was as if the war had never ended. He hoped this one would not be as long or as deadly. But no one was mentioning the word "war." If Gent was to be believed, the murders at the rubber plantations at

Sungai Siput were a short blip in an otherwise smooth transition to independence.

The door to the sparse room creaked open. Simon stripped and sank into the claw-foot tub, metal showing through the scarred enamel. He closed his eyes with a sigh as tepid water washed off the day's dust. His body ached. He hadn't ridden a bicycle for a long time. He might have dozed. Through the watery cocoon he heard banging, then a subdued voice.

"Frampton?"

Water dripped as Simon reached for a towel, not quite white but smelling clean. Wrenching the door open he saw the squat, athletic figure of James Landon, manager of the Phin Soon Mine.

"What the hell? Jim?"

"The ever-vigilant Sulung saw you from behind the bar. Trouble."

"The mine?"

"Not sure. I heard shots. Bastards. Can you come? Just in case."

"Give me a minute. You armed?"

"Yes. You?"

"Yes." Simon hopped on one leg as he thrust the other into his grimy trousers, a laborer once again.

"Hopefully we won't need to be. Did you happen to bump into Frank Hobbs?"

"I did."

"Good, then you understand why I'm edgy. Come on. Rumblings in the jungle."

Night was the scent of gardenias, the rustle of birds settling, the scuttle of a marauding mongoose heading back to its burrow, shadows dipping and weaving in the evening breeze and, in the distance, the sound of rapid gunfire.

"You've still got the Minx," Simon said, as they leapt into the Hillman.

"Yes, I didn't keep her safe throughout the war to have a bunch of bloody commies destroy her now." Jim spun the wheels of his precious car on the gravel drive.

"Stop shy of the gates," Simon said, numbed by an image of the mine, spindly on countless wooden trestles and struts, tumbling down with a well-placed bomb. He shook his head. "No point racing in. Let's see what's happening first."

"They'll have come through the back," Jim said, his mouth a grim line. "By the village. It's our weak spot. We haven't enclosed it yet. Mind you, none of the women want to be fenced in. Can't say I blame them. But this might change their minds. Christ, I hope young Ian Maclean's alright. Rather wet behind the ears. And very nervous after Sungai Siput. I shouldn't have left him."

"No point worrying about that now. Stop here. We'll walk the rest of the way."

Shots echoed over the dredge spoil, the naked ground to the side of the tin mine, and filtered through the trees—giant mahoganies—on either side of the gate. The men ducked behind the Hillman. Simon shut his eyes and clenched his teeth at the sound of panicked, screaming women. He'd hoped never to hear the sound again.

And then it stopped. The gunfire at least.

Jim straightened from his crouch.

"Stay down. Wait." Simon's voice was a hiss. "I'll go. I'm dressed the part."

"Be quick," Jim said. "That poor sod, Ian, will be in a tizzy."

***

A metallic smell lingered on the still air. An uneasy calm fell across the mine's quarters once the insurgents, their aim achieved, slipped back into the jungle, and after Jim's assurances of protection to his assembled workers.

"Baptism by fire, Maclean. Baptism by fire." Simon took the glass of *Chap Puteh* and raised the Dewar's whisky to the young man bent over the drink's trolley like a sapling. His red hair, a raked mess, made the pallor of his face more pronounced.

The decanter shook in Ian's hand, clinking the glasses as he poured, "Christ. I couldn't think straight." He drank deeply.

"Not many can. You did well, lad," Jim said. "All you could do."

"Really? I hid in the cupboard, along with Singh." Ian's voice was hoarse, his Scottish burr broad.

"Best place to be, I'd say," Simon said. "Doesn't seem as if they were intent on serious damage. More a warning."

"Why tonight? It's not pay day."

"Not a warning to you necessarily, Jim," said Simon. "More to your people. A 'we can get to you whether you're behind a fence or not' sort of message."

It was impossible not to be aware of Chinese endorsement of the communist cause. Many squatted on the edge of towns and villages, gathering information and supplying food to bandits living in jungle camps. Known members of the Min Yuen—the People's Movement, the civilian wing of the MCP—were being rounded up by the SF, the security forces made up of all races. It did not take long for news to travel the jungle grapevine, whispered from plantation to tin mine and back. Cooperate with the communists or face a merciless execution.

"Glad you were here, Frampton," Jim said after a moment's silence. "Not sure it was part of your plan but would you mind staying? Another gun might come in handy."

"I was heading this way tomorrow," Simon said, a smile not quite reaching his tired eyes. "I think my questions have been answered. As far as I know this is the first attack on a tin mine. But I fear it won't be the last. I wonder whether they'll go after any of the American concerns or whether they'll stick to British companies."

"God, in all the fuss," Jim said, "I forgot to ask whether you knew Gent has been recalled to London."

"I heard. Thirteen days after he declared an emergency. Must be some kind of record. Do we know who's replacing him?"

"Not yet," Ian replied, his color returning with the warmth of the whisky.

***

The narrow cot sagged, wedging Simon in the dip. He lay under a mosquito net, his hands behind his head, his pistol under the low bed, as he thought about the country he considered home. Called the Golden Peninsula by the ancient Greeks and Romans, Malaya had been dominated by Hindus and Buddhists until Muslim traders in the 14th century encouraged the adoption of Islam. And then the Europeans. It was always trade. And greed. First the Portuguese, then the Dutch and, not to be outdone, the British in the 1800s. Now, after rooting out the Japanese during the war, it appeared China was intent on taking over the country.

Despite Malaya being once again rolled in barbed wire, like stitches crisscrossing the very face of the peninsula, life in the cities remained relatively unchanged. Business as usual was being carried out to the fullest. "Can't let the buggers win" became the battle cry in the clubs, especially at The Dog, The Selangor Club, overlooking tennis matches and cricket on the *padang* in Kuala Lumpur, where *stengahs* flowed each evening.

But in rural areas life was not as sanguine. It was this last thought, and the memory of Ian Maclean's pale face, that accompanied Simon as he finally fell asleep.

Chapter 2

Townsville, Australia

THE SCENT OF EUCALYPTUS hung in the air as the paddle rested across her bare legs and the canoe scraped the bottom of the riverbed. Sunshine trickled through over-hanging gum trees and lit patches of iridescent blue on the wings of a pair of kookaburras. They watched Dee from their branch, bulging brown eyes gleaming through distinctive dark eye stripes like masked bandits. The male gave a low hiccupping chuckle before throwing his head back in raucous laughter. Dee smiled. It was hard not to.

After a disjointed night, she'd risen before dawn knowing sleep would not return, even on her day off. She'd tell them over breakfast. The canoe began to drift and Dee dug the paddle into the sand and held steady as an Eastern Gray hopped to the water's edge. She'd miss the 'roos, joeys peeking out of pouches until, in her humble opinion, they were far too old and quite able to hop themselves. The kangaroo jerked up from her drink, startled, then lurched around and took off.

"Righto, no putting it off," Dee muttered. She slid over the side, hauled the canoe high up the bank, and hid it under some brush. Other kookaburras had joined in the laughter and their strident exuberance followed her up the narrow path to the battered jeep, a gift from a former beau, a departing US Air Force pilot stationed in Townsville during the war—a gift she wasn't sure he had been at liberty to give, but one she accepted, nonetheless.

***

Showered and changed, Dee joined her brother and parents in the kitchen, the smell of sizzling bacon a reminder she had skipped supper the previous night, too tired, too excited, too terrified as she left the hospital after a twelve-hour shift.

"G'day, darl." Her father grinned around his mug of coffee. "You were up early for a working girl."

"George!" Her mother's voice was a suppressed rumble. "That is not an apt descriptor for your daughter. She is a nurse."

"Still a working girl, Ma," Dee's brother, Les, weighed in.

"Bit harder than you, mate," George said. "You sloped off the minute glasses were in the sink."

"That would be on account of Sally." Dee avoided her brother's glare.

"Who's Sally?" Fran, their mother, asked.

"The new teacher at the primary school," Dee replied.

"You're courting?" George asked.

"More than courting," Dee said. "Ouch!" She punched her brother back.

"Give it a rest, kids. Geez, you'd think you were still teenagers."

"Well, whoever she is, I need you at the pub until we're done. Got it?"

"Yeah, Dad, sorry. Can we have brekky now?"

Dee watched her mother break another egg into the frying pan and felt a pang. Six kids and a hungry husband used to necessitate a dozen eggs each morning. Now she cracked four. Dee sipped her coffee.

"Um, I've got something to say."

Her father put down his cup. "As long as you're not chasing that Yank over to America, it's okay. I know you still write."

"No, Dad. And you liked Seth."

George stretched his long legs under the scarred kitchen table and rubbed the morning stubble on his chin, a smile in his voice as he said, "Not that much. Never liked his name."

"I didn't," her brother said.

"You liked the gum. Now shut up," Dee said, standing.

Her mother looked up from sliding fried eggs onto plates. She clattered the pan back on the range and sat down with a plop.

"It's bad, whatever it is. You normally blurt."

"Oh, Ma, it's not bad. It's exciting and scary all rolled up together." Dee paused and gulped as tension tightened her jaw. "I'm going to Malaya!"

"What?"

Dee glanced at her father, not daring to look at her mother.

"You're bloody not," he said.

"They need nurses."

"Not you!"

"We need nurses. All those poor boys still in rehab hospitals. That big one north of Brissie. You could go there." There were tears in her mother's eyes.

"Come on, Ma. You know why I went into nursing."

"Doesn't mean you have to go halfway around the world to some other war. One that has nothing to do with us."

"It's not a war, Ma. It's a civil disturbance. They call it an Emergency."

"I don't care what they call it. It's got nothing to do with Australia."

"It would if the commies got to us through Asia," said Les.

Dee shot her brother a grateful look. The argument went back and forth until George and Les left to open up the pub. Fran stared into space from her chair at the end of the table, her finger tracing nicks in the old oak. Dee washed and dried the dishes, hanging the tea towel across the Aga rail to dry. She stoked the oven before sitting opposite her mother and taking her hands.

"Ma, nothing's going to happen."

"That's what Ronnie and Mitch said when they went off to war."

"I know. But I'm not going to a war. I'll be running a little clinic in a town. Safe as houses. You've got Les and Jimmy here. And David's not too far away. I've got to do this, Ma. I'm restless."

"I know, love. I just hoped you wouldn't go so far, or somewhere dangerous. What'll I do without you?"

"It's only for two years, Ma. It'll go in a blink."

***

The letter from the British Red Cross had come six weeks before Dee's departure date. Time enough to give notice, get uniforms made, and have qualms. She spent any spare time on the Ross River, canoeing up and down between the weirs, taking her fill of the sunbirds and drongos, the occasional osprey and, sometimes while trailing her hand in the waters, feeling the skim of the hard shell of a Krefft's turtle coming to the surface. She would miss the serenity.

Amid more tears, Dee had begged her mother not to accompany her to Brisbane to see her aboard the RMS *Mooltan*, her passage via Darwin to Singapore. Instead, her parents and three remaining brothers waved her off from the station platform in Townsville. She flopped into the seat and breathed a sigh. She was on her way.

In under a month her new life would begin. Weeks in which Dee would have a respite between worlds.

***

The RMS *Mooltan* had only recently been reconditioned after her war years spent first as an armed merchant cruiser, then as a troop ship. Her dummy stack, removed to allow a greater arc for anti-aircraft guns, had been rebuilt shorter than the original and she was once again painted in the traditional P&O colors of a white-banded black hull, her boot topping red, and funnels black.

Dee was grateful her two-bunk, second-class cabin was not shared, though she liked the company of some passengers. Men either returning to Malaya after a leave spent at home, or venturing into a new world, as she was. Others were families, the Ten Pound Poms who had flocked to Australia from Britain after the war, only to find it not to their liking and were heading back to all they knew.

Remorse prickled as the ship sailed north and neared Townsville, and her parents' grief immersed her in a desolation of her own. An image surfaced of the family before the war, bantering with her brothers over tea, immune to the magnificence of the bush spreading before them, sure that life would never change. A time when their lives stretched ahead and thoughts of distance and death never crossed their minds. Ronnie and Mitch killed in battles oceans away from home. The family had lost so much and now their only daughter was running away. Her mother, stoic and hardworking, had been unable to stop her tears or pleading. Her father had retreated to the pub, only for the argument to be replayed each meal time, until she was desperate to leave. Before her resolve wavered.

Only Les understood. His words returned to her, as if he were standing on the shore shouting them across the waves, "I sorta get it, Dee. You've always been the adventurous one. You've got more guts than me though. Good on yer." Words and tears flung away by the wind did not lessen the sting of her guilt.

She stayed on deck to give a final wave to everything she knew as they passed Magnetic Island, an important defense post guarding Townsville during the war. Known as "Maggie" to the locals, it was a place filled with childhood memories of days spent on the beach and nights under canvas, then later frolicking in the protected cove of Horseshoe Bay with friends in the armed forces.

Dee walked the wide decks twice a day, enjoying stiff breezes and views of the changing landscape as mountains melted into wooded flatlands around Cape York, the tip top of Australia. At times it felt like the ship was dodging islands as they sailed through the Torres Straits dividing Australia from New Guinea, then across the Gulf of Carpentaria towards the capital of the Northern Territory.

She shivered as they approached the wharf in Darwin, devastation still evident after the Japanese attacks on February 19th, 1942, the first of many throughout that and the following year. The same bombers had unleashed their cargo on Pearl Harbor two months earlier. Darwin, also unprepared and a less strategic target, had been bombarded by many more bombs than the American base in Hawaii, although fewer people had been killed.

Australia faded into the distance and RMS *Mooltan* wove her way north through the Java Sea. Dee felt her meshed emotions unravel as the miles between her and home lengthened. Relief that the shadows of her brothers' deaths no longer washed over her in an unending stream of sorrow allowed her to prepare, although for what she was not quite sure.

A couple of young men boarded in Darwin to head to a place called Raub where an Australian firm mined for gold. They were entertaining company who helped pass the time each evening. They all wondered what lay ahead as the ship approached Singapore and, just beyond the island, the Malay Peninsula.

***

Sunrise threw the world into a pink and gold cauldron that contrasted sharply with the uniform green of mangroves lining the shores. Silhouetted in the soft dawn blush, men balanced in the cross of pole stilts and fished in the waters surrounding Pulau

Belakang Mati, the small island off the coast of Singapore. An old Asian hand on board told Dee it meant the island of black death. Dee spotted several pillar boxes, some now with saplings growing through the slits of the concrete watching-posts dotted along the shoreline. The horror of being entombed in one made her shudder. She shook her head. Now was not the time to get cold feet.

Rounding the end of the island, the ship entered Keppel Harbour. Her entry to Asia.

Pandemonium surrounded Dee as she stepped off the gangplank. Stevedores shouted as trunks and boxes piled up on the wharf. Canvas sacks of mail formed a jumbled pyramid near the bow. Porters jostled as they elbowed and barged their way through throngs of bemused passengers, not all from her ship. A myriad of tongues swirled in a cacophonous babel. Sweat seeped down Dee's neck and she swallowed a bubbling panic. She jammed her hat down over her curls, picked up her small overnight case and, glad she had opted to wear uniform, pushed her way to what looked like the customs office. The pillar box red cross distinct against her gray dress helped clear a narrow path, which closed the minute she passed.

Foot by foot they crept forward until her passport was inspected and stamped by an officious man in a khaki uniform. She followed passengers through another set of doors to where more luggage was piled. The crush of people got worse. Seeing a grumpy toddler, she pulled a face at him. He stuck his tongue out then hid in his mother's shoulder, peeping to see if she was angry. Dee smiled, but before she could respond in kind she felt a tap on her shoulder.

"Hello? I say, excuse me, hello."

She turned to look into eyes level with her own.

"I say, I'm awfully sorry, but as you are the only person I can see in this melee in a Red Cross uniform, I assume you are Deidre Cunningham."

"G'day, yes, I'm Deidre. But my mates call me Dee. So if you want to be a mate that's what you call me." She stuck her hand out.

"Oh, goodness. Right. Of course. I'm David Gallagher, your liaison with the High Commission. I'm most awfully sorry not to have been here when you arrived. I got held up behind a damn trishaw."

"Oh, that's alright. I knew someone would show up sometime." Dee smiled at the very blond razor-short-haired and red-faced man, who looked even younger than Les but far less sure of himself. "What happens now?" she asked.

David glanced at his watch.

"We'll wait for your trunk then head straight to the station. You're on the night mail to KL."

"KL?"

"Sorry, Kuala Lumpur. The capital."

"I'm not staying in Singapore even a night?"

"No. Sorry. Orders from above."

Dee stifled a giggle and stopped herself from looking to the heavens.

"Righto. I think I saw my trunk on the wharf so it shouldn't take long." She smiled at his hmph. "So, Mr. Gallagher, what exactly does my liaison do? If you're in Singapore and I'm somewhere in Malaya, I'm not sure you'd be able to help much, if I needed it."

"Well," he paused, "it's a bit of an odd situation, really. You're our only girl to come from Australia. Normally they come in batches from Britain, so, well, you know, they can jolly each other along. Don't need a nursemaid. You're a bit of an oddity."

He blushed at Dee's peal of laughter.

"Wait till I tell my brothers that one. I've been called a lot of things but never an 'oddity.'"

"Oh, Lord, I'm sorry," David's color rose even more.

"Don't worry about it. You've given me a laugh for the day."

***

Dee had her night in Singapore after all. About to board the train, David Gallagher stopped mid- sentence as an announcement came over the Tannoy. She heard a snatched curse under his breath as he turned her back to the ornate station entrance. The line at Segamat had been blown up. Not an auspicious start, but it gave Dee time to get her bearings. To lose the roll of the ocean. To taste Tiger beer, and sweet and sour prawns at a market stall before traveling to the mainland.

"I assume you know a little about what is happening here," David asked, chopsticks poised.

"A little. The Red Cross was a bit sketchy with the details and we don't get to hear too much in the Aussie press. I know Edward Gent was sent back to England, then died in an air crash not far from where he was due to land. That he was replaced as British High Commissioner by Henry Gurney, and he at least seems to acknowledge there is a problem."

"Sir Edward Gent and Sir Henry Gurney," David corrected her, primly.

"Sorry." Dee hid a smile. "Oh yes, I remember something else. People were peeved Sir Henry brought men with him from Palestine. But they like that he seems to understand modern warfare. What do they call it?" She paused, her brow crinkled. "Guerrilla, that's right."

"Yes, well, it's never as easy as it seems to the press."

Next morning David Gallagher shepherded her back to the station, stopping on the way at a *kedai kopi* for coffee.

"You'll be met in KL," he said, handing her into the carriage.

"Like I was here?" She laughed as the earnest young consular officer colored, again. "I'm teasing, Mr. Gallagher, teasing. Thank you for liaising my way to Malaya."

She blew him a kiss as the train pulled out of the station, hearing his final words in a huff of steam.

"If the train stops suddenly, get down on the floor."

Chapter 3

THE *BASHA* LEAKED. Stakes holding the *attap* roofing were askew, palm fronds no match for the relentless rain falling in heavy splats, bouncing from leaf to leaf through the canopy overhead. Neither the smell nor the smoke from the tommy cooker they had risked lighting for char would travel through the storm, and a modicum of comfort came from the shimmy of warmth that steamed up from their tin mugs. Cigarettes, wild sage leaves gathered, crushed and kept dry in a tin, were rolled in strips of banana leaf. The harsh taste rasped their throats, but a smoke was a smoke.

The men looked over at Tenuk curled into a ball under a frond.

"That man can sleep anywhere," Simon said of their Iban tracker, a man more used to tracking animals in the jungles of Sarawak than communist terrorists on the Malay Peninsula.

"Lucky sod," agreed Frank Hobbs, drawing deeply on his cigarette, then stifling a cough.

"Who would've thought Force 136 would be back in business, eh?" Simon's voice was barely above a whisper.

"Better name now. Ferret Force. Just what we are, a bunch of ferrets rootling out guerrillas. Can't see the brass being that impressed, especially with us civvies back in the fold."

"I'm wondering that myself," Simon said. "It's October, guaranteed to piss down every afternoon. I'm cold and hungry. And this cigarette is godawful. Remind me again why we thought it would be a good idea to come nosing around here."

"If that SEP was being truthful when he surrendered, the CT camp must be somewhere in this swathe of bloody *ulu*. Though the police interrogation report of the chap did admit to an element of uncertainty." Frank choked back another cough and put the banana leaf stub into the dregs of his mug before tossing it into the jungle.

"Could've been a plant. Who caught the bastard?"

"No idea," Frank replied. "I didn't see the whole report. 'Only that which is pertinent to your brief' were, I think, the exact words quoted."

"Right, well, while I squat behind a tree to bury the evidence of my bully beef, you wake Tenuk. We've still got a few hours of daylight and the rain's finally easing. Best keep going. We needn't destroy the *basha*, the rain's doing a good enough job of that, and it might have been used by CTs at some stage. Not that they tend to use the same place twice."

"We taught them well during the war."

"I think the learning went both ways, Hobbs. Though we did arm them. A catchy name they've come up with for us in their propaganda pamphlets though—running dogs!"

***

Tenuk's signal, his thumb pointing down from his open palm, his fingers together forming an inverted vee between thumb and forefinger, had dropped Simon and Frank low into a spongy bed of dank roots, vines, and decaying leaves. The incessant hum of mosquitoes and stifling humidity added to the tension as they waited, weapons ready, for the tracker to ease forward to get a better look at the huts ahead. Long minutes later he gave the all-clear thumb up with a clenched fist.

The men crept forward to lie in the undergrowth with the Iban, waiting and watching. Simon shifted, easing his weight off one elbow for a minute without losing focus on the meagre CT camp he scanned through dull and dented binoculars.

Tattered tarpaulins stretched between trees in a low clearing in the jungle, the tree canopy above making it impossible to see the communist encampment from the air. A slit trench was visible at the back of the small compound and, to the eastern side, a thick length of bamboo dripped water to fall uselessly on the already soaked ground, probably piped from the spring they had passed half an hour earlier.

"Nothing, damnit!" Frank whispered, his Winchester held at his side.

Simon could smell the sour sweat of four days hard trekking on Frank and could only assume he was no better.

"I was sure we were on the right trail." Frank's disappointment was palpable.

"We were, Hobbs. Can't catch 'em every time. And even if the SEP was stringing a line, the intercept was good," Simon said, thinking of the encrypted message found in a tube of toothpaste in a captured CT's knapsack. He pointed to a smudged footprint not quite submerged in the quagmire. "They haven't been gone long."

"Which makes it even more infuriating," said Frank.

"I know," Simon agreed. "Come on, let's see what they've left behind." He took out his notebook, ready to take an inventory to be pored over by the desk wallahs looking for any clue to further operations.

***

Simon stretched out on his cot. He ached. Life on the rubber plantation whilst busy had not kept his fitness up to wartime levels. And his feet hurt. All well and good wearing hockey boots instead of regulation army boots—their tread being immediately recognized by CTs—but Bata boots, as some of the chaps called them, didn't provide much support, keep the feet dry or last long.

The recce had not produced anything tangible but sore feet, and for Frank a hacking cough that would keep him out of the jungle until gone, the risk of being heard too great. Simon's initial reservations about the appointment of Gurney lessened as it became obvious the new British High Commissioner respected Ferret Force's efforts, but how long he'd be able to keep the C-in-C on board with their unconventional tactics would remain to be seen.

Funny how he'd slotted back into jungle warfare. Well, not really. Skills might be a bit rusty but one never forgot—more's the pity. Two years, that's what the director of Sime Darby had said when he'd interviewed for the planter job back in Malaya six months after being demobbed. Two years to get the Malay Peninsula back to economic prosperity. Yet here they were three years later and back at war. All the energy put into getting production back up for both the rubber and tin industries being destroyed by a group of idealists. Though the powers-that-be continued to insist it wasn't a war.

Frustrating though, for those of them on the front line of a non-war. Getting ambushed. Shot. Blood sucked by leeches. Back on rations of tinned beef. Certainly sounded like war. This time Chinese squatters living on the edge of the jungle were not going to help security forces, with many doing everything they could to support the MCP. For two reasons, Simon complained to Frank as they'd shared dinner one night. Fear of reprisal, and politicians in London and their asinine way of thinking. And after the debacle of trying to repatriate vast numbers to China—people who didn't want to leave, to go to a country which didn't want them back.

***

Whenever able, Simon pushed through the swing doors of the FMS Club on Market Street in Ipoh, where he'd while away time with planters and managers at the L-shaped bar, hearing the situation on their estates and tin mines. It was not always comfortable listening, despite the soothing chimes of the old Victorian pendulum clock on the wall and the click of the abacus rattling up chits at the far end of the counter. Every now and then a burst of boisterous laughter would erupt from behind one of the curtained cubicles where dinner was served.

"How's Marina coping?" Simon asked, enjoying the smoothness of Chap Puteh trickling down his throat like syrup, noting the tiredness around his friend's eyes as he grabbed a quick *stengah* before heading to his plantation twenty miles away. "Hard being so isolated."

"Incredible woman!" Roger Tillman smiled. "She's determined to keep going. You know, business as usual. She now mans the Bren gun up at the house. Ah Loong, the cook, is also conversant with its idiosyncrasies, so between them they feel pretty secure. We're wrapped in barbed wire and have a sand-bagged safe room filled with supplies. The dogs are wonderful at giving early warning. But good God, man, every time I leave her alone to walk the lines or come into town for business, I wonder what I'll find when I get home."

"What a bloody life!" Simon sipped his drink wondering when next he'd see the pert wife of one of the first planters he met before the war.

Roger nodded. "I know Marina feels the same about me. Will I be ambushed? It was she who insisted I armor the old Ford. It's like a bloody tank now. Steel plated. Slits at eye-level. We've even got

33

Lifeguard tires, guaranteed not to deflate for three miles if shot, so I'm told."

"Hope they're not put to the test," Simon said with a sigh, looking around the bar. "You know they're running a sweepstake here? Who's the next planter to be killed."

"Yup. Never a dull moment in Malaya! But it's not going to be me." Roger downed the last of his whisky, shook hands, and headed off with an airy, "Look after yourself out there, Frampton. I know you're up to something."

"You too, Roger. Best to Marina!" Simon replied, thinking of the trim and attractive puckish woman lying on her stomach, firing off a machine gun. "I'm off soon, as well."

About to leave the bar, another planter he knew came in, his face pale.

"You all right, Watson?" Simon asked the lean man, his hair prematurely gray. "Looking a bit peaky, old chap. Here, have a drink. Beer or whisky? What's happened?"

The story that unfolded sickened Simon, the viciousness overwhelming. The fear instilled invidious as Malay rubber tappers were targeted on Dick Watson's estate. By nature a quiet occupation as a hundred trees per acre, planted in regimental lines, were tapped on alternate days. The white latex dripping richly into a small coconut cup tied to the trunk, urged from each tree by a slight downward nick to the bark, to be collected by the same tapper six hours later.

"The bastards just slit his throat," Dick said. "A good chap, excellent tapper, been with me for years. Before the war of course. The bloody gall of it." He took a long draught of Tiger beer. "It happened not far from the lines. Right behind the bloody village."

"Wasn't there any noise? Screaming?" asked Simon.

"Not a peep, apparently. Everyone just tried to run. Then, to make quite sure the message got through, the CTs grabbed another couple and did the same thing. Slit their throats, then vanished back into the swamp."

Simon felt the fury lifting off the man in waves. Another plantation where the workforce was driven to help the communists. No wonder the CTs were able to hole up in their jungle hideouts. They had a bountiful supply of fresh food being delivered by compliant tappers, Malays, and Tamils, terrified for their lives, becoming part of the Min Yuen—many unwitting communist supporters. A terror which no amount of reassurance from their British *tuans* could assuage.

"I know we're headed for Malayanisation but until independence comes, peacefully, they're not going to drive me, or any of us, away. Marjorie is just as determined to stick it out. She never goes anywhere without a pistol. And when driving she has a handbag full of grenades just for good measure. A cornucopia of weaponry." Dick paused, looking into his glass. "You know she's pregnant?"

"I didn't. Congratulations, old boy," said Simon, slapping his friend on the back. "And she's still staying?"

"Seems so," Dick said, a wry smile lightening his face. "Remarkable!"

"Not sure you deserve her."

"I'm not either," Dick replied. "Right, I'm off. Promised I'd be home well before sundown. Mid-morning and dusk are the favored times for an ambush on the roads around here. Bamboo bombs be buggered, is what I say!"

***

Lying under a net at the Guest House, loneliness engulfed Simon. He pulled out the worn photo of Woodland Farm, taken during the war. Tess standing at the front door. It was one of his favorite photographs. She was wearing Land Army garb of khaki dungarees cinched at the waist with a wide brown belt. It was summer, and her short-sleeved shirt showed tanned, muscled arms. Her smile was wide as if she was about to laugh. Something she did a lot of. She'd been lucky. Able to stay on the farm and help her father. Becoming mother hen to the various girls sent down from London as part of the Land Army, some of whom had never been in the countryside before, let alone known how to milk a cow or hoe a field.

Simon smiled at the photo, feeling her warmth over the oceans. He rolled over. Time to catch some kip. The next few weeks were going to be tough.

Chapter 4

Raub

THE LAND ROVER jounced along the rutted road lined with rubber trees that gave way, as they started climbing, to trees she couldn't identify. Miles and miles of jungle, menacing in its tangled density, made her shiver in the heat.

"This Banjaran Besar," Samsuari, the driver, announced, waving his arm at the hills.

Dee nodded and clutched the roof through the open window then glanced at the driver, marveling at his apparent unconcern, or perhaps his confidence in the red cross painted on the vehicle. She looked down at her uniform, smart and pressed when she'd climbed into the Land Rover hours before. She'd given up on the hat after the second time it flew out, only to be retrieved by the lad perched in the back on top of her trunk and boxes of supplies.

"Are we nearly there?" she asked.

"*Tidak lama lagi,*" Samsuari said, a gold eye tooth glinting through his grin as he saw Dee flick the pages of a dictionary she'd bought in KL. "Soon, soon, *mem,*" he translated.

Dee had been astounded to find out from the Red Cross liaison in the capital that she'd been posted to Raub, in the middle of Pahang state, near to where the miners she'd met on board the ship were headed. Part of her railed at the idea that the head office thought she'd need cossetting, but, as they wove further into the belly of Malaya, she began to feel more grateful.

The first Red Cross office in the country had been located in Penang and the push to bring nurses in, and to train local staff, was growing. Dee, determined to prove her worth, felt a flicker of doubt as they rounded a steep bend on a gravel lane and crunched to a halt in front of a dilapidated bungalow.

"This is it?"

"*Iya*, Sista," nodded the driver, getting out and stretching.

"This is the clinic? And where I live?" she asked again.

"*Iya*. I help," Samsuari said, starting to haul boxes to the ground. "*Saya pembantu anda.*" He laughed at Dee's blank look. "I am your ..." he paused.

"My assistant?" Dee asked.

Samsuari beamed. "*Iya*," he agreed. "Assistant."

"And Mohammed?" Dee looked at the youth carrying a box to the front step.

"He need get to Raub."

"Aah." Dee looked at the smiling Malay. She'd have to watch him, but she couldn't help be drawn to his unruffled manner. Some levity might be needed in this job. She stopped them moving her trunk and the boxes. "Just a moment. I want to look inside."

The front door creaked open. No key necessary. The rooms had been swept and rudimentary furniture dusted and pushed against the walls. She flicked a switch and was relieved there was a glimmer of light. The squat building consisted of one large room at the front that opened onto a verandah. At the back were three other rooms, and a lean-to bathhouse, thankfully with a dunny. A covered walkway led to a small cookhouse.

There was potential. But not tonight, after a long drive through bandit country and checkpoints. And not without a lock. Her nerves were stretched enough.

"Righto, lads, back into the Land Rover."

"You not sleep here?" Samsuari asked.

"Not tonight, Josephine," Dee said, climbing into the vehicle as shadows deepened and strange jungle noises loudened. "Where's the Rest House?"

***

A fan in her high-ceilinged room moved the air in languid whorls. She splashed in the chipped tub in the old-fashioned bathroom at the end of the corridor, then lay down in her underwear wondering how her first decision would be received. It didn't take long to find out.

A rap at the door then a note slid under roused her from a doze.

Welcome to Raub, Sister Cunningham.
Perhaps you would join me for a drink at the bar.
Jeffrey Gibbons, Administrator, Kuala Lipis

"Huh. Perhaps?" Dee muttered as she shook out another uniform. "Might as well look professional for my first confrontation."

She dawdled downstairs fifteen minutes later, a dash of lipstick doing wonders for her morale. A tall, angular man at the bar had one eye on the entrance. He hurried toward her with a wide smile and an outstretched hand.

Over an ice-cold beer, his apologies for the state of the bungalow profuse, he promised to have it brought to order immediately.

"A d-d-dreadful snafu," he admitted. "The message didn't get through until this morning. I drove down the road as soon as I heard, and just had time to get it cleaned."

"Sort of," Dee said. "If that's to be a clinic it must be spotless. But thank you for at least trying. Don't worry. I'll get to it in the morning. Just couldn't face it tonight. Now, tell me, my geography's not very good yet, where is Kuala Lipis?"

"Oh, about thirty miles east. As the crow flies. Somewhat longer in reality. Due both to the situation and the road." Jeffrey laughed. "That is our excuse for everything these days."

They chatted easily, and Dee was pleased to find the Administrator wasn't as stuffy as he had seemed at first, or as pompous as he'd sounded in his note.

"You know, Jeffrey, I might know a couple of chaps who could help with the bungalow. From the gold mine."

She laughed at his surprise.

"You've been here an hour and you've already met people?"

"No, you drongo! They were on the ship from home."

"Aah. Well, really we shouldn't be asking for help. It is the British Red Cross."

"Nonsense. It's worth a shot and we need any help we can get. You can say it was all my doing." Dee patted his arm and watched a blush creep up his neck. Were all Englishmen this uptight? Or maybe having five brothers had inured her to men's sensitivities. "Thanks for coming all this way, Jeffrey. I do appreciate it. But I'll be fine now. I might spend another night here but then we'll be hunky dory."

"One thing, Miss Cunningham—"

"Please, call me Dee," she interrupted him.

"Oh, right, thanks. Um, yes, well, Dee, I understand you brought supplies with you, in an open Land Rover. Rather foolhardy. What if you'd come across a roadblock? Medical supplies could have ended up in CT hands."

"That's what Mr. Gallagher said in KL. But I reckoned with that bloody big red cross we'd be right."

"You were lucky." Jeffrey looked into the dregs of his glass and frowned. "I'm afraid the bandits are not as altruistic as you might think."

"Well, Jeffrey, until they actually appear that way to me, I'm not going to worry about it."

***

Dee's bravado saw her through the evening until she made her excuses and went upstairs. Sleep did not come easily until, punching the pillow in frustration, tiredness won and she closed her eyes.

True to his word, Samsuari had the Land Rover pulled up outside the Rest House at eight. The boxes once again loaded into the back, along with brooms, mops and buckets, and disinfectant he got from the market on the way.

"*Selamat pagi, mem.*"

"*Selamat pagi,* Samsuari." Dee delighted in his gold-toothed laugh. "That's it, though. I can't say anything else, yet."

"I teach," the driver assured her.

"That's what I'm hoping." Clambering into the vehicle, Dee was glad she ditched her uniform and instead wore khaki trousers and a tan shirt. It was going to be a grubby day. "Now," she said, "we need helpers. But first I want to go to the gold mining offices."

It was worth the detour. Dee found the blokes at Raub Australian Gold Mining keen to help. One offered to introduce her to his wife who'd had a couple years of nurses' training. Much of the original mine village at Bukit Koman had been destroyed and the mine shafts flooded during the war, the expatriate employees interned by the Japanese. But the company returned in 1946 and was once again a major employer in the area. While they had their own small clinic at the camp, they were eager to support health initiatives in the town.

Dee rejected the offer of a cash donation—for the time being—but accepted cans of white paint and brushes which now nestled amongst the boxes and her trunk. She was even more delighted RAGM agreed to her spur-of-the-moment suggestion that they sponsor a couple of girls to work at the clinic. Dee left the office grinning, looking forward to joining the weekly company knees-up one Friday evening.

There seemed little concern about CTs and she wondered if the Emergency really was as desperate as she'd been led to believe—as dire a picture as painted by David Gallagher in Singapore and Jeffrey the night before. The township seemed to be managing just fine.

The drab little bungalow did not look much improved in the harsh brilliance of daylight. The windows had all been thrown open and, leaning against the crumbling balustrade of the verandah was a grinning Mohammed, smoke curling from a thin cheroot that smelled of cloves.

"What are you doing here?" she asked with a smile as he came forward to help unload the vehicle.

"Samsuari say me must come. You give ride from KL."

"But you paid him."

"*Tidak, mem.* Free ride. I work."

Dee looked across to the driver who shrugged and flashed a gold tooth.

"*Terima kasih*, Mohammed. I am glad to have you."

Each morning the young man lounged on the doorstep awaiting her instructions, with other youths appearing at different times of the day to help wash walls and paint. In amongst the smell of turpentine and paint, ladders and drop cloths, Dee interviewed five women and chose a girl to help whilst learning rudimentary nursing skills, and a young woman with some experience, along with an older Chinese to be her *amah* and cook, who would live in the quarters off the cookhouse. Samsuari agreed to step in if required for interpretation when dealing with any male patients, and Mohammed was employed to get the scraggly garden under control and to come whenever needed for odd jobs.

It took three days, a lot of scrubbing and painting, before Dee felt able to declare the Raub Red Cross Clinic open for business. Basic drugs sorted and stored in a cupboard that could be locked. Bandages rolled and ready with the help of Lucy Lim, who had worked at the hospital in Ipoh before her marriage to a local shop-keeper, and Putri binti Salleh, an eager Malay girl who wanted to be a nurse but whose father would not allow her to leave Raub. With Samsuari's help, Dee had persuaded the stern bespectacled man that she would not be putting ideas into his daughter's head but that Putri would be helping her people. He had left the clinic with a slight bow, murmuring, as Samsuari translated, "It is as Allah willed it."

After a final lingering bath in the claw-foot tub at the Rest House, Dee moved to the bungalow on the fourth afternoon. From now on her ablutions would take place with a scoop from the Shanghai jar in the lean-to.

Loneliness snatched at her throat when Samsuari sauntered off after he delivered her to the clinic, leaving the Land Rover to stand guard under the carport. She had never been this far from the ocean. Crickets and other jungle sounds had yet to begin their evensong as trees loomed behind the bungalow, casting it in shadows. Dee wandered through to the room she had chosen for her bedroom, touched to find her bed made up and a towel folded into an intri-cate swan sitting on the pillow. She unpacked her overnight case and put a jar of cold cream and a hair brush on the dressing table, the mirror shining spotless above. The photo of her parents and the boys, all of them, she put on the bedside table along with her alarm clock, although she doubted she'd need that.

"Righto, Sister Cunningham," Dee muttered, "this calls for a celebration." She went into the larger of the three back rooms, the one she had designated dining/living, and poured a glass of whisky which she took to the bamboo chair on the verandah, barricaded with sandbags. Sitting down, she raised her drink to the deep-ening sky. To Malaya.

Ah Sui, her *amah*, would move in the following day. Tonight she was on her own.

Chapter 5

"WELL, AS WE ARE NOT in full possession of the facts, let's leave it at that, Frampton. But I'd be careful how you speak about it if I were you." Frank Hobbs looked out at dugout canoes bobbing on anchors embedded in the sandy beach, waiting to be launched when darkness fell.

The men had been discussing the fiasco at Batang Kali, the village a known hotbed and supplier of food to CTs. It was also believed villagers had offered safe haven to those responsible for dousing three chaps from the 4th Queen's Hussars in petrol before setting them alight. In a ruthless response the SF had killed twenty-four civilians, mostly shot in the back. And worse, no absolute proof they had been Min Yuen sympathizers.

The argument for and against the brutality raged in hushed tones in bars and clubs. For Simon Frampton it was the latter, believing security forces should not be held accountable for heat-of-the-battle decisions, but Batang Kali had not been that. There were too many questions. Why no officer was present would be a good one to start with.

"You're probably right," Simon said finally, his gaze on a few bare-chested men in sarongs hauling down fishing nets, draped high on bamboo scaffolding to dry, in preparation for the night's catch. "But we are culpable for not doing more than basic training for conscripts coming out."

"You're right about that," Hobbs said.

The two men watched the sun set through a filter of casuarinas and coconut palms from the Mess verandah at the headquarters of Ferret Force, which overlooked the Straits of Malacca. Gentle wavelets lapped the shoreline leading up to Siginting Camp, near Port Dickson on the west coast of Malaya, not far from the home and training ground of the Malay Regiment. It would be easy to believe the country was at peace and not being held to ransom by the well-organized terror campaign of the Malayan Communist Party, and hard to marry their current location with the patrol from which they'd just returned after three weeks chasing a nebulous trail of whispers around Sungai Siput, north of Ipoh.

A nightjar's cloc-cloc broke their silence.

Frank got to his feet. "Another *stengah*? Then we can marvel at kismet and the timely demise of Lau Yew."

"Thank you," Simon said. He smiled at the thought of Two-Gun Bill Stafford. Of all the luck! The Kentishman, a barrel-chested, tough-talking, black-clad policeman whose name was synonymous with bravery up and down the Malay Peninsula after escaping imprisonment by the Japanese, had learned of the whereabouts of Lau Yew, a vicious and prominent member of the MCP. Or anticipated whereabouts. With a chain of informants—waitresses, barmen, trishaw drivers, and the like—Stafford, whilst having a haircut in Kuala Lumpur, had been told by his barber about a CT meeting slated to take place in Kajang, fifteen miles south of the capital.

With his squad of twenty Chinese policemen, also dressed in black, guided by the reluctant barber, Stafford crept through a rubber plantation overlooking a valley in which three huts nestled amongst *lallang*, the sharp thick-bladed grass that sliced bare legs and arms to leave streaks of blood like an alien web. The terrified barber, his hand trembling, pointed out the venue then melted back through the rubber trees to a waiting car to be whisked back to his barbershop.

Simon shuddered. From all reports, the operation could have been a disaster, with two unexpected events occurring. An early warning given when Stafford's crawling arrival was spotted by a woman sitting outside one of the wooden shacks. Her screams brought three men charging out, shooting as they ran for the hill behind the small clearing. Superintendent Stafford's men returned fire and the CTs fell. Two were dead. One was Lau Yew. A good kill. Five more women found cowering in the hut were handcuffed, including Lau Yew's wife. Stafford uncovered weapons, maps and two thousand rounds of ammunition in the main hut. He sent six men back to the road with the bounty and instructions to arrange transport for the prisoners.

Simon glanced up as Frank returned with their drinks.

"Stafford was a lucky sod, but you've got to give it to him. Quick thinking under pressure!" Simon said. "I wonder if the barber had known about a larger contingent of CTs close by. Probably not. Information seems to be kept to small cells of men and women. No one person knowing too much. Not a bad way to operate in the jungle. We should do it more often."

"That counterattack could have been catastrophic," Frank said. "Stafford and his merry men were vastly outnumbered. A stroke of brilliance, him screaming, 'Here come the Gurkhas!'"

"Not so fortunate for the women. Shredded by cross-fire. I bet that's not going to be highlighted in the CT *Battle News*, unless they write it up as an incentive against the British," said Simon. "I suppose anything can be twisted. Someone needs to find that bloody printing press."

"It's got to be somewhere. There is though rather a lot of *ulu* in which to look," Frank said, with a grin. "Here's to the Gurkhas that weren't!"

They clinked glasses.

"Indeed, chin chin," Simon said. "I have a vivid image of a platoon of Gurkhas rushing down the hill, *kukris* swinging. No wonder the CTs scarpered. I wonder what Chin Peng said when they realized it was a hoax."

"Oh, he would've spouted good old Mao—'When attacked, withdraw.'"

The men sat in the last embers of daylight, watching trees take on eerie shapes as the wind picked up. Crickets opened up the night with a short cantata, joined by frogs and the rustling of night critters. Barking deer heralded the full symphony from their position behind the Mess.

Dinner was a subdued affair, interspersed with appreciative murmurs as Ali, the white-clad waiter, presented plates of *kari ayam* and *pilau*, the curried chicken cooked in coconut milk, followed by ice-cold lychees and canned cream. They decided to have a final snifter before turning in. Clouds scurried to form a dull blanket—a good night for an attack. There was sure to be one somewhere. CTs or the security services. Men and women stealing through back streets or along jungle tracks, each sure in their own beliefs.

"Have you heard from Tess lately?" Frank asked, tapping his pipe on the verandah rail.

"Not for a few weeks, but mail is notoriously slow," Simon replied. "When we finally get back to Blighty, you must meet her."

"Assuming she'll wait for you!" Frank, his tone sardonic, smiled.

"There is that," Simon responded with a wry grin.

"Why, in God's name, didn't you marry her after the war?"

"Oh, I don't know. I wasn't finished with Malaya. She was engrossed in the farm. And, I think, in order to like Malaya or anywhere one has to want to be here, or there."

"You're probably right," said Frank. "Look at women like Marjorie Watson and Marina Tillman. I wouldn't want either of them coming after me. But Tess sounds pretty independent. Wouldn't she have adapted?"

"Probably, but she'd never give up Woodland Farm." Simon buried his nose in the snifter. "This is remarkably good brandy."

"It is, but don't change the subject. Did you ask her?"

"No. Now, no more interrogation." Simon put the glass down on the verandah rail and stood. "I've cadged a lift into KL so have got an early start."

"And I'm riding shotgun in a convoy to Ipoh at eleven hundred hours."

"Right then, I'll say goodnight. See you in Tapah on Friday, Hobbs. Ready for another jungle sojourn," said Simon. "I hope Tenuk'll be sober. You know what happens when he gets a bit of freedom. He somehow manages to find other Iban and the *tuac* flows."

"Not my chosen beverage, I must say. I suppose it's rather like Japanese sake but made with palm."

"Another drink I choose not to imbibe. Good night, Frank. A pleasant evening. Keep your head down out there."

***

Thoughts jostled in time to the bumpy ride. Talk of Tess had unsettled Simon. Why hadn't he asked her? Was it really because of the

45

farm? Most of their relationship—if it could be called that—was based on letters, often months apart during the war. Then a few idyllic months back in England before he'd left again. He couldn't blame her if she decided not to wait. Well, no point worrying about a maybe.

He hoped catching up with John Davis, who led Force 136 during the war and was now responsible for the formation of Ferret Force with many of the same men, and Bob Thompson would help to clarify the lay of the land. There was a lingering animosity between the army and police, and Ferret Force was considered by some as neither. It was a difficult situation. At the bottom of which lay the reasoning, and insistence, from corporations terrified their insurance policies would be nullified if they were dealing with a war rather than an insurgency. All very well for those sitting in London. Not such an easy façade to keep up in Malaya. Peace meant the police were in charge, with the army providing intelligence and support to them.

Simon had heard of some old codgers sipping gin and tonic at The Dog, safe watching cricket on the *padang* in KL, who seemed to think the Emergency was a lot of brouhaha about nothing. They weren't the ones being ambushed on lonely roads or being hacked to death on rubber plantations.

The jeep bounced to a stop at The Dog entrance. Simon thanked the driver and clapped his shoulder as he clambered out. Not bad time, he noted as he glanced at his watch, only a few minutes late for his meeting.

"I thought we'd be for the chop, but not quite so soon." John Davis stared gloomily into his glass. "How, in God's name, were we expected to form a viable force when the government wouldn't release, or provide, officers. We were promised twenty and only given nine. A travesty."

"It's the irregularity they don't like," said Simon. "We don't conform. Good God, we have both civilians and military in the Force."

"Which is why it worked," Davis said, his voice clipped. "Professional ferrets must be used against professional bandits."

"The Scouts are essentially Ferret Force, so not really much change," Simon said.

"Not for you, but for me there's a great deal more red tape." Davis lit a cigarette, curling smoke blunting his features. "I say," his mood lightened, "have you heard about Two-Gun's latest escapade?"

"Yes. Getting Lau Yew was quite a coup."

"No, no. Stafford's done it again. That man has more informants than anyone I know. All his underworld contacts from before the war, incredible."

"What's he done now?"

"Got word of an arms cache, not far from where his last fracas was. Brave chap, the informer. Not a pretty end if caught. The dump wasn't far from where the Bearded Terror slit the throats of six tappers. Lieu Kon Kim, or whatever his name, is a real bastard," John Davis said, referring to the man with a wispy beard responsible for terrorizing Kajang and southern Selangor in general. "I'd liked to have seen Stafford's face when they got to the spot. The informer pointed to a stand of saplings and told him the arms were under them. The trees had been planted after the weapons were hidden. Stafford and his men uprooted the trees to find a dozen pits, all lined with timber, and each holding circular metal drums filled with over two hundred rifles and ten-thousand rounds of ammunition, machine-guns and Stens."

"Bloody hell!"

"Now ask me how I know exactly what was in them," John said, laughter creasing his eyes.

"How?"

"Because, my dear Frampton, it was a load parachuted in towards the end of the war. For Force 136! But Chin Peng and his cohorts managed to get their hands on it first and hid it. Perhaps they knew, even then, the British would not honor their promises. Who knows?"

"There is a certain symmetry to the story," Simon agreed. "Did the informer get his reward money?"

"He did. A wad of it. $60,000. Stafford spent the day going from bank to bank collecting dollar bills. Then stuffed them in a basket, shoved the basket in a *beca* and went to the agreed *kedai makan*."

"What we do for King and country!"

"Indeed, but the story doesn't end there. Apparently, and I haven't spoken to Bill myself, the informer offered a present 'from the basket' for Stafford's men and proceeded to hand him $100."

"Oh my God." Simon chuckled. "I'll bet that went down well."

"Let's just say, that particular informant won't be helping Tin Sau-pah again."

"Who?"

"Tin Sau-pah. That's what the CT's call Stafford. The Iron Broom!"

Their laughter mingled with voices on the verandah, and Simon said, "It works both ways. Our chaps get a chuckle knowing Chin Peng is pronounced Chin Pong."

"Right, down to business," said John Davis, all levity gone. "Bob'll try and join us later. Your next foray, though that's arguably not the right word. I need you back in your old stomping grounds. Pahang."

"That's a big state," Simon said, with a smile. "Could you narrow it down?"

"I doubt you'll be dipping your toes in the South China Sea. Probably not going east of Temerloh."

"With all due respect, John, that's still a bloody large swathe of ground."

"It is indeed. And you'll be covering most of it. Starting near Raub. I need someone who can survive the jungle and handle the unexpected. In total six someones, including an Iban."

"Do I get to choose the team?"

"Within reason. You'll need someone with more than rudimentary medical know-how."

John Davis looked at Simon through hooded eyes, rather like a cobra waiting to strike. Gone was the bonhomie of a few moments earlier. A warning now carried in his words.

"Where exactly do you want us to go, sir?" Simon asked.

"I want to know where the hell those camps are. And where that damn printing press is. The regular SF seem unable to find them. Apart from popping off the odd bandit—more good luck than anything else—they are not producing results. The CTs are striking left, right, and bloody center, acting with total impunity. Around Mengkarak, particularly the Karmen Estate. It's got to stop. But first we've got to find the bastards. We're pretty certain it's Abdullah CD's lot. He's put the fear of the devil incarnate into the kampongs up and down Pahang."

"Well then, sir," Simon said, "I want Frank Hobbs, and Tenuk— he's used to us now, and we him. We'll need a CLO who can both liaise and interpret any Chinese if needed. I'd also like to include Haziq. He's from Temerloh. I trust him with my life. Have done many times. He's a good radio operator. And he's bored at base." Simon thought of the tough Malay he'd spent many months with in the *ulu* during the war. A small man with a huge heart. A man who hated anyone messing with his country.

"He might be bored, but he's efficient," Davis said. He was quiet, lighting a cigarette from the stub of the old. Drawing deeply, he held the smoke in his lungs before continuing. "Yes, all right, you can have him. But bring him back alive, please. Do you have a CLO in mind?"

"No, but needs to be someone from the area. And we'd all like to come back alive, sir," Simon said. "I'll be guided about someone medical, though both Frank and I are pretty good at patching. With that area to cover we'll be gone a while. It will have to be someone who can manage life on the move. Uncomfortably on the move," Simon stressed.

"I have given it some thought. I would suggest Robin Nancarrow. Cornishman."

"Never heard of him." Simon was dismissive. "Does he know Malaya?"

"Not like you and Hobbs, although his Malay is not bad. He came out just after the war."

"What's his story?"

"Chindits. Burma. Doctor."

"If he's a doctor, what the hell is he doing scrabbling around the jungle?" Simon asked.

"Like a lot us, Frampton, he couldn't settle back in civvy street."

Simon nodded, his eyes on the man opposite. "I assume I can meet him first."

"As luck would have it," Davis said, looking at his watch, "He'll be here in, oh, about five minutes. Another drink, old boy?"

Simon threw his head back and laughed.

"If that isn't a set up, I don't know what is!"

***

The Land Rover left the police escort and turned into the luscious gardens of the old Residency at Kuala Lipis, arguably the center of Pahang and once the state capital. Simon and Robin Nancarrow climbed stiffly out of the vehicle, bones jarred on the bumpy and often winding road from Kuala Lumpur. The drive had fortunately been uneventful, if long. The journey back to KL would be very much longer, and far more circuitous. It had, though, given Simon a chance to chat to the new member of the unit.

"*Selamat petang, tuan,*" the uniformed manservant greeted them.

The deep overhang of the old Edwardian building provided instant relief from the still, late afternoon torpor. The scent of jasmine hung sweet in the air as they followed the servant along the verandah and into the drawing room.

"Oh good, you chaps are here." The Administrator, a man Simon had briefly met with Bob Thompson at The Dog, stood to shake hands, as did Frank.

"Good to see you again, Gibbons," Simon said. "May I introduce Dr. Robin Nancarrow. Robin, Jeffrey Gibbons and Frank Hobbs. Sorry we're a bit later than expected."

"Trouble on the road?" Jeffrey asked.

"No. Just took longer to get ourselves sorted in KL." Simon took in his host's attire, a white dinner jacket and neat bow tie. "It appears we are meant to be dressing for dinner. This is as smart as I come, I'm afraid." Simon turned back to Frank. "Hobbs, you're looking rather spiffy. What do you know that I don't?"

"Not a thing, old chap," Frank said, with a grin.

"Not to worry, Frampton, we're a mixed bag this evening. But there will be one other guest," the Administrator said. "She should be here soon. Assuming she's back from her tour."

"She? Tour?" Robin asked.

"She's with the Red Cross. Spends half her life in a canoe visiting villages. She often stops in on her way home."

Chapter 6

THE SAMPAN SLIPPED along the subdued gloom of the tributary leading to the Sungai Jelai. Dee sat in the middle, ever on the lookout for both bandits and snakes, either in the water or hanging from low branches. She had nearly overturned the canoe the first time they had headed upstream when what she now knew as a mangrove viper had dangled in front of her, its eyes red and glowing against its gray-black body. Nor did she ever trail her hands in the river, having seen a number of banded kraits slither from the bank, their red heads vibrant against the opaque waters.

Samsuari sat in the bow and dipped the paddle in and out, raising barely a ripple. He only used the little outboard when they were in the midst of the larger river, the rasping sound of an engine too much risk of alerting CTs.

This deep in the jungle they would occasionally hear the muted roar of a tiger. Somehow that wasn't as terrifying as the prospect of snakes—many, Samsuari had told her, deadly. Sometimes, if they were far enough away from a settlement, they would talk. Their voices lost in the murmur of the *ulu*.

A few days before their first foray, Dee had glimpsed him through the window as she inventoried supplies to take.

"*Selamat petang*," she called to the hovering man and waved him in but he came only as far as the verandah. He refused a glass of water, barely making eye contact. "Samsuari, what is it? What has happened?"

He shifted his feet, kicking at a tuft of dry grass, finally glancing up and with no hint of gold, explained. His wife, Nur, was not happy about her husband taking a woman up the river, alone. For days. Maybe a week.

"What can we do?" Dee asked, wondering if it was danger or a white woman possibly accosting her husband that worried Nur.

"Mem, you come my house?"

"I would be honored, Samsuari. But does your wife want that?"

"She say no, but I think it good." He tucked a lock of black hair back into place under his *songkok*.

"Oh boy. All right. Tomorrow? After clinic."

"*Iya, terima kasih.*" His relief evident in the flash of gold.

"*Tidapa*, Samsuari, *tidapa*! But you must tell her I am coming. No surprise, nuh?"

***

Dee glanced back at Samsuari and smiled. They had come a long way since then. Nur had been gracious but guarded and accepted Dee's small gift with a hesitant smile, that first visit. The children shy but thrilled with the little cloth koala and kangaroo toys, treasures from the bottom of her trunk that Dee had shoved in as an afterthought before she left Townsville. Now, when she visited the kampong, she was welcomed as family and crawled over by Aminah and Ishraaq, each trying to outdo the other in garnering her attention. Dee loved visiting and, as her Malay improved, she and Nur began to have more involved conversations, often about the role of women in Malay society. A patrilineal culture but one in which women were often the lead in matters of commerce whilst still expected to manage the family.

A rush of sunlight as they eased into the deeper waters of the Sungai Jelai, and the outboard kicking in, brought Dee back to the present. They would be at the landing dock in under an hour. Another half hour to get the canoe on top of the Land Rover, now modified with struts to hold it. A welding feat mastered by a tough-looking Chinese from the RAGM. The company had continued to come through on their promise of help. Dee stretched. She was exhausted.

Perhaps they should head straight to Raub. Samsuari would be pleased to get home after five days away. But she had promised Jeffrey she'd stop in. Maybe just for a *stengah*. Then Dee remembered she was meant to meet with an Englishwoman the next morning, the wife of a planter from deep in bandit country. And Jeffrey's cook was excellent. Much as Dee liked Ah Sui, her culinary range was limited, and Dee was too tired most evenings to teach her new recipes.

"Do you want to take the Land Rover this evening?" Dee asked as they crunched up the drive to the Administrator's house.

"*Tidak, mem,*" replied Samsuari. "With sampan, better it stay here."

"Oh, yes, I wasn't thinking. Will you stay with your cousin?"

"*Iya.* I come here seven."

"Great. Thanks, Samsuari. It was a good trip even though I'm disappointed."

"Perhaps Tuan Jeffrey can make change," Samsuari suggested.

"Perhaps," she said, with a wave.

Sounds of merriment came from behind sandbags surrounding the verandah and Dee almost called the driver back. She looked down at her trousers caked in mud from the knees down to the top of her jungle boots. God knows what her hair looked like. Perhaps she could sneak around the back and slip upstairs to the spare room. She really didn't feel like socializing.

"Dee!"

"Sprung," she said under her breath, plastering a smile across her tired and, she was sure, dirty face. "Jeffrey," she called, "I'm filthy. All right if I nip up and change before I come and say hello?"

"Of course, my dear. You know the way. A *stengah* will be waiting."

"You're a dear. Thanks."

It was nice having a bath to soak in, rather than sluicing from the Shanghai jar. What would be even nicer would be the promised whisky balanced on the side, unlimited hot water and no social commitments. Dee lay back a few more minutes with her eyes shut, then dragged herself out, dripping on the tile floor as she towel-dried her hair.

She padded over to the bed and rummaged in the bottom of her rucksack for the shift she knew she'd shoved in at the last moment. She should've hung it in the bathroom to get some of the creases out. Oh well, too late now. She smoothed it down as best she could then slipped it over her head. The swirls of blue and purple batik fell like a waterfall tumbling. Lipstick and a comb and that was as good as it got. She wondered who was downstairs, thinking she could hear more than a couple of voices. She would have to try and keep her anger under control.

"Good evening, gentlemen," Dee said from the French door, taking in Jeffrey and the three other men on the verandah, who all sprang to their feet.

"My dear, so good to see you." Jeffrey kissed her cheek. "Let me introduce you to these reprobates. This dapper fellow is Frank Hobbs, the intelligent-looking one is Dr. Robin Nancarrow, and the ruffian is Simon Frampton. All due to head into the *ulu* tomorrow. Gentlemen, Sister Deidre Cunningham."

"From where, I gather, you have just returned," Simon said, shaking hands with a smile as Dee moved along the line of outstretched hands.

"How was the trip?" Jeffrey asked.

"I wish you hadn't asked," said Dee. She took the offered *stengah* and took a sip, trying to marshal her indignation.

"Why?"

"Perhaps you'd rather talk in private," Robin suggested, taking in Dee's heightened color.

"No, it's all right, thanks, Doctor. Jeffrey already knows what I'm going to say, don't you?"

"I'm afraid I d-d-do." The stutter, only occasionally apparent, showed the Administrator's discomfort as he studied his glass.

"Then why hasn't anything been done?"

"I'm sorry, I'm late to the party," Frank said. "Done about what?"

"Dredging. On the Sungai Jelai. The minute the monsoons fall the villages will be flooded again." Dee struggled to lower the stridency of her voice. "It's just not good enough, Jeffrey."

"You must understand, Dee, the p-powers-that-be have other more p-pressing things on their minds."

"More pressing than driving villagers into the hands of the CTs because they're sick of being drowned? Having their homes destroyed? I would've thought looking after people in the *ulu* would be a priority."

"If they would just b-build a bit further away from the areas that flood worst," Jeffrey said, looking helplessly at the others.

"Well, they won't. They're fishermen. They've lived there all their lives." Dee turned to the others with a rueful smile. "Sorry, fellas, I just get so riled up. And poor Jeffrey gets the brunt of it every time." She patted the Administrator's arm in apology. "Come on, no more talk about floods tonight. I'll harangue the poor man in the morning. Let's drink to the *ulu*!"

Lying in bed much later than was sensible, Dee smiled. It had been fun despite her initial tiredness, and anger. Dinner had been wonderful, and a welcome change from fish and rice. Jeffrey's cook had finished the meal off with a chocolate blancmange—where he got his stash of chocolate from only he knew. Then dancing! With them all, along the verandah. Jeffrey measured in his steps, just as in life. Frank, exuberant, and Simon fluid but not flashy. It was the good doctor who had proven a wonderful dancer, dipping and twirling her to the strains of The Andrews Sisters coming from Jeffrey's gramophone.

Laughter. Such a wonderful thing. Particularly in uncertain times. After her initial premise when she had first arrived in Raub that the Emergency might be overblown, her experience had taught her otherwise. The fellows tomorrow would be facing a difficult few weeks.

Chapter 7

"FUCKING LEECHES!"

Simon's head jerked up. The doctor rarely swore. He was killing the slugs, fat with his blood, from between his toes with dabs of salt. They had stopped for the night and built two simple *bashas*. The day had been tough, up and down escarpments that had slowed their progress, and they were all exhausted. Simon looked at the five men in various stages of undress, either checking for leeches or giving their skin some air. Even Haziq had lost his usual ebullience.

"Do you know what scares me more than CTs?" Frank asked the assembled group. "A leech crawling up my John Thomas!"

"Oh Christ. Thanks for putting that image in my head," Robin said. "I'm having enough trouble with them on my feet."

"I heard of one chap, I think he was with the Yorkshire Lights, who used to wear a Johnny on every patrol," continued Frank. A muffled snort came from the other *basha* as Haziq swallowed a laugh.

"You should've told us that before we left civilization," Simon said, checking his own feet for the swaying black slugs, drunk on blood. "How do they get through the eyelets of boots?" He looked across at Tenuk's almost naked body glistening with sweat, a web of tattoos stretching across his torso, a long pigtail hanging down his back, and bare feet, toes splayed wide. The sinewy little man, who often wore nothing but a loin cloth, seemed immune to the blood-sucking of leeches, mosquitoes, or anything else in the *ulu*. Tenuk turned and, seeing Simon's gaze, flashed a smile, his gold teeth dazzling in the lamplight. Simon grinned back. The pride of the Iban's life, procured just after he arrived on the Malay mainland from Sarawak the year before. The story of Tenuk's teeth had been told up and down the peninsula, providing moments of humor at times when most of the bars were filled with tales of destruction and death. Simon couldn't remember which dentist, in which town, had removed all Tenuk's real teeth and replaced them with a mouth of gleaming gold. Then, shinning up a coconut tree, they'd become dislodged and unwearable. His ensuing depression had persuaded those in authority it would be worth everyone's while for the British Army to replace his precious teeth.

"Right, I'll relieve Yi Wei on stag," Frank said, retying his boots. "His turn for some grub and shuteye."

"Two hours, Hobbs, then I'll take over," Robin said to Frank's retreating back as he went to swap guard duties with the Chinese Liaison Officer along the narrow path they had hacked earlier. "Remind me again why I'm in this Godforsaken part of the world," Robin asked the remaining men sitting around tommy cookers heating dried food and water for tea.

"Who doesn't like being sodden through from morning to night, night to morning?" Simon asked, slinging his sweat-wet uniform over a bush and unwrapping his drier ones from the waterproof poncho that all servicemen carried.

"How can one short dumpy man, not to mention his entourage of bloodthirsty commies, be so damn elusive? Abdullah CD's like a wraith," Robin said.

"Not to the kampongs he's terrorized into providing food and shelter. If I ever see his sodding *songkok* with the red star winking at me through the undergrowth, I'll shoot his bloody head off," Simon said.

Their voices were just above a whisper. Tenuk, his head cocked, listened to the shriek of a devil bat high in the tree canopy. Simon could see him counting the individual screeches. If he heard five from the same bat, Simon knew the Iban believed he would catch malaria and die. And he quite probably could. Die. The power of superstition often beating the power of Paludrine.

"My lady's brother, he say only one man find Abdullah." Haziq's voice came from the sleeping bag, into which he'd squirmed.

"Yeop Mahidin?" Simon asked.

"*Ya*." Haziq agreed. "They cousins. Go school together in Ipoh. Nuh! One man good, one man bad."

57

"A deputation from kampongs around Temerloh went to complain to the Sultan," Robin said, rubbing methylated spirits onto his feet before pulling on dry socks.

"Yeop'd have more chance than us. If we find Abdullah, it'll be a bloody miracle."

"Yeop boxer. Bantam," Haziq's sleepy voice chimed in.

"I thought he was a cricketer," Simon said.

"All sport," Haziq said. "Hockey, football, cricket, boxing."

"Handy chap to have around. Right, I'm going to get some kip," Robin said. "G'night."

"*Selamat malam, tuan*," returned Haziq.

Tenuk was already asleep, curled like a ball in the low angle of the *basha*. Despite being bone-tired, Simon lay awake for hours. He heard Robin creep down the track to relieve Frank, then Frank's muttered curse as he tripped on a root returning to the cover of the awning. Too soon it was Simon's turn to stand guard, and so another night passed on patrol.

It was difficult to know when day broke. The sky an occasional blue or gray speck glimpsed through the canopy. No wonder those living in the jungle were easy to spot in the villages and towns. There was a pasty pallor to their faces, whatever the color of their skin. Simon looked at the other five men. Apart from Tenuk, they all looked spent, the tedium of the patrol making them tetchy. They needed a couple of days rest, somewhere they could dry out properly. Get a little sunlight. Maybe even a wash.

"Haziq, I want to find somewhere to camp for a few days. We're about here." Simon pointed to a section on the map west of Kampong Batu Balai. "Any suggestions?"

"Old kampong near here, people gone after last flood. Maybe six, seven hours?" Haziq traced a route along the Sungai Chenderoh, a tributary of the Pahang River.

"Right. It's in the general direction. Looks remote enough. As long as the CTs haven't got there first. Now, that would be an irony. Is there an area for a drop?"

"Not know. Long time since I see," Haziq replied.

"What would be an irony?" Robin asked, trying to re-stick black nasty on his rifle to stop it glinting in any stray ray of light, the duct tape with which the army was held together.

"If, as we're looking for somewhere to hole up for a few days, we stumble onto CTs doing the same thing."

"Chance would be a fine thing. How's your arm, Haziq?"

"*Tidapa*," the Malay replied with a shrug. "No matter." He showed the doctor the jungle ulcer above his elbow, healing after an application of *kow-yok* taken from the depths of Yi Wei's kitbag. A substance Robin thought similar to Stockholm tar, and certainly more effective than the Epsom Salts he'd applied to the sore a few days earlier.

Shrugging on packs, with Frank carrying the Bren, they set off. It was another long, though uneventful day made a little easier by finding the river which they could then follow. Frustration was running high after nearly two weeks in the *ulu* and no sightings of CTs, or indication they'd ever been in the area. Tenuk scouted ahead as they neared the spot where Haziq thought the abandoned kampong was. He returned a short time later, grinning. It was CT free and appeared not to have been used.

Approaching with caution Simon could see why, but it would do for a few days respite from patrolling. Creeping lianas and saplings were finding footings and pushing through rickety wooden floors, reclaiming the kampong, inch by inch. The headman's house tilted over the river, giving the impression the slightest breeze would tumble it into the sludgy water. A hill rose steeply behind, either a good or a bad thing. Protection, or if a CT patrol spotted them, a death bowl.

"Where did they all go?" Simon asked Haziq, in Malay.

"Kuala Krau," he replied. "Young people want town. Government help them."

"It's not ideal," said Frank, coming back from a recce, "but it's better than where we have been sleeping. There's a house back there that's not too bad. Got a good line of sight just in case we have visitors. We'll have to be careful with fires. Easier to build here, but easier to be seen too."

"There's space for a drop," Robin said.

"I know, and with minimal hacking." Simon looked skywards, "But I'm inclined to ask for one further away. More work for us, but less chance of guiding CTs here."

"I take your point, much as I don't want to."

"Haziq thinks there used to be a small area downriver a couple of miles, and about a mile inland. We'll have a look tomorrow and, if it's suitable, clear as much as we can." A ten-yard hole in the jungle canopy didn't sound that large but clearing would still be difficult, no matter how sharp their *parangs*. "Meantime, let's get sorted. Then I'm having a dunk. If the CTs don't spot us, they could certainly smell us. Two at a time. No letting our guard down entirely."

Lying on a boulder, his faded uniform drying beside him in the last half hour before darkness descended like a theatre curtain and signaled the nightly cricket chorale, Simon closed his eyes. The first image to flicker in was not Tess, but Dee. He sat up, disconcerted, got dressed and hurried to their chosen hut. A supper of bully beef awaited, then an early night if the troop of macaques squealing in trees behind their camp ever shut up.

Finding the drop zone the next day took longer than anticipated. In the end, they doubled back and found it closer to camp than Haziq remembered, although far enough away to satisfy Simon's concerns.

Radio transmissions had less interference in the camp than in the midst of the jungle, and Haziq could soon be heard raising GLO RAF KUALA LUMPUR, giving HQ the Cassini Grid coordinates for near Kampong Batu Balai and their medical and food requirements, and wants.

***

Two days later, after a breakfast of char, oatmeal softened with water, and *pisang kechil* taken from the hand Tenuk hacked from a banana plant at the back of the kampong, four of them set off, leaving Robin and Yi Wei in camp. Tenuk, concerned he might have to climb trees to disentangle any wayward parachutes, once again removed his golden teeth. His toothless grin made the Iban look less fierce. He loped ahead, his blowpipe in one hand, poison-tipped arrows in a bark quiver strung across his bare back.

They made good time to the chosen drop zone and, after hacking back more *belukar*, the secondary undergrowth, settled down to wait on the edge of the small clearing. Coordinates had been received by the RAF, and Haziq would send up a smoke grenade to show position and wind direction as soon as the drone of the expected DC3-Dakota could be heard.

Tension rippled around the quartet as they waited. The timing and precision of the pilots never failed to astound Simon—the clearings they searched for often a pin hole in the midst of 200-foot-tall trees.

"I hope they put the Players in. I'd even settle for Woodbines," Frank said, looking at his last cigarette. "Otherwise it's back to banana and sage leaves."

Simon swatted a mosquito buzzing his head. "Do they never give up?"

"Nope ..." Frank broke off. "Is that it?"

"Yes. Quick, Haziq, fire up the grenade."

They watched the flare splutter and the trail of white smoke drift upwards as the drone increased.

"With a bit of luck any CTs in the vicinity will think it's a bombing raid and will take cover," Frank said. "There she goes. And here they come. What a beautiful sight."

They watched two parachutes fill like giant inverted teardrops and descend, oblong crates swaying below them.

"Bugger, one's blowing off course," Simon said, keeping his eyes on the straying parachute. "Frank, get the other one sorted. We need to get out of here quick as you like. Don't wait for us." He started running across the clearing, Tenuk close behind.

It didn't take long to find the second box. It had tumbled through the highest trees until the silk caught on secondary growth, its strings like giant tentacles holding the box at a precarious angle. An easy climb for Tenuk who shimmied out on a slim branch on hands and feet and had the crate crashing quickly down. It broke on impact, scattering tins of meat and fish paste, canned milk and peaches. A small sack of rice burst open. The hoped-for cigarettes were a welcome sight, along with some extra medical supplies requested by Robin, and a change of clothing for them all. Even Tenuk had a new loin cloth. Simon glanced up from gathering supplies and saw the agile Iban disentangling and wrapping the parachute in on itself before dropping it down.

Loathe to leave any sign of the drop, Simon and Tenuk broke down the rest of the crate and buried it, covering the fresh mound with rotting leaves. Then, slitting the silk parachute in two, they distributed the supplies evenly, tied them in bundles with the chute chords, slung them over their shoulders and headed back to camp, Tenuk leading the way.

Resting an hour into their trek, Tenuk held up his hand then crawled back the way they had just come. Simon nudged the bundles under dead leaves and lay behind a fallen log, his rifle aimed down the path, waiting for any sign from, or of, the Iban.

It came out of nowhere. A thrashing through the undergrowth had the hairs on Simon's neck standing to attention. But no shouts. A thump sent a shock wave along the ground. Lying still, Simon waited. Not long. Tenuk appeared and beckoned, his mouth a wide toothless maw. In voluble, lispy Malay interspersed with dialect words that Simon struggled to understand, he finally realized what had happened.

The Iban had shot a poison dart at a *babi liar*. The wild boar would provide a fine feast. CTs be damned. But first they had to get it home. Stripping a branch, they tied the hog's trotters to it, then with a grunt heaved it, along with the parachute bundles, up to their shoulders. Sweat drenched them as they stumbled back to camp with the coarse black-haired beast.

***

Confirming via radio the successful collection of the drop the day before, Simon learned the latest news of the area. A tapper had been found at the edge of an estate near Kuala Krau, tied to a tree with his belly slashed open. It would not have taken long for ants to find him. A warning to villagers in nearby kampongs. Support the communists or face an appalling death.

"Christ." Simon closed his eyes to the image before focusing again on new orders coming over the wire.

He missed a couple of words, "... remain at current base. Patrol east toward the Sungai Pahang." John Davis' voice may not have delivered the words across the airwaves but Simon heard his message loud and clear. Find the bastards. He pushed the headphones tighter over his ears, "... believe same band of CTs responsible for repeated attacks on trains."

"Tango Mike." Simon thanked the radio operator at HQ and handed the receiver back to Haziq. Simon said, "Right, chaps, trouble appears to be relatively nearby. Kuala Krau is having a hell of a time. Trains ferrying rubber and tin for transshipment in Singapore are being targeted.

"Abdullah CD's lot?" Robin asked.

"So says an SEP," Simon replied, "but no confirmation, although that particular murder follows his usual MO. We'll prepare today and head out before first light. There's a patrol to the east of Sungai Pahang. We're to search between here and the western bank. Weapons checked, kits pared down. Biscuits, clacky, and char," said Simon, referring to the chocolate bars and tea that fed the British Army on duffy.

"I think we, or at least Tenuk, would've seen signs if a camp was between here and the drop," said Frank.

"Yes," Simon agreed, "So we'll head due east. Means we'll have to cross the river."

"Upstream better," said Haziq.

Simon nodded. "The SEP said food supplies were low, his camp surviving on dried fish, with meat once a month for 'a treat.' Another treat, this chap said, was to be chosen for food collection parties, with the chance of a decent feed. At the expense of the villagers of course. So ..." Simon looked at their haul of supplies, "All provisions are to be buried. Just in case. Let's not leave anything for anyone apart from us."

"Sounds like hunger drove him to abandon the commies," Robin said. Rummaging in a tin, he unwrapped a piece of clacky. "Can't help feeling for the poor sods. Idealism only goes so far when you're a starving foot soldier."

"Well whatever it was, he doesn't want to stay around here. Abdullah'll be after his blood. Traitors come in for special treatment," said Frank.

***

Rain came down in torrents through the night, leaving the camp awash in trails of slippery mud. Dawn was a watery flush over the far side of the river. While the men rolled sleeping bags, and wrapped dry clothes in their ponchos, Yi Wei cooked up a conglomeration of tinned beef, rice, and jungle spinach he'd found the day before. There wouldn't be another meal until their return to camp, hopefully by nightfall. They ate in the flicker of the fire, breakfast washed down with piping hot tea.

Every patrol required preparation but there was an added urgency this morning. They each carried extra ammunition, extra radio batteries and an extra poncho, courtesy of the air drop, in which they would wrap their day sacks for the river crossing. *Parangs* had been sharpened the day before, and Robin double-checked his field dressings and drugs.

"It is at this stage, at the start of a patrol," he murmured to Simon, "that I feel most conflicted. On the one hand I'm checking medical supplies, and on the other I'm checking my weapons."

"I suppose it would be more clear-cut if you served as a medic, rather than a soldier or policeman, whatever we are, with extensive medical know-how," Simon said, patting Robin on the shoulder. He glanced around at the men for whom he was responsible, his stomach contracting. If he prayed, now would be a good time to seek a blessing. Instead he said, "Usual five pace formation till we reach the crossing point. It's likely to be harder than I anticipated, with all the rain last night. Typical."

"Should be okay this side of the river," Frank said, cheerfully. "But let's look sharp. No surprises in the form of CTs."

"Tenuk, after you," Simon said, with a slight bow. He was rewarded with a flash of gold.

Despite slick conditions along the banks, and ducking in and out of the tree line, they made good progress to their chosen spot. A slight narrowing of the river had made it seem a good choice on paper but, with the rain, it now gushed like shaken champagne. Logs lunged past like exploding corks.

"Up or down river?" Frank asked, looking at the hurtling waters.

"Buggered if I know," Simon replied, quietly.

"I'd suggest up," Robin's voice broke in. "Upstream the river's significantly wider. A longer crossing but hopefully not as difficult to stay on our feet."

"Right, decision made. But with only six of us, it can't be too wide."

Slinging their packs, with Haziq again lugging the radio, they moved further along the river until Simon called a halt. He studied the banks on either side. A herd of water buffalo luxuriated in the murky water, long, curved horns standing out stark against the gray of their just visible backs.

"They young," Haziq said, nodding to the herd, his voice hushed. "That good. Not angry."

"What happens if they get angry?" Robin asked.

"Only old bull charge," the stocky Malay assured him.

Tenuk's sing-song tones broke in. He rarely spoke, so they all listened. "Have buffalo race near my home. In Limbang. Many party." His voice tailed off as they all looked at him with interest, but he had nothing more to say.

"We could always cross the river on their backs," Robin said, with a quiet laugh.

"Not one of your better ideas, Nancarrow," said Simon. The water still ran fast but did not have the frantic eddying of their first choice. Simon untied a length of rope and signaled for them to cover their day sacks, rifles slung over their shoulders pointing skywards. "I'll take the Bren. Hobbs, you're in first, then Tenuk, Yi Wei, me, the doctor, and Haziq, you'll be last in, first out. Keep that bloody radio dry. Any questions?" He waited a moment. "All right then, tie on. I know it's not normal procedure but the river's wider than I'd like. We might not be able to maintain hand to wrist hold."

He tied one end of the rope to a sturdy tree higher up the bank, where the chance of a slide into the swirling river was less likely, then handed Frank the other end. Only when they were tied together did Frank get into the roiling water.

"I hate the fucking army," he muttered with a grin as water reached his crotch. "Good thing I didn't have a Johnny, my dick's too shriveled to keep one on."

Laughter exploded from Robin as, once Frank had a secure footing an arm's length into the river, he helped lower Tenuk. Holding the Iban's hand, Frank kept him steady as he shuffled past, but the surging turbid water pulled him under. Tenuk rose spluttering, clutching at Frank's hauling hand, but still he managed a gold flash to the concerned faces on the bank. Next went Yi Wei, his face enigmatic as he slipped in and joined the human chain.

Simon clambered down next and, hand over hand from Frank to Tenuk and Yi Wei, reached the middle of the river—the most vulnerable position. He fought to hold his place. The Bren unbalanced him and he angled one foot to the right as a wedge. The river reached his chin, muddy water splashing his face. Tipping his head back he tried not to take a mouthful, but his biggest concern was one of them being taken out by a log.

Robin followed him, and lastly Haziq, who was handed across the human chain as quickly as possible. Simon watched the rope slacken as Haziq let go Robin's wrist and lunged for the bank. He scrabbled up and quickly tied off his end of the rope around a giant bamboo cane the size of a man's thigh. He shrugged off his pack and the radio, then signaled Frank to cut his end of the rope.

Hand over hand, Simon saw Frank work his way across Tenuk towards Yi Wei and him. Simon passed him on to Robin, and then Haziq hauled him up the bank. Next went Tenuk, the CLO, then Simon, and lastly Robin. As they lay panting in the tree line, the threatening heavens gushed again.

"Thank Christ we made it over before that hit," Robin said, his voice almost drowned by the sound of bullfrogs.

"How's the radio?" Simon asked.

"*Baik, tuan,*" Haziq replied, but spoiled his assurance by adding, "I think."

Simon allowed them a short breather before they started hacking their way towards the next river. Somewhere between them and the Sungai Pahang they might find Abdullah's camp. With luck Abdullah CD himself. They could do with something to show for their weeks in the unforgiving *ulu*.

Chapter 8

FOLLOWING HER MEETING with the English planter's wife the day after the party at the Administrator's Residence, Dee sent a lobbying letter to HQ in Penang for permission to extend her region in which she wrote ... *"in order for the Red Cross to be effective, we must be seen to be countrywide and, with no medical facilities on the eastern side of the Sungai Pahang, I believe we are failing."* She advised HQ that Lucy and Putri, her assistants, were well able to take care of the day-to-day running of the clinic in her absence, and she would only be gone a week to ten days. Dee tapped her teeth with her fountain pen, a farewell gift from her father, then shrugged and wrote her final sentence. *"If you feel neither of my assistants are capable of running the clinic, I would suggest the Red Cross send a relief nurse to Raub from Kuala Lumpur."* She smirked, knowing the chance of that happening was slim to none.

Approval had been given, and Lucy and Putri prepped for dealing with most things. Ah Sui would stay at the bungalow as usual. Anything serious and they would call through to Ipoh for guidance. Mohammed was backup for anything practical.

Stuffing two blouses and a pair of trousers into her rucksack, along with spare knickers, a bra, socks and a couple of sarongs, Dee smiled. Good thing she wasn't particularly vain. She bundled her hammock and tied it to the top of the rucksack. After the first foray down the river when a cockroach had woken her on its probing saunter across her chest, she swore to never again sleep on a mat. Next went in a few toiletries and a small towel and she was set.

"*Siap?*" she asked Samsuari as he tied down the canoe.

"Ready!"

"Oh, hang on a moment." Dee went around to the back of the clinic and retrieved her wooden clogs to toss into the Land Rover along with her pack. Jungle boots were all very well for trekking but clogs were more practical once in the villages. "Righto, let's get going. Nur and the children are alright?"

"*Baik*," he replied, smiling. "They good."

After poring over the map the previous afternoon, they decided to drive as far as possible along a track off the Jerantut road, following the tributary which led to Sungai Tembeling. Sounded easy, but as they bumped along dirt roads, doubt jumbled in. She had let Jeffrey know they were heading out but had neglected to tell him where exactly. Dee knew he would make a fuss that their destination was deep in known communist country. Now she wondered about her decision. Oh well, too late now. She gave a chuckle. A good epitaph for her tombstone.

Samsuari looked over and grinned, his eye tooth a golden reminder of his delight. Dee knew he relished the departure from domesticity as much as she.

Three hours later they slithered down the muddy bank, the canoe between them. Dee ferried supplies while Samsuari tinkered under the hood of the Land Rover. She had watched him the first time he disabled the vehicle and she now knew how to disconnect the ground cable from the frame, then the slave cylinder arm from the transmission fork by removing the small cotter pin, one that looked just like a hair pin. This Samsuari clipped to the key chain around his neck. The technical jargon along with a diagram had been supplied by Les, her brother, in a letter after she'd described her initial adventure.

***

The sampan rode higher in the water now most of the supplies had been used. Dee felt drained. Permission to run a clinic always had to be sought from the headman, who would sometimes baulk but, with Samsuari's help, would eventually be given. Clinics started early and ended late as word spread to nearby villages that the Red Cross *jururawat* was there. As her Malay became less stilted, she felt more confident talking to girls and women about sanitation and nutrition. Her next challenge was to start pre- and ante-natal talks.

By the time she fell into her hammock each night she was exhausted. Not only from the volume of patients but from knowing that often her help was too late. Because of the risk of medicines falling into CTs hands, antibiotics were rarely in her arsenal but on this trip she had packed a small supply. They were the only thing that helped stop the spread of yaws, which the planter's wife had warned was a very real problem in the area. The painful skin infection, if not treated, spread through children in the kampongs and could affect the bones and joints for years, and sometimes cause disfigurement.

It was yaws that made her take a stand with headmen, if necessary turning to the curious crowd that always gathered as they arrived. Finding a child with yellow crusted sores, Dee would promise to help. Then she would drum into the mother the importance of covering the ulcer so transmission would be lessened.

And malaria. In her battery, along with quinine, Dee also carried colorful cards showing the cycle of the mosquito and how it was crucial to get rid of standing water. Some nights, after dispensing quinine all day, she longed for a shot of gin to go with a tonic!

"*Mem?*" Samsuari's hiss jerked Dee from her reverie. She spun around, tipping the sampan in her haste. She reached for her hat and jammed it back on. Not much use if it was a croc he'd seen, but if it was CTs, hopefully they'd see the Red Cross emblem and leave them alone.

Rounding a slight bend the *ulu* erupted in shouts and men waving arms and weapons. One had a red star on his cap. A platoon of screeching macaques joined in the ruckus. Dee spun to face Samsuari. There was no glint of gold.

"Go to the bank." Her voice was calm as three men waded towards them. "Let me talk."

She waited until they were alongside, reaching for the sampan. She glanced at her watch and saw it was past noon. "*Selamat tengah hari,*" Dee said, her smile not quite steady. She continued, not giving them a chance to respond. "*Apa kabar?*"

"*Selamat, mem. Tidak baik,*" replied the one in the cap. His skin was tight across his face, his eyes hollow.

It was not the answer she wanted. "What's the matter?" she asked.

"*Jururawat,* nurse, you come. He stay."

"No," she said. "He is my ..." her mind went blank.

"*Saya pembantunya.*" Samsuari helped with the word.

"Yes, he's my assistant," Dee said.

"No. You come. Now."

Samsuari put a hand out to stop her, but the younger of the two others pushed him back, then dragged the sampan to the mangroves.

"It's all right. I'll be alright. You stay here. I'll be back soon." Dee didn't know if she was trying to comfort Samsuari or herself. "What is your name?" she asked, as the one in charge pulled her arm. She shook him off and, taking hold of a branch, heaved herself up the bank. A row of faces watched from the trees. Not one was smiling.

"No name."

Dee turned in time to hear a grunt as a bandit knocked Samsuari back into the canoe and the youths tied it off. He lay still, winded, blood trickling from a gash in his forehead. "Don't you touch him." Her scream startled everyone. Her Malay deserted her and she shouted, "I won't do a bloody thing for you, if you hurt him."

Samsuari struggled to sit, and Dee waved him to stay down. "Do as they say. It'll be fine."

"Come. Now."

"Get my bag first, and those boxes." Dee crouched under the low hanging tree and pointed. "And my rucksack." The capped man moved nearer, his arm raised to strike her. She glared. Defiant. "I can't help without my things. Get them."

With a shrug he turned and shouted an order to the youths still in the water. Three men came out from behind the undergrowth and carried her bags up the tangled slope. Two more appeared and squatted on a rock. One casually pointed a revolver at Samsuari, still lying in the sampan.

Dee tried to smile at him. "Don't hurt him. Please. I'll come." A CT shoved her. "Oi," she said, spinning around, "don't push me." To Samsuari she begged forgiveness, "*Minta maaf!*"

The capped one slapped the youth, then urged her forward. Dee was glad she'd kept her jungle boots on in the sampan as she stumbled along the rough path following another man armed with a rifle. It was the first time she had been in the true *ulu*. The incessant hum of insects, the gloom, and the dense air surrounded her in angry swirls as sweat dripped down her face. She slowed to tuck her hair up under her hat and was again pushed. She stopped in her tracks, surprising the CT behind her.

"Once more, chum, and I'm sitting down. Then you'll have to carry me." She jabbed his chest. He grabbed her wrist and pulled her watch off. "I need that."

His indifferent grin curdled her stomach as he jammed the watch deep into a pocket.

Dee didn't know how long they hacked their way through the jungle. She'd been pulled down with a grimy hand over her mouth about an hour into the trek, a knife at her throat, and had lain in a twisted mess of limbs and terror for what seemed like an age before some signal was given that allowed them to move on. Her legs ached, and her breathing was shallow as she struggled for air in the suffocating humidity. Her clothes were soaked and torn from grasping vines and her hand was bleeding after clutching the spiny trunk of a giant kapok tree. Not even the brilliance of a giant tulip tree in bloom could lighten her fear, even for a moment. She longed for a drink. She glanced up but could see nothing but a blur of green. No patch of sky to indicate the time, but as the vague shadows deepened and the hum changed, she realized night must be falling. She swiped a filthy hand over her eyes, tears not far away.

Again she was stopped, jerked almost off her feet and pulled down to a crouch. They waited a brief time then moved forward. The path seemed better defined and suddenly they were in a camp hollowed out under the canopy. Another youth tugged her to a halt. Her legs buckled, and she sank to the ground looking around from under the brim of her hat.

In the half-light she could see a large raised structure, open on three sides, presiding over the trampled bare quadrangle. To one side was a ramshackle building, with a row of rough-hewn tables, next to it was a cookhouse. On the other side were two smaller structures, one with walls and a door, the other with waist high walls.

"*Selamat datang,* Nurse Dee."

Dee twisted her head to see a short man in a faded but clean tan uniform welcoming her. She didn't know if him knowing her name was more frightening than the look on his face.

His black hair was longer than fashionable. His skin was sallow and taut. His eyes tired, lines drawn tight around his mouth. She tried to rise but her legs refused to support her.

"You rest later. Come."

"No."

The man faltered. "Excuse?" His English was crisp, if abrupt.

"No. You have the bloody gall to say welcome after abducting me, hurting my assistant. Sod you. If I'm here to treat someone, I am not doing anything until I can wash and have a drink."

The man raised his hand and Dee shrank away. His lips curled, gaps showing where teeth had fallen out. Vitamin A deficiency flashed through her mind. Not much protein or calcium this deep in the *ulu*. He gestured to a woman wearing a grubby gray *samfu* watching from the cookhouse. She limped over carrying a bucket with a ladle.

"It good," the man said.

"Thank you." Dee wanted to gulp the water but managed to take sips so she would keep it down. "Now," she looked up at the man, "I am dirty and cannot treat anyone until I wash. Where are my things?"

Another woman, dressed the same way, brought her rucksack and medical bag.

"Ten minute."

Dee pushed herself up and followed the woman. There were few people around. Those in their party had melted away, and she noticed another building behind the central one. Bunk house maybe. A bamboo pipe trickled into a shallow metal tub behind a woven screen. The woman, who could have been thirty or fifty, nodded her to it, then stood guard.

Dee stripped off her shirt and scrubbed her face and arms. Her hand hurt where she had stabbed it on the thorns and she dabbed ointment and wrapped it in a lint bandage, tying the knot with her teeth. She pulled on a semi-clean shirt from her rucksack.

"*Baik*," she said to the silent woman, and was led back to the man waiting at the steps of the main building.

Strips of pandanus woven through bamboo and narrow planks made up a wall in which two flimsy doors hung crookedly. The smell hit Dee as the man opened one of them. A young man wearing only a loin cloth moaned on the low cot. In the glow of the oil lamp she could see one leg was a suppurating mess of shattered bone and skin from the knee down. A gunshot wound. The smell of rotting flesh made her gag. She pulled a mask and gloves from her bag and moved the lamp nearer. She lifted gauze pads to see his foot was a blackish-green, the color deepening as she looked. A bloody discharge oozed from blisters around the ankle.

"Hot water. *Sekarang.*" Now, she demanded from the hovering, bent woman who had stood from her place at the man's head. "*Cepat!*" Dee told her to hurry.

"It is poison, yes?" the man asked.

"Yes. You have morphine?" The patient's blistered skin crackled under her touch. His pulse beat rapidly and whilst he was sweating profusely neither his skin nor eyes looked yellow. There was hope.

"Two," the man replied. "You not have?"

"No. In case you lot get hold of it. Get it. He has gas gangrene. I have to cut the dead skin away."

The man stood still.

"Get it. Now. There's no time. Is there anyone here with medical training?"

"No. He surrender." The man's tone turned sour.

Shit, shit, shit. Dee looked down. She'd never done this before.

"All right. Where's the water? Lots. Hot."

"He is my son."

"I'm sorry. I'll try. Get the morphine. And get me a stool. And my bloody watch. I need it. One of your men took it." Dee was beyond caring if someone got punished. "What's his name?"

The man hesitated.

"Oh for God's sake, what's his name?"

"Tengfei."

Chapter 9

SIMON FOLLOWED HAZIQ, the Malay an excellent front man, always keeping Tenuk to pace by their special way of communicating—a kind of tongue click. Then Frank, laden down with extra ammunition belts. Yi Wei and Robin bringing up the rear with rifles at the ready, he and Frank taking turn and turn with the Bren.

The hell of jungle patrolling soporific, one foot in front of the next, until Haziq raised his hand, palm open and facing forward brought Simon to an instant halt as he sent the signal down the line. He tried to quiet his breathing, loud in his ears. The arms crossed signal came next, quickly followed by Haziq's clenched fist, his thumb pointing down. A track junction with signs of recent activity. It had to be CT. There were no other SF in the area.

Time froze as Simon considered his options, knowing the others awaited his decision. The jungle was always alive with noise, but any human sound became instantly recognizable. Thoughts jumbled. He was glad Frank's cough had gone. Silly. He wouldn't have been able to come if it hadn't. Cardinal rule. Never take a chap on patrol with a cough or a cold, no matter how minor. Simon motioned them to wait. He glanced at his watch, worn face inwards so no glimmer could bounce from it. Twenty minutes seemed an hour during which time Tenuk passed the message via Haziq that he had seen signs of two men.

With no further signal from Tenuk, Simon motioned them to proceed with extreme caution. Being so deep in the jungle and not coming from the general direction of any town or village, he was banking the CTs wouldn't suspect any SF activity in the area. Still, guards would be posted well out from the camp, particularly if a large training camp lay ahead. In which case they would be vastly outnumbered. Simon grimaced. Uncertainty bedeviled his waking and sleeping thoughts.

Tenuk melted back to Simon's side. He'd seen evidence of a small camp a quarter of a mile ahead, probably a staging post. Two guards. Haziq slid ahead and disabled the first without a sound, then gagged him. A kid of maybe fifteen. Simon watched him being tied to a tree, a wet patch forming at his crotch. He felt a momentary pang. Poor sod probably thought they were going to fillet him. A taste of CT medicine. Yi Wei and Tenuk settled down next to him.

Simon motioned Robin and Haziq to snake around and place a grenade necklace to encircle and cut off anyone making a run for it. A text-book maneuver they had discussed earlier, which had the added advantage of creating an impression of a larger force. Frank and he, sweat pouring down their faces, crept nearer the camp, no longer on the track but close enough not to lose it.

The glint of rifle where nasty black had peeled off, the snap of a twig, a footfall. Simon didn't know what spooked the next guard. But he fired and all hell erupted as the necklace of grenades went off and the guard ran backwards, flashes spurting from his machine gun in rapid fire.

Sound, though muffled by the *ulu*, still reverberated and it took Simon a moment to realize Frank had been hit. Frank stood, as if suspended, before falling forward over the Bren. His face smashed onto a log and Simon saw his head rebound. Heedless of further danger, he ran to his friend. Tugging the Bren out from under him, Simon fired a short burst of five rounds before flinging the gun aside. The stutter of shots fired could be heard from Robin and Haziq's direction.

He felt for a pulse before turning Frank over. But he knew. Simon's shoulders heaved. He didn't know if sweat or tears fell onto Frank's blood-splattered shirt. A bullet had entered just above his left eye and blown away his face. A single grenade exploded ahead, then silence. Struggling to haul Frank further off the path, he hoped it was one of theirs. He felt a hand on his shoulder and looked up to see Tenuk shaking his head, sorrow in his dark eyes.

"Goddamnit!" The words exploded from Robin as he ran towards the trio. He squatted next to Frank and felt for signs of life.

"I checked," Simon said.

Haziq burst through the undergrowth and fell to his knees, then looked down and bade his friend a blessed release, *"Inna lillahi wa inna ilayhi raji'un."*

"He wasn't Muslim," Simon said.

"Tidapa. Allah is merciful. All return to one God," Haziq replied.

The sounds of jungle life began again. Crickets. Frogs. The omnipresent mosquitoes whining. Somewhere, the bark of a deer. And further away the roar of a tiger.

Tension, anger, and sorrow encircled them as they waited for Simon to give the signal for Tenuk to crawl forward. The CTs might be playing possum somewhere close to the camp. It didn't take the Iban long to return and report the bandits had slunk off, leaving behind two bodies. Posting Tenuk as look out, Simon, Robin and Haziq moved into the camp.

Simon doubted Frank's death had been worth his sacrifice. A search of the camp proved him right. A staging post. A place to rest before carrying supplies deeper into the jungle. Not worth a life. Either theirs or Frank's.

His face grim, his rage only just in check, Simon took coordinates of the camp to relay later then searched for any papers. All he found were a couple of packs stashed under the low sleeping platform. He slit them with his knife. Haziq made an inventory of abandoned supplies, piercing cans as he went. They would be unable to carry much with them.

The camera was FUBAR and so Robin made a thorough examination of the bodies, making notes of sex, race, approximate age, height, build and any distinguishing features. One had a gold molar, and a jagged scar running down his left thigh. Both were thin, with a jungle pallor. They appeared to have been foot soldiers. Youths. No one of any import, save to their families. Watching Robin, Simon wondered if they had ever doubted their chosen life. Whether their comrades would return for them. Whether they had eaten rice that day. Before burying the boys in a shallow grave, they washed their hands and fingerprinted them. Simon had a brief image of decapitated heads. A practice he could not fathom but one which a couple of SF patrols had chosen rather than carry CT bodies back to base with them, but that had been before finger printing kits were distributed as a matter of course.

In silence, the three men chopped down branches, stripping them of foliage as they went, then lashed them together to make a stretcher for Frank, making sure to keep his body rigid. Covering him in a poncho, they headed back down the roughly hewn track to collect Yi Wei who was in some state, wondering what had happened. He'd spent the time, he told Simon, by convincing the CEP to talk and the kid, pimples standing out on his jungle-pale skin was singing like the proverbial canary. A part of Simon had hoped he'd been eaten by red ants.

The CEP, his hands bound but the gag absent, was prodded along by Haziq's rifle. Simon wished to Christ the promised helicopters were already in Malaya. He knew they'd never make it back across the river that night but they needed to get far enough away from any regrouped band of CTs out for blood. And they had to find somewhere for Haziq to get a message through to Port Dickson. They had to get Frank out. Bodies decomposed quickly and Simon decided, if they couldn't find somewhere for a landing strip, they'd try and get him down the river to Kuala Krau.

The weight of Frank's body stretched screaming muscles. Their senses dulled by emotion, Simon called a halt after a two-hour slog. Pushing off the track a short way, they crouched around a tommy cooker and boiled water for char. They ate rationed clacky and dry biscuits.

"You eat." Tenuk let his poncho slip and a cascade of small brownish fig-like fruit fell to the ground.

"What are they?" Robin asked, picking one up and sniffing.

"*Salak*," Tenuk replied. "Sweet."

"Same called snakefruit," Haziq added.

"I can see why," Robin said. "Here," he tossed one to Simon.

They watched Tenuk peel the fruit then sink his gold teeth into the firm white flesh. The Iban flashed a quick grin. "*Baik!*" he said, announcing its goodness.

Simon took first stag while the rest, including the CEP, once again gagged and whose jungle sores Robin had treated, tried to doze, propped against trees. Frank's body, shrouded in a poncho, a constant reminder of the terrible day.

After the last of the clacky and char, they set off again well before dawn and still without managing to get a message out. Exhaustion slowed them down, but at least they were following their own hacked path until the last hour back to the river. Simon wanted to be further south than their entry point, although, watching Haziq slowly scythe a path with his *parang*, he doubted any of them had the energy to clear an area for a landing strip, even if they could find a suitable site.

The river, turgid but welcome, came into view across a series of overgrown paddy fields. Simon reckoned, and Haziq agreed, that Kuala Krau was about six miles downstream. It would be easier, and safer, if they could steal a canoe and transport Frank to the police station there. Tenuk and Haziq scouted along the bank and on the edge of an abandoned kampong found a dugout. It would have to be bailed out all the time but it was something.

They could not risk balancing Frank's stretcher on the narrow prow and so hacked branches away to leave just two to keep his body firm, and hidden, in the base of the dugout. They split the last of the biscuits, and Simon, Robin and Tenuk watched Haziq, Yi Wei and the CEP clamber in. They had removed their uniforms and untied the CEP's hands. All concern about him giving them away evaporated the more he talked, giving Simon an idea of the location of the main camp though the boy hadn't known coordinates. Whilst it was not Abdullah CD's camp it was at least something useful to show for their disastrous patrol.

"No weapons on show, not to be used unless absolutely necessary. Just get to Kuala Krau." Simon shook Haziq's hand. "Be careful, my friend." He nodded to Yi Wei and thanked him.

Tenuk and Robin held the dugout steady as Haziq and the CEP tested the oars they had fashioned, then pushed them into the racing waters. Robin climbed the bank and stood with Simon as they saluted their dead friend. Tenuk, his golden grin absent, nodded as they watched the canoe disappear around the next bend.

"They'll be less of a target than if either you or I were aboard," Robin said, his voice weary.

"Yup. Right. Back to camp. We'll need a shorter crossing with only three of us. Thank God the rain's eased off."

"What then?" Robin asked.

"We'll rest up a day then head to Kuala Krau. We can get picked up there and taken to Temerloh. We're three men down. This patrol is over as far as I'm concerned."

The usual banter missing, somberness weighed them down as they hacked back to camp where they waited two days before setting off for the agreed pick-up point. Sweating through the *ulu* Simon found, to his discomfort, images of the vivacious young woman in Kuala Lipis persistently intruded on his thoughts, pushing past that of Tess. Like Tess, a sense of calm practicality ran through her, with both women fervent in their desire to right wrongs, but there the similarities ended. Dee, a petite water sprite who longed to see the world. Her hair a puff of blonde curls that refused to stay confined by pins and clasps. Her voice, surprisingly deep, held a twang of her Australian background.

The thought of Dee accompanied him through the misery of Frank's death and the pitiless jungle.

Chapter 10

HOURS LATER, her shirt clinging to her back, hair plastered in tendrils to her neck, Dee straightened on the stool, pulled off her mask and looked down at the bandaged ankle and foot. At her side was a bucket of decayed flesh and swabs of bloodied gauze. The agony of cutting away dying flesh and splinting Tengfei's leg roused him to consciousness. She had never felt so helpless and shot one of the morphine phials into the lad, anything to stop the screaming. The crone, his *amah* since birth, had wailed until Dee swore at her to shut up. The man, unflinching, had held his son's thrashing shoulders. She gestured for the woman to remove the bucket, then reached for Tengfei's wrist to check his pulse, counting the seconds on her watch. It had steadied a little but she was not confident the poison hadn't infused his entire body.

"Well?"

"I don't know," Dee said. She wiped her forehead with the back of her hand and rotated her shoulders. "I've given him penicillin. There is only enough for a day. Keep the wound clean, and try to control the fever."

"You stay."

"No. You don't want people searching."

The man sneered. "They cannot find. You stay."

"My assistant?" Dee looked at the man, tears of exhaustion and anger and fear trembling on her lashes. "Let him go. Please. He is a good man. He too has a son."

The man looked down at his son, then left the room. Dee shifted the stool to the top of the cot. "All right, Tengfei, it's up to you now," she told the unconscious man, dampening his brow with a cool cloth. The *amah* returned and, with a slight bow, handed Dee a tin mug filled with steaming tea.

80

"Thank you." She took a sip and sighed. "What is your name?" she asked in Malay.

The crone shook her head and returned to her position at her charge's head. She took his hand and murmured a discordant lullaby.

Dee shrugged, stood with her tea and went to the door, surprised to find it unguarded. But where would she go?

She flumped down on the top step and looked into the night. Tears trickled down her face. The woman in the grubby *samfu* touched her shoulder and beckoned. Dee heaved herself up and followed, the mug still in her hand. The woman pointed to a canvas cot with a rough blanket folded across it. She mimed sleeping, nodded then left. Slung on low metal legs, the cot had been placed behind a bamboo screen; a shield from the vacant eyes of the camp. Too tired and worried to care about privacy, Dee lay down fully clothed. Sleep did not come. Images of death from nursing manuals intruded each time she closed her eyes. She checked on Tengfei, and found the crone still at his side, still awake. Falling back onto the cot, exhaustion finally won.

***

Chanting woke her to a thin stream of daylight seeping through the *attap* roof. She listened. It didn't sound like Buddhist monks. Then a voice broke the rhythm, discordant and reedy. The chanting restarted, the pattern repeating, and Dee realized it was coming from behind the building. An incantation. Mao perhaps?

In the sick room, Tengfei lay still, breathing in shallow spurts, his fever raging. Dee shook off the fear he wouldn't last the day and whispered through her doubts, "Come on, mate, you've gotta fight." She sighed. She would bathe first, then rewrap his wounds.

Dee went down the steps and turned toward the washhouse, her surroundings clearer in daylight. She felt her arm snatched from behind and the straps of her rucksack bite into her shoulder. A bellow came from the man, ragged but clean, standing at the entrance to the smaller hut. Her arm was dropped. The offending bandit melted away, and the man approached.

"You stay," he pointed to the main building.

"I am going to wash." Rubbing her shoulder, she moved away.

"You wait."

"No. I'm going to bathe."

The man shouted for the same woman as the previous evening to accompany her.

"Really? Where do you think I can go?" she asked.

"You wait."

Each foray to the latrines and washhouse allowed her a glimpse into the prescribed daily lives of those in the camp. CTs got used to seeing her at all hours of the day and night and took little notice, although she was invariably accompanied though not guarded once she returned to the main building.

Constraints to independent thought and actions amazed her, though the man assured her on one of the rare times he answered a question, that all men, or women, were allowed to criticize the leader. Everything was structured. One morning, very early, she smelled the fires and, leaning up on an elbow, saw through gaps in the woven screen, cooks prepare breakfast for those leaving camp. Dee assumed messengers or food collectors. Sometimes a patrol, rifles ready, would march out with the dawn.

At first light a whistle blew and the rest of the camp stirred. It did not take long for them to appear on the parade ground because, Dee realized, they slept in their clothes. PE was followed by a clean-up brigade of the entire camp, then an hour or two of military training. But never shooting practice. Bullets were scarce, it seemed.

Breakfast was served at 0830 sharp, followed by an hour's rest. Then, as heat trickled through the canopy, educational programs started. It was that which had woken her the first morning. At midday, repairs were made to the camp, followed by another rest period before mending and bathing at four in the afternoon.

After the main meal of the day, singing lessons could be heard, which the man told her were good for morale. The day ended with another parade in front of the Red Flag before CTs were dismissed and permitted to return to the sleeping hut to talk and smoke until the whistle blew for lanterns out.

The monotony of their lives astounded Dee, their compliance even more so. But then hers was not that different. Days and nights revolved around Tengfei, as she and the *amah* took turns to sit with the patient. Mostly he moaned. Changing the dressing, as flesh came away with the gauze, became agony for everyone nearby. His fever continued to rage, the thinnest gruel spewed back and Dee, her nerves jangled, thought it was over.

A lantern in her hand, Dee went to the latrines one night, having sat with Tengfei for hours cooling his fever and trying to get him to sip water. On her way back to the sick room she saw shadows merging into solid shapes when a glimmer escaped through the opening of the man's hut. Surprised, she stood stock still and counted five figures before the *amah* hustled out of Tengfei's room and pushed her behind her screen. The crone put a finger to her lips and shook her head. Dee nodded, and lay down and wondered if they would talk about her.

The next morning the man disappeared. When he returned, five days later, he had morphine and penicillin. Dee did not ask where it came from, but shot antibiotics into Tengfei, and hoped.

Tengfei's father watched, silently from the door. "Your man. He safe," he said, as Dee straightened from her crouch by the cot.

"Where?"

"He released."

"Thank you. And me?"

"You stay. You help my people."

"No," Dee said. "A couple more days. Tengfei is recovering, and now you have drugs, but it will take time."

"You stay."

"Listen, mister whatever-your-name-is, you don't want the SF looking for an abducted nurse." Dee's anger dissolved and she turned her back on the man, refusing to let him see her fear. She looked down at Tengfei, sleeping more peacefully now. "I'll see anyone who needs help here, but then you must let me go. Please."

The man shook his head and moved to the door.

"For God's sake!" she said to the man's back as she followed him, "I haven't a clue where I am. I don't know anyone's name, apart from his and that could be fake for all I know. What could I possibly tell anyone?"

The door trembled on its flimsy hinges, as close to a slam as possible.

The cot became her haven. The nervous energy that kept her going through the day abated for a few precious moments before an exhausted sleep took hold. The moments often took the form of a slightly built Englishman. She did not dwell on why him, and not the dancing doctor who had whirled her along the verandah and made her laugh.

Dee didn't see the man for three days, but the morning following her outburst the first man, the one with the star on his cap, reappeared and lead her to a trestle table set up outside the mess hut. Men, and a few women, waited in the shade. She sighed. Mostly it was dysentery and diarrhea. Tropical ulcers, the omnipresent fever, and two minor wounds she knew were gunshots. One woman she suspected was pregnant. The dread that crossed her face as Dee questioned her symptoms indicated the punishment would be severe for breaking rules. As dusk fell on the sixth day of clinics and the last patient limped away, his ulcerated foot bandaged, she saw the man again.

"You must move the latrines further away from the water. That is why so many are sick."

"Next time," he replied. "Come."

Dee rose. Tired, she followed him into the sick room. Tengfei lay on the cot, awake. She slipped on gloves and looked at his eyes. No jaundice.

"Thank you," he said, his voice weak.

"You're welcome, Tengfei." She patted his shoulder and said, "When you can, you must leave the jungle."

"Come."

Dee wondered if everything the man said was an order. She followed him from the room and saw, through the gloom, her rucksack and medical bag silhouetted in the feeble lantern light.

"You go now."

Tears welled in her eyes. She brushed them away. Angry with herself. She nodded. The capped man was waiting, and four CTs, one of them a woman.

They trekked for three days. Dee's blistered feet bled despite dabbing them with methylated spirits each time they stopped, the sting taking her breath away. Her stomach rejected the slop they shared each evening, but she forced herself to swallow some. At dusk of the third day they reached a river. Dee didn't know which one. She sank onto a boulder and looked at the water flowing to somewhere. Tears dripped onto her boots as she removed them, her socks sticking to her bloody feet. Silence made her turn. She was alone. She scrambled to her feet, calling. Her rucksack and medical bag were by a tree, along with a flask of water and a handful of rambutans. She shouted again. Nothing. Fear slithered over her like a cape but without the comfort.

As night fell, noises sent her imagination to every dark place it could find. The emergency flashlight at the bottom of her rucksack gave a faint glow as she switched it on, then panicked and turned it off as she considered the already weak battery. She would keep it for a true emergency. "Hah!" The loudness of her voice startled her. "If this isn't an emergency I don't what is."

Mangrove roots buried in shallow graves by fallen leaves and mud made a soft bed but one likely to be shared with all manner of critters. She surveyed the water. And maybe crocs. Dee looked up convinced she saw snakes in every vine. "Oh, Christ, bugs or boas?" She snorted. "Boas." It took a number of attempts to find somewhere to hang her hammock, twisting branches away in an effort to stop something slithering down. "I am never leaving home without a parang again." Her voice offered some comfort.

She propped her rucksack behind her head and settled in the hammock with her rationed water and fruit, juice running down her chin as she bit the white flesh from inside the soft-spiked crimson shell. She sang snippets of remembered songs. She recited *Clancy of the Overflow*, her favorite Banjo Patterson poem. She thought of her parents. And Les, and Jimmy and David. Then flashes of Mitch and Ronnie as they marched off to war. She wondered if Les was still dating the teacher. And she cried. She longed for Frank, Robin and Simon to magically appear.

Her last thought as she slipped into a bushwhacked doze was that the man would not have abandoned her. Not after saving his son. She had seen an element of decency. She must stay put. Like in the bush back home. If you break down, stay with the vehicle. Stay put.

She woke to the squeaks of a laughing thrush on a branch above her, its chestnut-capped head tilted quizzically. Thankfully it had not rained overnight. Every bone and joint ached as she struggled down, startling the bird away with a squawk taken up by others in the trees overhead. Her watch had stopped at three fourteen but the sheen spreading across the river, a wide one, told her it was about six. She sipped from the flask, swallowing both water and panic, and remembered her mantra of the night before, "Stay put."

Chapter 11

"SISTER CUNNINGHAM, did you get a sense that the foot soldiers were tiring?" Her interrogator was a rotund man with a mustache whose ends wiggled as he spoke.

"No, not really. Not even when I held clinics for the camp, spoke to men and women who were sick, certainly hungry, and some injured. For people in pain they seemed remarkably contained. Not happy, but not discontent."

"Hmph. We are getting some responses to the offer of a reward for information."

"I thought that had been abandoned. After the outcry of $80,000 on Chin Peng's head."

"No. The cries of 'immoral' came from those safe in Whitehall. The reality is that rewards work. They always will. Thank God."

The questions had continued then doubled back for two days. Everyone had been very polite and accommodating, but Dee still felt they were disappointed in her inability to tell them where the camp had been. Her recollection of the five wraiths—all men, she was sure—slipping into the man's hut had provoked another barrage of questions but she could tell them little else. She learned that a pharmacy had been looted in Ipoh and assumed that was where Tengfei's drugs came from.

"Look, they could've been walking me around in circles for three days. I don't bloody know. But I'll bet you a quid wherever it was, it's not there now."

"Why do you say that?"

"Because when I told 'the man' to move the latrines further away from the water source, he said, 'Next time.'"

The Red Cross offered to annul her contract but Dee was anxious to return to Raub. To see for herself that Samsuari was alright. To get back to work. To forget.

After her abduction, and subsequent debrief in Kuala Lumpur, Dee no longer considered herself a neophyte in Malaya. Perhaps, she recognized, due to her limited exposure to expatriates, she found her sympathies often aligning more with the people around her, if not the CTs, rather than the mandates sent down by the colonial administration.

Her delight at finding Samsuari and the family waiting for her at the clinic when Jeffrey drove her home was visceral, as was her relief that Samsuari intended to continue accompanying her, with Nur's blessing.

Whilst Dee appreciated the financial and in-kind support of the RAGM, and Jeffrey's kind, but often ineffectual efforts, besides rescuing her, she decided if she was to truly serve Malaya she must spend more time in the jungle, and more time administering to the New Villages that were purported to be springing up around Raub.

These villages were the brainchild of Sir Harold Briggs, the Director of Operations, who believed the only way to win against CTs was to starve them of supply lines. The most effective way to do that meant resettling the predominantly Chinese squatters who had migrated from the towns during the Japanese occupation and now lived, not only on the edge of the jungle, but often of society. It was Sir Henry Gurney, the British High Commissioner, who persuaded the Sultans to agree to The Briggs Plan, and that giving squatters a permanent land stake in Malaya would limit the influence of communist propaganda.

At the end of long days, Dee wrestled with opposing thoughts as she sipped a whisky on her verandah, despite Jeffrey's protestations that she would be safer inside. She recognized the fine line she trod with regard to the apolitical code of the Red Cross, but satisfied her conscience that she was fulfilling the Hippocratic Oath, even if she wasn't actually a doctor.

On the one hand starving supply lines to CTs was crucial to bringing the maelstrom of the Emergency to an end, but civilians trying to eke out a living were caught in the web. And whilst it was mostly Chinese being placed behind wires, albeit only locked in at night, a large number of ethnic Malays were also corralled.

"I hear Chin Peng is trying to sell the plan as internment camps rather than permanent New Villages with standpipes for water, electricity, schools, health centers and so on," Greg, a miner at RAGM, said one Friday evening over sundowners at their clubhouse.

"It sounds to me like a win, win. Squatters get a piece of land, a home, the CTs get squeezed, and Malaya is closer to independence," commented another bloke.

"I imagine it will depend on who's in charge of the village," Dee said with a sniff. "Displacing people, herding them miles from their homes can't be good for morale. Breed even more discontent. And I can't help feeling most people don't really give a fig about communism, they just don't want colonialism. And who can blame them? And it's not going to be exactly free movement for people, is it? They'll have to show ID, they'll be body checked."

"For many, Dee," Greg argued, "it'll take away the terror of being targeted by CTs demanding either food or money. And have you thought about the incredible logistical coup of getting an entire country over the age of twelve identified with a thumbprint and a photograph? They've started that. Dangerous work too. I read a report of one village which had just been ID'd and the bastards swooped in and slaughtered some of the villagers, children too, then gathered up the IDs and burned the lot."

"I know there's no easy answer, but relocating people who don't want to be relocated seems draconian." Dee's thoughts flashed to her incarceration at the camp hidden in the jungle.

"Maybe, but they're indiscriminate bastards. That American running the orphanage, I can't remember where—the CTs shot him in cold blood, then set fire to his house with him in it. Hope the poor sod was dead first." The usually laconic Australian shuddered.

"Where are the SF? They must know where some of the camps are," asked another chap, pulling on a pipe.

"It's a bloody big jungle out there," Dee said. "I know."

"Have you heard Gurney speak, Dee?" Greg asked, easing the tension. "He's pretty powerful. His big question to Malaya is: do you really want to swap one rule with another? British colonialism with Chinese communism? I know which I'd rather have."

"I agree he wants *merdeka*, but it's taking too long," Dee said.

"Getting a country of Malays, Chinese and Indians to accept it's a plural society rather than an integrated one is a tall order. Now, enough politics. Another sundowner, Dee?"

"No, thanks, I need to get going. Sorry I got a bit heated."

"I'll follow you home," Greg said, standing.

"No, I'm right. I'm far safer than you. It's pretty obvious I'm Red Cross," Dee replied, her laugh a little forced.

"I can't believe you said that. And that you don't carry a pistol," he replied, "especially after what you've been through."

"I wouldn't be considered humanitarian then, would I, dopey? And the Land Rover's been covered in armor plate. Thanks to you lot. I can hardly see out the windscreen it's such a small slit."

***

Something didn't feel right. There was a glow from inside. Ah Sui never left lights on. Instead of driving straight under the carport beside the clinic, Dee reversed the Land Rover to face the track and left the engine running. She peered around the back of the vehicle toward the verandah. Shadows disappeared as the door to the clinic opened and light spewed into the garden along with the red flare of a cigarette.

"Who's there?"

"Simon Frampton."

"What the hell are you doing here?"

"I'm sorry. Ah Sui let me in."

"Well, she shouldn't have." Dee leaned into the Land Rover and switched off the engine. "What are you doing here?" she asked again. "This is not a rescue home. You can't just show up."

"I needed somewhere to go."

Something in his voice stopped her next words. She walked closer and saw his drawn face, his eyes bloodshot. But he didn't appear drunk.

"What's happened?"

"Frank's dead."

"Oh God! I'm sorry, Simon. So sorry. He was a lovely man." The image of Frank, white dinner jacket pristine against a backdrop of sandbags as they had laughed and danced on the verandah in Kuala Lipis, flashed in. Dee reached for Simon's arm. "Come on. In you come. Let's have a drink."

He held up his glass. "I'm afraid I helped myself."

"Good, pour me one whilst I let Ah Sui know everything's alright."

They talked long into the night. For the first time since her tears on the riverbank, Dee sobbed and admitted to Simon how terrified she'd been by the abduction. How guilty she felt to have put Samsuari through everything. Simon spoke of Frank. Their debrief in Port Dickson. And war. And fears.

As the night deepened, Dee asked, "How long are you here for?"

"A few days respite. Robin's gone to KL, Haziq to his family, and Tenuk to wherever he could find *tuac*!"

"You know you can't stay here, don't you?"

"Of course. I'm at the Rest House. I'll go now."

"You'll be alright, Simon. We both will."

"Yes, yes, I know." He stood then leaned down and brushed his lips across her cheek. "Thank you and good night. Can I stop by tomorrow, after work?"

Each evening as Lucy and Putri ushered the last patient from the clinic, printed instructions often clutched in hand, they would see Simon walk down the track from Bibby Street. "Here come the *tuan*," Lucy would call, a smile twinkling the girl's brown eyes. She, Putri, and even Ah Sui had taken to teasing Dee about her beau and fell into giggles at her blushes.

Dee looked forward to the company. Simon would wait in the garden as she washed and changed from her uniform into slacks and a blouse and they would sit on the verandah with a Tiger and watch *chichaks* stalk insects along the low wall then scurry around sandbags with their catch. And they talked. She was a good listener, and so was he.

"You know, it's the conscripts I feel for," Simon said. "The SF are stretched thin, not enough time to teach them to learn the ropes. Poor blighters, thrown in at the deep end, certainly in the early days. They had no understanding of Malaya, the political ramifications—*merdeka*—despite the army manuals."

"I can't help feeling for some CTs who signed up for an ideology. One, that after months in the *ulu*, most people would realize was unattainable. Christ, Simon, they have no food, no medicine, and yet somehow they keep their faith. How can people be so gullible?"

"People always want to hear of a better way of life, Dee. The British haven't always been honorable and yes, between you and me, the initial plan for independence was too long. And there is always someone who can drip feed notions of Xanadu. During the war it was the fascists. This time it's the communists."

"It's bloody depressing."

Not all their conversations revolved around the Emergency. Or Frank. They shared stories of their childhood. Simon told her of his early days in Malaya, before the war, as a naïve young planter. And it felt good to laugh.

On his final evening as they drank gin and tonic, Simon held up his glass, the slice of lime a splash of color in fizzing bubbles. "Do you know the first time I had this?" He dunked the lime with his finger. "It was on the ship when I first came to Malaya."

"Good grief, it must've been quite something," Dee teased. "I can't remember the first time I had a G&T. Probably illicit, out the back door of Dad's pub!"

Simon laughed. "Mine had been a memorable day," he said. "We'd just come through the Suez, and we'd been tossing coins for Arab kids to dive for. Incredible how they kept their breath. Then the gully gully man clambered aboard at Port Said."

"What's a gully gully man?"

"A conjuror. Magicians who'd entertain passengers by producing chirruping chicks from an onlooker's clothing, nearly always from a female! The first one I saw was really rather sinister wearing his jellaba and fez. For some reason I remember his filthy feet, with yellow toenails."

"Thanks for the image," Dee said. "What else did they do?"

"The finale was always a cobra charmed out of a basket by playing a kind of pipe. Scared the hell out of me the first time I saw it. Anyway, Port Said was the last stop before the Orient and I celebrated my new life with a gin and tonic. Never looked back." Simon gazed into his drink. "Thank you, Dee. I can't remember ever being this relaxed ..." he hesitated, "... with a woman. I feel rejuvenated."

"I told you I grew up with five brothers," she said, with a laugh, "You men hold no secrets for me." Her carefree tone turned to sadness at the memory of Ronnie, killed in Egypt, and Mitch in New Guinea during the war. "I miss them."

There was no awkwardness to the silences.

"You know, Simon," Dee said, breaking the quiet and thinking of the guilt of Frank's death that ate at him, "Shoulda, woulda, coulda—they're all a waste of time. None of us would get out of bed in the morning if we allowed ourselves to be swamped by them. And for you, and me, death is part of the job."

Simon stood, and drawing Dee into his arms, he kissed her goodbye.

"Come back soon, darling," she said. She smiled at his gap-toothed grin.

Chapter 12

THE FERRY, *TALANG*, was one of the Z-type tank landing crafts reassigned and converted after the war in an effort to get Penang reconnected to the peninsula, and was a vast improvement to the one he'd taken across in 1947.

The CT ambush at Sungai Panap on the island in January, believed to be the work of the notorious Labis gang, had shocked everyone. Eight SF men had been killed, including a British police sergeant, and six wounded. Up until then Penang had been considered a relatively safe area. And yet, standing at the stern of the ferry, Simon watched Butterworth dissolve into the morning haze as George Town neared and he felt the urgency of life on the mainland fade away.

Frank's death still lingered close to the surface whenever he was surrounded by solitude. Other friends had died, in the war and in the Emergency, but he'd always had Frank's irreverence and humor to help drag him out of the funk into which he was in danger of slipping. Now he was on his own, though Robin had become a stalwart. And Dee.

A laugh broke free as he lit a cigarette. Five days. No commitments. No phone calls and, although he'd had to leave his whereabouts with his CO, he'd been promised only the direst emergency would interrupt his well-earned leave. And more to the point, a grin played around his mouth making his brown eyes crinkle behind wire-rimmed glasses, five days with Dee.

He was looking forward to showing her Penang, the lesser known spots as well as the more obvious attractions of George Town. The Eastern & Oriental Hotel was a good place to start. The last time he'd been there, just after the war, the rooms, whilst still grandly proportioned, had shown signs of the Japanese occupation. He doubted the Sarkies, the four Armenian brothers who had built the hotel in 1885, would have approved of their wartime guests.

Simon had booked two rooms on the top floor overlooking the Straits of Malacca, and had stressed one of them had to have an adjoining bathroom. A luxury for Dee after her usual Shanghai jar ablutions. She'd wangled a lift to Penang with a convoy heading north from Kuala Lumpur. How she would return to Raub was open to conjecture, but she hadn't seemed in the least perturbed.

It was one of the things he liked about Dee. She didn't let life's minutiae get in the way. Whether it was work, or play. "What is the point?" she'd asked. "We might be blown up tomorrow. Though there's rather more chance of that for you than me."

Simon watched lines being deftly caught by stevedores amid the jostle and general chaos of Weld Quay as *Talang* nudged the wharf. He picked up his small leather suitcase and joined passengers eager to disembark. A Chinese woman, her hair scraped back in a tight gray bun, took a hesitant step onto the gangplank but pulled back as it swayed. An impatient businessman, his suit still crisp in the humid air, urged her to hurry. She turned and, although Simon couldn't understand the staccato Hokkien, neither he nor anyone was under any misapprehension as to what she was saying. The young man bowed, looked sheepish, and offered her his arm.

Pushing through those waiting to board the *Talang* for her return to Butterworth, Simon climbed into a *beca* and directed the driver to a tailor on Chulia Street in Little India. He assumed Rabindra would still be in business, his cluttered shop lined with bolts of fabric propped against all the walls, three sewing machines just visible through a bead curtain, thrumming as suits and dresses were stitched. Simon was certain the plump Gujarati would be able to find his original measurements in one of the many ledgers he stored under the wide, nicked counter on which he cut fabric. Three shirts and a new linen suit would do the trick. Simon would eat his hat if they weren't ready within twenty-four hours.

And there Rabindra was. Simon sauntered in, smiling at the tailor who rushed around the counter and pumped his hand.

"Good day, *tuan*," he said, his high-pitched voice unchanged. "You are back. Long time I not see you. You are well. You will take tea?"

"Hello, Rabindra. How are you? How is it the rest of the world ages and you do not?"

The Indian burst into delighted laughter, clapping his hands for tea.

"You are back to stop this foolishness. This commie nonsense not good for business."

"Well, we're trying. Tell me, how is your family? Your wife? Your daughters? They must be almost grown up now."

"Aiyee, and still they give me trouble." The man's eyes sparkled. "I am a man bowed by a house full of women."

Simon had known it would not be a short visit and an hour later, after much consultation about fabrics and colors intermingled with politics, he left with the promise his order would be ready next morning. "No fitting?" Simon queried.

"No need, *tuan*. You are the same size."

Another trishaw took him to the hotel. Glamor whispered out the doors of the E&O, the luxury of a bygone era evident in the hushed marble halls and chandeliers shimmering even in the broadest daylight. He registered, then, turning to follow the bellhop with his small case, saw Dee come in from the terrace, her blonde hair cut shorter and ruffled from the breeze. His breath caught as he took in her slim green skirt cinched by a wide red belt, above which a white short-sleeved blouse hugged her bosom. Her only jewelry, a gold bangle.

Her smile was radiant as she lifted her face for his kiss. "You're here, finally. I'm awash in coffee, I've been down here so long waiting for you."

"I stopped at my tailor on the way. Mold and moths have had a fine time with what few respectable clothes I have left. Although, for some reason, they have left my dinner jacket alone. Let me nip up to my room, then I'll join you." Simon checked his watch. "We could just about get away with a Tiger. If I dally a little, it will be eleven, we could pretend we are having an early tiffin."

"Sounds lovely. Hurry up. I don't want to waste a minute."

Simon wondered which of the rooms along the corridor was Dee's. The bellhop, who stood a discreet distance away as he and Dee met, unlocked the door with a hefty brass key, put the suitcase on the rack, drew back the curtains from the door to the small balcony and bowed as he spirited away the dash Simon gave him, smiling his way out.

Splashing water on his face, Simon saw his eyes were bright. Nothing like the thought of five days leave in one of his favorite places with a lovely woman to push dark thoughts aside. And Tess.

"Let's just have a lazy day," Dee said, sipping a Tiger beer, nibbling from the bowl of *ikan bilis* that had come with it, the fried anchovies giving a delicious salty crunch. "No sightseeing. I know you want to show me Penang, and I want to see it, but I think we both need to wind down a little."

"Of course," said Simon. "But I insist we go out for dinner."

"You insist, do you?" said Dee, her voice teasing. "Did I not tell you I grew up with five brothers, insisting does not go down well."

"I'm sorry. Let me rephrase. I would very much like to take you out to dinner. To Hameediyah's. Please?"

"Ah, well, that's better. In that case I would be delighted to accompany you to wherever you just said. Thank you." Dee's smile was wide. "You do know you can't play the pompous Pommie with me, don't you, Simon? Snooty doesn't go down well with us Aussies."

"So I'm learning. But I think you'll enjoy the restaurant. It's been around forever. At least thirty years. And it serves wonderful southern Indian food. I am happy to be quoted as saying the best *nasi kandar* in the country. How's that for sticking my neck out?"

"If I knew what that was, I'm sure I'd be impressed."

"It's aromatic steamed rice, surrounded by lots of little side dishes. It is quite spicy though, more so than Malay curries. Is that alright?"

"Well, if my eyes start watering and I roll on the floor in convulsions you'll know it's not."

"Oh dear, I'm sorry, Dee. I wasn't thinking. It's just that I normally eat there my first night in Penang. A kind of tradition. Last time I was with Frank. We can go somewhere else, or dine here."

"Don't be silly, Simon. I'd love to go. You're not used to being teased, are you?"

He lit a cigarette, confused. "I didn't have sisters, so no, I suppose not. Brothers tend to be rather more physical," he replied.

"Don't I know it. You would have very little chance against me in a pillow fight!"

They shared a plate of club sandwiches and, after another beer, Dee rose, picked up her handbag and said, "If I don't move, I shall fall asleep. I don't usually drink at lunchtime. I'm going to change, then I'm going for a swim. That water is so tempting. And I am open to temptation."

Simon stood, not sure if there was an invitation buried in her last sentence, or whether the mercurial woman he was with wanted to be alone.

Dee reached up, pecking his cheek. "You are most welcome to join me."

"I'll just finish my cigarette," he said, watching her leave.

"You do that!" Her words drifted back.

Instead he ordered another beer and watched the nearly deserted beach—sensible people being indoors during the heat of the day. Simon saw Dee reappear and wander along the sand until she was not in direct sight of the verandah. Even in a batik sarong and under a coolie hat she managed to look chic. He moved his chair and watched as she untied the sarong to expose a halter swimsuit, the color of the turquoise sea. She tossed the hat onto her towel, kicked off flat shoes and, careless of wetting her hair, dived into the shallows and swam, her arms a rhythmic arc in and out of the water. Dee had told him that growing up in a coastal town had allowed her to spend half her life in, or on, the ocean. It showed. She could certainly outswim him. He wasn't used to being bested, or ribbed, by a woman.

***

The yellow and green storefront of Hameediyah's drew them in and, seated amongst mainly Indian patrons, the women's saris bright as parrots, they ate their way through *nasi kandar*. Dee, after an initial gasp at the searing heat of chili, appeared to delight in the mix of tastes and textures. Simon watched her charming the young Indian waiter, who rushed her an extra bowl of *riata*, the cucumber and yoghurt dish designed to cool the most inflamed throat. He marveled at how people were drawn into her orbit. Even a fractious infant whose eyes brimmed with tired tears and who, to Simon's mind should have been in bed, was dandied and calmed on her lap.

Simon directed the trishaw to take them back to the E&O through streets coming alive with vendors serving Chinese, Indians, and Malays, and noisy squaddies from Minden Barracks released for a night on the town.

"Where is Love Lane?" Dee asked, watching the scene with delight.

"Why?"

"Just curious. It's the red light area, isn't it?"

"Er, yes, I believe so," Simon said, looking anywhere but at her.

"You believe so?" Dee said, with a laugh, digging him in the ribs. "You're being stuffy again, Simon. Let's ride through it."

"Now?"

"Why not?"

"It'll be noisy, and coarse and full of drunks," said Simon.

"Oh, come on, just for fun."

"Very well. But we are not stopping."

"Scared an old flame will recognize you?"

Her teasing voice made him laugh. "Really? You are incorrigible. I cannot believe you ever lost at anything with your brothers."

"Not often," Dee agreed. "I was the youngest. The older three spoiled me dreadfully, the younger two took it out on me. I had to learn fast. And be warned. I wasn't above cheating."

"Where did your father fit in?"

"He wasn't around much. Long hours running a pub."

Their conversation was cut short as Dee gazed at people milling around on Love Lane, garish lights and signs in enormous Chinese characters urging entry. The smell of burning braziers cooking satay over hot coals, steam rising each time water was tossed on skewers of chicken or beef. Hustlers called punters through beaded curtains. Women sashayed down the street in sleek *cheongsams*, or tripped along in flirty skirts. Drunk squaddies staggered as they pushed into dance halls, eager for the touch of a woman. Music blared out through the same doors—The Ink Spots or Doris Day competing with the latest Chinese or Malay or Hindi hits—an assault on the senses. The street awash with color, life full of vibrancy.

Dee turned to Simon, her eyes shining. "What fun. Let's stop and have just one drink, oh please? Who knows if I'll ever get to Penang again."

"That is bribery of the cheapest kind!"

"Uhuh, I warned you I don't always play fair," she said.

About to stop the trishaw making its stuttering way through the throng, they heard the shrill blast of a whistle. Peering around the side of the *beca* and along the road behind, Simon saw two MPs running toward a bar they had just passed.

"Not tonight, and no, I'm not being stuffy, but there is no need to get caught up in a fracas. I have enough of them in the *ulu*!" Simon smiled. "Honestly, Dee. MPs behind us."

"Very well, but don't think I'll forget."

"I'm sure you won't. Let's get a bit closer to the hotel then stroll the last few blocks."

Simon liked the feel of Dee's hand tucked into the crook of his arm. The brush of her breast. He didn't know what, if anything, would transpire over the next few days, but he did know he enjoyed her company.

"Would you like a nightcap? The bar might be a little more sedate than Love Lane, but I'm pretty sure I can guarantee no MPs," he suggested.

"Mmm, lovely. I'd like something decadent."

"Oh Lord! What constitutes decadent for a publican's daughter?"

"Something an Australian publican wouldn't serve! I know, what's that green liqueur? I'll have one of them, please," Dee asked, hopping up onto a bar stool.

"Chartreuse. Made by French Carthusian monks," Simon replied, distracted by the flash of bare thigh.

"Well if monks make it, it can't be too potent."

"I wouldn't bank on that," Simon said, ordering her drink, and a Dalwhinnie for himself. "Here, and The Raffles in Singapore, are the only places I have found that serve my favored single malt. Would you be more comfortable at a table?"

"No, thank you. I like sitting at a bar. You hear all sorts of interesting things."

The barman, not in the least wilted in his buttoned-up jacket, put their drinks in front of them with a smile, nodding as Simon asked him to put it on his chit.

Simon tapped out a cigarette.

"May I have one, please?" Dee asked.

"I'm sorry, I didn't think you smoked."

"I don't, often. Just occasionally with a nightcap. Something else I can blame my brothers for." She drew in, released smoke in a slow spiral, then took a sip. "Goodness, that's sweeter than I expected. But also pungent. Umm, I like that."

They talked quietly, laughing at the imagined chaos of MPs hauling squaddies back to barracks. Finishing her drink, Dee slid down from the barstool, picked up her handbag, leaned across to kiss Simon's cheek, and thanked him for a lovely day.

"Hang on a minute, Dee, I'll walk you upstairs."

"No need. I'll see you in the morning. G'night!"

Simon's shoulders slumped as he watched her reflection in the mirror behind the bar saunter towards the door.

***

Dee, meeting him for breakfast on the dining room terrace, had, Simon noticed, drawn every man's eye with her loose-limbed walk, legs encased in tight red capris, paired with another white blouse and flat red shoes. Her blonde hair curled around a sort of bandana more usually seen on doughty British chars, but which on Dee looked pert and enchanting.

They spent the day sightseeing around George Town—Fort Cornwallis where Captain Francis Light first stepped foot on Penang in 1786, the blackened hull of the famous blue Cheong Fatt Tze mansion bombed during the war. They wandered along Beach Street admiring the cream buildings of the old financial district, copper-colored panels glinting in the sunshine. They ate lunch standing at a *tok-tok mee* vendor selling wanton noodles, and so called for the tok-tok noise made by a wooden block being struck to announce his arrival as he pushed his cart along the streets. Then further down Beach Street they walked along Love Lane, in daylight more seedy than romantic. They carried on to Cannon Square where the opulent clan temple of the Leong San Tong was approached through an alley, deliberately narrow in the hopes of preventing infiltrators.

"The Penang Riot started here," Simon said.

"Recently?" asked Dee.

"No, in the 1800s. I can't remember the exact date. It broke out between two clans fighting over the monopoly of the opium and arak trade.

"What's arak?"

"A drink made from the sap of the coco palm."

"I'll stick to chartreuse. So, Mr. History, who were the two clans?"

"Am I boring you? I can be a bit pedantic."

"No, Simon. I love it. You must get used to me pulling your leg. So, who were they?"

"The Kean Teik and Ghee Hin, Chinese secret societies. Amazingly Malays got in on it too and took sides. The Red Flags supported the former, White Flags the latter."

"I wonder how they decided. How did it end? Who won?"

"It took about nine days and was eventually stopped when the Governor General brought in sepoys from Singapore. But hundreds had been killed by then, and a great many houses destroyed. Rumor, or legend, says a cannon was fired, the hole of which can still be seen in one of the minarets of the Acheen Street mosque. It was quite a tidy end really, because the clans were fined and the money put towards financing four new police stations."

"You do love this country, don't you?" Dee said, linking arms with Simon. "I think it's wonderful. You make me realize I've been taking it too much at face value."

"Are you teasing me, again?" Simon asked.

"No, darling, I'm not. But I've had enough culture for today. Let's collect your clothes from—what was the tailor's name—then go back to the hotel and have a swim. You didn't have one yesterday and you can't possibly stay on such a lovely beach and not dip a toe into the water."

***

"What's on the agenda today?" Dee asked, sipping coffee the next morning. "I love starting our days on this terrace. The jungle is going to feel very claustrophobic."

"That it is," Simon said. "I'm pretty sure I'll be going back in next week."

"Sorry, we said we wouldn't talk about work." Dee squeezed his hand across the table. "All right, Tuan Tour Guide, what's on?"

"I thought we could wander along Weld Quay, look at some of the Peranakan houses."

"I keep seeing that word, but am not actually sure what it means," Dee said.

"The Peranakan are descendants of early Chinese immigrants, 16th century, who married Malay women. The men are called *babas*, the women *nyonyas*. And Peranakan really is a distinct culture."

"Sounds great. If we're going to walk, let's not dilly-dally, otherwise it'll be stifling."

"Let's see how we go." Simon nodded to the *beca* driver and helped Dee in.

"Damn, it's hot. Why don't you ever wear a hat, Simon?" she asked from under her conical dome.

"I do in England," Simon said.

"I didn't think you had enough sunshine to warrant a hat there."

"Very funny!"

"Oh, we're back near the ferry," Dee said. "I thought these were shophouses rather than Peranakan."

"A bit of both. Not all Peranakan were stinking rich."

"Aren't they narrow? Much narrower than the shophouses in Raub, or Ipoh, or even KL," said Dee.

"Here, and in Malacca and Singapore—the Straits Settlements—people building along the waterfront were taxed on the width of their property. Hence long and narrow. They go back 200 feet sometimes."

"I'd love to go into one. One like that blue mansion. That looked as if it was once incredible."

"A pity much of Penang was destroyed in the war. The Japs gave the island a hell of a pounding in December '41. Not our finest hour. We up and left. Not just the RAF but your lot too."

"Were there many casualties?" Dee asked, as they wandered along Bridge Street.

"Sadly, yes. Particularly in the ethnic Chinese population. About 600 civilians were killed in those air strikes, and over a thousand wounded. That, and the shameful way Britain capitulated in Singapore—the whole of Malaya really—spelled, to my mind, the end of our, what shall I call it ... invincibility for want of a better word, within the minds of locals."

"So why is it taking so long to grant independence?" Dee asked, stepping around an elderly Chinese clad in striped pajama bottoms and a white tee-shirt, puffing a long pipe as he watched the world pass his front door.

"Because there has to be a functioning middle-class to sustain any country, and clear and cohesive leadership. None of the states want to give up their autonomy."

"Surely there is a middle class—shopkeepers, business owners, all those working in government," said Dee. "And there are many who are very well educated. Doctors, lawyers—it seems lots did their training in England and Scotland."

"The start of one for sure. But look at the ethnic tensions. Britain is not going to sit back and watch the communists take over the peninsula. Quite apart from the moral question, consider all the commercial interests."

"They let the Japanese walk over the country."

"*Touché.*"

They walked along in silence. Simon, rather than being disgruntled, was intrigued. Dee brought up questions many skirted. She didn't follow the blanket assumption that Europeans had all the answers. Searching his conscience, Simon didn't think he felt that way either, and yet he often subscribed to the common belief that Malaya needed a long lead in to *merdeka*. Maybe they didn't.

Dee took his arm.

"Look, there's a bloke selling *chendul*. Let's have some."

"Have you ever tried it?"

"Of course. I plucked up courage once I got over thinking the rice flour jelly things were green slugs."

"Thanks for that image. I think I'll wait for a Tiger."

Spooning the flavored ice shavings into her mouth, Dee asked, "Have you ever seen a tiger in the *ulu*?"

"No. I've heard them though."

"So have I. The last time I went upriver. Part of me desperately wants to see one, the other part knows I'd be terrified. I'd probably tip the dugout over, lose all my supplies and generally cause chaos. Poor Samsuari."

Simon laughed. "Somehow I can't see that happening. You're far too self-assured to let a cuddly creature scare you!"

"Hah, you're teasing me. You see, I'm a good influence," Dee said, with a laugh.

"You've got a green tongue!"

"I have no response to that, so I shall maintain a dignified silence."

The walk back to the hotel was hot, but much easier than getting in and out of a *beca* each time Dee wanted to go into a shop. Her Malay impressed Simon. He could tell she had been working hard to learn, with Samsuari's help. She bought some pale green silk in one shop, floral cottons in another, a sari in a third.

"Thank you for being so patient, Simon," she said, with a grin. "My brothers would have retreated to the nearest bar by now."

"Not at all, I've enjoyed it. You don't take long to make up your mind."

"Well, I either like something or I don't."

"Do you like that?" Simon asked, pointing to a delicate jade necklace coiled amongst amulets and figurines in the window of a Chinese emporium. "I'd like to give you something from Penang."

"Don't be silly, Simon. I'll never forget this. Come on, it's time for a swim. You promised."

"You're a hard woman to spoil," Simon said.

"Nonsense, all I want is to cool off."

***

Laughing, they ran into the water. Dee again dived in and powered out toward a junk rocking lazily at anchor. Simon, not having grown up near the ocean, swam at a slower pace to a wooden raft, climbed up and turned to watch her swim back. Clambering up the ladder, her curls flattened, water streaming down her face and body, he couldn't think of anyone else he knew who was so completely unaffected. Throwing herself down next to him, she reached for his hand, and kissed it.

"Simon, I really am having the most wonderful time. Thank you."

"I am too. Penang will never seem the same again."

"Then you'll only ever have to come here with me." She laughed. "Come on, I'll race you back." She leapt up and dived in before he could reply.

He followed, his pace methodical and, walking up the beach, smiled to see her already lying on a towel.

"I think that would be called a false start at the Olympics," he said, sinking down next to her.

"Or you could just call it cheating. I did warn you."

The sun, past its afternoon intensity, cast waving palm frond shadows over them as they dried.

"Where would you like to have dinner this evening?" Simon asked.

"You choose. You haven't been wrong yet," Dee murmured, her eyes closed.

"I can't win. When I choose you accuse me of being high-handed, when I suggest you choose, you tell me to."

"Welcome to a woman's mind, darling."

Simon leaned up on his elbow to look at her, a few droplets still trembling on her brown arms and legs. He ran his finger along her inner arm.

"You are lovely, Dee."

"So are you."

Simon laughed. "I don't think anyone has ever said that to me before. A bit battle scarred, I'm afraid," he said, glancing at the puckered skin showing above his trunks.

"A bullet?" Dee asked.

"Yup. I got sloppy. Nothing too serious."

"The war?"

"Uhuh."

"That's it. You get shot and all you say is 'uhuh'?"

"Not much else to say." Simon grinned and changed the subject, "I'm feeling idle, let's just eat at the hotel tonight."

Dee sighed, recognizing there would be no further explanation. "Perfect. I think I've had enough sun for today. Are you staying?"

"No, I'll come in too."

Shaking out their towels, Dee tied her sarong around her chest, and Simon tugged on his shirt, and hand in hand they walked up the beach to the hotel and their rooms.

"Shall I knock on your door on the way downstairs, let's say, a couple of hours?" Simon asked.

"Yes, please. We can make an entrance together. I brought one rather fancy outfit, I shall wear it this evening."

His rap on the door was answered by Dee's voice telling him to come in. The scent of fresh lime wafted along the short corridor.

"I ordered up some gin and tonic," Dee called from the bathroom. "Help yourself, there's ice as well. I'll just be a minute."

Simon poured a couple of drinks, dropping a slither of lime in each glass. He looked around the room similar to his, though he did not have an adjoining bathroom. She was tidy, or she had tidied up. Just a pair of shoes and her handbag were on display. He sat down in one of the wicker chairs facing the ocean through the open balcony doors and waited.

"Hello." Dee's arms curled over his shoulders from behind. The scent of lime was stronger, as if she'd floated in a bath of them. He smiled.

"Hello, to you too. It's been a long time since I've seen you. At least a couple of hours."

"Actually, you've never seen me like this." She moved in front of him and took the glass from his hand.

Simon laughed. "No, but I have imagined. And my imagination did you a disservice." He stood and reached for her. "My darling, darling Dee, you're beautiful." They kissed and his erection strained against her nakedness.

"You have too many clothes on," she said, unknotting his tie, then, undoing the buttons of his shirt, slid it off his shoulders. She traced his scars with her lips. "Not just a flesh wound then."

"That's the trouble with getting naked with a nurse," Simon said, his fingers circling her hardening nipples. He bent to kiss them and groaned as she arched back. She eased away and lay on the bed watching him undress, her fingers caressing her thighs.

He knelt over her, and kissed her again, then sketched a line down her neck to her breasts. She reached for him, her hips rising to meet him, her arms pulling him closer.

"Hang on." Simon reached for his trousers, fumbling for his wallet. Dee took the Johnny from him and rolled it on, stroking him all the while. Then she eased herself onto him, and watched his excitement match her own as she pushed his shoulders, her breasts tantalizingly near his mouth. She rode him until, very quickly, their breathing changed and they were spent. Dee collapsed on top of him, her breasts flattened against his chest, their bodies cooling under the fan. "My God," Simon said, his arms tightening.

"You will have noted I am not a virgin," she said, into his chest.

"Thank God for that," he replied. They lay quietly, until Dee rolled to his side and again traced the indentation reaching from his waist to the top of his leg. "I think I need that drink," he said. "Madam, may I offer you a gin and tonic, though really we should be drinking champagne."

"I did think of that," Dee said, getting up with a lazy smile, "But I thought that might be considered forward! I mean, what if you had rejected me?"

"There was absolutely no chance of that," he said, watching her walk to the table and add more ice to the glasses before bringing them to bed. "You are tanned all over."

"I am."

"Dare I ask how you manage that?"

"You may. You know the back of my compound is walled. Ah Sui graciously turns a blind eye. There is your answer. There is nothing quite so nice, apart from this," she pointed to her glass, "Oh yes, and this," she tickled his penis, "as lying in the sun, starkers."

"I wholeheartedly approve."

They loved again. This time slowly, intimately, with none of the previous urgency. Then bathing together. Simon soaping her and she him, they watched each other's bodies buck and thrust in the mirror.

"I'm hungry," Dee said later, from her position tucked in by his side, but I can't be bothered moving. "Shall we order room service?"

"No. Come on, you have an entrance to make and a reputation to uphold."

***

The next three days their area of sightseeing widened. Simon borrowed a car from a chum at Minden Barracks and they drove up Penang Hill, the top of the coolie hat, as Dee called it. They wandered around the gardens at Kek Lok Si Temple, the cornerstone of the Malay Chinese community at Ayer Itam—a smile passing between them when they learned it was also called the Temple of Supreme Bliss. On their last day, they took a picnic prepared by the hotel, and found a secluded spot along the north shore where they drank warm champagne as they frolicked, naked, in the water. Returning to the E&O as night fell, they bathed, and loved, and this time, ordered room service with another bottle of Taittinger, this one chilled.

"I have something for you, my dearest one," Simon said, reaching into the bedside table. "I thought it would look rather nice with that green fabric you bought."

Dee opened the box to see the jade necklace nestled on dark green velvet—the beads glistening like trembling dewdrops.

"Oh, Simon, thank you, darling. They're beautiful, and will always be treasured."

He fixed the clasp and turned Dee around in his arms to look at her. "And this is an image I shall always cherish," he said, taking in the green necklace against her naked body.

"I won't cry tomorrow," Dee promised Simon later. "But I will be crying inside."

Chapter 13

"Do YOU THINK anyone in Britain even knows what's happening here?" Robin Nancarrow asked. He and Simon were in the Manchu Milk Bar in KL—a less than salubrious establishment, but entertaining nonetheless, not to mention misnamed. Milk was about the only thing unavailable.

"I doubt it. But sending Harold Briggs out as the civilian lead was a masterstroke." Simon gazed into his tankard, then glanced around the bar. The long narrow room was divided into alcoves by low wooden partitions, each alcove decorated with pink cushions, all adding to the general seediness. "No country wants to be run by the military, our friend Boucher has certainly been curtailed, and Gurney is getting on with the politics of the whole thing, insisting we are in a war of political ideologies—armed support for a political war, not political support for an army war. Got a nice ring to it. *Merdeka* or bust!"

Robin snorted. "Did you hear Boucher's response?"

A waitress interrupted their conversation when she delivered their refills. All the waitresses were Malay and wore white blouses and short white skirts, their nylon-encased legs shown off by three-inch heels, their staccato clacking across the wooden floor adding to the background hubbub.

Simon nodded his thanks, his thoughts on the General Officer Commanding, Major General Charles Boucher, before replying, "Not verbatim."

"Well, verbatim, he said he didn't think 'a bunch of coppers should start telling generals what to do.' I'd like to have been a fly on the wall." Robin took a sip. "Seems a bit unfair the resettlement program is called The Briggs Plan. It was Gurney who came up with it."

"I doubt he cares. Just that it gets done," Simon said. "I'm bloody glad I'm not involved in the actual process. Christ, moving that many people, by stealth almost, must be a logistical nightmare. The squatters don't know where they're going until they're on the buses or in the trucks. Unsettling for them. But the CTs would have a field day if they had that information. Time will tell the effectiveness of the New Villages."

"You know they're recruiting Australians and New Zealanders to help run them—some medical personnel, but many eager to do anything they're asked. Incredible the number of people who've applied. And it's got the full support of both their governments. I suppose the Antipodes would be high on the red peril list." Robin looked at Simon. "Speaking of Australians, and nurses, how goes it with the lovely blonde in Raub?"

"She's very well, thank you."

"When do any of us get to see her again?" Robin asked.

"Whenever we can coordinate her humanitarian patrols with my less altruistic ones. I find it incredible she is still willing to visit communities in the *ulu*, along the rivers, after her abduction. Eighteen days in a CT camp. Not sure I'd be so sanguine."

"You'd have been shot!"

"Very probably," Simon agreed.

"Why don't you try and get her down for the dance at The Dog next week?"

"Didn't know there was one," said Simon.

"King's birthday, old boy."

"Of course. That would be fun." The thought, one that now beat an uncomfortable tattoo, surfaced again. He had to tell her.

***

Dee did manage to arrange a couple of days leave, and a free billet at the RAGM house on Lorong Kuda, behind the race track in KL, fortuitously empty. It was one of the smaller black-and-whites, the old Colonial style houses that dotted the peninsula—what Dee called an upside-down house, with the sitting room upstairs to catch any breeze that whispered through the grove of mangosteen trees.

At the appointed hour, Simon drove up in Robin's car. The iron gate to the entry hall was opened by a bent black-and-white *amah*;

so-called for their chosen uniform of black ankle-length pajama-style trousers and long-sleeved white *samfu*. Ah Yong was tiny, even next to Dee, and she sparkled, from her oiled hair and dark eyes, to her crooked-tooth smile. She showed him upstairs to where Dee waited, an elfin vision in a simple dress of fern green. At her neck was the jade necklace. Simon ran up and pulled her to him, ignoring the disapproving tut from the *amah*, her gray hair scraped back into a tight, coiled bun.

"Maybe we should go now, otherwise we might not make it," Dee said, drawing away from his kiss with a smile.

"I suppose so. I'd rather stay here. In fact, I know so!"

"What? After me calling in every favor imaginable. I am going to the dance, even if I have to be Cinderella. In fact, let's make a pact. We'll be home by midnight!"

"Barefoot?" asked Simon, with a leer.

"Bare everything!"

The Dog, that bastion of colonial living, though even from its first days it was a club whose membership was based on social and educational standing rather than race, provided a touch of rare glamor for both Simon and Dee. Simon watched as she charmed men and women alike with her wicked, throaty laugh and teasing sense of humor. He wondered if it was because she was a publican's daughter or whether it was because she was Australian that she seemed so completely at ease with everyone, with no preconceived ideas as to where people fitted in society.

Jealousy tingled as he watched Dee dance with Robin then laugh at something the tall doctor said. Simon groaned quietly. He had to tell her. But not tonight.

***

"Dee?" Simon trailed his hand across the bed in the half-light of dawn easing its way through the shutters, missing the cool touch of her skin. A sarong around his waist, he went out to the small verandah off their bedroom. "Hello," he said, kissing her neck. "You're up early."

"Good morning," she replied, stroking his face. "Force of habit. Even after a late night." She looked up at him. "And there's something the matter, isn't there?"

Simon looked down at her upturned face, a face he knew he loved. Would always love. He dragged the other chair nearer and sat down. He bent over, hands clasped between his knees.

"Is this how women's intuition works?"

"Don't tease, Simon. What's going on? You've been reposted?"

"No. But yes, I do have to tell you something. And yes, I have been cowardly. It is something I should have said months ago."

"Months ago, or before we got to this stage? The stage where whatever it is, is bound to be painful?" Dee's green eyes were awash with tears waiting to fall. "All right, spit it out but don't give me any claptrap about not wanting to hurt me. It's going to."

Simon kept his head down. He cleared his throat. "When I left England the last time, it was on the understanding that, when I returned, I would marry a wonderful woman and would take over the running of her family farm. Not that she isn't capable of doing that herself. She is. More than me, probably." Relief washed over Simon. The words were out. He looked at Dee.

"What's her name?"

"Does that matter?"

"Of course, it matters. I'm not going to think of her as 'a wonderful woman,' am I?"

"Tess. Her name is Tess."

"How very apt. Of the d'Urbervilles?"

"Dee," Simon said, "be angry, but not at her."

"Listen, mate, I can be angry at whoever I bloody like." Dee held her hand up as Simon started to speak. He longed to kiss away the tears trickling down her face. "Just shush. I don't want to talk for a minute."

They sat in silence as the sun sent fingers of light through the mangosteen trees, throwing soft shadows of mauve and blue over the scythed grass. The sound of snorting and bridles clinking as horses were led out for exercise rides around the track came across from the stables next door. Simon wondered if it was a race day.

"All right," Dee's voice broke their silence. "Tell me."

"Tell you what?"

"Everything. I'm assuming Tess doesn't know about me."

"No."

"Do you write?"

"Of course."

"Oh, of course. You're fucking me but writing to another woman back home in bloody Blighty."

"Come on, Dee, it wasn't like that. It isn't like that. This isn't some jungle fling, and you know it."

"In that case, just so I understand, why are you telling me about Tess now. Why didn't you just break it off with her?"

"Because I didn't know where this," Simon waved helplessly at them both, "was going. I didn't know if there was an 'us.'"

"Oh, hedging your bets. Don't ditch the girl back home until you know what's with the girl currently in your bed." Dee stood and from the door to the bedroom said, "In that case why did you tell me about her? Some sense of British fair play? You're pathetic. I'm having a bath, and by the time I'm out, I'd like you gone." Dee slammed the French door, then opened it again. "You know, Simon, I might not have been a virgin, but I do not leap into bed with every man I meet."

***

Simon's neck jerked, and he opened gritty eyes as the train juddered to yet another stop. His gaze took in soldiers sprawled over the bench seats, National Service conscripts, all so young. Fresh faced. None of the jungle pallor they would soon get. Some were trying to sleep on bunks lining the sides of the next compartment, like rows of mummies in a metal tomb.

He wasn't part of the platoon but, needing to get out of KL, he'd decided to head up to Ipoh and have a poke around. See if he could pick up anything from his old contact, Ah Tok. Four days kicking his heels in KL was too long. He needed to be busy. Dee had refused to see him. A letter from Tess had finally caught up with him, which had added to his confusion. Full of enthusiasm for life in Dorset, it had made him homesick. Or maybe he was heartsick.

In a week he'd be back in the *ulu*. No time to think then, just act. He and Robin were due to meet up with Haziq, Tenuk—and another chap, Andy Robertson, who none of them knew—the following Wednesday when they would patrol west of Temerloh.

A couple of squaddies jumped down, laughing and shoving each other as they lit Woodbines. Simon wondered where their sergeant was. If they weren't on guard as the train was being refueled, they should be staying in the carriage.

Refueling and re-watering was always risky. With the engine idling they were sitting ducks, made easier by the fuel stations all being clearly marked. Not that ambushing a moving train was difficult; they were so slow.

Simon caught a movement. He turned his head, his hand going to his pistol. He pushed a young private out of the way as he leaned across to peer into the gloom of dusk. The *belukar* running alongside the rail tracks was a mass of shadows and waving fronds. He hissed at the soldiers around him to be quiet, keep down but look sharp. Their scared faces made him feel old.

Then it came. The stuttering fire of a Bren gun. And a wail. One of the laughing privates lay writhing on the gravel next to the train. His friend leapt aboard, screaming. Simon could see three or four shapes approaching the train, fire spitting from their weapons as the men on board struggled to find theirs amidst the confusion and shards of broken glass.

"Do not get out on the other side of the train," Simon roared. "Stay down. Return fire when able."

He saw men jump to the tracks anyway and the ambush erupted from both sides. A CT staggered then collapsed. Good, one down. He grabbed a private's rifle and shot through a hole in the window. The CT lurched, turned and ran back into the *belukar*. Fire spluttered from all along the train. Someone threw a grenade that lit the edge of the jungle in a flash of red. Another exploded near the woodpile. As suddenly as it started, the ambush was over. The CTs had made their point then slunk back under jungle protection.

"You're hit, sir," a medic said, taking in blood dripping down Simon's arm as he went along the carriage checking on soldiers. "Here, sit down. Let me see."

"Glass rather than a bullet, I think. I'm fine. Just put on a field dressing. I'll get it seen to later. Is everyone back on board? Any dead?"

"Yes, sir."

"The private first hit?"

"Yes, sir. And another. Four wounded."

"What the bloody hell was he doing? He and another chap got down off the train. No weapons. Nothing."

"Don't know sir, they were all told not to."

"Goddamnit!"

"Yes, sir. Right, that's a patch until we get north."

"Right, thanks. Keep your head down out there," Simon said and shook the medic's hand.

"Yes, sir."

"Are you going all the way to Butterworth, sir?" A subaltern came along the carriage, a young soldier with blood dripping from his neck draped across his shoulder.

"No, Ipoh."

"Well, thanks for the help. Here, Sampson," he lowered the soldier onto a bench and spoke to the medic, "this chap needs attention."

Simon nodded and moved along the swaying train. He found an empty space and brushed glass off the seat. He leaned his head back, touched his bandaged arm and closed his eyes but did not sleep.

***

Ipoh was a washout on firm information on CT movements, but Simon whiled away the time until he had to meet Robin and the others, much of it in the FMS bar. He also learned that Marjorie Watson—she of pistol and grenades in her handbag fame—had left Malaya. Frightened, after the birth of their daughter, by the incessant attacks to which their rubber plantation was subjected.

"I don't know if she'll ever want to come back," Dick, her husband, told Simon. "And I don't know if I can ever settle in England. What a bugger's muddle this bloody Emergency is causing."

Simon could only agree. "I can only imagine how difficult it is for the wives on isolated plantations. Defending their homes. Malaya."

"We're all fighting the same battle, old chum."

Chapter 14

GATHERING AT THE police station the afternoon before the patrol, the unit met Andy Robertson, Frank's replacement, and their new Chinese Liaison Officer.

"I am Mr. Chin Chan Tan," he said, his tone pleasant if a little grandiose.

"Welcome," Simon said, shaking hands and introducing him to the others. He asked Mr. Chin a few questions about his experience, and where it had been, then said, "Right, here's where we're going. Ready for the highlife, chaps?"

Laugher trickled around the chart table but not from Mr. Chin. Instead he took a step nearer and leaned in to listen, his eyes following the pointer as Simon traced their route on the map.

"Always subject to change, of course," Simon said, watching Mr. Chin for any reaction. No smile tweaked, even as the others laughed.

***

Much of the night was spent tossing on the lumpy cot, trying to put his finger on what irked him about the new CLO. Simon fell into a fitful sleep as options churned to the backdrop of bullfrogs croaking their pleasure after a deluge battered the roof of the Rest House.

Morning brought no answers, but Simon could not shake his unease. Mr. Chin stood aloof, disdainful of the easy banter between Haziq and Robin.

"Ready?" Robin asked, watching Andy toss his pack into the back of one of the Land Rover.

"Aye, as I'll ever be," the burly, balding Scot replied. His beret jauntily cocked over one eye. "Extra jocks, extra socks. What more does a man need in the jungle?"

115

Simon listened from the other side of the vehicle. Andy sounded the right sort of man to have with them. Not Frank, of course. But a good chap, nonetheless. He hoped he was right. They'd be thrown together for at least three weeks, probably more. Haziq, back from his wedding, was buoyant, his black hair oiled whenever in town now flopped freely over his forehead. The smell of oil in the jungle was a sure-fire giveaway to any vigilant CT. Like coffee. Tenuk, his long hair a black streak down his bare back, looked a little the worse for wear but Simon knew, once they got to the *ulu,* the Iban would shake off the effects of a night of drinking and again become an expert tracker.

The question mark hovered over Chin Chan Tan. Simon saw him check his watch, again, and glance at the vehicles and the Malay police drivers and constables, who would return to Jerantut once they dropped off their passengers. What was it that made him uneasy? He felt Robin's eyes on him. Simon shrugged and bent to pick up his pack.

"Mr. Chin," he said, straightening, "there has been a change of plans. We have no need of your services. Thank you. Tell your superior I have released you from patrol. Direct any questions to the police commissioner's office."

"But, sir, I have been assigned. You will need my assistance." His voice was high, agitated.

"Don't argue, Mr. Chin. That is an order." Simon could feel the combined breath of the others being held, surprised at his tenor. "We have a different location, and a new brief. If there are any issues with your dismissal from this patrol, they will be dealt with on my return. Good morning to you."

"Right, everyone in." Simon climbed into the seat next to the lead driver, Robin in the following vehicle. The others piled in the backs, Haziq and his radio behind Simon. The canvas sides of the Land Rovers were rolled up, allowing them greater visibility, but also the CTs. The roof was still on. It was always a trade-off. Like everything in Malaya.

The road was more a track; any laterite long washed away. Simon studied the map and listened with half an ear to Haziq's vivid telling of his wedding, the two other Malays chuckling at his descriptions.

"*Tarik balik.*" Simon interrupted, telling the driver to pull over, as he flagged down the Land Rover behind. They were just short of Sungai Lompat, a tributary of the Pahang.

"*Tuan*, this is not the place," the driver said, his face concerned. "Many miles short."

"*Ini baik-baik saja*, this is fine," Simon said. He climbed out, followed by a puzzled Haziq, already unloading his radio.

"What's up?" Robin asked, leaning out his window. "Engine trouble?"

"No. We'll start here."

"Really? Why?"

"As good a place as any," answered Simon, his voice neutral. "Unload, we'll let these fine men head back."

Robin shrugged and swung the door open, saying, "Right you are. Out you get, chaps." Once again Simon thanked the day John Davis put the two men together. It was trust. And there had been something about Mr. Chin Chan Tan that he had not trusted. He was sure to have been vetted, as well as anyone could be, but something had been off. Something about him checking his watch, more than once. His intense study of the map the day before. And his pack had been small too. More a day sack than a pack big enough for a stint in the *ulu*. There was whittling down, but Mr. Chin's had been too pared.

They watched the Land Rovers judder forwards and back as they turned around on the narrow track, then waved the policemen off with a smile.

"What's all this about, Frampton?" Robin asked, hefting his pack and moving off the road into thorny *belukar*.

"Mr. Chin didn't add up and I'd rather we didn't walk into something unexpected. Just going on a hunch. We've a longer trek but I think a safer bet."

"Are we still heading to the estate?" Andy asked, swatting a fly.

"Yes, the objective is the same, but we'll arrive from a different angle. When we get to the river, Haziq can radio in our change of plans."

"Good, I know Tommy and Louise are looking forward to some company. It's been months since anyone's been there. Apart from CTs, that is. They're giving them hell. Most nights. Tommy also said we are only welcome if we bring up-to-date copies of *The Straits Times*!"

"Did you bring some?" Simon asked.

"Of course! Except by the time we get there it'll be old news."

"Newer than they're used to, I suppose," Robin said.

117

"All right, we're a man down but I think better off. Usual formation. Tenuk, Haziq, Nancarrow with the Bren, me and then you, please, Robertson. You and Robin to change out after rest periods. Everyone clear? Good, move out."

***

The day unfolded as expected. A long, hard slog through jungle and the encroaching *belukar* of abandoned rubber estates, and across paddy fields that bordered tributaries of the Sungai Pahang. A different kind of patrol. The risk of exposure great as they crossed treeless, soggy ground, trying to keep to small berms surrounding the rice being cultivated. It was Simon's least favorite type of patrol. Here they were easy pickings. At least the *ulu* hid them. As well as it hid CTs.

Shadows lengthened and the sun lost its heat as they headed southeast and reached the mighty river, the longest in Malaya. Soaked with sweat and the slipping and sliding through rice fields, Simon didn't want to think about the number of leeches sucking the blood between his toes. As long as that was the only place they were. He had an image of Frank telling the story about the Yorkshire man and the Johnny, and smiled through his weariness.

Hiding in a coconut plantation, they waited for the brief dusk to fall into night, the next two days a repeat of the previous one, the jungle grinding them down with its tedium.

The fourth day on patrol, slips of paper appeared tacked on trees on the periphery of an abandoned and isolated estate. Ripping one down, Haziq read the Malay aloud but kept his voice quiet. It exhorted tappers and miners to inform, and to provide food to those fighting for *merdeka* from the jungle. The threat "or else" was implicit.

"And just to make sure, it's written in Cantonese and Tamil as well," Andy said, scanning another ragged slip.

"Look at the actual print." Simon squinted at the muddy page and showed Robin. "I'd say it was produced on the same machine as *Battle News*. See the ink here. Smudged in similar lines."

He and Robin had read confiscated copies of the CT newspaper when they'd been in KL. Written by the communist's answer to Too Chee Chew, but always known as C. C. Too, Osman China was also a top propagandist who knew how to elicit terror in those living in kampongs and estate housing.

Tenuk beckoned from behind a row of overgrown rubber trees. Easing through an outcrop of banana plants, they joined the tracker. He pointed to a leaking wound where a hand of bananas had been cut. The sap only just congealing. Simon nodded his thanks; aware his focus had been elsewhere, his lapse of concentration corrected by the Iban.

They followed the tracker, keeping low, weapons ready. Light filtered through the swaying trees, and macabre shadows moved in a dance of maybes. A wooden shack, perhaps a rest place for tappers long since gone, appeared as a dim outline at the far end of the row. Simon tried to slow his breathing as they dropped to a crawl. He steadied his binoculars on his elbows and searched every inch of the lean-to. From a distance it looked deserted, *attap* roofing dangling from one side, planks jutting at angles. About to give the all-clear, a glint caught his eye. Perhaps a piece of corrugated iron. Perhaps a rifle. He saw Tenuk edge nearer, stop and signal.

Robin touched Simon's shoulder and waved his hand in front of his face, his signal asking if they were to ambush. Simon nodded then waited as he and Andy crept around to encircle the hut. Haziq planted the radio in the underbrush, and inched forward, the Bren ready.

A flash came from the hut. Simon ducked, then heard rapid fire coming from deeper in the trees. Not sure if it was Andy and Robin shooting, he and Haziq leaped to their feet and crashed ahead, firing as they ran. A movement to Simon's left spun him around, shooting. A body fell. They moved forward. A high-pitched scream sounded, then another deeper cry came from behind the hut. Shouting. Then silence. Haziq doubled back to the body and Simon watched Tenuk creep closer to the hut. His signal came. One body.

Squatted beside Simon, Haziq whispered his report. "Dead." Canteen at his feet. They'd surprised him. His rifle was still slung over his shoulder.

Simon, his heart beating, nodded, and together they ran on and fell to the ground behind two trees mere feet from the hut. Sweat stung his eyes and he blinked, gathered his breath and inched closer, covered by Haziq.

A whistle sounded and Simon eased his grip on the pistol. Three CTs, one with blood oozing down his leg, appeared with Andy prodding them from behind, the Bren trained on their backs. He moved away to guard the rear of the hut, the direction the CT's had been running, as Haziq bound and gagged the men. Tenuk scouted further into the jungle behind the plantation.

Simon looked down at the body of a woman crumpled amongst a scattering of dirty blank paper by the hut window, her rifle across her chest in a sinister parody of defense.

"Another one out back. An older man. Though hard to tell when they've been in the jungle. Emaciated," Robin said, crouching by the woman.

"She doesn't look very old," Simon said, as Robin began his examination. "Shit. Is it really worth it for them?" He picked up one of the pages.

"The beauty of indoctrination, old chap." Robin looked up. "I'll do this, take fingerprints and photos, you look around."

The hut was bigger than it looked. A rickety table in the corner of a windowless back room was covered with a tarpaulin. Before lifting it Simon got down on his hands and knees with his torch and knife to search for trip wires.

He eased the flap up and let out his breath in a low whistle.

They'd found it. They'd bloody found it.

The printing press.

***

Simon, anxious the shooting might have alerted more terrorists and knowing their movements would be hampered by the prisoners, wanted to destroy the press and get away from the area before a CT party attacked. The chances were it would be a stronger unit than the five of them. The press, no matter how ancient and cobbled together, was still an important part of the CT propaganda war. He wondered why they kept it in a relatively unguarded area, and not in the midst of a larger camp.

"Should have begged forgiveness," he muttered. Their orders, given over the radio when Haziq reported the find, were to return to base with the portable press. "What, in God's name, could anyone learn from this? Bet the sod at HQ's an ARAB with MINTUA."

Robin snorted at Haziq's puzzled look. "Arrogant Regular Army Bastard with his Mind in Neutral, Thumb Up Arse!" he translated.

"Bloody hell, that'll weigh us down," Andy said, looking at the bulky machine.

Tenuk reappeared to report there was no camp within the immediate vicinity, but there were signs of activity deeper in the *ulu*.

Simon was quiet, watching as Robin treated the youth's leg wound. "Right," he said, and nodded to the two uninjured CTs, men in their thirties, "they can carry the sodding thing. Haziq, you and Tenuk are on stag while we sort this out. Keep lively, I don't want any surprises."

He glared at the CTs lined against the flimsy wall, then gestured for Andy to follow him. "We'll build a kind of sling. Use the tabletop as the base. It'll add weight but keep the bloody thing stable. Use tree branches for stretcher handles." He looked away as an image of Frank in a similar stretcher flashed across his mind. "Right, you get the branches. I'll dismantle the table. Look sharp. The sooner we're out of here the better."

"Aye, ain't that the truth," the Scott said, unsheathing his knife as he went outside.

The captured CT's dug shallow graves for their comrades' final resting place, and Robin logged and photographed them and the area, as well as the CTs.

"How bad is it?" Simon nodded to the wounded man groaning behind his gag. "Can he walk?"

"Yes, and it's not bad enough for that racket," Robin said.

They watched Haziq lean down and say something. The groaning stopped.

"What did you say?" Robin asked.

"I tell him if he make noise, I cut his belly open."

"A taste of their own medicine, I suppose," Simon said. "But not something we are going to do."

"He not know that," Haziq said.

The mood was somber, despite the find. With the wounded man, and the CTs carrying the press, the going was slow, with frequent stops. A successful patrol for a change, if killing two people could be counted a triumph. Lives cut down, for what? The question followed Simon as they hacked their way out to a hastily arranged pick-up zone.

And never far from Simon, the pain on Dee's face.

Chapter 15

DEE SAW LUCY AND PUTRI exchange glances as she dragged herself, eyes dull and blurry, into the clinic the day after her return from KL. All she wanted was to hide in bed. Even the kitten, Harimau, more often shortened to Hari and so named for his tiger stripes, who had purred his way into her heart, could not ease her pain. There was no bright smile, none of the usual crackling energy that invigorated everyone.

"Thank you." Dee took the mug of tea from Ah Sui, but rejected the papaya neatly sliced and sprinkled with lime, ignoring the *amah's* tut. "I'm not hungry this morning. All right, Lucy, Monday morning means babies and infants. Are we ready?"

"Yes, Sister. I mixed more sulfur ointment."

"Well done, thank you. And the sluice room?"

"Is ready, Sister," Putri said.

The controlled pandemonium of the morning helped Dee focus. Toddlers with scabies was a constant problem and Lucy was kept busy washing them in the sluice room before slathering the squirming infants with sulfur cream. Printed notes assuring the mother that scabies was not a product of poor hygiene but a mite, and instructions in Malay, Chinese, and Tamil on bathing the child before reapplying the cream for three nights were given with a tub of the unguent.

A four-year-old girl lay listless in her mother's arms, her eyes shiny with fever. Her breath smelled of vomit. These were the ones Dee hated. Malaria or polio? She manipulated the child's arms and legs and whilst they didn't appear to hurt, they were floppy. The inflamed throat decided her.

"*Ibu*," she said to the mother, "I am worried about Jenab. She must be checked by a doctor." The panic in the woman's face twisted like a *kris* in her heart as Dee stroked the child's clammy forehead. "I will arrange it, and Samsuari will take you to Ipoh."

"Ipoh?" The name of the town nearly eighty miles away jolted the woman from her alarm. "*Tidak*. No can."

"*Ibu*, please, you must. Your mother, she can care for the others. Your husband can go with you. Yes?" Dee turned to call Samsuari and ask him to take the woman back to her kampong, then to the hospital in Ipoh and to stay with her until they knew what was happening. "Be careful, nuh."

The specter of her abduction, not yet buried deep despite her public nonchalance, and the fear that Samsuari would again be punished for helping her, made her wary of any movement around the country. All that effort, the geeing up of nerves, to get to KL to see Simon for the weekend. All for bloody what? The mother in front of her, wiping sweat from the child's forehead, and Samsuari's concerned glance, brought Dee back to the clinic. She couldn't be certain, but she had a feeling word might have been spread by "the man" to leave her Land Rover alone. She had to hope so.

"Polio?" Samsuari asked, his voice subdued as the woman gathered her things.

"I'm not sure. But Jenab is very sick."

"*Tiada masalah,* no problem," he replied. "I tell Nur."

"*Selamat jalan.*" Dee wished him safe travels.

The day limped on, and she forced herself to eat the sandwich Ah Sui prepared for a late lunch. Dee was tempted to cancel her talk to expectant mothers about the benefits of breast milk over diluted tinned Carnation milk. All she wanted to do was fall into bed, even though she knew Simon's face would float in the minute she relaxed. "God damn the man," she muttered, getting to her feet and helping Putri set out chairs for the pregnant women.

At last the day was over, the clinic tidied, and a supper of curried chicken and rice swallowed down. Ah Sui's anxious face had disappeared to her quarters behind the cookhouse.

Dee poured a slug of whisky, foregoing any soda, and taking it out to the verandah kicked one of the hated sandbags before slumping into the bamboo chair. Her anger had lessened with the day, but misery threatened to swamp her. She hadn't known where their relationship would go. So many variables. Malaya,

England, Australia? But after Penang, she had known she was in love with Simon.

Rage flared again as she thought of the hours spent talking about life, and death. Simon's insistence she talk about the abduction, and her guilt about Samsuari had helped sort some of her tangled emotions. And he had talked about Frank. But never Tess. Actually, not very much about England at all. Always Malaya. Bloody Malaya. Tears fell, the damp patch spreading on Hari's fur until he jumped down in indignation and stalked off. His departure made Dee cry more.

Even after her foray to the CT camp, Dee had not thought to run back to Townsville, despite the Red Cross willing to void her contract. Now, that was all she wanted. Home. The sound of her brothers roughhousing. Her mother's voice. Night noises intruded as she seesawed through options. They all came back to duty. She was needed in Raub.

***

Gravel flung from a vehicle speeding along the track drove Lucy to slam the clinic doors, as Putri and Dee yanked windows shut, yelling to the few remaining patients to get down on the floor. About to peep through the glass she heard her name.

"Dee!"

"Jeffrey?" She smiled at the nervous group. "*Tidak menagapa*," she said, urging them back to their chairs.

"Dee?" Jeffrey called again, his voice urgent.

"Christ, Jeffrey, what's up? You scared the life out of us, screeching in like that."

"Sorry. But all hell has broken loose. Gurney's been murdered. On his way to Fraser's Hill. Don't know the details. I'm on my way now. Just wanted to warn you. Be careful. Must go."

Dee reached up and kissed Jeffrey's cheek. "Do you need me to come?"

"No. Absolutely not. Medics are there. But thank you."

"You be careful. Stop in on your way back. Doesn't matter what time."

She watched him drive off. Sir Henry Gurney? God, who next?

"*Ayiee*," Lucy said from the door. "He good man."

"Yes, he was," Dee patted her arm. "Come on, let's finish up, then you must both get home. I don't know what's going on, but it's best no one is out after dark tonight. Putri, can you stop by Nur and tell her Samsuari probably won't get back? The roads will be blocked with SF."

A few patients stayed to see Sister Dee, but most slipped away, horrified at the latest tragedy in their country. This, one that would impact them all.

Again, Dee sat on the verandah in the dark. She must have dozed, because the subdued crunch of tires startled her awake. She rubbed her cricked neck and stood as Jeffrey came to the verandah, his usual rigid bearing dejected.

"Come on, you need a drink. Have you eaten anything?" Dee looked at her watch. Three in the morning. Even the cicadas had hushed. She led him through the clinic, stopping to pour a whisky before going along the walkway to the cookhouse. "How does an omelet sound?"

She cracked eggs and, about to start whisking, saw Ah Sui's puzzled face at the entrance. Dee shook her head and shooed her off. "It's all right. You go back to bed. I've got this."

Jeffrey, his hands around the tumbler, started talking as Dee chopped onions.

"He was in his Rolls. You know, the black Silver Wraith? The envy of us all. In convoy. An armored scout car, a police wireless vehicle and Land Rover with six Malay policemen. The wireless van broke down but Sir Henry didn't want to hang around, so they continued on."

"Well, I doubt many would stand up to him and insist he wait," Dee commented, slicing tinned ham.

"The ambush was at that S bend at Mile 56 $\frac{1}{2}$. What a stupid marker. Now forever immortalized." Jeffrey's voice was harsh. "They opened fire with Brens, Stens and rifles. Killed his driver instantly. His aide grabbed the wheel and stopped the car careening down the ravine. He and Lady Gurney weren't touched. But Sir Henry was. He managed to get out, slammed the door shut and staggered along the road towards the CTs, who mowed him down. Christ," Jeffrey rubbed his eyes, "either an act of supreme bravery or supreme foolishness."

"He was trying to save his wife," Dee said, with certainty. "He was that kind of man." Her thoughts flew to Simon. "What about the Land Rover? The policemen?" Dee asked.

"Five wounded. The scout car edged around the Rolls—it's riddled, Dee, riddled. How Lady Gurney and the aide survived unscathed is incredible. Anyway, the scout car took off for the next police station to get help but met reinforcements on the way. They'd heard the gunfire."

"Any CTs shot? Captured?" Dee asked.

"Doesn't seem so. A bugle was sounded and they disappeared back to wherever the hell they came from. Goddamnit, Dee. He was the right man to see Malaya through to *merdeka*."

"I know, Jeffrey." She pushed the omelet across the kitchen table. "Eat. Then we'll talk some more. I'm going to refresh your drink."

Dawn was sending teasing rays through the palms when Jeffrey finally left. He'd fallen into a troubled sleep on the sofa, with Dee sitting guard over him.

"Thank you, my dear," he said. "October 6th, 1951 will go down as a day always remembered in Malayan history."

Sir Henry Gurney was buried two days later in the Cheras War Cemetery in Kuala Lumpur, his murder mourned by the vast majority of those in Malaya—Malays, Indians, Chinese and Europeans—from kampongs and towns. And as news filtered out it seemed the ambush was a random act—a roadblock to stop whoever drove by.

The assassination of a wise man who wanted what Malaya wanted. Independence. *Merdeka*.

The subdued mood throughout the country suited Dee. She didn't know where Simon was, and didn't know if she wanted to know.

Chapter 16

MALAYA WAS IN LIMBO.

Speculation rumbled up and down the country, around the bars and *kedai kopis,* over beer and coffee, as to who would replace Sir Henry Gurney. With the electoral success of the Conservative Government in Britain and under Winston Churchill's leadership, Malaya became more an immediate issue in Parliament. Churchill sent his new Colonial Secretary, Oliver Lyttleton with instructions to report back.

With friction between the military and police rampant, and morale low amongst the police force, Lyttleton's first recommendation was the immediate recall of Nicol Gray, the Commissioner of Police.

Appeasing planters and tin miners, understandably exhausted by the continual threat to their plantations and mines, became another task. Lyttleton believed their demands for greater penalties for captured Min Yuen would be a cynical move and told them, "At the point of a gun, you would pay rather than be murdered, and so would I, and you know it."

Lyttleton suggested a new role be created, that of Deputy High Commissioner who would manage the day-to-day running of the country. It became the Colonial Secretary's job to persuade the Sultans to agree, which they did, although there was tangible disappointment when the role was not given to a Malay.

However Lyttleton's most dramatic recommendation proved the hardest to fulfill—that the country be led by one man, preferably a general, who would have authority over both military and civilian issues. Churchill, frustrated at the lack of momentum and whilst in Canada for a council of war on Colonial issues, asked for the army list and found his man. Demanding his presence in Ottawa, Churchill spoke one word to his definitive choice, "Malaya!"

General Sir Gerald Templer arrived in Malaya a few weeks later. He despised outdated colonialism and his distinctive administrative style shocked within moments of arriving at King's House, the British High Commissioner's residence. He shook hands with all the servants, then insisted funds set aside to gussy up the residence instead be used to upgrade the servants' quarters. He demanded even the smallest and poorest plantations house their laborers decently, saying that to do less provided breeding grounds for communist recruitment. He was exacting, expecting compliance with mandates almost before the words were out of his mouth.

And Templer stressed that the Emergency and civilian affairs were not "two entities." That both were inextricably linked.

Leaning against the Long Bar at The Dog, Simon and Robin discussed the latest Templer tale wherein he got wind of an incident at the Lake Club in Kuala Lumpur when a Malay had been refused entry to a function. He, Templer, called the Club committee together, all old white wallahs, and told them to open membership to all. They refused and resigned en masse. The new committee was of a different ilk.

"The irony of the story is that the chap in question actually owns the land the Lake Club is on." Robin chortled and indicated another round to Yi Ling, the barman.

"Templer is certainly a proponent of the carrot rather than the stick. Essentially told the Sultans, yes, you should have *merdeka* but first you have to help get rid of the communists." Simon drained his drink as the barman set a fresh glass down.

"The reality," Robin said, "is that he realizes the outcome of everything he does here will impact the whole of Asia."

"You're right, of course, Nancarrow," agreed Simon. "What I admire is that he is not trying to put his name to anything. Not trying to come up with new plans, just implement those of Gurney, and Briggs."

"When you're not admiring our leaders, how are you feeling? About Dee?" Robin asked, not looking directly at his friend's face.

"Oh, you know," Simon said, gazing into his drink. "I'd rather be in the *ulu*, and that's saying something."

***

Three days after their idle banter at The Dog, and later a long night of carousing at the Happy World, Simon was given details of his next patrol. He and his usual squad of Robin, Tenuk, Haziq, and now Andy, were to patrol the area north of Kuala Lumpur, around the township of Tanjong Malim, deep in the midst of rubber country. Fast becoming a hot spot of sabotage, where residents often complied with CT demands rather than face the terror of torture, or worse.

"No one seems able to find the blighters," Bob Thompson, now Permanent Secretary for Defense, said to Simon. "No trace of a camp. No whisper from people in the town. The Min Yuen are doubtless a strong support, but nothing we say compares to the constant barrage of threats rained down on the town. See if you can root out any sign of a camp, or tracks—frankly, Frampton, anything."

"I didn't think this was your bailiwick anymore, Thompson," said Simon, with a smile.

"It's not, but I keep my ear to the ground. Said I'd be seeing you anyway. So here I am. Seven Gordon Highlanders, eight policemen and seven civilians killed so far this year, and it's only bloody March. And the bastards have cut the water supply I'm not sure how many times since this fiasco started."

"All right. Population is sparse on both sides of the road. We'll have a nose around. I'll need a CLO, in case we can get anyone to talk to us. Any chance of Yi Wei?" asked Simon.

"Every chance I should think. You tend to get results." Thompson paused. "By the way, old chap, your instincts served you well. Chin Chan Tan, the CLO you kicked off patrol, was indeed dealing with both sides. The blighter is currently residing at Her Majesty's pleasure in Changi, awaiting trial." He looked down, smoke from his cigarette hiding his eyes. "I can't get used to saying Her Majesty. A sad day for us all when the King died. May her reign be as beneficent."

***

Two weeks jungle bashing produced nothing definitive, even when they followed possible tracks that started near the water supply pipes. Old paths. Old *bashas*. A lot of leeches salted or burned off. Clothes sodden either from sweat or the lashing rain of the Northeast Monsoon which hadn't yet abated. Their feet were a constant soggy and wrinkled mess that never dried out no matter how much methylated spirits they poured over them each night. There was no argument from any of them when Andy said, "I hate the fucking *ulu*!"

Deciding it was a wasted patrol, they started back on the four-day trek to the pick-up point.

"You alright, old chap?" Robin asked, handing Simon a mug of tea. "You've been guzzling Paludrine."

"We all guzzle Paludrine. I'm fine," Simon answered, wiping sweat from under his hat. "You know what Andy says, we're fodder for every imaginable insect in the *ulu*."

"All the same, I'd like to have a look. Come on, over here."

"I'm fine, Nancarrow. Leave it."

"No can do. Stop being an ornery bastard." Robin was obdurate. "Shirt off, Frampton."

"Oh, for God's sake, Robin, I'm fine."

"Shirt off."

Simon, his arms and neck aching, tugged his shirt over his head.

"I presume every bone hurts." Robin said, examining the rash. "You are not a pretty sight. Probably dengue." He kept looking. "Aha!"

"Sounds like a eureka moment," Simon said, trying to smile.

"Scrub typhus. This little scab here," he prodded Simon's back, "is evidence. It's a chigger bite. Nasty. Right, we've got to get you out of here."

"I'm fine. Shoot me full of whatever I need."

"Your pain is going to get worse. Your fever is going to get worse. You could well begin to hallucinate. And frankly, Simon, you're a risk for us all if we run across CTs. So no, you're not fine. I will not get myself killed because of scrub typhus." Robin helped Simon back into his shirt, then called Haziq.

"Radio in. We need the RAF."

***

Simon remembered very little of the next ten days. The hospital in Ipoh was a blur of swirling white and blue and black as nightmares became reality, and reality was conflated with nightmares. When the fever finally abated, it was Dee's face that intruded.

"Lucky sod. Some people get all the breaks."

Simon turned his head to the ward door.

"They're sending you to the Cameron Highlands. To recuperate. Hah!" said Robin, coming in and shaking Simon's hand. "And just to ensure you do rest, I have informed Dee of your recent predicament."

"What?" Simon groaned and tried to speak.

Robin ignored him and continued, "She took some persuading but agreed to meet you there. How that girl manages to get time off to flit around the country to see you is beyond me. Even more so, the question, why!"

"You shouldn't have done that."

"Nonsense. You need some sense knocked into you. She is just the one to do it. I told her it was touch and go for a few days."

"You shouldn't have said that."

"Actually, old man, it's true." Robin stood looking down at his friend. "Now, there'll be a vehicle here at 0900. Be ready. See you when you get back. You've only got a week, so make the most of it. Sort out whatever it is that is going on between you two." Robin hooked the chart back on the foot of the bed, winked and said, "You'll be fine."

"Nancarrow," Simon called after him, "thank you!"

***

Simon had not been on patrol since his bout with scrub typhus and, after his week in the Cameron Highlands, had been kicking his heels in Port Dickson. He enjoyed spending time at the Malay Regiment headquarters—a refreshing mix of Malay and British officers—working on training manuals for British conscripts being sent with little knowledge of the country they found themselves defending. After a month of desk duty he was ready for what he considered real work.

"How were the Cameron Highlands?" Robin asked, when Simon arrived at The Dog in KL for the weekend.

"Wonderful. Short walks elongated as the week went on."

"And the Aussie?"

"She's wonderful too. We listened to Édith Piaf followed by Joan Sutherland, the Australian soprano."

"All back on track?"

"It would seem so," Simon said. But he wasn't entirely sure. Nothing definitive was said or decided. Both of them skirting around the thoughts uppermost in their minds.

"You're a lucky bastard. Don't fuck it up again!"

"Thank you, too, for those erudite words." Simon sipped a Tiger, and watched a batsman hit a six over the *padang* before saying, "You know, Dee was saying Lady Templer is pushing to open a lot more Red Cross branches, for better services for the villages. Trying to get a kind of women's institute started. Dee has nothing but praise for her."

"There'll be knitting brigades and jam-making competitions, soon," Robin said, grinning.

"Don't let Dee hear you say that. She'll have your guts for garters."

Robin threw his head back and laughed. The barman looked over with a smile. "I could respond to that comment but will refrain— only because I value my good looks!"

"No, I'd leave your face alone, but I would stamp on your feet, twinkle-toes. I never did ask where you learned to dance."

"I have—had—a twin sister. She bullied me into helping her become the best dancer in St Austell. Served her well when a US military field hospital opened there. Not far from our farm."

"Had?" Simon asked. "I didn't even know you were a twin."

"Yup." Robin closed his eyes. "An accident. Up in London. September 16th, 1944. She was a driver for some senior wallah in the army. Got flung from her Land Rover when it hit rubble and flipped. Broke her neck. I was in Burma with the Chindits. But I knew something had happened."

"I'm sorry, Robin. What a bloody tragedy."

"Yes, it was. She'd have made someone a wonderful wife and been a first-class mother. I still miss her. It's almost physical."

Robin gazed out across the cricketers to the minarets of the federal buildings beyond. Simon was quiet.

"You'd have liked Helen," Robin said, eventually.

"I'm sure I would have."

"All right. Enough." Robin shook his head. "That's why I don't talk about her. Let's have another *stengah*. On your chit."

"I am sorry," Simon said again, signaling Yi Ling for another round. "And right on cue, here is Andy. I suppose you'd like a drink too," he said.

"Aye, I would. Thanks. You're not bad for a Sassenach. Either of you, I suppose," the Scotsman said. "Anyone up for a visit to the Happy World? I heard there's a good jazz band playing."

"Not, the pipes, the pipes are calling?" Robin asked with a grin.

"Sod off! And that was Ireland anyway."

"Why not," Simon agreed. "My ears haven't been assaulted for a while. I've never known a place that plays so many kinds of music under one roof."

"I've never known a place like it. Full stop." Andy said. "Aberdeen's going to be a wee bitty tame after all this."

"You mean there aren't taxi-girls wearing pajamas in the pubs? I'm sure there are in Plymouth, I just haven't found them yet," Robin said, his mood lightened by the Scot.

"I hear you've been passed fit for the *ulu*," Andy said to Simon, when the laughter subsided. "No more high living in the hills for you."

***

And then Tanjong Malim in April 1952. A name that became synonymous with a brutal ambush in hills above the town, and harsh punishment meted to the townsfolk. One that caused General Templer's brand of governance to be questioned in Whitehall. This time less of the carrot. Lyttleton continued to support him though, saying the man had to be allowed to do his job and that it was all very well for people in London to decry methods used but what about the people being targeted in Malaya. Templer was unrepentant, and his tactics proved two things. He was a man of his word and that, if people felt safe, they would inform and sign up to help defend themselves.

The incident involved a pipeline, once again sabotaged. The repair party sent in were ambushed. Most were killed—a district officer, an engineer, fitters and seven policemen. Those still alive fought bravely until a counterattack was launched when reinforcements came after hearing gunfire. The CTs fled, taking with them as much weaponry as possible.

"We should've found some trace of them," Simon said bitterly to Robin when he heard of the one-sided battle.

"Forty of the bastards, and only two killed," Andy said. "Did you hear? Templer hotfooted it to Tanjong Malim and lambasted community leaders—Chinese, Malay and Indian. Called them cowards for not coming forward with information, for helping the CTs. Not just monetarily and with supplies, but with their silence. Telling them that if the communists won, Malaya would only be changing hands, and that the Chinese would not be nearly such easy masters. Told them the entire town—20,000 people—would be punished."

Simon, looking into his half-empty glass, said, "A stroke of genius."

"Half rice rations for men and women is pretty extreme," Robin said. "A twenty-two-hour curfew. No one in or out, which meant no supplies."

Simon had been in two minds. "It could either have worked, or failed spectacularly and sent them flocking to the MCP."

"The children were probably the only ones delighted. No school," said Andy. "It must've been like a ghost town."

"Templer promised he would be the only person to read any information given. Police and soldiers delivered paper to every household and told them to write down what they knew. A day later the papers were collected, put in sealed boxes and taken to King's House, accompanied by community leaders who watched the general read them."

"I bet a lot were blank," Andy said.

"I don't suppose we'll ever know. Apparently he made a few notes, then destroyed all the papers."

"The whole ghastly business could have been avoided if we'd found something," Robin said. "I know, I know." He raised his hand as Simon started to speak. "Can't look at things that way. But just sometimes it would be nice to be proud of stopping something without people getting hurt in the process."

"Aye, it would," Andy agreed.

Templer's dictatorial punishment garnered a number of arrests within eleven days of the initial ambush. One town, Kampong Simpang Ampat, was demolished. Despite sitting on the water pipeline, it had never been targeted. Unheard of. The daytime curfew on Tanjong Malim was lifted, and to ensure the town felt secure from possible retaliation, Templer had the entire place surrounded by two wire fences, with look-out towers and a lit perimeter. It was the safest place in Malaya.

***

To the amazement of the naysayers, General Templer's strategy, and subsequent protection of Tanjong Malim, galvanized over 3,000 recruits for the Home Guard. It also heralded a real period when people felt the tide was beginning to turn. Helped by a propaganda magician.

C. C. Too knew the communists' mind like no other. A cheerful Malayan Chinese with a brilliant intellect and an expert cryptologist, it was he who persuaded those in authority that, in order to keep waverers from joining the MCP or the Min Yuen, there had to be no censure. That to encourage those in the *ulu* who were hungry and whose commitment might be wavering, or realized they'd made a mistake, or just missed being with their families, there had to be no "I told you so," no preaching, no theoretical arguments. His premise was that everybody could make mistakes but those errors in judgment shouldn't determine the whole trajectory of a life.

When composing leaflets to be dropped over the jungle, Mr. Too used snippets gleaned from informers and SEPs, niggles that could be played upon when the air filled with sand and brown colored paper drifting from the sky, suggesting surrender. His argument for not using white paper, like many of his suggestions, came from understanding the enemy. Paper that merged into the jungle floor could be glanced at by a passing CT, without drawing the wrath of a superior.

Chapter 17

OVERHANGING MANGROVES gave little protection and rain bounced off Dee and Samsuari like nails hitting a rock face, leaving them sodden and miserable. Nightfall dropped, the velvet sheath adding to the unspoken tension rippling up and down the sampan.

"Will we make it in time?" Dee's voice hurtled back at her through the torrent.

"Can," Samsuari called, tweaking the throttle. "Rain stop soon. Not far."

His cheerful voice did not fool her. Their riverine adventures had lost much of the initial allure since their encounter with CTs and they had an unspoken rule of being at their chosen site well before dusk. They would be foiled this evening. Dee still believed she had an element of protection and had treated others with questionable injuries but never again had she been taken to a camp. Instead those hurt or ill were carried to one of the villages along the rivers to which she ministered. She never mentioned the incidents to Simon, and he never asked. And Samsuari had no desire for anyone to know.

Dee pushed dripping hair back under her canvas hat, drooping low over her brow. "The rains are early," she muttered, and wiped her streaming face as the monsoon downpour churned the river in widening eddies. "You're sure?" she asked Samsuari.

"Sure. *Tiada masalah.*"

"Hah, no problem, he says." Dee spoke aloud and glanced up at Samsuari's laugh, his gold eyetooth a spark in the storm.

"It alright, *mem.* No worry."

"Great way to end our last trip, nuh?" she returned, trying to grin.

"*Iya.*" Sad agreement replaced his smile.

Samsuari was right. The rain ended like a closed stopcock and, despite slithering and slipping up the bank where the track lead to the Land Rover, they got the canoe and their packs loaded before the next lashing. Another hour, *insya'Allah*, and they would be home. No stopping at Kuala Lipis to see Jeffrey this time. She would see him and the RAGM crowd the next night at her farewell bash.

Three years gone, mostly in a heartbeat. Part of her wanted to extend her contract again but letters from home, even one from her father, had her concerned. Nothing definitive said, just a feeling. And Les was about to become a father. Much as the thought of leaving people she had come to care about hurt, not to mention Simon, Dee knew it was time to go. Time to reconnect with the family, and time for both her and Simon to see what time apart would bring. Her mouth dried and her throat ached at the thought.

Simon would arrive for one night before his next patrol. Her final evening would be spent with the people who had gone out of their way to embrace her. The people of Raub. Samsuari and Nur, the children, Ah Sui, and Lucy and their families, Putri and her father who probably wouldn't speak to her now that his daughter had decided to ignore his wishes and go to Ipoh and train at the hospital. And others like Mohammed, who had helped her and whom she had helped. There would be children running around, food cooked by the community, and Dee knew they would have whisky for her, despite many being Muslim.

Clutching the roof as they swerved around puddles and skirted full ditches, Dee dreaded the coming five days, two of which would be spent handing over to the new nurse.

***

"Hello, my darling." Dee felt Simon's rough hands through her blouse as they drew her close. He breathed her in. "You smell delicious. Fresh and limey."

"You're a smooth talker for an Englishman!" Dee stepped back from his embrace, her fingers going to the jade necklace resting in the hollow of her throat, a pulse jumping erratically. She could feel her stern words, spoken in the solitude of her bedroom as she dressed, going up in flames. Or down the dunny. She wasn't sure which. Either way, she did not want to waste the night crying.

"You are also quite, quite beautiful."

"Only 'quite'?" She glanced down at her emerald green capris and white broderie anglaise blouse as she led Simon into the bungalow. "Let's have a *stengah* out in the garden before supper. Ah Sui magically had to visit her auntie and won't be back until the morning."

"They are all going to miss you. But no one more than me."

"Simon," Dee turned and took his hand. "The only way I'm going to get through this is with humor. Please, I'm begging you, don't make this harder than it already is."

"I know, darling, but we have to talk, a little."

Dee kicked off her flat black pumps and sank onto a bamboo lounge chair as darkness settled over them like a warm shawl. Simon moved the other chair closer. Smoke from their cigarettes drifted toward the stars and words which had never been spoken, promises never made, struggled to find voice.

"I'm going to have to cut down on these. I've never smoked so much." Dee paused, waving the cigarette at Simon. "You'd like Australia, you know. You can be a bit stuffy, but really you're not half as pompous as you pretend. And my brothers'd knock the rest out of you."

"What a delightful prospect," Simon said, reaching across the narrow divide to hold her hand. "I will come, darling. As soon as my tour is over. I'm about done with being shot at."

"And shooting?" Dee asked.

"That too. The occasional rabbit is all I want to aim for."

"We haven't got many of them. Not since myxomatosis was introduced to kill the bloody things. Although in his last letter, Les said they're becoming immune to the virus and breeding again."

More unsaid words hovered in the sultry air.

"I'm not sure what I'd do there." Simon broke the silence, hesitance in his words.

"Farm, you drongo! That's what you do. Sugar, wheat, sheep. Who cares? Depending on where you want to be."

"I want to be with you."

"Well then, we can work it out. I'm not married to Queensland. I've always wanted to see more of the country. We can explore together."

"What about your job? You can't just take off whenever you feel like it."

"That's why I'm going to supply nurse. I could do with time at home. See what's up with everyone."

"Would you come to England?"

"Yes. But Australia first."

Supper was subdued. Crickets, cicadas and nightjars accompanied the click of chopsticks as they ate Ah Sui's *nasi kebuli*, her specialty made up of rice cooked in coconut oil mixed with chicken, raisins, cloves and lemongrass. The deliciousness was lost on them.

"Did you know a nightjar's call is called 'churring'?"

Simon looked at Dee, a hint of amusement replacing the sadness. "I can't say that I did know that. Thank you." He looked into his glass, put it down on the table with a clunk and said, "Come on, let's not be miserable. Malaya, Australia and England are all in our future."

They cranked up the gramophone and danced on the verandah as Édith Piaf sang *Hymne à L'Amour*. Simon sang too, his pleasant tenor sending tremors through Dee.

"My French isn't great," Dee said, her voice a whisper. "But I don't want the sky to fall or the stars to fade, or to forget the time we have loved."

Water from the Shanghai jar was chilly, and Simon wrapped Dee in a sarong before they padded into the bedroom. Harimau curled up in comfort was put out the door with an aggrieved yowl. The scent of night jasmine wafted in and covered their loving with sweetness. Their limbs intertwined, Dee drifted to sleep, to wake to the caress of lips on her skin as dawn filtered through the louvres and, in their urgent sadness, they made love.

Sleep swathed Dee again but she was jarred awake by the sound of a jeep on the gravel. She reached for Simon but instead felt the delicate petals of a *bunga raya*, the red hibiscus, and the crinkle of paper. He had gone.

My dearest one,

I couldn't face the day, or any days ahead, with the image of tears in your eyes. Forgive me. You have my love, always, S.

Angry, she scrunched the paper, only to smooth it out against the pillow. He was right. She would have cried. She was crying now.

***

The farewell party organized by the townsfolk of Raub was a feast for the senses. Women were festive in brilliantly colored *baju kurung*, the knee-length sleeved tunic worn over a long skirt. Some wore the hijab, some went bare-headed, among them Nur and Putri. Lucy and Ah Sui, and many of the other Chinese women wore lithesome cheongsams. The men more subdued in trousers and white shirts though Samsuari was resplendent in his *baju melayu*, the tunic layered over trousers and under his *sampin*, the sarong tied at his waist. His *songkok* sat on freshly cut and oiled hair. He grinned at Dee's delight, his gold tooth once again in full view. She was glad she had dressed up for the occasion but still felt like a sparrow in a hall full of orioles, her wide-skirted sapphire blue dress relieved by a black patent belt, and her jade necklace.

Children, many of whom Dee had treated for illnesses, others she had just treated with treats, gathered excitedly, vying for her attention. Aminah and Ishraaq believed they had the monopoly and clung to her hands as she circled the room. She hugged Nur, pregnant and sad it would not be Dee who delivered her baby.

"You promise you will write and tell me, yes?" Dee said.

"*Sudah tentu*, of course," she replied. "Maybe it will be a girl. We shall call her Dee!"

"Oh God, please don't." Dee noticed Nur's hurt surprise. "Oh Nur, that would be a great honor," she corrected, "I just meant my name is not beautiful enough for your baby."

Trestle tables lined the community center. Mounds of rice interspersed with tureens of beef and chicken curries, plates of diced cucumber and tomato, bowls of grated coconut—a panoply of color and tastes welcomed Dee as she piled her plate, urged to take more than she could possibly eat by the proud women behind the feast.

Then the music and stately dancing. There was no violin, but an accordion, and the *rebana* or drum, and a brass-knobbed gong. Dee delighted everyone by joining in, her steps guided by Nur. She was grateful they played the faster *inang* and *joget* rather than the slower *ronggeng*, knowing her emotions would not survive the more soulful style.

Darkness dipped the trees in black and before people drifted away, eager to be home before deep nightfall, the crowd was brought to attention and Dee led to the center of the circle.

The headman, also wearing *baju melayu* and a *songkok*, his authority etched in lines across his face, presented her with a gold medallion. It was her undoing. She read the inscription, *To Sister Dee, 1952,* and on the obverse, *In token of services rendered, from Raub villagers, Malaya,* and tears flowed unchecked down her face.

"*Terima kasih.*" She thanked them, her voice breaking. "*Saya rindu kamu,* I will miss you all, so much. Thank you."

Around her people responded, *sama-sama,* it is nothing, and wished her *selamat jalan*—safe travels.

Samsuari, Nur and the children, Mohammed, Putri, Lucy, and Ah Sui walked her home where she had gifts for all of them. A watch for the man who had guided her so well, a silk scarf she found in KL for Nur, and toys for the children. A dictionary of nursing for Lucy and Putri, a singing kettle for Ah Sui, and for Mohammed a shiny new parang in a leather sheath. Each would also receive an envelope to be distributed by her replacement once she had left Raub. They left her in a smudge of tears as she kissed Aminah and Ishraaq goodbye.

Ah Sui shuffled out the cookhouse to make tea for the *mem*, and Dee wondered as she buried her face in Harimau's fur, if a heart could break twice. If it could, hers was a good candidate.

***

David Gallagher, her liaison in Singapore, had dutifully met her night train from Kuala Lumpur and driven her to the airport. This time it was he who had tried to lighten the mood but Dee could find little to amuse her, even his blushing reminder that this time he had been on time for her arrival.

Her stomach was a kaleidoscope of butterflies and she couldn't decide if it was because of leaving Simon and Malaya or trusting her life to the giant metal cylinder that would fly her home. The glass and steel tower of Kallang Airport, one of the layovers on the Kangaroo Route from London to Sydney, rose in front of her in all its modernist glory.

"The Scottish architect, Frank Dorrington Ward, designed the columns and railings," David said. "He was the chief architect here for years."

"Nice," Dee said, eyeing the Qantas Empire Airways plane waiting on the runway. "Have you flown?"

"Not yet, but soon, I hope. You'll be on a Lockheed Constellation. They're wonderfully roomy."

"Not as roomy as a ship." Dee had been looking forward to a few weeks of nothing. Not having to talk. Not having to think. Time to just be. Time to nurture her memories. But instead she was going to be hurtled through the sky to Darwin then on to Brisbane. She would get home before her letter.

"You'll be home in no time. Marvelous. They had to extend the runway beyond Mountbatten Road for the bigger planes," David struggled on. "Traffic lights had to be installed to stop cars trying to beat the planes."

"Nice," Dee said, again. "Look, David, it's very good of you to ferry me around but would you mind just dropping me off, rather than coming in?"

"Oh." He blushed, his earnest eyes clouded with disappointment. "I thought we might have a drink at the bar. I hear it's rather good."

"David, you're a dear man, but really I just want to sit quietly. Please."

"Yes, yes, of course. Well, here we are. Bon voyage, et bonne chance." He called a porter to carry her suitcase.

"And to you, David. And thank you." Dee shook his outstretched hand, turned and went into the terminal, the hustle of Asia closed behind the sigh of the doors.

Part Two

Now

Chapter 18

England, 2010

MAX'S CHIN FELT strangely smooth. A clean shave was the least he could do for the old boy; his grandfather had never taken to the designer-stubble look. Countryside hurtled past in a murky haze, pierced by occasional car lights waiting at level crossings, or dimly lit single-platform stations too minor to warrant stopping the Exeter-bound train. Max pushed back into his seat as if it could absorb all the dramas of the previous week.

Lisa's image flickered through the passing trees like an old-fashioned stop-motion cartoon. A symmetrical face surrounded by a wave of dark curls. Violet eyes awash with angry tears. He'd told his sisters about the break-up. His younger sister, Emma, had not held back, her mass of blue hair bobbing in time to her words. "I never really liked her. She tried too hard." Susie, older by four years, had offered him a room in their overflowing house in Clapham. A gesture for which he was grateful but not eager to accept. Fifteen-month-old twin girls, though much loved by their uncle, were not conducive to thinking. No, the best place for him was out of the way in Dorset. Perhaps then Max could work out where the hell he wanted his life to go. He was tired of drifting.

The train slowed. Sherborne, and Simon Frampton, known by his three grandchildren as Fa, were next. Max hoped he'd be allowed to take the wheel. His grandfather drove as if he was still in the jungle dodging bullets and bandits and not on narrow country lanes. A black and white photograph seen years ago of Fa as a young man wearing camouflage, squinting through cigarette smoke, a carbine held loosely across his body, and leaning against a mud-splattered Land Rover, sprang to Max's mind. Had his grandfather ever had doubts about where his future lay?

Max hauled his rucksack and computer case down from the metal shelf and lurched along the aisle to collect his suitcase. All his worldly possessions. Emma had been furious he'd left so much in the flat he'd shared with Lisa. "What about your bed?" she asked, muttering to his careless shrug, "well, speaking as someone who is currently couch hopping, I could do with a bed." But he was happy to be rid of most things. Start afresh.

He didn't blame Lisa for being livid. He'd been lazy. It was when his footsteps faltered the closer he got home that he realized it was time to leave. Being grilled as to when he'd be moved from his current advertising account to one she considered more appropriate had become a night-time routine he dreaded.

"It's embarrassing," she'd said one night after a party where they'd both drunk too much. "Demeaning, somehow."

He remembered pointing out the whole world couldn't be in banking like her, but the whole world did need loo paper, and just under half needed tampons. The comment had not gone down well. Max grinned. It was quite funny, now. But Lisa had been right. Marketing wasn't for him, in any form.

The train slowed and he grimaced as Lisa's flicker-fusion image was replaced by that of his parents. There would be constrained disappointment when he told them about Lisa, and that he'd quit his copywriter's job. A double whammy for his mother. His girlfriend had been diligent in her desire to be everything he could possibly want. In his mother's eyes at least. Max wasn't sure he knew the real Lisa. That was part of the problem.

Sherborne's mid-nineteenth century station, particularly in winter, didn't look as if much had changed in the intervening years. Dried twigs poked out of forlorn hanging baskets creaking on rusty chains. In the misty January evening it was cold and eerie, sinister almost. Even his grandfather, leaning on a walking stick under the weak lamplight, a tweed trilby hiding his face, could have been a character from a Cold War novel.

"Hello, Fa." Max dropped the suitcase and, ignoring his grandfather's outstretched hand, hugged him.

Abashed, but pleased, the old man patted Max's shoulder. "Good to see you, my boy. Come on, it's colder than a witch's tit. Is that all your luggage?"

Rain turned to sleet, and the roads became slushy. Max was glad he was driving the Range Rover and not Fa's low-slung Jag, much as he loved the twenty-year-old convertible. Nearing the turn for Melbury Bubb and braving the cold, he wound down the window and yelled, "I'm going to Hell!"

"Will you children never tire of that signpost?" Fa asked, with a laugh.

"I doubt it. I bet it's the only place in the world with a sign saying, 'Hell Corner.'"

The hamlet, little more than St Mary's Church, a smattering of houses, a rather grand Jacobean manor, and Woodland Farm, had always represented fun, and a kind of peace. Away from his child-hood house in London, where rules had been firm and expectations seemingly unattainable. The car fishtailed to a muddy halt at the entrance to the stone farmhouse. A warm glow cast from the porch light across worn gray steps, boxed yews clipped into tall rectangles played sentry to the cheery red door.

Max loved the old farmhouse. Flagstone floors covered in Persian rugs and runners. Wide armchairs, chintz covers, now faded, had cradled them as children or been used as fort walls on wet and windy days when playing outside had lost its appeal. Dormer windows in the attic, through which sun streamed on long summer nights, had kept Max and his sisters wide awake. The minuscule bathroom tucked under the rafters, pipes with barely enough oomph to gurgle tepid water.

When they were little, he, Susie and Emma had pretended they were *The Borrowers*, Fa and Nana turning a blind eye to bits and pieces that disappeared from downstairs and the biscuit crumbs that led a trail upstairs.

"Mrs. Bartlett thought you'd be more comfortable in the blue room, Max. Rather than the attic. Hope that's all right." Fa snapped the latch, hushing a dog's vociferous welcome.

Max rubbed the roan cocker spaniel's ears. "Hello, Bacchus, you're looking very silky considering the weather. And God bless, Mrs. Bartlett!" he added. The stout farmer's wife, hair permed into submission, was the reason his mother worried less about Fa living alone. She, and Joe Tine, who had bought the fields around Woodland Farm, kept an eye on him.

Fa smiled. "Take your things up while I heat the casserole Mrs. B. left. She holds my cooking in very low esteem."

The bedroom door opened to toile curtains, Chinese scenes depicted in blue and white replicated in framed prints on the blue walls. Beside the high bed, a pillar box red armchair with a brass swing-arm light to the side promised lazy afternoons of reading. He opened the heavy oak wardrobe doors and memories of hide-and-seek wafted out on a hint of camphor, along with he and his sister's never-ending hope of a Narnia-like experience.

Swamped by an overwhelming sadness, Max flopped onto the bed. It must be lonely for Fa, here on his own since Nana died. Then it struck him. He had been lonely in London. Surrounded by people, and Lisa.

Max went down to the kitchen where opera engulfed the room in rich eddies. "Let me guess—Carreras? Here you go, Fa." He plonked two bottles of whisky on the weathered pine table. "By way of thanks, for taking me in on a day's notice."

"Don't be silly, my boy! I am delighted you can tell your Carreras from your Caruso—good to see something stuck. And thank you for these. Talisker?"

"I know you're a Dalwhinnie man, Fa. I like the Highland malts, too. But after visiting the Talisker distillery on Skye last summer, I'm a convert."

"Always happy to experiment, Max. Now, would you like a beer before supper? Help yourself, you know where it is."

Conversation remained neutral as they ate but Max knew the real talking time was coming. Fa poured whiskies then lit a cigarette.

"I thought you weren't meant to smoke indoors?"

"Extenuating circumstances. Mrs. B. won't be in tomorrow, so I'm safe. Right. What's happening? Considering you usually bring a rucksack for a week, I rather think you anticipate a longer stay. Which, by the way, is absolutely fine, and Max, nothing goes outside this kitchen. Bacchus won't breathe a word." His grandfather sniffed, sipped and swilled the Talisker. "Mmm, not bad. Thank you. Right, now I shall shut up."

Max leaned forward. Chestnut hair flopped over to hide heavy eyebrows above gray eyes. His fingers drummed the whisky tumbler as he wondered where to start. Fa sat quietly, smoking, one hand toying with the dog's ears.

"I told you I'd bailed on Lisa. She thought we were heading down the aisle. Why, I don't know. We not once talked about marriage. She's always been set on a career and I didn't know she was getting broody. I guess moving in together said it. Stupid."

"Not really. I think you young people have it right. Much better to know each other's foibles before getting to the ring stage. Anyway, on you go. Just don't be too hard on yourself. You're not a cad, my boy."

"Here's the kicker, Fa. I left the agency. Left them in the lurch so probably won't ever get another job in advertising. At any of the big ones, at least."

"Well, you weren't happy there so I shouldn't worry. Though it is a stroke of luck your parents are still away. You'll have time to get your story straight." His grandfather paused. "Have you ever considered, how rather strange it is your mother, my daughter, is so very conservative, one might almost say parochial? How did that happen? Her mother wasn't. Sarah doesn't seem terribly interested in anything but wretched curtains and wall colors, though I know it's her job." He looked across the rim of his tumbler. "Oh Lord, I'm sorry, Max. She is your mother, and I have no right to speak like that."

"That's all right, Fa. She does love us—most of the time. It's a good thing Susie is more like her. Mum can at least feel she succeeded with one of her children. Emma and I are no hopers. And Dad thinks every man should be 'in the City.' Financiers like him and Giles. I'm not knocking it. It paid for our education, and a lot more. But it's not what I want."

"What do you want?"

"Ahh, there's the rub. Isn't that what you say, Fa?"

"Shakespeare, actually. Hamlet. '… To sleep: perchance to dream: aye, there's the rub.'" Fa lit a new cigarette from the still glowing stub of the last, blew a smoke ring and winked at his grandson. "Too late to stop now, so don't bother. Now, how's this for a plan? The byre is full of trunks and boxes filled with God knows what. I have neither the energy nor inclination to do anything about them so, in lieu of bed and board, you have the unenviable task of going through everything. A mindless undertaking which will give you plenty of thinking time and, my boy, take as long as you like."

***

The smell of coffee lured Max to the kitchen next morning. The pot warming on the Aga and crumbs spilling across open pages of *The Telegraph*, proof Fa had eaten before heading out with Bacchus for a walk. Though who took whom was always up for debate.

His phone vibrated and he saw Lisa's smiling face. He turned it over, ignoring the brrt brrt, brrt. They'd said all that needed to be said. But still he felt guilty. Max took a mug from the dresser and poured coffee. Milk, veins of cream, testament to its freshness, glugged from the blue and white stoneware jug. The only jug he ever remembered seeing. The kitchen had always been the heart of the house. The only thing missing was Nana. She'd have known how to handle Lisa.

The phone vibrated again. Would she never give up?

"Hello," he said, his voice distant, his eyes on the hills beyond the leaded windows and not on the phone.

"It's me."

"Oh, hi, Susie. I thought it was Lisa. Again."

"You have to talk to her. She's been on the phone to me constantly. For over an hour last night and again this morning. Clean breaks don't happen, Max. Not in real life. Speak to her. You owe her that."

"Jesus, Susie. I thought you were on my side."

"I am. But I haven't got time to listen to her every day. She doesn't believe you're not staying with us. Answer the goddamn phone next time she calls. Tell her it's over."

"I have."

"I bet you pussyfooted around. Trying to be nice. Be plain. Let her rant and call you a pig. She'll feel better."

"Fine!"

"So," Susie's voice gentled, "apart from Lisa, how are things?"

"Fine," Max repeated. "I feel a log has been dislodged and I can breathe again. Lisa and I have been wrong a long time, Suse."

"Not in her mind. And Fa?"

"He's great. Same as ever. He was smoking indoors last night but looked a bit shame-faced. As if Nana was going to pounce. I'm going to help him sort those trunks in the byre."

"Good. That might mean he's considering a move."

"Nope, don't think so. Lessening the burden for us when he dies, is what he said."

"Oh, for God's sake. What is wrong with this family?"

"Nothing. He's being pragmatic. And, I think, he's a little curious. Some of them haven't been opened for fifty years. Perhaps there'll be something about Malaya. He's been reluctant to talk about his time there on the odd occasion it has come up in conversation over the years."

"We have enough day-to-day dramas without skeletons emerging!" Susie said, her sniff audible over the phone.

***

With Fa dozing in his armchair by the fire, glasses askew, a copy of *The Oldie* face down on his lap, Max beckoned Bacchus.

"Come on, I know you've had one walk but another won't kill you," he said to the reluctant dog. He found wellies in the boot room, then cut behind St Mary's and tramped through the trees and up Bubb Down. A moment of pure contentment swept over him as, leaning over a wooden gate at the top of the ridge, he surveyed the Dorsetshire countryside spread like a giant higgledy counterpane. The simplicity and order of nature. Life didn't need to be complicated. Maybe he'd give up London completely, move to Woodland Farm. Help Fa. Get a job in the pub at Chetnole. What would his parents say to that idea? A smile twitched as he petted Bacchus, returned from chasing a rabbit. But first, Lisa.

Max hunched deeper into his jacket hoping the cold would keep his thoughts clear. Or maybe penance. A grin flickered. "Shoulda been a Catholic," he muttered as he pressed her number. "Hello?"

"So you've finally decided to speak to me." Sarcasm dripped through the pain in Lisa's voice.

"I thought we'd said everything," Max said.

"You might have. I haven't. Where are you? At Susie's?"

"No. I'm in Dorset."

"Scared I'd show up on her doorstep? Make a scene?"

"Not at all. You have every right to be upset."

"Don't be patronizing. What about work? Your precious tampons and loo paper?"

"Cheap shot, Lisa. I quit." Max kicked a clod of earth and watched Bacchus snuffling at something.

"What?" Surprise and curiosity outbid the vitriol. "Why?"

"Time for a change."

"Ditch the girl, ditch the job. A twofer?"

"This is silly. You've been phoning Susie, what did you want to say?"

"You're a shit. Do you know that? All that façade of being a decent bloke is crap. You're a fake. All that bullshit about traveling and seeing the world. It was all talk. What do you do? Run away to your grandfather."

Max listened in silence. Isn't that what Susie had said? Let Lisa get it out of her system. But it didn't make for comfortable hearing.

"What about your parents? Do they know? About us? Your job? I bet they don't."

She knew him well, he'd give her that. "No, not yet."

"Hah! A gutless shit!"

"They're still away actually, Lisa. Have you finished? If so, would you please stop calling Susie? It's not fair to drag her into this. If you want to rant some more, call me. I promise I'll pick up. But we are over. And Lisa, I am sorry. Truly. Look after yourself." Max snapped the phone shut and gazed over the rolling hills, searching for his earlier serenity.

***

After a couple of lazy days and evenings with his grandfather and fortified by one of Mrs. Bartlett's cooked breakfasts, Max pulled on an old jacket, jammed a wonky beanie on his head, knitted by Susie when she was an earnest twelve and, standing in the doorway, faced the bracing wind swirling sleet around the yard. Digging his hands deep into the pockets, he found gloves.

"Whatcher goin' out in that for?" Mrs. Bartlett's soft burr, her deliciously rolling r's, followed him into the mud room.

"Might as well start now. At least sort out what I can bring in and what can be left out there for a warmer day."

"Well don't you go draggin' things over my clean floors."

"Wouldn't dare, Mrs. B."

Pushing open the rickety door, he ducked into the byre. The smell of cows lingered though it must have been twenty years since they'd been milked in there. Dim light from the single bare bulb showed trunks, three deep along the back wall, on top of which were numerous boxes and a few suitcases. A rustle came from behind the bank and a mouse scuttled out before disappearing back into the maze coated in dust and cobwebs.

"Bloody hell!"

"I told you it would be a mindless job."

Max spun around, surprised to see his grandfather. "I thought you were out."

"I was. Don't panic, my boy. I'm sure most of them can be glanced through—no decisions needed. The newer boxes on the very top and the suitcases are Nana's clothes. I couldn't face getting rid of them. But it's time they went. Would you mind taking them into one of the charity shops in Sherborne?"

"Of course, Fa. I'll run them in this afternoon. What do you think are in the trunks?"

"Memories, Max, and probably a few things best left forgotten. Well, I'll leave you to it. You decide if I should see anything."

***

It took Max a month to whittle down the bank of trunks and boxes. Numerous trips to the charity shop and the tip had left him with one small tin box, a wooden crate and three dented trunks. One, just legible, was stenciled with his grandfather's name: *Maj. S. J. Frampton, Malay Regiment.*

The hinges creaked, then locked, until Max forced the lid open. Inside were albums of black and white photos, letters and papers, programs and leaflets from Fa's time in Malaya. He flicked through one album, smiling at an image of his then wiry grandfather, standing proud in a uniform of long baggy shorts—Bombay bloomers, he remembered hearing them called—short-sleeved jacket, Sam Browne complete with pistol, and a strange black, oval-shaped hat, perched in a devil-may-care fashion atop his very short, short-back-and-sides and clean-shaven face. Clutched under his arm was a swagger stick. A few other photos showed a disheveled man with longer hair covered by a stained straw hat, wearing wide black trousers and a loose shirt and sandals on what looked like grubby feet. Holding the photo to the weak light, Max saw it was also his grandfather. Yet another showed him in jungle fatigues with a group of men around something covered in a tarp on what looked like a table made into a stretcher. Towards the end of one album images of a woman began appearing.

***

Not having been seduced by Talisker's peaty flavor, his grandfather had reverted to sipping the oakier Dalwhinnie after dinner. Two bottles sat on the coffee table between them. Shoving Bacchus away from the hearth, Max built up the fire then settled back in the chair, picked up his whisky and eyed his grandfather over the tumbler's rim.

"I found your old army trunk, Fa."

"Good Lord! I thought that had gone years ago. A few ghosts in it, no doubt."

"Tell me about them."

"Are you really interested, or are you being polite?"

"No. I want to know," Max replied.

Chapter 19

"YOUR TRUNK SAID Malay Regiment. Were you still in the army?" Max asked.

"No, I went back a civilian. Which I was before the war. I'm essentially a farmer, as you know. In Malaya, I was a planter. Rubber."

Max looked at his grandfather. His military bearing still evident, despite the cane.

"But you were in the army during the war?"

"Sort of. I was a useful chap to have around. I knew the place, spoke Malay and Mandarin, so, yes, I was given a uniform. Not that I wore it much. I did more skulking around than anything else. Just bloody lucky I didn't end up in Changi, or on the Burma Railway."

"You were a spy?" Max asked.

"No, not really."

"Bloody hell!" Max laughed. "My grandfather, a spy."

"Nonsense," Fa said. "More a scout."

"Wasn't it hard—to come back to Dorset, to farm?"

"In a way. But I was done with fighting. Lost too many friends. And some who came back, who had been in Changi or on the Railway, well, they were never quite the same again. What I hadn't realized was that I wasn't quite done with Malaya."

Fa shuddered and gazed at the fire, his glass resting on his knee, sadness slackening his face. Max put the grate around the glowing coals and, calling Bacchus, let the dog out for a last sniff around the garden. He stood in the doorway, a thousand questions surging, before he returned to his grandfather.

"Come on, Fa, time for bed. Another history lesson tomorrow," said Max. "I'll close up. Hide the evidence from Mrs. B." He picked up the ashtray and tossed the butts in the fire and watched them sizzle then splutter out. Not much point really. The housekeeper had only to walk into the sitting room to know his grandfather had been smoking in the house.

***

The shrill jangle of the phone followed by his grandfather's measured and neutral tone gave a clue to what was coming.

"Good morning, my boy," said Fa, dropping into his chair at the head of the kitchen table and reaching for the coffee pot. "That was your mother."

"Morning, Fa. Thought it was."

"What, a good morning or your mother?"

"Both," Max said. "Well?"

"Your parents will be gracing us with their presence tomorrow."

"Bugger."

"Succinctly put. But yes, I tend to agree. However, you couldn't possibly have expected them to accept your career decision without some kind of concerted battle."

"No, I suppose not. What else did she say?"

"Not much. Though I am given to understand she lays some of the blame at my door, which seems a bit tough. Something about filling your head with romantic notions."

"Sorry, Fa." Max slid the butter dish across the table to his grandfather, then poured himself another coffee.

"Oh, not to worry. One of the pleasures of old age, and there are not many, is being able to ignore one's children's sillier comments. However, I imagine you are in for a torrid couple of days."

"Is Emma coming?"

"Didn't say. Why?" Fa asked, slathering butter on his toast.

"She likes a drama, particularly if she is not in the midst of it."

"I think that a little unfair. Boisterous was too mild a word for some of the shenanigans you two got mixed up in."

"Yeah, I know. Actually, I hope she does come. Might help deflect any flack. Mum's still seething over Emma not finishing her degree. I've got that one up on her." Max looked out to where daffodils had started to push their way through the lawn, and beyond the garden wall where oaks with gnarled branches were shaking out their spring finery. "At least the weather's improving," he said.

155

"I can disappear for a walk when the going gets tough, can't I, Bacchus?"

"Thank you, Max. And leave me to deal with the fallout. Good thing Mrs. B. is coming today. She can prepare their room. You might have to make a run into Sherborne for supplies." Fa bit into his toast, a splodge of marmalade falling onto the plate. "On second thoughts, I'll come with you. I've got to see Smithers sometime. Might as well be today. He can always squeeze me in. We can grab a pub lunch."

"Who's Smithers?" asked Max.

"My solicitor. A couple of things to sort about the farm."

***

"Fa?" Max paused, his back to his grandfather as he washed their supper dishes. "Why did you go back? To Malaya?"

"Aah, now there's a question."

Max turned to see his grandfather swirl his whisky, the amber liquid glistening. He looked weary, and guilt twinged. There were many evenings ahead when the story could unfold. He was just about to suggest they call it a night, when Fa spoke again.

"Why did I go back? For the adventure. The excitement. Being in any country on the brink of *merdeka*, independence, is an interesting time. An optimistic time. Though 'brink' was more hopeful than actual. And I loved the country. The people. I had no idea Malaya was also on the verge of madness."

Max nodded.

"It's always about the people," Fa continued.

"I wish I'd paid more attention in school; I don't remember hearing anything about independence or an emergency."

"A war that wasn't a war. Probably not much written about it. Ready for your delayed history lesson?" Fa asked but didn't wait for a response. "In 1946 the Malay States, all nine of them, and the British Straits Settlements of Malacca and Penang, agreed to form a crown colony to be known as the Malayan Union. Didn't last long. Any of us on the ground could've told those around the negotiating table it wouldn't." Fa laughed and lit another cigarette. "The nationalists didn't like the Union, so then the Federation of Malaya came into being a couple of years later. It was Edward Gent who led the corralling of the sultans. No mean feat, I'm sure."

"What was the difference? Between the Union and the Federation?" Max asked, wishing his grandfather had taught him history, rather than the dry old codger who'd tried to hammer dates and facts into their disinterested teenage heads.

"The Federation restored symbolic positions, symbolic you will note, back to the State rulers. The sultans were loath to relinquish any of their royal trappings. Who could blame them? And now, my boy," Fa said, putting down his glass with a laugh, "in preparation for tomorrow, I shall say goodnight."

***

The crunch of tires on gravel and Bacchus barking alerted Max to his parents' arrival. He sighed, closed his book and uncurled from the armchair. The rumble of Fa's voice welcoming them drifted up the stairs, then Emma's voice calling, then singing something about coming down from his ivory tower. "Hah, Van Morrison!" Max muttered, then grinned as he heard his sister being shushed by their mother.

"Really, Emma. Must you?"

"Oh, Mum, lighten up. This might be the last time Max smiles this weekend."

He hoped not. Tucking in his shirt, he smoothed his hair and glanced in the mirror before tugging open the door. Best get it over with. Though he knew it would not just be one conversation but rather a drawn-out rolling attack picked up with irritating regularity over the next two days.

"There you are, darling," his mother said, reaching up for his kiss.

"Hello, Mum. How was the drive? You managed to get away before Friday rush hour."

"We had to juggle a few things, but yes. And here we are. Go and help your father with our luggage while I put the kettle on and talk to Fa. Emma, go and help too."

"I've got my rucksack," said Emma.

"You can bring in the groceries," her mother said, glaring at her daughter and pointing to the door.

"Really, Sarah. We do have shops in Dorset," her father said mildly, his mustache twitching.

"Yes, but not Fortnum's, Daddy. And, before you get snippy, I brought you some Gentleman's Relish!"

"Ah, that's all right then." Fa smiled. "It shall be my own stash, jars not to be opened when visitors are here."

"No fear of me stealing it, Fa," Emma said, giving him a hug. "It's disgusting. Far too fishy. And you don't like it either, do you Max? Okay, okay," she said to her mother's raised eyebrow and slight nod towards the door, "we're going."

"Good thing I brought the Land Cruiser," said his father as he and Max shook hands. "Can't see a bloody thing over these Dorset hedgerows in anything lower."

"Oh well, Dad, a Chelsea tractor can be useful when it's not cruising in London."

***

Once Mrs. Bartlett's hearty steak pie was finished, Max knew there was no longer any chance of avoiding the discussion for which his parents had traveled from London. He sent a silent plea to Fa, and Emma, both of whom appeared to be engaged in an ardent study of the remnants of crusty pastry flecking the pine table.

"Let's have pudding in the snug after we've cleaned up," his mother said. "Max you can help clear. Off you go, Daddy, Emma. Would you pour me another glass of that rather good merlot, please, Michael?"

The three worked in silence, loading the dishwasher, scrubbing pots, drying sherry glasses. Folding the tea towel, Max called Bacchus in the hopes of escape but his mother's hand on his arm stopped him.

"Sit down, Max," said his father, pushing a glass of wine across the table to him. "You too, Sarah."

"How could you, Max?" His mother's eyes filled with tears as she reached for her glass.

"Are we talking about Lisa, or the agency?" Max asked.

"Both." His father, for the first time, looked exasperated. "We've had that poor girl on the doorstep more times than I care to think about, Max. You do not seem to have behaved very well."

"Would you like to hear my side of it, Dad? Aren't you the one who always says, 'it takes two'?" Max could feel his temper start to bubble. They had already made up their minds. Why was he always the shit? He took a deep breath, then a slug of wine.

"Really, Max. Lisa expected to be walking down the aisle next year." His mother sniffed. "And I thought so too. You moved in together, for God's sake. Wasn't there a message in there?"

"Not at all. And I never gave her any intimation of marriage. The whole point of living together is to see whether one can. Whether one is compatible."

"One?" Michael asked.

"Okay, me. Whether I can," said Max. "And guess what? I found we're not and I couldn't. Surely it's better to find out before the noose is tied?"

"Don't be flippant, Max."

"Sorry, Dad. But you can't deny it's less expensive. In all manner of ways. And frankly, Mum, Lisa is wrong to involve you. Susie put a stop to it straight away. I would've thought you would too. A little family loyalty."

"Max, darling, she was perfect for you. Clever, beautiful, amusing."

"No, Mum, she was perfect for who you think is perfect for me. Our visions of perfection are somewhat different."

"All right. And I'm sorry if you think we've been disloyal. But the poor girl was hysterical."

"Unlikely. Her makeup would've smudged," Max said.

"That comment is beneath you, Max. Right, no more on Lisa. I mean that, Sarah," Michael said as his wife began to speak. "But what about your job? You were making your way up the ladder, Max. You could have made marketing director someday. If not there, then some other agency. I know you wanted a different account but for God's sake, you won a Clio for your last campaign."

"Again we differ, Dad. You, Mum, Lisa, you all wanted me on a different account. I was quite happy flogging tampons and loo paper. If I had to market anything, at least it was something needed. Rather than some flashy vehicle with no chance of seeing a dirt road, or a ridiculous kitchen aid for a kitchen never used in an upscale flat in Islington."

"But couldn't you have just changed agencies?" Sarah asked. "To walk out like you did was so unprofessional. So angry. Are you angry, darling? Do you need to speak to someone? A counselor or someone?"

Max looked at his mother, astounded.

"For God's sake, Mum. Get a grip. I'm neither angry nor in need of counseling. What I needed was time to think. And that I have here. With Fa."

"You're running away." His mother's statement was bald.

"No, Mum, I'm not. I'm running to something. I might not know exactly what it is yet, but I know it's not in London."

"Is there someone else?" She reached across the table to touch his hand.

"I thought we weren't going to talk about Lisa anymore," Max said. "But no, there is no one else. I'm quite happy to be single."

"You're not gay, are you?" Sarah asked, the glimmer of a frown showing under her fringe.

"Really, Mum? No, I'm not gay but would it matter if I were?"

"No, of course not, darling." His mother paused, "Well, it might a little."

"At least you're honest, Mum. But relax. I'm as much a heterosexual as Dad. Oh, you are, aren't you, Dad?"

"Max! That's enough," his father said, though a dimple showed. "I think we should leave this conversation for the moment. Simon and Emma are probably longing for whatever is on offer. Sarah, what's for pudding?"

"Thanks, Dad." Max stood. "I'm going to take Bacchus for a quick walk. I have plenty of chance to eat Mrs. B's puddings. It'll give you a chance to grill Fa about my waywardness."

***

Max had been right. The conversation about his career had rumbled on and off all weekend. Over breakfast, while waiting for drinks to be delivered at the pub in Chetnole on Saturday, on the walk to church, mercifully short, on Sunday. It had been Emma who sounded the *coup de grâce*.

"Mum," she said, as they drank coffee after the Sunday roast she'd prepared, "I don't know why you keep on at Max, and me. We're both following in your footsteps. We're both artistic. Just like you. Only in a different medium."

Fa had laughed out loud, whilst Max had snuffled into his cup. Michael merely looked resigned. His parents and Emma left shortly after lunch, with his sister promising to return soon.

"I say," said Fa, rustling the paper and relaxing into his chair once everyone had left. "Did you hear the news this morning? I haven't had a chance to ask you. The BBC, in their wisdom, has decided to cut their Asian Network. Let's hope we never need the Malays or Chinese or anyone in Asia to stand up for us again. Bloody fools. Run by a bunch of left-wingers with no idea of what made Britain great. The BBC being a large part of that."

"No, I didn't hear that. Do you really think there will ever be another time when the world is at war?"

"I hope not, lad, I hope not. Anyway, the weekend didn't seem to go too badly, eh?"

"Not for you maybe, Fa. What, by the way, did you tell them? On Friday evening?"

"That you were sorting my papers and would be writing my memoirs."

"Oh, God," Max said, a laugh erupting. "No wonder Mum kept on at me. The family history being exposed to the public. Whatever next?" He paused, looking down. "Do tell me there's something scandalous."

Fa took off his glasses and, his voice sapped, said, "No, not scandalous. Just a little sad."

Chapter 20

FA'S WORDS NIGGLED Max all day. It wasn't a word he'd heard his grandfather use often. Even when Nana died, his grief had been private. And did it really matter what happened sixty years ago? He battled with his conscience as he wiped down the kitchen counter.

"Why sad, Fa?" asked Max, before he had time to reconsider.

"Whenever a country one loves is attacked, it's sad. You're a fortunate young man, Max. You were a baby when the Falklands War started. But it becomes personal. And we all felt Malaya was our country. Most of us had spent years there. Some in dreadful conditions."

"And yet so many of you went back after the war," Max said. "That's the bit I struggle with, Fa. I don't know if I'd want to go back."

"Of course you would, Max. You don't just abandon a place because it gets a bit sticky. People have put their lives in your hands. Your comrades, the tappers, the miners, the house staff. They all looked to us to help them. Christ, they put themselves on the line often enough to help us. It was up to us to ease the way to independence. And it could have gone smoothly, taken longer than many wanted, but a plan was in place. Just the wallahs in Whitehall messed it up. Like politicians mostly do."

"You mean the Chinese thing?"

"Indeed I do." Fa scowled, and levered himself up. "Right, I'm off to bed. Let Bacchus out will you, please?"

Max watched his grandfather leave the room. He didn't seem as spry. Getting shot was what had finally sent him back to England, and Max knew he still occasionally felt the repercussions. And more often as he aged.

Bacchus ran off chasing something, imaginary or real. Max stood at the door waiting for the dog to return and, when he didn't, he wandered over to the cowshed. He switched on the light and, in the gloom, pulled down a tin box he'd found at the bottom of the last wooden crate. Spiders had built webs on top of webs, it had been there so long.

The chill of a spring night was made colder by the metal trunk Max sat on. He held the box on his lap, his fingers toying with the flimsy clasp—the one he'd broken. He didn't know what to do. Show it to Fa. See if he wants it. Or if he even remembers. Of course he remembers. In the split second he'd seen the contents the previous afternoon he knew the box was full of envelopes. He'd slammed the lid back down quickly, sensing—no—knowing, they were from a woman.

Oh, to hell with it; Fa had said to go through everything. Max opened the box and looked at the top envelope, without touching it. The writing was cursive but blunt, no trailing ys or js. He lifted the box closer, something stopping him picking up the letter addressed to his grandfather in Malaya, and peered at the stamp. Australian. Australian?

The box clattered to the floor as the dog's wet nose nudged his hand. "Bloody hell, Bacchus. Now look what I've done." Max scrabbled to gather the slew of envelopes scattered around his feet. "Oh, shit!" He stuffed everything back in the box and tucked it into the crate. "Come on," he said, bending to pet the spaniel's ears. "I think you've just saved me from the unforgivable."

***

"Max?"

"Mmm, yup." He wished he'd ignored the persistent ringing of his mobile phone.

"Are you still in bed? It's late." His sister's voice reeked of censure.

"Six-thirty is late for you these days, Susie."

"No, it really is late. It's gone ten. What's wrong?"

"Late night," Max said, rubbing his eyes, gritty from lying awake for many hours. His breath tasted sour.

"Were you and Fa up drinking? Never mind. I've got something to tell you."

"Can I call you back? Give me half an hour."

"No, can't wait. And anyway, I've got to take the twins for their MMR jabs in half an hour."

"Fine," Max said, shoving another pillow under his head. "What's up?"

"It's Lisa," Susie said.

"What now? Susie, I can't keep taking her calls. It's been months and I'm tired of being called a misogynistic prick."

"I know, I know, but you do need to know this. Max, she took an overdose last night. Her mum just called me."

"Fuck. Fuck, fuck, fuck!" He kicked the bedding off and sat up.

"Helpful, Max. You're going to have to come up to London."

"Why?"

"Now you are being a prick. The woman you lived with, not that long ago, has swallowed a bottle of tequila along with a fistful of tablets."

"Oh shit. I know. I'm sorry. Who found her? Is she okay?"

"Her friend Alison. She was worried when Lisa didn't answer her phone, or her messages. She's got a key. They pumped her stomach, so yes, she's okay, physically."

"Suse, I didn't see this coming. She seemed—I don't know—less vitriolic last time we spoke. More sad. Which, come to think of it, made me feel worse."

"Well, she's obviously a mess. Mrs. Cartwright is too. Not surprisingly. You have to come."

"Won't me rushing up to London send the wrong signal? The last thing I want is to let her think we'll get back together."

"I know. But you need to come, if only to prove you aren't a total wanker."

"Thanks, Susie. I feel so much better." Max pulled the curtain open and gazed out at the fields. "Okay. I'll get the two o'clock from Yeovil. Can I crash with you? I don't think I could face Mum. Bugger! Does she know?"

"I haven't told her but Mrs. C. might have rung. They seem to have got more pally since you broke up. And yes, of course you can. The girls will be thrilled to see their uncle. Stay as long as you like."

"Thanks. But it'll only be a couple of nights."

***

Max watched the passing landscape through half-closed eyes. Even seeing the grime of London change to rolling fields dotted with cattle and the happy yellow of rapeseed failed to lift his spirits.

A couple of nights had turned into nearly two weeks. One of his conversations with Lisa replayed in his head. A field of buckwheat appeared to undulate and it took him a moment to realize it was alive with honeybees darting from blossom to blossom. A brief distraction before her words rattled in time with the train.

"But, Max, I don't want to sell the flat. We worked so hard to make it ours." Lisa had looked through from the sleek kitchen to the sectional sofa they'd bought after much discussion, and after they'd had the dividing wall knocked down to make one large sunny room that opened onto the tiniest terrace in the world.

Max had been making her a late breakfast—her favorite—scrambled eggs and smoked salmon. She'd still looked pale but had lost the translucency of when he'd seen her lying in the hospital bed ten days earlier. That, her hair a stringy mess and her eyes listless, along with a tube dripping fluids into her thin arm had shaken him.

"I know, but doesn't it, well, you know, bring back bad memories?" He'd buried his head as he beat eggs and chopped parsley.

"I don't care. And they aren't all bad."

"Lisa," he tried to be patient, understanding. "It's just a flat. Bricks and mortar."

"Really, Max? Is that what you'd say about Woodland Farm? It's just a building."

"It's not the same. My childhood, all our childhoods, are etched into the walls there." He'd sighed. "Even if we'd stayed together, we wouldn't have lived here that long." He'd watched the butter melt in the pan, then added the eggs, letting them set just a little before stirring. "What if," he paused, trying find words that would not send her over the top, "what if we put the flat on the market, and you take three-quarters of the proceeds? I need some cash to get me through until I get another job. I don't want to sponge off Fa." He'd been surprised at the silence and as he slid the scrambled eggs onto a plate had glanced up at Lisa. He recognized the look. Sheer stubbornness.

"Buying me off?" Her tone surprisingly mild, almost bantering. "I am not selling. I love the flat."

He'd sighed. "I can't help with the mortgage much longer, Lisa."

"I'm not asking you too. Alison is looking for somewhere else to live. I'm going to clear out the study and turn it into a bedroom. Her rent will help with the mortgage." Lisa picked up her knife and fork. "Aren't you eating?"

"No. I promised Mum I'd pop up and see her."

"Okay. Thanks for this," she waved at the breakfast. Her throat caught as she asked, "Will you come and see me before you run away to Dorset?"

Max nodded, turned away and picked up his rucksack before her tears threatened to spill, again.

"Templecombe. Next stop Templecombe." The conductor's bored voice broke Max's thoughts.

Quite apart from Lisa's depression, he was exhausted from living with Susie. His admiration for his sister had grown daily as he watched her juggle work and the girls, as well as enjoying quiet evenings with Giles when calm finally descended on the chaotic household. They were a real family. Max sighed. He couldn't remember life being like that at home. Only at Woodland Farm.

And Fa. It would be good to see him. Time away had helped Max sort out his guilt at almost overstepping the line by reading the letters. First thing in the morning he'd take the box into his grand-father's study. If Fa wanted to tell him who they were from, he would.

"Hello, my boy." Fa's voice, deep and mellow, wrapped around Max as he hugged his grandfather. "Been a tough couple of weeks, I imagine."

"Yeah, you could say that."

"How is she?"

"Stable. On tablets to make her sleep, then more to liven her up," Max answered, noting the hanging baskets had been planted, dainty fuchsia showering delicate pinks and vibrant red and purple blooms along the station platform. Happy colors.

"You can tell me more later. I was late leaving the farm and have to pick up a couple of things, then I thought we'd have a pub lunch. How about the Half Moon, we can sit outside? We'd probably miss the Chetnole Inn—ridiculous they close at two."

"Yup, sounds good to me, Fa. Do you need some help?"

"No. Might as well leave the car here. I'll meet you at the pub."

Max slung his rucksack into the boot, then walked to the pub. Taking his tankard into the courtyard he sat at one of the platform tables, a pint of best bitter in front of him, watching bees dart and dive amongst tubs of snapdragon and calendula. He smiled. Mum'd be impressed. He could thank Lisa for that. They'd planted their handkerchief-sized garden last summer full of plants that would attract honeybees. "We're in the middle of the city, they need somewhere to feed. They're endangered," she'd said. Typical Lisa. She'd set off on a quest to find out everything she could about what to plant. They'd even set up a bee bath. Twigs and stones carefully placed in a shallow terracotta saucer to give the bees somewhere to perch as they drank. Give her her due, she'd changed the water every morning before leaving for work.

Max sighed. Susie had been right. Seeing Lisa, spending time with her, seemed to have lessened her anger. Sitting on the tiny terrace, watching the bees, they even laughed a few times, reminiscing. And they'd talked, really talked.

Organ music floated over the town. Max glanced up the street and, not seeing Fa, downed the rest of his pint and ambled across to the Abbey, where Susie and Giles had married, a building he'd always admired. The fan-vaulted ceiling and stained-glass windows were magnificent. Even the more modern reredos fitted into the hodge-podge of styles of the ancient Abbey. As a boy, going to services with Nana, his mind roaming as the sermon washed over him, he'd wondered in a ghoulish kind of way whether Alfred the Great's sons really were in the tombs, and what they looked like. Shriveled like walnuts? Or preserved? Max smiled as he wandered along to the North Choir Aisle. He might not have remembered the sermons but he'd remembered their names. Ethelbald and Ethelbert. They'd sounded like Disney characters. He leaned against a pew, music from the organ in the North Transept swirling around the arches and chapels in joyous abandon, as if the organist was playing purely for his own pleasure and not for a congregation whose voices could never match the glory of his chords.

Max took one last look around before walking back to the pub. Fa should be there by now.

Bacchus bounded up as the Jaguar slid through the gates to Woodland Farm.

"Get down," Fa roared through the open window as the spaniel made to jump and scratch the precious paintwork.

Max leapt out of the car and knelt to receive the dog's delighted greeting.

"I've missed you, you daft dog," he said. "I bet you haven't had a decent walk since I've been gone."

"Hah, I'll have you know we went up Bubb Down Hill the other day."

"Do you ever stop to think about the names around here, Fa?"

"Bubb or, as it was, Bubba, is a Saxon name."

"Sounds more American," Max said. "Think of that golfer, Bubba Watson."

"I'd rather not. A good walk spoiled."

Max laughed as he put groceries away and the kettle on.

"Do you remember, Fa, when we used to tramp up there, to Bubb Down, looking for dinosaur fossils? We were convinced we'd find some. Emma still is."

"I do indeed. I think Emma could say 'cornbrash formation' and 'Jurassic' before 'cat' and 'dog.' She was by far the most diligent in turning stones over. You just liked digging and getting dirty, didn't matter if you found anything. Susie always had a doll to look after. But Emma, she loved the search."

"She said she might come down in the summer—get out of London for a while."

"She'll soon tire of two crusty bachelors," Fa said, with a laugh. "Speaking of which, Max, I trust you know you are most welcome to invite friends to the farm. You don't need to be saddled with an old man."

"Really, Fa? Dad outcrusts you any, and every, day! But thank you. I haven't though felt the need of any other company, and nearly two weeks in London has cured me, if I needed curing, of ever wanting to work there again."

Max pulled out a chair and plopped down, turning his mug of tea around in his hands.

"Actually, Fa, I wanted to talk to you about that."

"About what?" his grandfather asked.

"Me staying here. I can't go on sponging off you forever."

"Nonsense, Max. You're helping me by sorting out the cow byre. You pay for most of the groceries."

"Fa, I'd like to stay, please. But on a formal footing. Pay rent. I've spoken to Ted. His barman left just before I went up to London. He can give me evening work from Wednesday through to Sunday at the pub. Chetnole gets busy in the summer—weekenders, tourists. It won't bring enough to buy a Maserati, but enough to pay rent and board. And it will give me the days to write."

"Aah, I thought you might be putting words down." Fa lit a cigarette. Through the smoke he looked at Max. "A book?" he asked. "I haven't wanted to pry."

"Yes. I feel a bit of a fraud. Some days I think I'm pretending to write. Others I feel on top of the moon and really believe I've got a chance."

"I would imagine, my boy, that is what all writers feel. May I ask what type of book."

Max hesitated.

"It's quite alright, Max. You don't have to tell me a thing."

"Thanks, Fa. I'm not quite ready." He looked into his empty mug and wondered if he ever would be.

"Right then. Here's the deal. You need to finish up in the byre. There are still a few boxes of papers that need going through. Most I'm sure can just be junked. Old ledgers from the farm which even the taxman wouldn't be interested in now, but I suppose they should at least be glanced at. Nana was not wont to throw anything out. When that's finished, you can start paying rent. Let's say £100 a month." His grandfather held up his hand, "No, Max. That's the deal."

"That's ridiculous, Fa."

"Take it or leave it!"

"Fine. But I buy the beer and whisky."

"Now that sounds an ideal solution, my boy. Good, that's settled. And Max, it is an arrangement that can last as long as you like. I think we've proven we can rub along quite well together."

"There is one other thing, Fa." Max paused, searching for the right words. His grandfather looked at him, waiting. "Er, I found an old tin box, then with the business with Lisa, I left it alone. But I think you might want to look through it. Letters. From Australia."

"Good Lord," Fa said. "I thought that was long gone."

"I haven't opened them. Just the box. They'll look jumbled because I dropped it and stuffed them back in. I'm sorry."

"Not to worry," Fa said, his voice distant.

"Would you like me to get it?" Max asked, watching his grandfather's face.

"Perhaps later. I think I'll take Bacchus for a walk."

"Hang on a minute, I'll come too," said Max, getting to his feet.

"Thank you, Max, but I'll go on my own, if you don't mind."

"No, no, of course not, Fa."

His grandfather slapped his thigh and Bacchus bounded after him as they went out through the boot room. Fa seemed deep in thought, and Max hoped he hadn't opened up old wounds.

***

Working in the Chetnole Inn five nights a week, the easy pace of life at Woodland Farm changed and Max's days took on an urgency. As if proving to himself his chosen path was the right one. A path that would only be justified if he could get something published. Not just in his parents' eyes, but in his own. So far his inbox was filled only with rejections. Short stories that weren't hitting the mark.

"Why don't you write something for *The Oldie?*" Fa suggested.

"I don't think I qualify," Max said, wiping the kitchen table after dinner one Monday.

"No, but you live with one. Have you ever read it?"

"Can't say I have," replied Max.

"Well, try it. There's always one lying around somewhere. It's not just for geriatrics. Rather it lampoons much of the youth culture of today—something you do already at the grand old age of 29! I think your humor would translate well."

"Okay, I'll have a look."

"Speaking of looking," said Fa, pausing to light a cigarette, "I haven't opened that box yet."

"You don't have to, Fa. It can be tossed or put back in a trunk and left alone."

"No, I will get to it. It's rather stirred up a few things."

"About Malaya?"

"Yes."

Max paused then, wanting to lighten the mood, said, "Oh, I forgot to tell you, a chap came into the pub the other night. He was a conscript out there. One of the last, apparently."

"Poor sod. Can't have been easy. From England's green and pleasant lands to the fetid humidity of jungle patrols."

"He spoke more about the trip out there."

"What was his name?"

"Didn't ask. He was rather a bore. He told me about his first gin and tonic, in Colombo I think he said. He's still drinking it, in rather copious amounts the other night. Said it was his summer drink."

His grandfather laughed.

"Mine was in Port Said. Did I ever tell you about going through the Suez?"

"Don't think so. What happened?" Max looked up as his grandfather snorted.

"Christ, we nearly capsized the ship."

"What happened?" Max asked again.

"There were hundreds of men working along one side of the canal—don't forget the British were not their favorite people—well, they all downed tools, and their trousers ..." His grandfather's face turned red as, through his laughter, he went on, "... and proceeded to give us a demonstration of massed masturbation. God, it was funny. There were rather a lot of nurses on board, most of whom thought it equally entertaining. Anyway, there was a mad rush to the side of the ship to get a better view, which tilted the poor old tub, rather alarmingly it has to be said."

"What did the captain do?"

"Screamed at us to get back from the rails. He was livid."

"There, you see? That kind of thing would never happen now. More's the pity," Max said. "They'd probably shoot you today. And my generation are so damned PC."

"You're not. Write for *The Oldie*, my boy."

Chapter 21

A SKYLARK TRILLED a sweet song that suffused the garden in the soft evening air. The warmth of the day lingered, and Bacchus rolled on his back, head lolling, his tongue hanging out and his eyes closed—a picture of pure canine pleasure.

Max and his grandfather sat on sun loungers, a tankard of beer in their hands. A platter of salami, manchego and cheddar, and a bowl of olives—wrinkled black jostling with plump green ones stuffed with pimentos—on the low deck table between them. Françoise Hardy's voice singing "Tous les Garçons et les Filles" mingled with summer sounds.

"What a way to spend a Monday evening," said Max.

"Wait till you retire," his grandfather replied, "All evenings are like this. In summer, anyway."

"I've got a long wait ahead of me then," Max said. "In the meantime, I'll just enjoy my Monday and Tuesday nights off. Hey, Fa, have you ever heard Madeleine Peyroux? You'd like her."

"No. But if she's like some of the voices I hear on the radio, I'm not interested."

"She's not. She's mellow jazz. American."

"And now you've lost me," he said.

"She grew up in France."

"So there might be some hope!"

"Really, Fa? What about Billie Holiday? Or Louis? How about Ella?"

"I'm talking about now. Most of them caterwaul rather than sing."

Max got to his feet, picked up their tankards and moved toward the house.

"A refill, and a change of songstress. Bacchus, stop tripping me up."

Max watched his grandfather from the kitchen window. Curiosity niggled even though he'd promised himself he wouldn't broach the tin box. He ran upstairs, shuffled through a stack of CDs and found *Careless Love*. As he returned to the garden "Dance Me to the End of Love" drifted out the windows.

"Well, what do you think?" he asked.

"Rather pleasant. Far more French than American!"

Max settled back on the lounger with a laugh, and they sat in companionable silence, listening to the music.

"I got around to opening that box, Max," Fa said finally, his gaze distant. "It's rather rumbled a lot of old emotions."

"Good ones?" Max asked.

"Yes." Fa petted Bacchus, back from slurping his supper. "I'm getting lazy, having you here. Can't even feed the dog."

"Don't be silly, I just happened to be in the kitchen at his supper time," Max said, letting Peyroux's voice fill the void that followed. He closed his eyes, his mind wandering to the last time he'd been to Paris. Anywhere really.

"The letters were from a woman I met in Pahang," Fa said suddenly.

Max kept his eyes closed.

"Kuala Lipis." His grandfather continued. "She was with the British Red Cross, although she was Australian. It was the evening before we—Frank, Robin, Haziq, Tenuk, Yi Wei and I— headed into the jungle. We were staying with the local administrator. Can't remember his name. His chaps were going to drop us off the next morning at a track not far out of town. Strange evening."

Max heard the cigarette lighter snap shut.

"Must have been odd for her too. Sitting down to dinner with a rag-tag bunch of men, Robin and I not even dressed properly. All of us fell in love a little that night, though our host was obviously hoping for more than the friendly banter they shared. Easy to fall in love when there aren't many suitable women around."

"What was she like?"

"Sharp! I don't mean hard. But she didn't suffer fools, and she thought most of the British administration were filled with them. The administrator, poor chap, must have had a hell of time whenever she wanted something. She'd just returned from a trip to villages along Sungai Jelai—that's the river that joins the Lipis at Kuala Lipis. Kuala means confluence," Fa explained. "She could only get to the villages between the two monsoon seasons. So that must've been August '49. What a long, long time ago, Max. She was furious there hadn't been any dredging of the river after the last floods. Didn't matter what Jeffrey said—that's it. That was his name: Jeffrey Gibbons. Sometimes had a stutter. Anyway, she was scathing, and sad."

"Why sad?" Max had heard his grandfather use the word more in the last few weeks than ever before.

"Because if the river did overflow its banks again there were bound to be deaths. There always were. The kampongs were set close to the banks, up high, but still only on flimsy stilts most of the time. There was a reason all the government buildings in Kuala Lipis, anywhere that flooded, were set on the highest ground they could find."

"Fa, what was, is, her name?"

His grandfather looked surprised. "Sorry, Max, here I am telling stories about a nameless, faceless woman." He laughed, took a sip of beer, and munched a slice of salami. "Her name was Dee Cunningham. Deidre. But she hated that so was always called Dee. She wasn't beautiful. But she had the sort of looks that would stay with age. Not like some ravishingly pretty girl whose prettiness wears away with the years. And tiny. Maybe that's why she was so forceful, had to make up for her size."

Fa snorted, took another draught of beer and went on.

"Anyway, we all had a jolly evening once Dee had got over her anger. She was a good sport and danced with us all. Turned out Robin Nancarrow, the doctor, was a rather good dancer and twirled and dipped her along the verandah. The Andrews Sisters singing "Rum and Coca Cola" comes to mind. I'm sure we were noisy."

"Sounds fun," Max said.

"Yes, it was. A much later night than we should've had, considering we were heading off the next day for God knew how long."

"Or maybe it was a perfect send off," Max said.

His grandfather's smile was vague.

The music drifted over their silence until Max said, "I picked up one of the books in your study, Fa, *The Jungle is Neutral*. It doesn't sound it to me. Smaller patrols seemed far more effective."

"That was proved after Tasek, that place just north of Ipoh. Eight hundred SF men, supposedly well-trained and with superior firepower, failed to quell fifty CTs. A bloody fiasco."

Fa drummed a cigarette out from a pack lying beside him but didn't light it. "I knew Freddie Spencer Chapman—the chap who wrote *The Jungle is Neutral*, it's about the war in Malaya by the way, not the Emergency. He was Force 136. His premise was the *ulu* should be perceived as neither good nor bad and that to survive, it was one's state of mind that contributed to the body's ability to manage deprivations, and bounties. And he lived by his credo." Fa lit the cigarette. "He was a brave chap, killed himself in the early '70s—didn't want his wife to nurse an invalid."

"I don't get that."

"Hah, says a young chap. Imagine, if you will, Max, being utterly dependent on another for the most basic of human needs. How can that be considered a good life? I'm all for euthanasia. We do it for our pets." He glanced at Bacchus. "We should be able to make that decision for ourselves. If I decide to take a trip to Switzerland, you'll know why."

"Dignitas?"

"That's the one," said Fa. "Should it come to that, Max, I would like you to come with me."

"Bloody hell, Fa. Come on!" Max stood and walked to the garden gate, his eyes watering. He couldn't imagine a world without his grandfather. He shook his head. Silly. They'd celebrated his 90th birthday a couple of years before. He looked back at Fa lying in the lounger, smoking. It was probably living with Fa that kept his mother off his back. Someone to keep an eye on her father. When really it was the other way around. Fa showing him the path, without saying much. "You are okay, yeah?" he asked, sitting back down.

"Don't get maudlin on me, Max. Death is coming. I just want to meet it on my terms."

"Okay," Max looked at his grandfather. "But you must tell me if there is something wrong. No sudden surprises."

Fa nodded, "Fair enough. Now enough of that. It's cooling down, let's go in. How about a whisky? Do you know, we used to carry a ration of rum on patrol, they'd even include it in air drops? The army did some things right."

They settled in the drawing room with their drinks. Fa lit another cigarette and gazed into his tumbler.

"In your wanderings through the study, have you come across the expression 'have you eaten rice today?'" Fa asked.

"Not that I can remember," Max said. "What's it mean?"

"It's a greeting. A kind of 'how are you?' It had an added poignancy for anyone coming from the jungle. SF or CT. Hunger had a lot to do with some surrendering."

Fa took his glasses off and rubbed his eyes. Max noticed wrinkles did not smooth out as quickly as they used to. He waited, knowing his grandfather would continue when memories sorted themselves out.

"Friendships. Like I said, Max, it was all about the people. You must remember, we weren't a regular army or police unit. We were ex-Ferret Force, well, Frank Hobbs, Haziq and I. We'd been together through the war, when it was Force 136, knew each other's foibles. Robin and even the CLO, Yi Wei, fitted in just fine with our rather casual approach. Not to the job at hand of course, but the manner in which we functioned. There was little 'yes, sir, no sir.'" Fa paused again. "They were all good men."

"Did you stay in touch?"

Fa ignored the question. "The *ulu* is exhausting. Boring. Unforgiving. Thorns catching your clothes. Roots tripping you. Vines forever reaching, twining around your rifle even as you're hacking your way through. In swampy jungle we had to contend with *meng kuang*." Before Max could ask, Fa explained. "That's a leathery kind of long, wide grass with thorns that curve along each edge, and to make sure you really didn't want to go near it, there was another row pointing the other direction along the central ridge. Capable of shredding a man. And mosquitoes."

Max was quiet, waiting.

"You laugh, Max, at the Hell signpost. The jungle really was hell. We lived in the twilight. A glimmer of sunshine might leach through occasionally but mostly we stumbled along in a grimy soup of grayish-green. Each rest break was an exercise in checking you didn't collapse onto a scorpion, or an ant's nest, or disturb a snake. Malaya has arguably the most deadly snakes in the world. Over thirty, I seem to remember. The pit viper was one which terrified me. Hardly distinguishable from the undergrowth, with long fangs and able to launch amazing distances. Robin always had generic anti-venom but different snakes require different sera."

Max shivered. "You mentioned the RAF and supply drops. Couldn't they spot camps, the larger ones at least?"

"Not a hope. In 127,000 square miles of mostly jungle it was well-nigh impossible to see anything on the ground, especially if they didn't want to be seen. No, foot slogging, informants, and dashes of luck found the camps."

"What happened when you did?"

"Kill or be killed often. Not sure about us, but for the CTs capture was always preferable. You can't get information from a dead man. And after a few months in the *ulu*, capture was sometimes a blessing. Good food, dry clothes, relocated far enough away from his, or her, area of operation to feel secure. It really was hell. But interspersed with moments of heaven. Hah, I'm a romantic old fool!"

A catch in his grandfather's voice made Max look up.

"No, you're not. Just reliving extraordinary events." Max paused, "Fa, what happened to Dee? You haven't mentioned her again."

"I've been thinking a lot about her lately. She'd be 87. Probably not still alive."

"You are, and kicking!"

His grandfather laughed. He closed his eyes and sighed, "She was my moments of heaven. Then we hit a rough patch. My fault, of course. It normally is, Max, even when one thinks one is doing the right thing. I told her about Nana, Tess. That we had an arrangement. I was confused. Deeply in love with Dee, but very fond of Tess not to mention, in essence, promised to her. I'd given her a ring. I suppose it was an engagement ring." Fa paused. "It was a confusing time. I didn't want to hurt Tess; she didn't deserve that after promising to wait for me. I didn't have to go back to Malaya but I was a young man and still looking for adventure. I liked the idea of farming, especially here at Woodland Farm, but knew if I stayed I'd never leave. Never see anything more of the world. So, I ran. Never expecting to meet someone else."

"I've got to ask, Fa, why did you tell Dee?"

"I suppose I wanted to know whether she could ever see herself living in England. For all my interest in other places, I knew I wanted to end up here. Initially, after I'd told her, she wouldn't have anything to do with me. Can't say I blame her. I'd been clumsy. An oaf. She tossed me out, then I was back in the jungle. She was busy. She really was a dedicated nurse, Max. Never armed. Would not let me drive with her because of course I always had a pistol. And she was right in the midst of bandit country. She had a driver cum boatman. Samsuari, a wonderful chap. A delightful Malay who thought the world of her. His children used to crawl all over her whenever she went to his kampong. And his wife, who at first was very mistrustful, came to be a great friend."

"So, while you lot were armed to the teeth she never had anything. Wow!"

"Yes, it was wow. She was abducted once, on one of her forays upriver. Taken to a CT camp to treat a young man. She was there about ten days then released, alone, on the banks of a river. I am certain she treated others. She never told me. And I never asked. As far as she was concerned if someone was ill, or wounded, she would treat them."

"And what about Nana, Tess?" It felt strange to Max to call her by her name. "When you were in Malaya, I mean."

"I was that despicable man. Writing to and receiving letters from one woman whilst desperately longing for another. Just as Dee had accused me. Hedging my bets. Not something of which I'm proud. Don't misunderstand me, Max. I cared for Tess. Very much. But ours was not a grand passion, even in the early days. Our letters were not of yearning. More friendship. Practical. What was happening on the farm. Tess's father was getting on a bit and she was managing pretty much everything. Hah, I remember one of her letters telling me she had stripped down the tractor! Another remarkable woman."

Max was vaguely uncomfortable. His grandfather's eyes were closed, a smile tickled his mustache and Max asked, "But you and Dee got back together?"

"Yes, we did. I had Robin to thank for that. He, like most men Dee met, fell a little in love with her. She was a wonderful dancer, I was not. They used to dance together—it was rather magical to watch, though I was eaten up with jealousy. She was great fun. Totally unpredictable, except with her work. There was a vibrancy about her that was irresistible." Fa's voice trailed off before he said quietly, "But who knows, Max, maybe after time familiarity would have bred not contempt, but a less charged time together. I don't know. And until you found those letters, I hadn't thought about it for years."

Max saw his grandfather's eyes were moist. Guilt almost stopped his next question. "So how did you get back together? You said Robin helped."

"Yes. I had a rather bad time with scrub typhus. Once I could leave hospital, I was sent up to the Cameron Highlands to recuperate. Robin let Dee know and she joined me. We hadn't seen each other for a few months. We were rather cowardly, I suppose, and skirted around the subject of Tess, and us." He smiled at Max. "She tried to talk me into going to a fortune teller. But I wouldn't. Bloody rubbish. She went in though. Came out smelling of incense from all the joss sticks being waved about."

"What did she say?"

"Don't know. She wouldn't tell me." Fa was quiet, then said with a chuckle, "We used to listen to Édith Piaf. And Dee loved opera. It was she who introduced me, not literally, to Joan Sutherland, the Australian coloratura soprano—they called her 'La Stupenda.'"

"What the hell is 'coloratura,' Fa. Never heard of it."

"Trills. Not my favorite, it must be said. I find it shrillish, rather than trillish, but Dee loved listening to her. And Mario Lanza, the American tenor."

"Ha, there's another American artiste you admire!"

"Indeed." His eyes misted and Max looked away as he said, "We loved each other, deeply."

"I can't begin to imagine, Fa." Max's voice was wistful.

"You'll find it, my boy. What you need is an adventure of your own. You've been holed up down here too long. Not that I don't like having you here. I do. Very much. But you must not be tied."

"I'm not, Fa, this is the place I feel most at home."

"Well, it'll always be here, Max, so feel free to roam," Fa said, lighting a cigarette.

Chapter 22

SLEEP WOULD NOT COME. Stories of Malaya chased around in his head. Tales of a grand passion. Max grinned in the dark. Sounded like one of the romance novels Susie used to read. Underlying his thoughts was that he couldn't imagine the fear that had spiked many of his grandfather's days. The jungle. Every day an uncertainty.

He clambered off the bed and gazed out the window at the rolling Dorset hills, silhouetted in moonlight. He loved it here. But if he stayed, would he ever leave? Ever have his own adventures? They could never be his grandfather's but he had to delve into discomforting territory. Stop being afraid. Fa was right. He stood a moment longer, then opened the door and, careful to avoid the creaky floorboards, crept upstairs to the attic. He pushed open the dormer window to a blast of autumnal air, switched on the lamp and computer and began to type.

Max woke to the chittering of sparrows and saw two sitting on the windowsill. He groaned and lifted his head, then realized where he was and sat up. It was late. His sudden movement startled the birds. He looked at his computer and beamed.

A dunk under the shower freshened him and, hauling on clothes, he ran down to the kitchen.

"Morning, Fa." He bent to pet Bacchus.

"Morning, my boy. You're late. Everything all right?" His grand-father twitched the paper and continued reading.

"Fine, thanks." Max put a muffin in the toaster, then slathered it with marmalade and poured coffee.

Fa folded the paper and, with a wink, asked, "Have you noticed Mrs. B. has given up haranguing me? She popped in earlier, unexpectedly, to drop a cake off and didn't say a thing about me smoking. One battle with a female I have won. There haven't been many!"

"Did you win any with Dee?"

"Not many. Just the ones she allowed me to win. Rather like your grandmother. Most of us are putty, my boy, when it comes to arguing with women."

"What happened, Fa? With Dee?"

Simon sighed. "She'd extended her tour once and that was coming to an end. I was, in many ways, a fool. Head in the sand, still hedging my bets. I never did write and tell Tess. I just thought it would all sort itself out."

"You just let Dee go?"

"I suppose I did. Malaya wasn't done with me. Despite the *ulu*. I liked the people. And it's always about the people, Max. Always. I've said that before. Local and expatriate. I'd met some of the Australians involved in gold mining around Raub. Naturally enough, Dee knew a lot of them. It was they who kept her supplies of Vegemite topped up. Disgusting stuff. Give me Marmite any day."

"What about the Australians?" Max tried to guide his grandfather back.

"They made me think. They were hard working, fun, often irreverent. But I just couldn't imagine myself farming there. Queensland sounded very different to Dorset. And farming was, is, all I know. That and the jungle. And killing."

Max sat quietly. A lot of what Fa had told him had seemed abstract. But hearing him say 'killing' gave him a jolt. Up until then it had been a sort of 'kill or be killed' exercise.

Fa's voice brought him back to the kitchen table.

"But I was building up to going to Australia. I really was. Before I returned to England. Just to see. I knew if I went straight back to England, the trajectory of my life would change. Tess had been understanding about me going back to Malaya after the war. I doubted she would be again. Despite all this with Dee, I kept on writing to Tess. What kind of cad does that?"

Max didn't speak.

"I went to Raub. Cadged a 24-hour pass. Our last night was probably the unhappiest night of my life. We talked. We made promises. We danced. That was the last time I listened to Édith Piaf. "Hymne à L'Amour." How's your French, Max?"

"Not brilliant. A-level and bust. But Josh Groban did a cover a few years ago."

"Oh yes, I like his voice."

"The Americans you like are adding up, Fa. Have you heard his version?"

"Can't say I have. I think I've avoided the song for the last fifty odd years."

"Would you like to?" Max asked. "I can probably find the Édith Piaf one too."

"Not sure I would, Max. Thank you all the same."

Max poured coffee for them both, let the dog out, then sat across from his grandfather, his face alive with excitement, tinged with hope.

"Fa, I finally have my story. Malaya." He leaned back in the chair and waited.

Simon lit a cigarette and, through the smoke, said, "I thought you wanted your own story. Your own experiences, Max. You have to live your own life. Not live it through mine, or anyone else's." His eyes were sharp.

Max had expected the response, had his thoughts marshalled, but Fa went on.

"I hope it's not about me. I was joking when I told your mother you were sorting out my papers for a memoir. To get her off your back, might I remind you? There is nothing to be written about me, even when I'm six feet under. Though I want to be burned to a cinder."

"No, Fa. Not about you. But your stories, your experiences are unique."

"No, they're not. Every one of us out there had similar experiences. Robin, Andy, Frank, Haziq. All of us."

"Okay, unique is the wrong word. I'm sorry. But they are mostly unheard, certainly by my generation. It's a novel, Fa. Not you, not Dee. But based there. What do you think?"

"Well, you'd better hurry if you want me to read it!"

"Don't be silly, Fa. There's years in you yet."

Max stood, and putting their mugs in the dishwasher, glanced at the clock above the door. It was almost lunch time.

"We've talked the morning away, Fa. Fancy a pint? I'm working this evening but a pint at lunch won't kill me, or you."

"Why not! We'll take Bacchus, seeing as he hasn't had a walk yet."

Max laughed. "This'll help him. A walk to the car and a walk into the pub. Let's go to The Acorn instead of Chetnole. Ring the changes."

The pub was almost empty. Taking their pints to an old oak table near the fire, in front of which Bacchus immediately stretched, they sat down and picked up their earlier conversation.

"I mean it, Max. Nothing about me in this book of yours. I'd feel a fraud."

"Nothing, Fa. What your stories have done is trigger a different story. Of course the historical bits will be there but nothing related to you. I promise." He paused, looking at the glowing logs. "Did you stay in touch with Robin or Andy, any of them?"

"Yes, of course. In the days of letter writing. Andy stayed in Malaysia, after *merdeka*. The thought of returning to Aberdeen was too much. He married a Malay girl. Fatima. She looked a lovely woman. They had a couple of sons. One of whom I met when he came to university here. Andy died about ten years ago, I think."

"What about Robin? Did he eventually go back to medicine?"

"He did. Research into tropical diseases, malaria mostly. Based in London but spent a lot of time in Africa. He used to stop in on his way down to St Austell to see his mother. Tess was most taken with him. It was his damn dancing that the women loved."

"Did he ever marry?"

"No, but he had a string of women, we met a few, but none seemed to last longer than a year or two." Fa was silent, his hands idling with the cigarette packet in front of him. "Life's a bugger sometimes, Max. Robin died of complications to hemorrhagic dengue on a trip to Sarawak. Poor sod."

"Doesn't seem fair."

"No, it wasn't. He saved my life a couple of times. Once getting me out of Pahang when I had scrub typhus, then when I got shot."

"Fa, before you tell me about that, I have got one question. Well, lots, but one major one."

"All right."

"You talked about being in the army, but were you always? I mean, right to the end? I thought the army was subordinate to the

183

police by 1950. And you never seemed to have to go on parade, or wear uniform, or, frankly, really follow orders."

Simon was quiet. Then he laughed. "Oh, I followed orders alright! But you're right. Sort of. After the Ferrets were disbanded, a number of us were quietly seconded to the police, to Special Branch. I'm sure in part due to a good word from Bob Thompson. I spoke Malay and Mandarin, could melt into my surroundings, and knew the *ulu*. Really the only requirements."

"How about knowing how to shoot?"

"Well, that too."

"So," said Max, a smile playing around his mouth, "You were a copper?"

"I suppose I was. The locals called us *mata-mata*. Eyes. Though really I spent most of my time mooching around the jungle. Went where we were told but left pretty much to our own devices. It was a strange situation. As you know, Frank, Robin and Haziq had been army too. Frank and Haziq in Malaya during the war, like me. Robin in Burma."

"Where did Andy fit in?"

"He was police all along. And stayed on after we all left, in the Malay Police Force. Became very senior. Took Malay citizenship and ended up a *datuk*. Impressive."

"A what?"

"It's a Malay honorific title. Datuk Andy Robertson!"

"But you weren't just a copper were you, Fa? You were much more cloak and dagger."

"Yes. We were Special Branch, which was part of CID. We were syphoned off after '52. Technically British officers, and people like Haziq remained army, and were paid by them. The true 'coppers,' as you call members of the police," Fa said, with a laugh, "those part of Special Branch, were paid by the Malay government who also picked up their not inconsiderable expenses."

"Sounds complicated, and very political."

"I suppose it was. Not my area, and by 1952 Templer was in charge, with the next most powerful man being the head of SB. You know they called Templer 'The Tiger of Malaya?'" Fa paused. "We weren't always successful and despite not capturing as many CTs as we'd have liked whilst on patrol, we did a lot of digging. Of putting together a map if you like, of what the MCP looked like in the jungle. That's why Tenuk, and Yi Wei and other CLOs who worked with us were so invaluable. Those Chinese who did help us, both the army and the police—and there were many—were very brave. They were the ones who most easily infiltrated the camps. Women as well as men. Women are often better than men, Max. They can be brutal, with no compunction about using violence. But they can also get close to people far easier, both men and women, and win trust. And often are better interrogators. A real softly, softly approach. I had nothing but admiration for them."

"Why did you leave? The end of '52, wasn't it? I mean, the Emergency didn't officially end until 1960, did it?"

"You have been doing your homework."

"A lot more to do, Fa, but I've made a start. And all my notes from your stories are incredible. Raw research."

"That's me. Raw!" Fa said. "And in need of a cigarette. If you want to continue this conversation, you'll have to come outside."

"Okay. Let me get another couple of pints."

"I'd call that delaying tactics, but as you're paying, I'll accept." Simon snapped his fingers to Bacchus who grudgingly followed him away from the fire.

"Ah, good man," said Fa, taking his pint from Max. "It's not too bad here, we're out of the wind at least."

"Still bloody cold. Hurry up!"

"I got shot again."

All thoughts of the weather left Max. "I knew you'd been shot. On your side, right? I remember seeing the scar when we used to go swimming. We made up all sorts of tales about it. I think mainly to do with pirates."

"I seem to recall being made to wear an eye patch at one stage."

"Oh yes, that's right. I'd forgotten that. You scared Emma. She must've been tiny. How did you get shot, Fa? Wouldn't twice be considered careless?"

Simon laughed. "Good old Oscar Wilde. That was losing parents, my boy. Lady Bracknell, I believe, 'To lose one parent, Mr. Worthing, may be regarded as a misfortune; to lose both looks like carelessness.' But yes, we were probably a bit gung-ho."

"Not a word I readily associate with you. But go on." Max drank deeply, enjoying the taste of the local bitter, and watched as his grandfather was taken back to another time. He saw his eyes open and asked before he could speak, "By the way, Fa, does Mum know much about any of this?"

"Very little. She never showed much interest. That's probably why I've been gushing on for so long to you, Max. It's been a very happy time having you to stay, if a little poignant." Fa smiled. "You're a good listener."

"I'm rather ashamed I never asked before, Fa."

"Don't be. The time obviously wasn't right. Now, where was I? Oh yes. Robin and I were driving up to Ipoh from KL, there'd been a bit of bother around Sungai Siput. Remember, where it all started?"

Max nodded, laughing. "For 'a bit of bother' read ambushes, shots fired, grenades launched."

"Well, yes, I suppose so," Fa agreed. He looked into his beer. "There was no escort that particular afternoon. I can't remember why. Anyway, we were following *The Straits Times* delivery van and felt fairly secure. Driving through Tapah late in the afternoon, the driver stopped, delivered some newspapers, then told us there'd been trouble up ahead and that he wasn't going any further. Wise chap. We would have been sensible to follow his lead. But as I said, we were gung-ho. Wanted to get to Ipoh before nightfall and it was only thirty miles. So, on we went. Bloody silly. You were right, Max. We didn't always follow protocol but, by God, we were hauled over the coals later."

Max was quiet.

"Anyway, I was driving and Robin had the carbine. We had pistols of course, and grenades. He was hanging out of the window, easier to see at that time of day prior to dusk than peering through an insect-smeared windscreen. He saw something ahead and told me to either gun it or reverse very quickly. Once you leave Tapah the road starts to wind, or it did then. We weren't far from Batu Gajah. We were lucky. For some reason the CTs hadn't got the ambush ready. Unusual. But we weren't a convoy so the Min Yuen hadn't known about us. Maybe they were preparing for the following morning. Whatever the reason, the log hadn't been dragged all the way across the road. Reverse wasn't an option so I put my foot down, swerved around the log and went for it. They managed to get a few shots off. They were all on my side of the road, so Robin was trying to fire across me, then he climbed out of the window to shoot over the roof of the Land Rover."

Max looked at his grandfather. He would have been a few years older than Max was now, and he couldn't imagine the kind of life and death decisions being made, on a daily basis.

"You must have surprised the hell out of them."

"We certainly did, but not enough to make them run for it. They emptied a few more rounds into us, and I managed to keep going. Not sure how. Most of the roads weren't sealed, and even if they had been once, they were full of potholes. Regular deluges, heavy vehicles, the odd grenade all made driving in Malaya a challenge."

His grandfather's hand went instinctively to his tummy as he continued. "Then it all got blurry. Robin took over. Driving from his side of the vehicle because he didn't want to stop. Good thing he had long legs. I remember thinking him very pushy. We got a bit further on and did stop. He patched me up as best he could. Shot me full of morphine, put me in the back and raced for Ipoh. Bouncing around on the bed of a Land Rover is no picnic and I do remember thinking he was a bloody awful driver. That was the end of Malaya for me!"

"Your decision or theirs?"

"A bit of both. I was in a bad way. Lost a lot of blood."

"Where were you shot, Fa?"

"Through the belly. Lower abdomen to be precise. Why you never saw the scar as kids." He laughed. "Lucky it wasn't higher, or lower!"

"Jesus, Fa."

"That's rather what I thought."

"Did you tell Dee?"

"Of course not, and made Robin, on pain of everything I could think of, promise not to either. She was back in Townsville. What could she do? I didn't want any decisions made because she thought I might croak."

"So what did you do?"

"Oh, we kept writing. She wanted me to go to Australia. Just to have a look. I'd had long leave due. Three weeks. I had been seriously considering it but I was in hospital in Penang longer than I'd expected. I told her too much was happening and my leave had been postponed. Something I knew she'd understand. She wrote about going to England. We were both trying to find a way. Distance had not lessened our feelings."

Fa paused. He closed his eyes. "Things rather fell out of my hands. Our hands, I suppose. I wasn't healing and it was decided I should be shipped out. I was trying to pluck up the energy, and the courage, to tell her I was going back to England. Explain why. Being shot, the whole thing. Throw myself at her. Promise her I'd go to Australia when I recovered. The courage I needed, was to write to Tess. I was going to come clean. Then I didn't need to."

Max waited. The wind was eating into him, but Fa seemed unmoved by the cold. He lit another cigarette. Coughed, then inhaled.

"A letter arrived. Telling me she couldn't leave her mother. She wasn't well. There was no one else to look after her. Her father was busy with the pub. Her three remaining brothers all had lives of their own. Families."

Max waited again.

"I don't know why I kept all those letters. I've gone to read them again and again since you found them. But I can't. Do you know what she said, in her last letter? I don't need to read that one. It's been ingrained in my memory since the day I opened it. Dee said it was time to grow up and face her responsibilities. Her grand adventure was over, that she'd had the time and love of her life."

Tears glistened behind Fa's glasses. He took them off and rubbed his eyes. "What an old fool I am. Take no notice, Max."

"Never! Fa," Max stopped, not sure he had the right to ask but what the hell, "Have you been happy?"

"Oh, my boy, of course I have. What wasn't there to be happy about? Tess, Nana, was a wonderful woman. It took me a long time to recover, and she bore the brunt of it. We shared a long life together filled with combined respect, a gentle love and pride in our daughter, in Woodland Farm, in you three ragamuffins. Of course, I've been happy."

"Did you ever hear from Dee again?"

"Never."

"Fa, did Tess ever know about Dee?"

"No. What was the point in hurting her?"

Chapter 23

DAYS FOR MAX FELL into a rhythm of reading and writing, interspersed with meals with Fa, walks with Bacchus and the occasional run, as well as his shifts at the pub. His grandfather had clammed up about Dee and so Max kept silent, although the more he read about Malaya the more questions accumulated, and the more he wanted to see the country himself. Confident his grandfather would reopen the door to his memories, Max, in the meantime, couldn't think of any other time he had felt so chilled, so at one with what he was doing.

West Country papers published a few articles, and a short story appeared in an online magazine but so far no one wanted to pay him. But, he comforted himself, clippings all helped. And then an email appeared in his inbox from *The Oldie* showing interest in his query about a light-hearted piece on inter-generational living. Their response sent Max flying down from the attic to swing Mrs. Bartlett around the kitchen, an action which left her primping her permed hair in a fluster of delight. Fa also showed pleasure as long as it made no actual reference to him.

***

"Morning, Fa."

"Good morning." Simon shook the newspaper then tossed it onto the table catching the edge of his plate. Honey seeped through the pages. "Bugger, now look what I've done."

"Here, have another coffee," Max pushed the pot across the table, "what are you up to today?"

"I'm nipping into Sherborne. Anything you'd like?"

"No, I'm fine, thanks. What are you going for?"

"You're worse than a wife sometimes, Max," his grandfather said, his words softened with a smile.

189

"In other words, none of my business."

"Exactly. How on earth I managed on my own will, I'm sure, remain a mystery for the entire family. You can add that to your next article for *The Oldie!*"

"Oh, come on, Fa! I just asked."

"On a more interesting topic, and one that will require your assistance," Fa said, trickling honey on another slice of toast, "is the imminent arrival of your sister."

"Which one?"

"The smaller, wilder one."

"Emma's coming down? That's fantastic. When?"

"Tomorrow," Fa said. "I gather she intends to spend the winter in the West Country."

"What?"

"For a writer, you are remarkably short of words this morning."

"But how come? What happened to her belief the only place to be was London, Paris or Florence?"

"I don't know; you'll have to ask her. All I know is that she arrives tomorrow, when, she assured me, she would tell us everything."

"Did she browbeat you, Fa?"

"No more than you, my boy." His grandfather laughed at Max's face. "Emma will liven us up. It will be nice for you to have someone younger to talk to."

"I like talking to you, and listening," Max said, sounding a trifle petulant. "Chaos follows Emma."

"Well, maybe you need shaking up. You need a little more in your life than your grandfather and the pub. I am expecting a phone call from my daughter any moment now. She will almost certainly accuse me of taking her children away from her. Sarah is incapable of seeing that children need freedom to explore, and not just little children."

"We're hardly children, Fa."

"Perhaps not in years, but both you and Emma are still searching for something. And if living in the depths of Dorset, or wherever she's going, helps you find it, then that's fine." Fa looked at his grandson a moment, "And Max, I earnestly believe you are on your way to finding it. Aha, right on cue. The phone. Odds are it's Sarah!"

"No bet!"

Max listened to the phone call taking place in the hall. One side of the exchange anyway. Although his grandfather said little, it was not difficult to imagine the other end of the conversation. His mother would be furious, even though she was the one always on at Emma to stop working odd jobs, and couch surfing. Max smiled. It seemed he was now the one doing odd jobs. What on earth was Emma up to? He pulled out his mobile phone and tried to call but, it just rang.

***

Barking sent Max and Fa to the front door in time to see Emma emerge from a powder blue VW Beetle, one that had seen better days.

"Emma, my darling." Fa enfolded his granddaughter in a bear hug. He was not tall, but she still only came up to his chin.

"Hello, Fa. Thanks for taking another orphan in. It's just a few days, and I'll be the better-behaved one."

"That I doubt!" Fa said, with a smile.

"Hi, Em." Max lifted her off her feet and swung her around, Bacchus leaping at her flying legs in delight. "Where'd you get the wheels?"

"Long story. Isn't she pretty? Her name is Skylar."

"Of course it is," Max said, laughing. "Come on, I'll help you with your stuff."

"Am I in the attic, Fa?"

"No, Emma, your brother has taken that over. None of us dare go in there for fear of dislodging the great many papers scattered over the beds. God help him if there's a gale."

"Great. It'll be warmer downstairs."

"My God, I never thought I'd hear the day when my grandchildren complained of being cold. Take your things up, then come to the kitchen. Max has swapped shifts in honor of your arrival, and so you don't have to tell the same story twice. And Mrs. Bartlett has made your favorites, steak and kidney pie and a peach cobbler."

"She's a sweetheart."

"So," said Fa, pushing back from the table, "we've covered all the family except you, Emma. Which, I must say, is most unlike you. Would you like to go into the sitting room or stay around the table?"

"Let's stay here. It's cozy. We'll clean up first, though."

"Right, you do that. I'm going outside for a cigarette."

Max and Emma cleaned up the kitchen, chatting about mutual friends in London.

"God, wouldn't it be funny if Suse appeared on the doorstep?" Emma said.

"Fa would love it; not so sure Mum could cope. All her children deserting her."

"She wouldn't even notice. She's far too busy swanning about telling minions what to do."

"That's a bit harsh, Em," Max said.

"Not really. That's what she does, and why you and I always got in trouble. Susie was the smart one. She did exactly what she wanted, never got caught, and always kept her trap shut. You and me, we never learned. That's one of the reasons I had to get out of London."

"There are phones in the country."

"But, Max," Emma fluttered her eyelashes at him, "the reception is so bad in Cornwall."

"Right," Fa said from the kitchen door, "Bacchus and I are ready for our bedtime story."

"I'm over my abstract phase," his granddaughter announced.

"Thank God for that," Max said. "I never understood your paintings."

"That's because you're a philistine," his sister retorted, flicking her brother's hand.

Simon and Max listened, charmed by Emma's excitement. A grant through Wings International in partnership with the Audubon Society, to not only study painting but avian conservation under, as she described, one of the greatest living bird painters. Christopher Dale lived near the Marazion Marshes in Cornwall and they would be spending their time studying birds there, along the Hayle Estuary and in the Scilly Isles. The grant covered her accommodation, transportation, and living costs, which was how she could afford to buy Skylar. Emma bubbled with joy as she explained Mr. Dale had never had an apprentice before, that he had a reputation in the art world for being cantankerous and exacting and that her essay and portfolio had beaten out other applicants.

"Emma, that is fantastic," Max said, glancing at their grandfather.

"I'm delighted for you, darling. Now, what do we know about this man?"

"That sounds terribly pompous, Fa."

"That is as may be, but I'd like to know the man with whom my granddaughter is going to spend so much time. Didn't your mother want to vet him?"

"Nope. She's just thrilled I've found my 'direction.'" Emma laughed.

"But Emma," said Max, a wolfish grin curling his lips, "Fa is an expert interrogator."

"I know. Don't you remember how he could always get a confession out of us when we were younger? Probably still could."

"Don't you want to know why?" Max asked. "Our grandfather was a spy."

"Really, Max. What bollocks!" said Fa, standing to refresh his whisky.

"A spy?" Emma asked.

"Yup. In Malaya," replied Max, studiously avoiding his grandfather's eye.

"Really, Fa?" Emma asked.

The bantering continued long enough for their grandfather to finish his drink. Then, as he headed up to bed, Max and Emma took Bacchus out for his last rootle around the garden.

"Do you think we upset Fa? Teasing him?" Emma asked.

"No. He quite likes us knowing he wasn't always a stodgy Dorset farmer."

"Hardly stodgy, Max."

"No, I know. But to look at him now, you'd never believe all the things he's done. We just know about the associations with farming, and the environment, of course. It's fascinating listening to his stories. He was, is, amazing, Em. All the things he'd done by the time he was my age. It overawes me."

"Don't be silly. You've just done different things. Brr, I'm getting cold," Emma said. "You can smell autumn in the air."

"Not brave things." Max took the conversation back. "Like trekking through the jungle for weeks at a time. Being shot at. Having to shoot people. Christ, I don't think I could do it."

"Well, thank God, you don't have to. It's because of people like Fa that we can be who we are. And it was quite brave ditching Lisa!"

"Yeah, you're right." Max laughed, then whistled Bacchus, "Come on, boy, time to go in." A roan shape hurtled towards them, tail wagging in the half-light leaching across the lawn from around the curtains in the sitting room. "Hey, Em, are you sure about this chap, Christopher Dale? He sounds a bit difficult."

"I'm fine."

"You always say that when you're not," Max said.

"I haven't met him."

"What?"

"I had to write an essay about why birds are my passion, tell him what I hoped to gain from the five months studying under him. And promise my first born to Wings International. All the interviews were done at WI headquarters in London. I think he's feeling his mortality or something. Wants someone to carry on, carrying on. He is a really good painter, Max, really good. I'm going to learn such a lot."

"How old is he?" Max asked, and slung his arm over Emma's shoulders as they headed back to the farmhouse, a frown skimming across his face.

"Dunno, late forties maybe?"

"And this is really what you want to do? Traipse around the countryside photographing birds, then painting them?"

"Yup."

"Perhaps there's more of Fa in you than any of us! Do you want me to come with you? I could drive down with you and get the train back."

"That's sweet, Max, but no, I'll be fine. I'm a big girl now."

"Still my baby sister, Em!" Max said, as they took their boots off in the mud room. "Another drink? Or a hot chocolate?"

"Ooh, yes, let's have a chocolate."

With their elbows on the kitchen table, and Bacchus under it, they sipped the frothy drink, and Emma said, "Tell me Fa's story. Are you writing it down?"

"Yes, I am, actually." Max didn't mention the hours of research into literary agents. That somehow seemed too presumptuous with the book nowhere near being finished. Or with a decent title. "Does he know?"

"'Course he does."

Chapter 24

WITH EMMA GONE AND set on her new path, his grandfather still not really talking, another article sent and accepted with a few minor edits by *The Oldie*, Max found his new-found equanimity evaporating. Another sleepless night had been spent lying on top of the bed in the attic. Max had scrawled his grandfather's words down, as close as he could remember, when he'd come up after dinner the night before. He pulled the pad closer and read the words prompted by, he thought, a gentle probe about Dee.

> *The mind's an amazing thing. It shuts out what it doesn't want to remember. I wonder sometimes, in today's world, whether it really is good to rehash old mistakes, old horrors. Does it put them to rest forever, or does it keep them lingering to infest our current days? Don't we all have a right to forget pain? Forget anything if we want to. Isn't it our right to control our minds? Our thoughts? I don't know.*

Max didn't know either. It was so ingrained for everyone to spill their guts, not just on social media, but to anyone who would listen. The more he'd thought about it, the more he'd come to the conclusion his generation were pretty gormless. He smiled. Not his word. His grandfather's. But, the argument had raged in his head, hard to compare. The millennials had not fought a world war, though there were plenty of 'small' wars going on. Fight a battle, get injured, write a book. Fight a battle, be brave, write a book. He shook his head. Isn't that what he was doing? And he hadn't fought any battles.

Under Fa's words he'd written a brief list of names and addresses in Australia. He turned on his computer, pulled up the drafts he'd written in the early hours and hit send on the top two. He slipped

195

downstairs to make coffee, hoping Fa hadn't got up early. He didn't want to talk this morning.

Carrying his coffee back up, his unsettled thoughts kept time with his steps. Emma had unsettled him. Fa's story had unsettled him. Max shrugged, and muttered as he put his mug down, "Basically you're unsettled."

A ping drew his attention to the computer. He clicked on email.

Hi Max! Wow, talk about out of the blue. How did you find me? Silly question, everybody can find everybody these days. First thought was that you were some weirdo, but I've looked you up and you seem reasonably sane though why you're writing for a magazine called 'The Oldie' is a bit of a mystery. You can't be that old. Okay, I'm rambling.

Max smiled.

Yes, I am Deidre Cunningham's granddaughter. Bloody hell. I knew she'd nursed with the Red Cross in Malaya but nothing much else. Truth be told, I never really asked. She went back to med school and became a doctor.

But I'm going to stop there. I want to talk to my brother about all of this. Or perhaps he's on your list. Another stab in the dark, maybe? I'll get back you.

Jessica

P.S. Does your grandfather know you're doing this?

Max looked at his watch. Nine hour time difference. He knew because he'd checked the minute he hit send, less than half an hour ago. So it was 3pm in Queensland. He'd found a few possible names trawling for anyone the right kind of age to be either Dee's children, or grandchildren. Cunningham wasn't that common a name but he didn't know if she'd married. He'd started in Townsville then traced a few to Brisbane. Out of eight names, he decided to try two at a time. Jessica Johnson Cunningham and Robin Cunningham. The first because he liked the name, the second had a little more thought behind it. Robin Nancarrow had been Dee's friend too. A tad lucky, really. He stopped smiling. Jessica hadn't answered the one question he wanted to know.

Hi Jessica,

Great to hear from you so quickly. Thanks. One thing, is your grandmother still alive?

Max

He waited.

Yes. More later.

About to go downstairs for another coffee he was drawn back to the computer by another ping.

Does your grandfather know?

Shit!

No, not yet.

Max hurried away, not wanting to answer any more questions. Questions like, why not? Best not to say anything to Fa until he had a bit more information. Dee might be gaga. Or dying. Guilt punched him. Who was he doing this for?

The lid of the dog food bin clanged and Max knew his grandfather was puttering around in the kitchen. He tensed. Fa had an almost inhuman ability to divine guilt; none of them had been able to get away with much as children. He must not mention Dee.

"Morning, Fa. Sleep well?" Max stepped over Bacchus lying across the doorway. "Any coffee left?"

"Good morning, my boy. I've just put some more on. You were up early. Everything alright?"

"Yep. Couldn't sleep."

"Funnily enough, I couldn't either. Must have been our conversation last night. All this gnashing of teeth in public is sickening. It's voyeuristic. A generation living vicariously through people whose lives are beyond shallow. Bloody celebrities. Most of them couldn't find their way out of a paper bag. It's like the military, or policemen, bleating on about being wounded. That's the job."

"Damn, you are on a roll this morning, Fa."

"It is each and every government's responsibility to ensure their people are cared for, and educated and, as much as possible, kept safe. Like mandating seat belts. But no one can account for a madman taking a knife to a stranger, or a gun to a roomful of children. All we can do is try. We must stop wanting to blame someone, anyone. Some things just have to be sorted out privately. Then whatever decision is made, must be lived with. Graciously. By all parties."

"Are we still talking about life in general, Fa?"

"Hmph." Fa lit a cigarette and glared at his coffee cup.

"What about bringing pressure to bear on rogue governments?" Max asked, leaning against the counter as he waited for his toast to pop up. "There has to be a line somewhere."

"Yes, of course. That's why we've fought two world wars, and countless other small ones. That's a collective issue. I'm talking, at the moment, about how we conduct our private lives." Fa coughed. "Now, would you get the paper for me, please? I heard Pat drop it through the letterbox."

The only sound was the crackle of the newspaper, as Max read the sports pages and his grandfather the news.

"A few of these idiots who don't want to allow prisoners to vote should take a leaf out of C. C. Too's book," Fa said.

"I'm not sure I agree," said Max. "If you've done something bad enough to warrant a jail sentence, shouldn't you lose privileges?"

"Yes, of course, particularly for a heinous crime. But if one loses everything that relates to the world outside prison, how on earth can one be assimilated back into that world at the end of a sentence? Remember C. C. Too. Everyone makes mistakes, those mistakes shouldn't dictate the remainder of a life. Rehabilitation is paramount, and being able to vote is part of retaining a stake in the country. Actually, I think the bigger issue that should be addressed by our Whitehall mandarins is the fact that so few people bother to vote. And then they have the gall to bleat."

"You're saying make voting mandatory?"

"I am," Fa agreed.

"I'm with you on that one," said Max. "I'll have to think a bit more about the prisoner voting. On a different topic, Fa, I'm thinking of going up to London sometime."

"Good idea, my boy. Change of scene, and I really don't need babysitting."

"I know, but why don't you come too? You can stay at Mum's, I'll stay with Susie. You haven't been up to town for at least a year. You've been saying you want to see *Les Mis*."

"I'll think about it," Fa said, before adding, "Joe or Mrs. B. could look after Bacchus."

Max spent the rest of the morning trying to lose himself in his manuscript but kept checking email. He'd done a lot of that lately. Firstly waiting for a response from agents. Any agents. Then two nibbles in one day. One more of a bite. It had taken all his self-control not to burst in on Fa with the news. No jumping guns. Instead he punched the air and told Bacchus. Now the wait for an email from Australia. Nothing came before he was due at the pub. He wasn't surprised, just impatient.

Ten days later he heard.

> *G'day Max,*
>
> *Sorry it's been a while. You must've been wondering. I had to wait till I could see Mitch. My brother. Named after my great uncle. He's a lawyer. That's all you need to know. Everything has to be by the book which is why I had to speak to him in person. He's living in Sydney. I'm in Brissie, Brisbane, and DeeDee is back in Townsville. He took a bit of persuading. "Why rock boats after all these years?" is what he asked. And I get that. Have you spoken to your grandfather yet? I bet you haven't. Which I sort of get. No, I do get.*

Max smiled at the screen. He wondered if Jessica spoke as fast and furiously as she wrote.

> *You might not have heard from me again. Then where would you be? Up the proverbial creek. And no, before you ask, I haven't mentioned anything to DeeDee.*
>
> *She brought us up you know. Our parents died in a car accident when we were little. Now, don't get all weepy on me. I was five and Mitch was seven. A long time ago now. And we couldn't have had a more loving childhood. We lived in Townsville, then Brissie.*

I think I told you DeeDee went to medical school after her mum died. She was a GP, and a wonderful one. You should've seen her farewell party from the practice—one she started. She only truly retired about ten years ago. We'd been trying to talk her out of working for years. So she compromised—not something she's good at—and worked part time until she was seventy-five.

Then she stunned us and buggered off back to Townsville. Somewhere she hadn't lived for twenty years. She even bought back the old homestead house. It's not out in the country anymore. Townsville's grown so much. But it's still a nice area. Amazing, eh? Ending up in the house you started in.

So what happens now, Max?

I suppose you'd better tell me a little about your grandfather. His name would be a start. You didn't say much in your initial email. Just that DeeDee and he had been friends. I kind of think more than friends, mate. If, after all these years, you think it a good idea to get in touch. Just saying.

Max laughed. She was crazy.

I'm guessing he's widowed. Otherwise you really would be a weirdo. Talk about causing feathers to fly if your grandma was still around. Or maybe he's divorced. DeeDee was. Way back when. Though actually they were separated for about ten years before they got around to divorcing. Mum was only about five when they split. Anyway they stayed mates and shared custody of Abigail—that's my mum. He died years ago. Tom was his name. I remember DeeDee being upset. They stayed in touch even after he remarried. And of course when Mum and Dad died, he came back up north. He was a nice man. Moved to Adelaide when he remarried.

Max was beginning to feel he needed to draw a flow chart.

Maybe it was because of your granddad that she never remarried, or that her marriage failed. Huh! That would explain all sorts. She was a stunner. Still is actually. Had men falling over. She loved to dance. You know how as we age our eyes fade? Hers never have. Still a beautiful green.

Anyway, Max. That's probably enough for now. I've got late shift and need to catch a few zeds. Tell me a bit about your granddad.

See ya,

Jessica

Max looked over his shoulder. Not sure why. Fa never came up to the attic.

Hi Jessica, great to hear from you. I was beginning to wonder but didn't want to be pushy. Things have b

He deleted and tried again.

Dear Jessica, delighted you got back to me

Max looked at the words typed and erased them too. He'd been spending too much time with Fa. Much too formal. He started again.

Hi Jessica,

Great to hear from you, and glad you spoke to your brother. His name didn't make my list, maybe because he's in Sydney. And I don't blame him for being cagey.

So a little about Simon. We all, my sisters Susie and Emma, and I call him Fa. Can't really remember why. Maybe one of us couldn't pronounce 'grandfather.' Anyway he's a farmer in Dorset. Hah, maybe because he was a farmer. In a place called Melbury Bubb. Or was. He sold the land about fifteen years ago but kept the old farmhouse and a couple of acres. He's 92 and amazingly well considering he smokes like a chimney.

Oh yes, I live in the country with him. Not to baby him, as he calls it, but because I was done with London and it suits us both. I'm his general factotum and dog walker. He is regaling me with tales of the Emergency, some of which I'm using in a novel.

When I was going through old boxes and trunks in the byre I came across one filled with letters from Australia. I gave them to him without of course reading them. Oh, yes, and there were a couple of photos of Dee in an album. She certainly was a looker. You're right about their friendship, it was pretty intense and then I think got messed up through time and place— circumstance, I suppose you could say. Makes you wonder what could've happened.

Nana died about eight years ago. Her name was Tess. They always seemed a great match, solid. No rows, at least none that we heard and, as kids, we spent most of our holidays down here rather than in London. When I asked Fa about her, he said they shared a comfortable kind of love, which I thought rather dismal. But it lasted so maybe that is the best kind to have. No major highs, no major lows.

He told me that in Dee's last letter she wrote that she had to stay and care for her mother and that, 'Her grand adventure was over, that she'd had the time and love of her life.' Isn't that sad? Maybe that's why I started this. Though I'm not exactly sure what 'this' is. Are you?

I'd best get back to work. What do you do that involves night shifts?

And, where do we go from here? I'm not sure I want to break any of Fa's confidences, more than I have already by getting in touch. I obviously didn't think this through.

More later,

Max

Chapter 25

WORDS JUMPED AROUND the page and Max could bring no order to them. Instead of writing he spent hours gnawing his fingernails and pacing the attic, or the hills. Bacchus curled into a donut whenever he appeared downstairs, exhausted from multiple walks a day.

The question, what next, seared itself behind his eyes to swivel into place the moment he closed them. He was tired and irritable but also hungry.

"Where's Fa?" Max asked, lifting the lid on soup bubbling on the stove. "That smells good, Mrs. B., it's what brought me downstairs. Is that for lunch?"

"It is. Your grandfather's out with Joe Tine talking about cows," she replied, her hands deep in soap suds as she washed knives and chopping boards. "And he'd better not walk manure over my clean floors."

"He wouldn't dare," Max said, with a laugh, "And neither would I. I'll tell him lunch is on the table."

"Leave him be, he'll come in when he's ready. It's good for him. Outdoors. Now it's not so cold. And man-to-man talk."

"I'm famished."

"Then you'll have to wait. Read the paper." She dried her hands and hung the towel over the Aga rail.

"You're tough, Mrs. B. No wonder we all love you."

"Get out of here. I've work to do. You'll hear your grandfather when he comes in."

Max wandered into Fa's study and saw the small tin box on his desk. He closed the door and moved along the hall to the sitting room. If Fa was reading Dee's letters, Max didn't want to intrude. Guilt preyed. He'd already intruded. Jessica's emails were proof.

He lay on the sofa, his legs dangling over the arm and, with his hands under his head his mind drifted, for some reason at ease for the first time in days. His story, if he could get words down would, he realized, mirror what little he knew of Fa's fellow copper, Andy. Based in the final days of the Emergency, it told of a battle with dueling loyalties—that of his birth country and that of the country he'd come to love. The conflict largely erased when he falls in love with a Malay girl.

"Lunch." Fa's voice interrupted his thoughts as it bounced down the uneven flagstone floor.

Max ambled along to the kitchen, his mind off his grandfather and Dee and back in Malaya. Not Fa's Malaya, but his. His story.

"Where's Mrs. B.? I thought she was having lunch with us."

"Not today, she has errands in Yeovil. Though why anyone would choose to go to that hellish place, I'll never know."

"Would you like a beer, Fa? I picked up some Fursty Ferret when I was in Blandford St. Mary the other day."

"How nice. And how very apt!"

Max laughed as he poured two glasses of the amber ale.

"Did you miss Ferret Force? I mean, it seemed you had the run of the country."

"I suppose so. But we only lasted about five months. And it was the right decision. Don't need a bunch of soldiers telling civilians what to do, and how to do it. Much more sensible to be an adjunct to the police, even if we did have vastly more men in the army than they had in the Police Force, initially at least. But they were mostly Brits. Until the Fijians, Aussies, New Zealanders and Rhodesians came to lend a hand. Commonwealth countries anyway. Better by far to have those living in Malaya fighting for their way of life."

"You mentioned a special SB facility. Where was that? And, I suppose, more to the point, what went on?"

"Hidden deep in a rubber plantation on the outskirts of Kuala Lumpur. Astonishing, patient work was done there. Dismantling ancient battery sets and rebuilding them using only old wires and muddying solder, and so on, so they could be surreptitiously put back into the public domain which then, with luck, would fall into CT hands. When the radio was tuned into Peking or Radio Malaya a signal was sent to any nearby monitoring teams, ergo a direct lead to a camp. Ingenious."

"A Malay GCHQ," Max said, referring to the government communications citadel outside Cheltenham.

"Yes, I suppose so," said Fa. "But it wasn't just a listening station. There were boffins, what you'd call tech geeks, coming up with gadgets in the machine shop. A document processing lab, cells with two-way mirrors and listening devices. And, in some ways, the most important thing, it was the repository for files on all known CTs—being added to all the time. Painstaking work, done in the shadows, about which most people knew nothing."

"A veritable 'Q' from James Bond films," said Max. "I wonder what 'Q' stands for?"

"Quartermaster, I should think."

"Do you remember when we were kids, Fa, trying to make invisible ink?"

"I do. It used to drive Nana mad to find you all in the kitchen with lemon juice, and vinegar and God knows what else spread over the table. I'm amazed you didn't set the house on fire trying to read each other's messages with a candle under the paper."

"She wouldn't let us use the iron."

"I can't quite figure out the logic of that, but I'm sure she had a reason," Fa said, his face softening as he thought of his wife.

"You haven't mentioned Chin Peng for a while. What happened to him? I assume he was captured, or shot? Or did he eventually surrender?"

"No. Went into exile. With a band of loyalists. Crossed over the Thai border and set up camp in the jungle there. That is, I think, when the heart went out of the Emergency, even though it dragged on for another six or seven years. That happened after I'd left. Those die-hards left behind, people like Osama China, who'd been instrumental in spreading communist propaganda, must have felt utterly demoralized. Abandoned. Remember Lau Yew had been killed, as had The Bearded Terror of Kajang, and a number of other major players."

"Why didn't Thailand send them back?"

"Thailand was neutral. After a few minor skirmishes during the war, they formed an alliance with Japan. There was apparently no desire for further confrontation with anyone."

***

Research papers were piling up on the beds, the floors, every flat surface in the attic. Often Max would head back up after a shift at the pub and lose himself in the story forming under his fingers. Always with one eye on the inbox.

G'day Max, sorry for the delay—I've been on nights. I get messed up and life apart from work gets put on the shelf. Oh yes, I'm a doctor. ER. Trauma. That kind of thing. If a shrink got hold of me, I'm sure he'd say my choice of profession is a direct correlation to our parents' accident. But, surprisingly for someone who can be a bit of a ditz, I'm good in a drama. Mitch can't understand it. DeeDee can.

So, you're a writer? I imagine that requires calm. You and I can never be more than friends. That's a joke! I live in a carefully coordinated sphere of chaos, or that's what Mitch calls it, anyway. Funny really. I suppose we've both chosen jobs that require a cool head. Mitch can be a bit of a dag. I could be mean and call him boring.

What about your sisters? Have you told them yet?

I know we agreed to take things slowly, but it occurs to me that neither DeeDee nor your Fa are spring chooks. We might not be able to afford too much 'cool.' And how are we going to do this? DeeDee's comfy with the tech side of life. I suppose because of work. And has an email account. Which is good, because she is a bit deaf and never answers her bloody phone. Or maybe she chooses not to. She can be stroppy!

What about Simon?

Right, I'm off to bed,

Hoo roo,

Jessica

P.S. Just realized I haven't said much about DeeDee. Sorry. I'm stuffed.

A few words jumped out at Max. He supposed a "dag" was the opposite of "cool." "Stuffed"—was that full or knackered? His laugh bounced back at him from the screen. "Hoo roo?"

Hi Jessica,

If you and I are going to be more than friends—that was a joke—I'll have to find an Australian dictionary! I think George Bernard Shaw should have added Australia to the list when he described America and Britain as being two countries separated by a common language. I figured out most but "stuffed" stumped me. Ate too much? Exhausted?

No, I haven't said anything to Susie or Emma. They are both tied up in their lives. No, that's not true. They would be instantly enthralled and want to butt in. Which would be fine, except the more who know about this before I, we, bring it up with Fa and Dee, the more likely it is that the gun is jumped.

Am I hedging? Yes. I honestly don't know how Fa will react. He has been so open about his time in Malaya, part of me feels I'm breaking his trust. Shit. I am. It all seemed a great, romantic idea. Now I'm not so sure. It's not like it's going to turn into a Mills & Boon reunion. They're still on opposite sides of the world, for Christ's sake.

Sorry. Feeling guilty.

Oh yeah, Susie is in PR. She set up her own business after the twins were born. Chloé and Olivia. They're almost two and a half. Gorgeous. She's married to Giles. He's in the City. Would that qualify him as a "dag"? Nice bloke and perfect for Suse. She's great. Kind and calm and able to handle our mother with practiced ease.

Emma is the crazy younger one. She's an incredible artist and has recently decided she wants to spend her life tramping around in estuaries and swamps photographing birds and then painting them. And conservation.

I'm in the middle.

That sounds pretty negative about Mum. Mum's okay, as is Dad, and hey, aren't we lucky to have them, especially considering you didn't. It's just that every now and then I wonder if they are actually my parents. Emma and I are utterly different to them. They're very conservative, with both a lower and upper case C. We're much more like Fa. And Mum is like neither him nor Nana. Must be a throw-back.

Yeah, Fa's surprisingly good on the computer—when he realized he had more chance of his letters to the editor being published if they were emailed rather than snail mailed he got computer savvy.

Right, back to work.

Max

"More curry, Fa?" Max asked, stirring the casserole dish. "There are a few chunks of lamb left."

"No, thanks, my boy. That was delicious. Hotter than a Malay one, but good nonetheless."

"It is one of the few things I cooked better than Lisa. Though she said I used too much chili. I had to make extra raita for her. There's some of Mrs. B.'s chocolate mousse, if you'd like."

"No, thanks." Fa rolled his napkin and tucked it through the silver ring, his initials still visible despite years of polishing. "I'll go and put my feet up in the sitting room, if you don't mind cleaning up."

"Sure. I'll join you in a while."

Max went to the dining room to pour a glass of whisky for each of them, then joined his grandfather.

"Thought you might like a snifter, Fa," said Max, putting the Dalwhinnie in front of him before taking his Talisker to the armchair opposite.

"Good idea, thank you. Do you want the television on?"

"No, not tonight, Fa." Max paused, gathering his thoughts, and his words. "I want to tell you something."

"Sounds serious. What's up?" Fa lit a cigarette and waited for Max to speak, smoke forming curlicues above his head.

Simon had always had an endless supply of patience when dealing with miscreant grandchildren. The silence used to get so painful, one, or all of them, would admit to whatever misdemeanor they were being accused. It felt a bit like that now.

"Fa, I've done something thoughtless," Max began.

Fa waited, his brown eyes magnified behind his spectacles.

Max continued, "I mean, I might have overstepped the mark. Shit, this is hard."

"Why don't you just spit it out?"

Max looked at his feet. "I went online and found Dee. Well not her exactly, her granddaughter."

"You did what?"

"I found Dee." Max met his grandfather's gaze but held his tongue.

"And what gave you the right to do that?" Fa asked, his eyes now blazing though his voice calm. His face pale.

An outburst would have been easier.

"Nothing, Fa. Absolutely nothing. I started by trying to find out if Dee was still alive. She is. Then I thought it might be fun."

"For whom exactly, Max?"

"You, Fa. Truly."

"Goddamnit, Max, you had no right. That was the past."

It was Max's turn to be quiet. He watched Fa, lighting cigarette after cigarette. The sitting room becoming a fuggy swirl of liquid nicotine. His grandfather finally broke the silence.

"It was the past," he repeated. "My past."

"Yes. But a very important part of it."

"That is as may be. But it was not yours in which to interfere. And, more to the point, Max, I trusted you with it."

Max looked down. His Talisker drained as his grandfather continued.

"You, as yet, have not met someone for whom the world stops. I hope someday you do. The pain of when that is taken away is an anguish I hope you never feel. You had no right, Max, no right at all, to do what you have done." Fa paused again. He took a sip of whisky. "I presume you and this woman are in touch."

"Yes. By email."

"Does Dee know about this, this meddling?"

"No. At least I don't think so. Jessica said she'd wait until she went up to Townsville. She lives in Brisbane."

"Good. Then you are to write to ... what was her name?"

"Jessica."

"To Jessica, and tell her in no uncertain terms that she is not to mention any of this unfortunate nonsense to her grandmother. Am I clear, Max?"

"Yes. And, Fa, I am truly sorry to have upset you. It wasn't meant to." He got some comfort from petting the dog's silky ears.

"I'm sure it wasn't, Max. But it has. I am now going up to bed. See to Bacchus, please. And also email the woman."

Max waited until he heard Fa's bedroom door close. He poured another whisky and took it with him to the garden as he waited for Bacchus. He leaned against the far gate, the one leading to the fields and on to Bubb Down Hill. Even in the dark the hillside looked dry. The grass crunched when Bacchus came running to his whistle, hopeful for a bedtime treat.

Max watched the dog settle on his cushion near the range, then gave him a pat. "I've fucked up, Bacchus. Badly. G'night, boy."

Chapter 26

G'day, Max, or I suppose I should say "good evening" because it's almost daylight here. I'm in Townsville. I got some unexpected time off a couple of days ago and decided to fly up and see DeeDee. It takes over 15 hours to drive and I've only got a few days. I've been up for hours. Couldn't sleep. The trouble with coming off night shifts, and excitement.

I told her, Max. I know we said we'd let each other know before we said anything, but it just sort of came out. She has that effect on me.

Max groaned and could hardly bear to read the next sentence. Whatever it said, it was not going to be easy to control the outcome.

It was bloody amazing. I was nervous as hell. But as soon as I said Simon, her eyes lit up. I swear, Max, she looked young again. It was gnarly. And then she had a thousand questions, not many I could answer. I said I'd ask you. But in true DeeDee style she told me not to be bloody silly. She'd ask them herself.

So, me old mate-in-crime, you'd better tell your Fa.

Right, there's no surf around here but I'm off for a swim. Let me know quick as a spit.

See ya,

Jessica

Max sat, mesmerized by the blinking cursor. "Oh fuck, what have I done?"

Jessica, I've blown it. I told Fa, and he's beyond livid. I can't remember a time he's ever been so angry. After reducing me to the size of a flea, he went to bed. No shouting, just cold and calm. I have no idea how to fix this, especially as Dee now knows.

We're as bad as each other. Both blurters. Shit.

Max

He hit send then paced around the attic, the space for once not giving any comfort. The dry air sucked what was left of his vitality. If they didn't get rain soon, summer would be long and arid. Typical England, a hellish winter, and now the driest spring since records began. A sad chuckle escaped. Talk about typical English, here he was worrying about the weather.

Max opened the Velux skylights as far as possible. The night was bright with stars. Another reason not to live in London. Way too much light pollution. A shooting star jolted him from his reverie, reminding him of nights spent lying on rugs on the lawn when they were down for the summer. The three of them would try and stay awake as long as possible, counting them. Fa used to lie with them sometimes.

Papers and files, rocks holding them down, covered the beds and Max emptied one onto the floor and stretched out. His eyes felt red and sore, but each time he closed them, Fa's disappointment swam into vision. An email pinged and woke his ragged sleep, and the previous night flooded his conscious. Instead of stars he could see dawn filtering through an array of pinks and mauves, as if deciding which best fit the mood of the day. His head felt groggy, his mouth dry and fluffy. As if he was the one who'd been chain smoking. He rubbed his gravelly eyes and brushed fingers through his hair. He needed a haircut. Tugging his shirt down, Max went to the computer, not sure he wanted to read what Jessica had to say. Whatever it was, it wouldn't help with Fa. With luck he'd still be asleep and Max could avoid him until he could have a coffee before dealing with the day.

He listened for his grandfather from the top of the stairwell. Stepping over the squeaky step, the fifth one down, he paused at the bottom of the flight. Carpet from here on. A quick swill in the bathroom helped clear his head. Opening the kitchen door he saw Fa, leaning on his cane as he waited for the coffee to finish spluttering, and realized his caution was pointless.

"Morning, Fa. Couldn't sleep?"

"No. Good morning, Max. Coffee? It'll be ready in a minute."

"Yes, please. I'll let Bacchus out."

"Then we are going to talk."

"Yup," Max agreed, opening the door for the dog. "I will do anything I can to make this right, Fa."

"Did you contact the woman?"

"Jessica. Yes." Max stopped, not sure how to go on. Before he could continue his grandfather started speaking.

"Max, your contacting Dee notwithstanding, I just want to make one thing quite, quite clear. Just in case you misunderstood anything I might have said. Your story, your book, you haven't told me much about it. But I want to be certain it has nothing to do with my life. Or Dee's."

"It doesn't, Fa. It really doesn't. If it parallels anyone, it's Andy. But it's not him. Just a character who stayed in Malaya. It is pure fiction based around the facts that you've told me, and upon my research. And, it is more to do with *merdeka* than the Emergency."

"They're intertwined."

"Yes, I know. But the story really starts in 1954, after Templer left, and the lead up to the general election in '55. It's about a country coming into its own after being colonized, essentially by Europeans since 1511. You know, first the Portuguese, then the Dutch, then us."

"I am aware of the history, Max. All right. Good. I shall look forward to reading it." Fa lit a cigarette.

Max realized, perhaps for the first time, that the action was often a delaying tactic.

"What you did, contacting Dee's granddaughter was such a breach of trust, Max, it almost took my breath away. And I was disappointed in you. I've never felt that before. I'm too old for dramas, Max."

Max pulled the chair out next to Fa and sat, hunched around his coffee mug. He looked down at the table, the place where so many happy memories were etched, literally in some places. A scratch here, a splodge of paint there.

"Fa, never, ever would I want to disappoint you, and I am so very sorry. If I could undo all of this, I would. I've been a complete prat."

"Yes, you have, rather," Simon said. "But the reality is there is an ocean between us and the whole thing can just go away. Die down."

"I'm afraid it can't."

"Why not?" Fa looked at Max. "She knows."

"Yup. Jessica got time off and flew up and, a bit like me, blurted it out."

"Oh, bloody hell," said Fa. "She'll be angry as a hornet. I probably didn't mention she had, and I imagine still has, a temper."

"No, actually. She's delighted," said Max, watching his grandfather's head jerk up. "Jessica said she glowed, suddenly looked younger."

"Bullshit."

The word stopped Max. He'd never heard Fa swear like that.

"No, really, Fa. I can show you the email."

The silence around the table was broken by Joe Tine rapping on the glass at the back door. He held up two bottles of milk, and pushed the door open.

"Morning, all." His jovial face took them in. "Uh oh, looks serious. You alright, Simon?"

"Good morning, Joe. Yes, all fine. Thanks. Do you mind if we don't chat this morning?"

"Right you are." Joe put the bottles on the counter. "Oh, Bacchus is in the byre if you're wondering. Okay, be seeing you." The door closed behind him.

"Dee really wasn't furious?"

"No. She was delighted."

"Well," said Fa, looking so nonplussed that Max laughed.

"It's not often you're short of words, Fa."

"Don't think you're out of the doghouse, my boy."

"Oh, I know that. But at least one of you isn't irate. She has lots of questions apparently."

"She always did."

"Um ..." Max said, then cleared his throat and started again. "Fa, she wants to email you."

"Humph. She does, does she? She never wrote again, you know, after she told me she had to stay and look after her mother."

"But you didn't write. What could she say? She didn't know you'd been shot. That you'd been shipped home. I think you're being a bit unfair ..." Max stopped at his grandfather's glare.

"I think you should shut up, while the going is reasonably good."

Simon stood, stuffed his cigarettes and lighter into his pocket, gathered his cane, and said, "I'm going to the study. You can bring me a fresh cup of coffee, please. And then I do not wish to be disturbed. For anything. Understood?"

"Yup. Loud and clear. I'll make a fresh pot and bring it along."

"You do that."

"Um, Fa?" Max stopped his grandfather at the door, "What if Mum calls?"

"I'm out. I have no desire to speak to anyone, least of all your mother."

***

Flinging soft green cloths over tables in the garden and holding them down with crystal bowls of summer roses—peaches, pinks and soft mauves all jostling for prime position—Max was happy to be out of the kitchen. His father was setting up the barbecue. They had exchanged resigned looks and gone about their appointed jobs. Giles was keeping the children entertained whilst their mother bustled about in the kitchen, with Mrs. B. being gracious at the intrusion into her domain.

"Nana would've been happy," Fa said, wandering over to Max. "She did love her roses."

"Hi, Fa. You can command operations from over there," Max said, pointing to a chair shaded by apple trees. Ida Reds. It was the only variety he could remember apart from Golden Delicious. Something about the name made him smile.

"I don't mind where I am as long as it isn't anywhere near the kitchen. Sarah has gone all out. Even Mrs. B. seems to have caught the bug. I thought we were having a quiet family barbecue. But I suppose it's not every day her daughter heads off to Africa to chase birds. With a man none of us have met."

"True." Max squatted down beside his grandfather's chair and asked, his voice low, "Are you going to mention Dee to Mum?"

"No. There's nothing to say."

"Okay. But she has inherited your ESP and knows something is up. She asked me this morning."

"What did you say?"

"I told her you were tired."

Fa's laugh sounded more like a bark, and brought Bacchus running. "It might well be extreme fatigue before the day is out."

It all ended in tears. Susie and her mother sobbing as Emma and Christopher left Woodland Farm, his beaten up Land Rover spewing dust and pebbles as they accelerated through the gates. The little ones, overexcited and exhausted with no afternoon nap, followed suit. Giles scooped up Olivia, and Max carried Chloé back to the garden, followed by Fa and Michael. The girls calmed down and with thumbs in their mouth leaned against their father and uncle as the four men stretched out on sun loungers.

"That went well," Fa said. "Until the end."

"Destined to happen," said Giles. "Even Emma looked a bit teary."

"I don't think a family gathering can be called a success unless there are tears," Max said. "Even Mrs. B. got in on the act. Did you hear her muttering, 'Africa, Africa, why Africa?'"

"Sarah is upset because she doesn't know when they'll be back and, despite liking Christopher, can't quite get her head around him taking her daughter away." Simon gave a chuckle. "Susie is crying because she really will miss Emma."

"Yeah, she will," agreed Giles. "They speak at least two or three times a week. That was why she was so pissed off when Emma told you, Max, about Christopher before her."

"They can always video call," said Fa.

"Really, Simon? I didn't realize you were so up on technology." Max's father looked up in surprise.

"Just remember, Michael, when your grandchildren are tormenting you to stay up with the times, that I was there first," Fa said, looking across at Max. "Well, it's been a long day, I think I'll join those two," he nodded to the sleeping children, "and head off. I'll stop in at the kitchen and say goodnight to the girls, and thank Mrs. B. Good night, all."

The men watched him go.

"Is he okay, Max?"

"Sure, Dad. Just weary. He's almost 93."

"I know, I know. Your mother is convinced he's avoiding her."

"Don't be silly. We all know there is no avoiding Mum." Max struggled to his feet, Chloé in his arms. "Come on, Giles, I'll help you put these munchkins to bed. Leave the women to their tears and, I'm sure, another bottle of bubbles over the kitchen table. Be back in a bit, Dad. Enjoy the peace."

***

Max sipped a cup of tea and waited on the lounger for Bacchus to patrol the garden as daylight finally faded. He felt relaxed. The weekend had gone well, despite the tears. Emma and Christopher were leaving in a couple of days and a part of him was deeply envious.

"Come on, Bacchus. Time for bed," he called the dog, softly.

Pushing the door open to the attic he saw the glow from his computer. He hadn't checked email over the weekend.

G'day, Max,

How'd the farewell barbie go? Thought I'd leave you alone whilst all the family stuff was going on. But I've got to warn you DeeDee is getting nervous. Reconnecting all seemed a great idea when I first told her but the longer it is before they actually communicate the harder it's going to be for her. She told me yesterday it was Malaya all over again. He's a ditherer, she said, and wondered why she'd ever thought he would've changed. Seemed harsh to me. But I don't have the whole story. She is surprisingly reticent, still. Do you know what went down? At the end?

Hah, it's rather nice having a pen pal. Did you ever have one? I wrote to a girl in France for years—we still exchange the odd email. But the point is, it's easier to spill one's guts to someone you'll probably never meet.

So here comes the gut spill. I've started dating. A doctor. Something I said I'd never do again. But who else am I going to meet? It's either medical people or patients. And that really is a non-starter. He's nice. And just so you know how fickle I've been in the past, he's not particularly good looking. More cuddly than cute. But he's kind, and he makes me laugh. He's a gynecologist / obstetrician. Good thing I'm a doctor and don't get squeamish at the thought of him peering up vaginas all day long.

Max pushed his chair back, almost spilling his second cup of tea as he burst into laughter. He felt a twinge of pity for the chap. Jessica reminded him of Emma. Incorrigible. And he hadn't had the courage to ask Fa whether he'd thought any more about writing to Dee. But he had to.

Too much information, Max?

Max glanced over his shoulder. It was uncanny how Jessica seemed to know his reactions. He laughed again. In four years with Lisa he'd never had such a frank discussion.

If you're going to continue to be my pen pal, get used to it. You're cheaper than therapy. Anyway his name is Ian. He's 42, which is old. But nothing compared to your Emma and Christopher, so you won't be shocked. Never married. No kids, that he knows of. What about you, Max? You with anyone? I sort of get the impression you're not. Are there even any women in Dorset?

Right gotta go. Back on nights from tomorrow so have a shit-load of stuff to do. Won't see Wonderman either for a while. That is the advantage of dating a doc—he understands.

Hoo roo,

Jessica

P.S. Tell Simon to stop messing around. It's not fair.

Hi Jessica,

Yes, thanks, the weekend went well. No dramas except the expected tears as Emma and Christopher (such a mouthful but he doesn't like being called Chris) drove off into the sunset. A picture that would've been far more dramatic if it had actually been an African sunset and not a Dorset twilight. I am a little envious. She is totally stoked about the whole thing. Didn't even blink at all the shots they had to have. Amazing. She used to be such a baby.

You're right about Fa. He needs to get it together. I've been on tenterhooks but I'll have a chat with him tomorrow. He does seem to have calmed down but then there've been people all over the place for a week. Susie and the girls came down early. It was kind of funny at the weekend. Mum kept saying he was avoiding her. I kept saying he wasn't. Just enjoying being with Emma the last time for a while, and seeing his great-grandchildren. But he definitely was.

Good for you. Glad you've met someone nice. No, I'm not seeing anyone. Had a long relationship with a lovely woman. I just realized we wanted different things. That's why I came down to Fa. To get away from London for a while. Amazingly, I've been here over a year. And I love it. Don't think I'll ever go back to the city. But Emma going off has made me realize I can't bury myself here forever.

Right, will let you know tomorrow how it goes with Fa. If you're on nights I won't expect anything from you for a while.

Nope, never had a pen pal.

G'night,

Max

"Morning, my boy. Sleep well?"

"Not bad, thanks. I never realized two little beings could create so much noise. So much general mayhem. Thanks," Max said as Fa pushed a coffee towards him. "What are you doing today?"

"Nothing much. A bit of paperwork."

"Fa?" Max looked into the steaming black mug for inspiration. "Um, I was wondering what you'd decided? About Dee?" He asked, his eyes firmly on his coffee.

"Ah, you were, were you?"

Max glanced up.

"It's just that Jessica mentioned it in an email last night."

"You seem very chummy." His left eyebrow arched above his glasses.

"She has a boyfriend, Fa. We're just writing about you two."

"Not something I recall asking you to do."

The men sat at the table, scene of so many family events.

"It's been a strange time, Max. I don't mind telling you. Our talks about Malaya brought a lot to the fore, which was interesting for me, as much as for you. But this business with Dee. It's unsettling." Fa lit a cigarette. "Don't glare at me. I'm nearly 93, if I want to smoke in my kitchen, I damn well will."

"You're getting stroppy, Fa."

"Stroppy?"

"Okay, grumpy," Max said, with a laugh.

"I'm allowed to be grumpy."

"Yes, I suppose you are. You know Mum was convinced you were avoiding her."

"I was."

"I know. I ran interference for you."

"That was the least you could do." Fa smiled, and Max felt a shift in the air, as if they were back on their old footing. "I have spent the last week or so, before the family descended, reading old letters. It's been rather odd. Like I've been reading about someone else's life. It was all such a long time ago, Max. I was a different person."

"I don't think you were, Fa."

"All right, I was a young man. Your age. A lot of life has happened since then. What is the point in going back?"

"Fun, Fa, fun." Max tried to lighten the mood. "Tell DeeDee things you didn't tell her before."

"DeeDee?"

"That's what Jessica and Mitch call her."

"Oh." Fa was quiet, puffing on his cigarette.

"Write to her. What harm can it do?"

Chapter 27

Hi Jessica,

They are off and emailing. Well Fa is and now he's chomping at the bit waiting for an answer. I hope to God Dee answers soon otherwise he'll be impossible to live with.

Just remembered you're on nights so probably won't get this for a while. Just wanted you to know he is, in Fa's words, "rekindling a romance."

What a day.

Max

Max was startled by a ping.

G'day Max, you still there? Yeah, I know. DeeDee phoned me at work. Nearly gave me a heart attack. She's never done that. I had to rush out of a consulting room I was so worried. She sounded like a kid, Max. So excited. Didn't know what to say. I told her not to be a galah and asked what Simon had written and she told me 'none of your business!'

Galah? Idiot, Max assumed. He looked it up, rejecting the first definition—a word used amongst Jews to describe a Christian cleric. But Google's second definition gave him pause to wonder. The rose-breasted cockatoo, known for its intelligence and fondness for humans, might not be the right one after all. He grinned. He was having fun.

What have we started? She did say Simon told her about

being shot. Again. And being shipped back to England. Strewth, Max, we really don't know how good we have it, do we? I mean, I see people in ER all the time, who've been in accidents, knifed, occasionally shot, but DeeDee seemed so matter-of-fact about it. Though she was pissed he hadn't told her. Said something about it not being his decision to make. She nearly bit my head off when I disagreed. I'm learning, when she asks a question these days, it's rhetorical.

Have you told your sisters yet? Mitch is keeping his distance. Doesn't want to get involved. Mitch all over. He's a great guy, but distant. And not just in miles. No, distant is probably the wrong word. Disengaged, maybe. You're the writer.

Okay, gotta get some sleep.

X J

P.S. 'Stuffed' is tired beyond thinking.

Max stomped mud from his feet before he entered the kitchen through the boot room, managing to catch Bacchus before he trailed dirt over Mrs. B.'s floors. He'd seen her car parked around the side of the farmhouse. Kicking his shoes off, he dried the dog's paws, then gave him a treat for suffering the indignity with relative resignation.

"Morning, Mrs. B. All well?"

"Morning, dear. Yes, thanks. Coffee's on. Not like you goin' out without having a cup first."

"Yeah, I know. But I was a bit late and Bacchus was hustling me."

"You both spoil that dog rotten." She glared at the dog.

"And you don't, Mrs. B.? I've seen you 'drop' things from the chopping board," Max said. "Fa up?"

"Haven't seen him. He's in the study. Spending a lot of time in there these days, last couple of weeks, anyway. What's he up to?"

"Oh, just research, Mrs. B. Checking some dates and things," Max answered, avoiding her curious look. "I'll take him a coffee."

Knocking on the study door, Max heard the computer being closed before his grandfather's voice.

"Good morning, my boy. Ahh, thank you. Just what I wanted. Sit down. Or better yet, go and get yourself a coffee then sit down."

Max returned to the kitchen telling Mrs. Bartlett that Fa didn't want breakfast just yet, and assuring her that he would get it sorted.

"He needs to eat, regular-like, you know," she said.

"I know. And he does usually."

Closing the door on her hmph, he went to Fa.

"Okay, what's up?"

"A couple of things, Max. Both of which will need your help, I'm afraid."

"All right, if I can."

"Number two is that I want you to tell your sisters all of this." Fa pointed to the computer in front of him, then added, "And your mother!"

Max almost spilled his coffee, laughing at the grin across Fa's face, his eyes crinkled in glee behind his glasses.

"Bloody hell, Fa. That's a tall one. Susie and Emma no problem, but Mum. Don't you think you should tell her?"

"No." He grinned. "You started all this. You can tell her."

"Does she really need to know? I mean, Suse and Emma can keep their traps shut. They'll be pissed I haven't told them already, but that's okay. But Mum? Oh boy."

"Don't you want to know the first thing?" Fa asked, his grin getting broader, if that were possible.

"I'm not sure I do, Fa." Max thought his grandfather looked decidedly smug.

"I want you to also tell your mother I am going to Penang."

"No way!"

Max just got the words in before Fa continued. "Yes." Fa grinned, again. "And Dee is meeting me there."

"What? This is getting out of hand, Fa. You can't go to Malaysia. Neither can she. I mean, shit, you're both in great nick but that's a long way to go at your age."

"Really?" Fa laughed. "I'm not a complete fool. You're coming too. And Jessica can help Dee."

"Oh, my God, what have I done?" Max watched his grandfather light a cigarette. "You know, Fa, you can't smoke on planes anymore. How will you cope?"

"I've thought of that. And I've done some digging. That nicotine gum stuff should do the trick. I've looked at all the risks. Nothing wrong with my heart, which seems to be the main issue." Fa smiled. "Now, I've also decided that we'll do the trip in mini hops. Here to Rome. Never been there, always wanted to go. There's a hotel near the Spanish Steps that looks rather nice. Rome to Dubai. That doesn't thrill me, but a couple of days in a tinsel metropolis won't kill either of us. Then we'll fly into KL. Have a look around there for a few days. Don't suppose I'll recognize much. Then I'll meet Dee in Penang. What do you think?"

"I think you're barking mad. That is a hell of a trip for anyone. Let alone a 93-year-old. Come on, Fa. Please."

Max watched the grin on Fa's face dissolve. His eyes closed, just briefly, before opening to blaze at him like two pieces of glowing coal.

"Now you listen to me, Max Taylor. You started this. And I am going to finish it. I am going to Penang. So, you can either be a bastard—what's the word you use—aah, yes, a prat, about it, or you can help."

"Oh hell. Fine. Malaysia will probably be the safest place for me for a while. Mum is going to kill me."

"Yes, I think there is the distinct possibility murder will be on her mind."

Max snorted. He got up and went around the desk to his grandfather and hugged him.

"Oh God, Fa, does Penang know what's about to hit it?"

Their laughter brought Mrs. Bartlett and Bacchus to the study door. The dog rushed in, his tail wagging at the noise. He jumped up, pushing his wet nose at Fa's hand. Mrs. B. looking askance, shook her head at the tears pouring down the men's cheeks and went back to the kitchen, tutting. Max saw a smile flit across her face before she turned. She might not be smiling when she found out what was going on. Mrs. B. was known for her firm distrust of anything foreign.

***

"You could've warned me." Max could hear Susie's voice before the phone reached his ear.

"What about?"

"Fa, you idiot. I've just had Mum on the phone. One minute she's spitting tacks. Livid with you for raking up old things. The next, dying of curiosity."

"Why?"

"Why? For God's sake, Max, she finds out her father adored another woman."

"Oh."

"Oh, he says. Max, what did you think Mum'd say?"

"It was years before she was born. That's like saying all your boyfriends before Giles were more important than him."

"God, you men can be so obtuse." Exasperation came across the ether in waves. "Doesn't matter if they're dead, they're still competition."

"Oh my God, I will never understand! And don't be judgmental."

"I wouldn't. I won't." Susie was indignant. "What did Fa say to Mum?"

"I don't know. But thank God he finally agreed to be the one to tell her. I wasn't privy to the conversation, but probably normal Fa, words of wisdom. Happiness doesn't come in one size, sort of thing."

"You've been with him too long. How is he, by the way?"

"Winter gets to him. And, of course, smoking. But he's energized too."

A wail came through the phone.

"Gotta go, someone's hit someone on the head with something, I imagine. Stay in touch. And don't keep anything else from me. Promise?"

"Yup."

"Promise, Max!"

"Okay, I promise. Go, I can hear the noise from here. Give those girls a cuddle from their uncle. I'll be up to see them soon. Fa's got to get his passport renewed, it'll be easier if he applies in person." Max moved the phone away from his ear as Susie bellowed at Giles. "I now have no eardrum, Suse!"

"Can it! You'll survive. Right, I'd better go. Seems like lights out is not going to be a simple affair tonight. Max?" Susie said.

"Yeah."

"Don't go all country squire on me, will you? You've changed. You're more, I don't know, calm somehow."

"Is that code for dull?" Max asked, laughing.

"No. I dunno, you just seem different. Gotta go, sounds like a riot is about to break out upstairs. Love you, bye!"

***

Max looked across at his grandfather, one eye on the A30 taking them towards London. "You awake, Fa?"

"I am now."

"Sorry."

"No, it's alright, I was just resting my eyes. Did that on stag. It helped make the world clearer, the *ulu* less confusing. What is it?"

"You mentioned women working for Special Branch. Did you work with any?"

"Once. I was called down to KL. SB had been having very little luck, though that isn't the right word for the meticulous work they did ... Where was I?" Fa asked, losing his train of thought.

"Working with women."

"Oh yes. It was thought that if we found the chap running the couriers we'd disrupt Chin Peng's entire operation, and perhaps be able to find a few more camps, which were being pushed deeper and deeper into the jungle. Templer was getting fed up with the lack of progress. And that was never a happy state of affairs, for anyone."

"The police woman?"

"I'm getting there, Max. A whisper reached SB that the courier lead might not be a man. They didn't have a lot to go on, but in a list of names was a woman working out of Singapore which, for some reason, seemed suspicious. They called me in to wander down the peninsula and help keep an eye open. But it was Irene Lee who brought the goodies. The fastest draw in Malaya," said Fa, his voice admiring. "Against anyone. SB boffins, who manufactured all sorts of gadgetry, made her a special holster. More like a padded bra, I suppose."

"Did all the women have them?"

"Not that I know of. Irene was rather flat-chested and so couldn't wear a regular holster. She nearly always wore a black *samfu*, which had poppers instead of the more common frog knot closures over her left breast. My God, she could whip her Beretta out faster than a blink."

"Were there many women officers? Operatives?"

"I don't know. We didn't have company parties, Max." Simon's tone was sharp. "But I think it's fair to say most women become part of an undercover organization for personal reasons. Think of Violette Szarbo or Odette Sansom during the war. In Irene's case, her husband had been murdered by CTs early on. She had remarkable instincts. There probably wasn't a safe she couldn't crack, or a lock she couldn't pick."

Max found it difficult to concentrate on both the road and his grandfather.

"Can't remember how they found out the woman used to shop at Robinson's—it was, still is I imagine, a department store in Raffles Place where women loved to shop. All women. I was to be another pair of eyes. I could hang around some of the departments but would've looked a bit conspicuous in the lingerie area more than once!" Simon laughed. "We did have some fun, occasionally."

"Did you spot a drop?" Max laughed with his grandfather. Then glared at him and shook his head when he pushed in the Jag's cigarette lighter. Fa had grudgingly agreed to a no-smoking policy in the car.

"Fine. You've been watching too many spy films. But yes, that's exactly what happened. Irene saw the woman meet another, each carrying an identical bag, which they switched. Irene followed her by trishaw and on foot, all the while being shadowed by the SB car I was in." Fa added. "When it looked like we might lose her in the crowd, Irene caught up to her, nodded to us, drew her gun and bundled the woman into the car." Fa chuckled. "Real cloak and dagger stuff. Rather fun."

"Not for the woman! I'm surprised she didn't bolt, or scream."

"All happened too fast. Irene was a pro. We whisked her off to a house behind Tanglin.

"Okay, but how did you know you'd be able to turn the woman? CTs, agents, operatives, whatever you want to call them? Weren't they scared witless about being found out?"

"Precisely, Max. That very fear kept them careful. A photograph was taken of the woman between two grinning *mata-mata*. Then she was told that if she betrayed them—the SB—50,000 leaflets with that photo would be dropped in the *ulu*. A good deterrent, I'd say."

"Did you ever get the main man?" Max asked.

"I heard Irene kept following the trail and yes, did get her man, through a few more women first. I told you C. C. Too was a wonderful tactician. So was Irene. After putting the fear of God into another woman, Irene walked her into a brightly lit room with women in white coats and trays of odd-looking implements. At first glance it could have been a torture chamber. It was in fact a beauty parlor. Which, bear in mind, would have been pretty enticing after the *ulu*, and after a ... What is that term they use on the television, ghastly phrase?"

"A make-over?"

"Yes, that's it. After that, the woman promised anything and was turned. A major notch on Irene's already full belt. Then she turned a chap called Chen Lee. In August, I think it was, after I'd left Malaya, the trail eventually led Irene to the main man, or in this case, a woman. Lee Meng. I don't know all the ins and outs of the whole operation but to answer your original question, Max. Yes, I was honored to work with a woman at SB. Arguably, the best."

At Hyde Park Corner both men fell silent as Max dodged buses and taxis. As they neared Hampstead, mixed with Max's pleasure at seeing old haunts were the feelings of constriction that marked living with his parents. He recognized those rules now defined him but Susie's more relaxed household was more pleasant than their childhood home.

"You alright, Max? You've gone very quiet. Thinking about your meeting tomorrow?"

"I'm fine, Fa, thanks. And yes, a bit." He paused, awaiting his chance to slip into the traffic heading up Fitzjohn's Avenue. "Do you ever wonder how Mum became so rigid? She grew up in an easy-going home."

"Perhaps that was the problem, Max. Some children like more definition to their imposed limitations. The three of you didn't. Well, Susie maybe a little more. But certainly not you or Emma.

And Sarah hated the countryside. Marrying your father was the making of your mother."

"Wow, Fa. That is so sexist."

"It is, but it's also true. It gave her the freedom to find out who she really wanted to be. Michael was wealthy enough that she didn't have to work, and ironically, once you lot were all in school, she realized she really did. And she is extremely good at what she does. I'm very proud of her, Max. I might not always agree with her way of doing things, but she has been the best mother she could be. And look at you all. You turned out so-so!"

Max laughed. Turning left onto Arkwright Road, he felt the pull of home. The car had barely stopped before his mother ran down the front steps, the dark green door wide in its welcome behind her.

"Darling," his mother pulled open his door, "How lovely. I don't think you've ever been gone from home for so long."

"Hello, Mum." The familiar scent of Joy wafted up as Max bent to kiss her. "How's tricks?"

Sarah rushed around to the other side of the car, and waited as Simon organized his cane.

"Hello, Daddy, I'm so glad Max persuaded you to come. It's been too long."

"My darling, lovely to see you. And looking charming as ever." Fa raised his hat as he kissed his daughter. "Yes, I thought it was time."

"Come on, let's get inside, it's chilly on this side of the house when the sun goes down."

"Mum, can I leave the Jag here? I don't fancy trying to find somewhere to park in Clapham. I'll get the Tube down to Susie, once rush hour's over."

"No need, darling. They're all coming up for an early supper. The girls too," Sarah said as they went inside, the smell of apples cooking suffused the hall. "Mrs. Wolford has made your favorite meal. Isn't she sweet? Never forgets. Chicken and mushroom pie, without the mushrooms, and apple crumble. You know you could've stayed here, Max."

"Yum. And I know, Mum, but most of the people I need to see are south of the river. It'll be easier. And you get Fa all to yourself. Did you get tickets for *Les Mis*?" Max distracted his mother.

"Your father did. The four of us are going on Thursday night."

"Thanks, Mum. We've been looking forward to it."

Supper was fun. The twins a diversion from any serious conversation despite both his parents asking who his meetings were with a number of times, in different ways. It was Fa who eased the tension.

"Sarah, Max will tell us when he is ready. Every young man needs a few secrets. Now, I am going to say goodnight. It's been a long day." Fa got to his feet, delighted the twins by blowing them kisses then catching theirs in return, and left the room.

"Well, that was neatly done," Susie said. "You'll have to wait to grill him, Mum."

***

"What's up, my boy? Your mother is standing next to me, curious, and not a little disgruntled that you wouldn't speak to her. And then had to wait for me to shamble over."

"I wanted to tell you first. I got one!"

"One what, Max?"

"An agent. I've a got a bloody agent."

"Oh, Max! Congratulations. Wait a moment, please tell your mother before she expires in front of me. Which as we all know would go against the natural order of things. Here, my dear," Max heard him say, "take the phone."

Max told Sarah, then listened as she demanded to know when the book would be published.

"Mum, Mum, it's an agent, not a publisher. And I'll tell you everything. But not right now. A few things to figure out first." Max listened a moment before replying. "Yes, it's a novel. I just wanted to tell Fa, and you, of course. Put him back on a moment, will you please?"

"Max?"

"Hey, Fa. Whisky's on me!"

"That it is, my boy. Well done!"

Chapter 28

Townsville, Australia

FIVE GALAHS PERCHED on the verandah rail, their pink breasts and gray backs a foil to the gum trees and a red blooming bottle brush that shielded the house at the back. White heads and beaks bobbed as they shuffled from foot to foot. From the open double doors they looked, to Dee, as if they were conferring about the array of clothes littered on the bed, hems frilling under the whirl of the fan. She stood in her bra and knickers, holding dress after dress against her slim body, occasionally trying something on, only to rip it off and toss it on the pile.

She padded through to the kitchen and cut a lime, adding a slice to the ice-filled glass before pouring in gin and a whisper of tonic. She held the glass to her forehead and closed her eyes. In emails it had sounded a grand plan. Now, three days away from flying across the country and up Malaysia's spine, it didn't seem quite so feasible. Or sensible. Dee looked down at her body and groaned. What was she doing? Why spoil the image Simon had carried all these years? She put a hand to her hair. At least that was still there. Was he bald? And teeth. She had her own teeth. But where the hell had all the wrinkles and lines come from? And when?

She straightened her shoulders and caught the reflection bouncing back at her from the kitchen window. Through a screen in a dim light she could pass as, what? How about 87? Dee chortled. What the hell? He'd had bad eyesight nearly sixty years ago ... unless he'd had laser surgery. She laughed out loud startling the birds, who rose in a flutter only to land back on the rail determined to see the end of the fashion show.

There must be one dress that would do. She shook her head. Lots would 'do' but she wanted more. The colorful mound confronted her again and picking her way over scattered shoes, no longer in pairs, she grabbed an oversize tee-shirt and puttered outside with her drink. The herb garden always soothed her. A sweet, pungent aroma suffused the air when Dee nipped flowers off a basil bush with her fingers. She swirled a basil leaf in her gin and wandered over to the pergola. Two rocking chairs reflected the pinks of the Rangoon creeper and swaddled her in a fragrant bower. Flashes of yellow, and high-pitched tweeting alerted her to sunbirds flitting and feeding in the vine. Dee eased onto a rocker and watched two geckos posturing over territory on a raised bed wall. They reminded her of another time, of memories she had quashed even then.

Sitting on a river bank. Stay put! She snorted. Perhaps that's what she should be doing now. Staying put. Why go traipsing back? Into the unknown. Dee rocked, her bare toes tickled by ferns each time the chair came forward. The rhythm transported her back through the decades.

Fighting for Tengfei's life, she hadn't had time to be afraid, though worry and remorse about Samsuari swamped her whenever she closed her eyes and hoped for sleep. Waiting on the river bank had been when fear had almost choked her. Even the sweet juice of rambutans left by CTs had not driven the bile from her throat. The jungle noises she had learned to feel comfortable amongst became menacing. A rustle had her straining to see snakes in the branches overhead, or eeling their way down the bank. Even a troop of clowning macaques had failed to quiet her terror. Stay put. The mantra had sent her into a dazed sleep. And then, as dawn misted the river, the faint putt putt of an engine.

The relief of seeing Jeffrey at the prow and Samsuari holding the tiller as the sampan appeared around the bend had been so immense she had burst into tears, her sobs broken only by the sound of her shouts.

Dee sipped her gin, the basil leaf adding piquancy to the drink.

In the slow ride back down the river, which Jeffrey told her was Sungai Tanum, deep in the Pahang forests, she heard Samsuari's story. CTs had taken him in the opposite direction from her departure and kept him for three nights before blindfolding him and leaving him, hands bound, on a track not far from Kuala Lipis. Found by an SF patrol, they had dropped him off at the Residency where he told Jeffrey of Dee's abduction. Samsuari had also delivered a letter, scrawled on newspaper, advising the Administrator neither he nor the SF were to look for the Australian nurse. She would be returned. Samsuari had been driven home to his frantic wife and there he had waited until a message arrived, late at night, telling him to meet Tuan Jeffrey, at the clinic at first light.

Ten days later Jeffrey received another missive, the note tucked under the wipers on his Land Rover, from someone Dee supposed was "the man," advising him where she could be found. No SF were to accompany him. Only he and the boatman were to travel the waterway. They would be watched. If SF were spotted the nurse would be killed.

A shudder spilled Dee's drink.

Simon's face, drawn from sorrow at Frank's death, came into focus. Each evening spent in the garden behind the clinic, talking over *stengahs*. The first and last time she'd spoken about her abduction, except to the authorities. Malaya, the first and last time she'd been in love.

Her glass drained, Dee sighed and returned to the kitchen for a refill. The galahs had given up. She was going to Penang. She just had to find the right dress.

"What happened to that green silk one?" she muttered to the mess on the bed.

"DeeDee?" Jessica's voice came from the front of the house. "Where are you?"

"Bedroom. Come and help."

"Oh my God, what happened?" Jessica pushed open the door and looked at the welter of colors, then crossed over to hug her grandmother.

"I can't find anything to wear." Dee sank onto the love-seat by the window. "To, you know, to meet him. Oh yes, hello! Good flight?"

"Hello, to you too. Yep, everything good. Just let me wash up, grab a beer, and we can try again. I had no idea you had so many clothes."

"Neither did I."

***

The plane left the tarmac and Dee watched Townsville disappear as they headed south to Brisbane.

"It was crazy, you coming home only to fly back to Brissie two days later. I am quite capable of flying on my own."

"I know, DeeDee, but I didn't want you bailing at the last minute!"

"I wouldn't have done that."

"You were on the brink the other night."

Dee ignored the comment and accepted a glass brimming with bubbles from the flight attendant, wearing a uniform inspired by Aboriginal motifs. Jessica raised her drink to her grandmother, "Here's to Penang!"

"Do you know what air hostesses wore when I first flew on Qantas? It was QEA then. Qantas Empire Airways. Back in the early fifties." She didn't wait for Jessica to reply. "They looked more like nurses. White dresses with a wing flash above the left breast. And a cheeky little black cap. It actually gave me some comfort. I was terrified of flying."

After changing planes in Brisbane, and wine with dinner, Dee kicked back on her fold-out bed and shut her eyes, not expecting to sleep, but not wanting to talk any longer. She woke a few hours later, the night sky drifting by her window. Clouds like puffs of palest gray cotton wool morphed into shapes before dissipating back to a carpet of fluff. Dawn tickled them a soft pink and mauve, promising a beautiful day.

Jessica was curled like a kitten on the bed next to her. Dee smiled. Some things never changed. Simon didn't sound as if he'd changed. Still the same way of writing, and probably talking, serious but ever ready to laugh. Maybe they should have video called. It might have mitigated the shock.

She smiled again. The closer she got to seeing Simon the less panicky she felt. Dee knew she looked okay for her age—how she hated that expression. But there was no getting away from the word age. Too late now. She noticed the clock on the monitor and changed the time on her watch, the same one the CT had tried to steal, still going strong with only a couple of repairs along the way.

Curiosity nibbled. Jessica had been very circumspect about her correspondence with Max, insisting it was only about Simon and her. Dee wasn't so sure. And why had Jess ditched the doctor before she left Brisbane, although he had sounded dull. Not nearly strong enough for her granddaughter.

Mitch's phone call of the night before played in her head. So concerned, so sure she was going to be disappointed. The problem with both Mitch and Jessica was that they had never had a grand affair. One that changed the world for them. Dee closed her eyes and remembered the last time she and Simon were together. And the morning she found the *bunga raya* lying on the pillow next to her. She'd had hope still, hope they could work out the geography of loving each other a world apart.

The despair came when she'd seen her mother, so stoic, so ill. Then nothing from Simon. No letter, no nothing. Anger had followed soon after. The cycle between the two had got her through med school once her mother died. Then life had taken over. A good life. Apart from Abigail being killed, that had been another kind of hell but she'd had two little beings to care for and not much time to think, let alone mourn. Dee shook the memories away and watched the flight attendant deliver breakfast trays through the first-class cabin. Luxury all the way she'd told Jessica and had laughed when Simon told her he'd said the same to Max. She worried about his journey, very much longer than hers.

"I wonder if David Gallagher will meet the plane?" Dee said, seeing Jess stretch and yawn. Her grin showed even teeth.

"Who the hell is he? Honestly, DeeDee, do you have beaux scattered around Asia?"

"Oh, not just Asia, sweetheart!" She laughed. "David was my liaison when I arrived and left Malaya. Funny man blushed every time he opened his mouth. He'd be dead now."

"Why? You're not!"

"I might be by the time this little frolic is over."

"That is not in the least funny."

Dee's exuberance waned into exhaustion as the plane landed in Penang. Clutching Jessica's arm, she walked up the steps of the E&O Hotel, her face pale. It had been a long few days and she was relieved she would have time to gather herself before Simon and Max arrived. But first thing she was going to do was wallow in a bath, then climb into bed and sleep. Jessica was going for a swim then a wander around George Town and also had the night market in her sights. Dee reached up to kiss her cheek at the door to her room.

"I'll see you in the morning, sweetheart. And Jess, thank you!"

The smell of lime drifted from the fruit bowl and the bathroom. The room had been refurbished. "Of course it has, you silly woman, but it's still lovely," she muttered as she flung open the French doors. And the view. Memories flooded Dee. Her hand flew to her cheek as an image of her standing in front of Simon, stark naked, flashed before her eyes. "Hussy!" she murmured through her smile.

Chapter 29

HEAT HIT MAX LIKE a flannel. His sunglasses steamed up the instant they left the air-conditioned comfort of the terminal and sweat trickled under his rucksack. He glanced at Fa, leaning on his cane, his jacket draped over his arm, and marveled. The old man did not look as if he'd just stepped off a plane after a week of travel and into what felt like a sauna. His tie, knotted perfectly, had already been commented on, much to his delight.

"*Selamat datang ke Malaysia, tuan.*" The customs official had welcomed Fa with a huge grin and pointed to his green and yellow striped regimental tie. "My father was in the Malay Regiment. Port Dickson."

"*Terima kasih,*" Fa thanked him.

"You are on holiday?"

"We are. I am showing my grandson your beautiful country."

"Welcome back." The official handed their passports over with a three-month visa. Waiting for their luggage, Max asked, "How much Malay can you remember, Fa?"

"I don't know yet. I looked through an old language book and was surprised how words came back. But reading is not hearing, as you very well know. So, we'll see."

"I don't suppose you'll be taking that tie off," Max said, with a grin. "It might open all sorts of doors."

Their stay at the Mandarin Oriental, the closest Simon could get to where Dee and he had stayed on Lorong Kuda, the whole area since demolished for the Petronas Towers, lived up to its reputation for luxury. Unless Max sold a great many copies of his book, as yet unpublished, he doubted he would ever sleep anywhere as opulent.

Fa was resolute. "I've got my membership card for The Dog. I found it in one of the boxes." Max's suggestion that perhaps it would not be honored, his grandfather not having paid dues for sixty years, was overcome with a laugh. "Of course it will. I just won't be able to sign a chit." And he had been right.

The black and white Tudor-style building had welcomed them, the doorman delighting in the dog-eared piece of cardboard stating the bearer, Major Simon Frampton, was granted entry to the Royal Selangor Club. The Club secretary, who happened to still be onsite, was tickled and, with much laughter, promised a new laminated card to replace the dilapidated one would be ready before they finished their first drink. "On the house, of course, Major Frampton."

Gin and tonics on the long verandah sent Max to an earlier time. White-clad teams played cricket on the *padang*, framed by palms and bougainvillea. A few people stopped to talk to Fa, commenting on his tie, and welcoming him back with tales of their parents and grandparents during both the war and the Emergency. Max grinned as he shook hands with yet another well-wisher and wondered if this was the pride a parent felt. All concerns of the adventure being too strenuous for his grandfather disappeared.

Fa was right. Much of Kuala Lumpur was changed. Knocked down in the name of progress, but enough remained to not be depressing. The railway station with its striking mixture of Eastern and Western architecture, minarets atop slender columns supporting Mughal arches, might only be a stop for commuter and goods trains now, but its spectacular façade drew the tourists. They took a taxi to Carcosa, what was once King's House and which, after *merdeka*, had first been returned to the new Malayan government, only for them to hand it back to the British as an act of good faith and friendship. It remained the residence of British high commissioners until 1986 when, Fa told Max, the idiot Foreign and Commonwealth Office decided it was too expensive. Carcosa was then used for visiting dignitaries, before becoming a hotel.

"Did you ever come here?" Max asked.

"A few times. In Templer's day. It was a wonderful building, a grand central staircase that, so rumor had it, was on occasion used for tray races."

"By you?"

"Now that would be telling, wouldn't it, my boy?"

Selamat petang, Max,

Jessica's email blinked as he shrugged off his tee shirt. Fa had gone to bed early and Max had a pleasant, if hot, evening wandering around the Connaught Night Market at Cheras after a short train and bus ride. He assumed it was the same Cheras where Sir Henry Gurney was buried. Touted as the longest street market in Malaysia, selling everything imaginable, it had been a noisy conglomeration of nationalities, though remarkably few tourists. Max ate curried noodles washed down with a Tiger beer before taking a taxi back to the hotel. He finished up the evening in the bar, astounded the barman could produce Talisker.

> *Well, we made it. DeeDee was stuffed so went up for her 'beauty' sleep. She is in the same room. Can you believe it? I spent the arvo wandering around Penang. I am in sensory overload. I ended up taking a trishaw to the Chulia Night Market—it was filled with hawker stalls, and I have just eaten the best satay in the world. Though no doubt the next stall holder would say the same thing. The peanut sauce almost knocked my head off, but a Tiger came to the rescue.*

Max laughed. A fleeting image of Lisa sitting at a food stall drinking beer from a bottle interrupted his reading. He laughed again. Never ever would that happen. She hadn't even liked having a Mr. Whippy from the ice-cream van on Brighton Pier on a hot summer's day.

> *Speaking of tigers. Did you know there used to be a lot around? Bet there aren't many now. DeeDee said she used to hear them, particularly when she was holding clinics along the rivers. And did you know—I'm becoming a tiresome travel guide but suck it up—that if you were to plant sugar-cane along a river, or in an area elephants consider their own they will just come along and rip it up? My patch. Move on, sort of thing. I'm rather with the elephants but it must be a terrifying sight—seeing a mad nellie on the rampage.*

Max laughed again. He didn't know any other family who called elephants "nellies." It was always "ellies." Why, he used to ask

Lisa, would you call them "ellies" when the song is "Nellie the elephant packed her trunk" ...? A question to which she had no answer, much to his satisfaction.

Hey, I've just realized we're on the same time zone. Are you awake?

Yep. Hi Jessica. I'm just back from the night market here. Fa went to bed early too. It was a good idea to stop here a couple of days. He's tireder than he's letting on. But he insists he wants to take the train to Penang. No CTs this time, he told me. What a strange and different life they both led.

Yeah, I know. DeeDee's been more talkative than ever before since this trip has been planned.

Oh, and no, I didn't know that about nellies! Thank you. I shall tread carefully around any sugarcane fields I happen upon.

Idiot! Hey, Max? Are you nervous?

Yes, I am a bit.

God, you sound so posh. "Yes, I am a bit."

Sod off. How's that?

Better. Thank you. Though we say "rack off."

You say a lot of weird things. If you don't mind me saying so.

I do.

Tough! But back to your original question. Yes, I'm nervous. Although maybe more anxious. I just don't want there to be an awful let down.

Yeah, I know. I offered DeeDee a valium tonight, and she just laughed and told me to take it.

I can't wait to meet her. She sounds a cracker.

She is. And she can spit like one too. I suppose, Max, it's a bit weird we didn't video call either.

'Spose so. You might have bailed if you'd seen me first.

Don't think that would've been an option—Fa and Dee were determined. Right, bedtime. G'night, Max. Oh, what time do you think you'll be here?

Train to Butterworth. Then the ferry across to George Town for old-time sake. So probably at the hotel about 2:30. Good night, Jessica. See you tomorrow.

Max tossed and turned a long time. It wasn't only jet lag keeping him awake. He couldn't believe Fa was so unconcerned. So sure of their old feelings. He turned the light back on and sent a quick update to his mother, and another joint one to the girls. The last thing he remembered was hearing a cockerel, then the hotel phone rang.

"Good morning, my boy. Are you getting up? The train leaves in just over an hour."

Max's eyes looked haggard in the mirror as he splashed water over his face. About to forego a shave, he thought better of it. Better a few minutes late than appear in front of Fa disheveled, this of all days. Stuffing his sponge bag in his pack, he rolled his sarong, bought at the night market, and shoved that in an outer pocket.

Fa, his Panama hat at a jaunty angle, his cane tapping briskly, followed the porter along the platform chatting in Malay. His grandfather's fluency continued to surprise Max. Settling into the comfort of the first-class compartment, Fa sighed.

"This, my boy, is infinitely better than the goods carriage."

Closing in on Ipoh, Fa told him that Ah Tok, the man who had given him a room for the night right at the beginning of the Emergency, had been mown down in an ambush not long after Simon had left Malaya. Bob Thompson had believed it was a targeted attack.

"Easy pickings, Max. Easy pickings. Ah Tok was a good man. He had five children. Many of those in the SF were known to the CTs because they had worked together against the Japanese during the war."

The closer the train got to Butterworth, the quieter the elderly man became.

"You okay, Fa?"

"Yes, my boy. Just remembering."

The ferry across to George Town was made in almost total silence. The hotel, after Max's phone call the day before, had sent a car to meet them and he was delighted to see the gleaming Rolls Royce.

"I wanted to take a *beca* through Little India, past Rabindra's." Simon was petulant.

"Come on, Fa. You want to arrive feeling cool and calm," Max cajoled.

"I am cool, and calm."

"Fine, I want to arrive at least cool. I am not in the least bit calm. And I have never been in a Rolls. Give me a break, okay. Please, Fa, get in."

If Max thought the Mandarin Oriental in Kuala Lumpur was deluxe, the colonial grandeur of Penang's Eastern and Oriental spoiled him for any other hotel.

"Glad we're not in the new wing. But," Fa said, looking around as they were being checked in, "It certainly looks spiffier. The Jap occupation had worn the old girl down. All the linens and crockery had disappeared. Imagine." They followed the bellhop to the lift. "You're on the second floor, my boy. I'm on the third. We're meeting Dee and Jessica for tea in the Planters Lounge in …" Fa glanced at his watch, "… an hour. I shall meet you downstairs."

"When did you arrange that?" Max asked.

"It has always been part of the plan," replied Fa, a grin showing the gap in his teeth. "Later, Dee and I will have dinner together, alone. Here at the hotel. You young ones may do as you please. Can I suggest a slightly more formal attire?"

"Sure, Fa. I won't let you down. But I'm not wearing a tie!"

***

Max felt as if he was preparing for a job interview. His one pair of good trousers were uncreased but he set up the ironing board and pressed a long-sleeved shirt. Rolling the cuffs up to his elbows he felt his stomach churn the gallon of water he'd drunk to relieve his dry mouth. He paced the room, watching the clock.

"Good, you're ready. And thank you, Max. You look presentable. Though a tie would finish the ensemble rather well."

"Don't push it, Fa. This is as good as it gets. Come on. You, by the way, look very debonair," Max said, taking in the lightweight tan suit, white shirt, ubiquitous tie and polished shoes. His cane even looked as if it had been shined. His white hair was smoothed back, showing the barest of receding hairlines, and his eyes glowed. "And, Fa, I'm impressed you haven't had a cigarette since London."

"Nicotine gum, my boy. Should've tried it years ago."

The mâitre d' showed them to a low table surrounded by library chairs in the Planters Lounge. On the wall behind hung a sepia map of Malaysia. Mirrored Peranakan cupboards stood guard either side and elegant brass lamps shed pockets of light. An oriental teak screen separated the area from the rest of the room, giving privacy but allowing air to circulate. Celadon jars lined a long sideboard, adding a subdued splash of color to the simple palette.

It was perfect. Straight out of Maugham. Max was itching to take notes.

"*Selamat petang, tuan,*" the waiter said in greeting, his smile taking in the old man's tie. He continued in English. "My father, he too Malay Regiment."

Max listened as his grandfather responded, then rattled off an order, all in Malay.

"You're good, Fa. What have you ordered?"

"Champagne, to be followed by afternoon tea."

"Perfect. That's perfect." Max realized he'd have to come up with a different adjective. He looked around in silence and wondered at Fa's complete ease. "You're really not in the least concerned, are you?"

"No. Strangely, I'm not, Max. We loved each other then. We love each other now. It's really very simple."

"My God, I hope I have that some day, Fa. I really do."

"I hope so too, my boy. Aah, here's the champagne. *Terima kasih*," he thanked the waiter.

"And right on cue, here they are."

Max knocked the table in his haste to stand. Fa got to his feet and, leaning on his cane, moved forward, his eyes glistening as he watched the petite woman approach the table. Her silver hair curled gently at her neck. Her face was lined, each one a laugh remembered. Her eyes too were bright. Pools of cool mossy green. Her lips were a pale peach color. She had a slight tan. She wore a plain, short-sleeved, white shift dress, a simple gold bangle shone on one slim wrist, on the other a dulled watch with a black strap. Her low-heeled pumps and bag were neutral. At her neck she wore a jade necklace. She was beautiful.

Dee walked straight into Fa's outstretched arms. "Oh, my darling, I've waited a long time for this," she said, reaching up to kiss him as he enfolded her, his gnarled fingers holding her close.

"And I," he replied.

Max took a step back. So personal was the moment. Only then did he look at Dee's companion, her granddaughter. They smiled.

"G'day, Max, I'm Jessica."

***

Champagne and afternoon tea. The most natural combination. Flutes filled with chilled Taittinger, complemented thin-cut cucumber sandwiches, smoked salmon on slivers of brown bread— each topped with a delicate spot of sour cream mixed with chives, melt-in-the-mouth shortbread and an array of tiny cakes. And Lady Grey—an exquisite hint of bergamot coming through the hot tea—a more subtle and elegant version of Earl Grey.

Fa and Dee spoke and ate very little, but sipped champagne, a current encircling them. Fa leaned across the narrow gap between their chairs and caressed Dee's cheek. An intimate touch that made Max blink.

Conversation was polite, yet desultory. A rundown of their journeys so far. Rome, marvelous; Dubai, glitzy; KL interesting. A soft laugh emerged when Max related the story of Fa's membership card at The Dog. Brisbane to Singapore on Qantas, long but pleasant flight. Singapore, vastly changed, lost some of its charm but certainly cleaner. Max, for the first time ever in his grandfather's company, was uncomfortable. He now understood how a gooseberry felt. He sensed Jessica felt the same.

"Shall we order another?" Fa asked, nodding to the ice bucket in which the Taittinger bottle was now upended.

"Not for us, thanks, Simon." Jessica's voice beat Max to the moment. "I'd like to see more of Penang."

"Yes, good idea," Max said. "Such a pleasure meeting you, Dee. I look forward to speaking more tomorrow." He watched Jessica lean down and kiss her grandmother's cheek, then smile at Simon. "Shall we?" he asked, gesturing to the entrance of the Planters Lounge.

"We shall," Jessica said, grinning. "Have a lovely evening, you two."

"Yes, see you both in the morning." Max smiled at his grandfather.

"Bye, darlings." Dee's words seemed totally appropriate.

Chapter 30

MAX AND JESSICA WERE silent as they wove through the clusters of tables, filling now with visitors eager to experience high tea in the glamor of a bygone era. A variety of languages rippled around the high-ceilinged room as waiters slipped between tables with hushed ease. A woman, her hair a shining black bob, chic in the palest blue lace *kebaya*, paired with a midnight-blue batik sarong, stood to greet her guest, another woman of a similar age in a sleek, cream cheongsam sprigged with tiny flowers. A man, his suit in complete accord with his black *songkok*, looked far more at home than a tourist in a flamboyant Hawaiian shirt, though thankfully his legs were encased in trousers and not a pair of shorts. Max didn't need to hear him speak to know he was American. A thought crossed his mind as they crossed the room. His powers of observation had become far more acute. Lisa would be impressed. He wondered why her name kept springing to the fore.

Max gestured to where Fa and Dee sat, oblivious to anyone else, and asked the maître d' presiding over the lectern to put the bill for the table on his room. He pulled the key from his pocket, "Er, Room 212. And anything else they may order."

"Certainly, sir." The man smiled, "Your grandparents?"

"Sort of," Max replied.

"That was a nice thing to do," Jessica said. "Thank you."

"I've never felt quite so unwanted. Have you?"

"They barely noticed we were there. Right. Where shall we go?"

"How are you about walking?"

"Fine. I've flatties on." Jessica waved a slim ankle in Max's general direction.

He could not fail to notice her toned legs in the snug skirt that skimmed the top of her knees. Cerise or claret, maybe fuchsia?

Emma would be amazed he could name so many colors. A simple white tee accentuated the curve of her breasts.

"Okay." He pulled his mind back with a shake of his head. "Er, there's a hotel, The Blue Mansion, built in the 19th Century that looks worth a visit. I read about it on the train. The owner wanted to honor his heritage so built it in the traditional Chinese style rather than the more common Anglo-Indian. Feng Shui and all that. Anyway, I don't think it's far from here. How does that sound?"

"Good for me. Let's go. Have you got a map?"

"No, but I've got my phone," Max said, patting his pocket.

"I like proper maps."

"They are proper maps."

"No, they're not. They don't crinkle, or get torn. Or get ice-cream spilled on them."

"But you're less a target with a phone. Looking at a map smacks of being a tourist."

"And whipping out a mobile phone doesn't yell, 'steal me'?"

Max sighed. "Can we start again?"

"Yeah. Sorry. I'm a bit uptight. Didn't think I would be. I wonder if this is what it feels like when your ankle biters start dating?"

"Ankle biters I'm guessing are kids." Max laughed. "I can't wait to call the twins that! But yes, it does feel strange. Sixty years, Jess, that's a long time to be in love. Especially when fifty-eight of them have been apart. Not to mention other people in the picture."

"You called me 'Jess.'"

"Sorry. Not sure why, but that's how I think of you."

"Very few are allowed to call me that. But strangely, you can. Must be your Pommie accent."

"Oh, okay. Thanks." He grinned as they turned out the hotel gates and he moved to the curbside of the pavement.

"Does it feel weird? I mean you only know Simon married to your Nana. And here comes DeeDee waltzing in. It's like she's obliterating all his life since Malaya."

"No, not really. Because of Mum, and my sisters. We're testimony to the life he's lived since then. And he was happy. Like I said before. A calm and relaxed happy."

"Did you see their faces? I wanted to cry. And I don't do that very easily."

"I know. I did too. Very manly."

Jessica punched his arm, then grabbed it as he stepped off the pavement and into the path of a trishaw.

"Get out of the road, dopey. And actually, it's kind of refreshing a man wanting to cry. Are we going the right way?"

"We're looking for Leith Street. Should be up there."

They walked in silence until reaching the mansion.

"Well, there's no doubting it's blue," Jessica said. "I guess to show his wealth. Organic indigo was incredibly expensive. Think of the Tuaregs. The blue men of the Sahara."

"I've heard of them. Have you been to Africa? To Morocco?"

"Yeah, I volunteered in a hospital for three months not far from Tarfaya, in the south."

"Huh! Lots of things to learn. Come on."

"You reckon we can just wander around?" Jessica asked.

"I don't see why not. It's a hotel. And we'll end up at the bar. Look, here's a brochure. Hah, I couldn't remember the guy's name. Cheong Fatt Tze."

"Can't imagine why not. It rolls off the tongue." Jessica laughed, then read "Thirty-eight rooms. Five granite courtyards. Seven staircases and, get this, Max, 220 vernacular timber louvre windows. I'm glad I'm not cleaning them. I thought you said he built a Chinese house. It says here, eclectic. The tiles came from England, and the cast iron work from Scotland. Oh, and Art Nouveau stain-glass windows from Europe. Eclectic alright."

"It's won awards for conservation and cultural preservation," Max said, looking at plaques along a wall in the reception. "Impressive."

Each archway lead to another courtyard of delight, bamboo benches covered with cushions begging to be sat on, pots of palms and ferns, fronds gentled by a cooling breeze filtering along walkways, circular staircases leading to balconies protected by wrought iron railings.

"It's magical, like walking through a child's picture book," Jessica said. "I'm half expecting fairies and elves to pop out from behind one of the plants."

"Let's see if the magic continues in the bar," Max suggested.

Stools lined the long granite counter, glassed Peranakan doors shielded liquor bottles, and a smiling barman greeted them.

"Oh, yum." Jessica studied the cocktail menu. "I'd like a Sir George, please. I like rum, and infused with *pandan, gula melaka* and *cendol*, it can't be bad, though I have no idea what either *gula melaka* is, or *cendol*, but who cares."

"*Gula melaka* from bud of date or sago palm," the barman told her. "Very sweet."

"And *cendol*?"

"Like jelly made from green rice flour."

"Beauty! Thanks," Jessica said to the grinning barman. "Why Sir George?"

"He first governor of Penang."

"That figures," she said.

Max closed the menu with a snap. "I'll just have a Tiger, please."

"Don't be a dag, Max. You've been drinking champagne." She picked the menu up. "Here you are in this gorgeous bar and you want a Tiger. Have a cocktail."

"My God, you're bossy." Max tempered his words with a smile as he tugged the menu from her and scanned it. "Fine, nothing creamy though. Okay, I'll have a lychee martini, please."

Conversation drifted from topic to topic with ease. None of the awkward silences of a first meeting, the months of emailing having taken away any necessity for idle chit chat. They had a second cocktail, then decided satay from a street hawker was needed.

"Whoa," Jessica said, "that was stronger than I thought. Thanks." She took Max's outstretched arm. "I'll be right in a minute. But need food."

Walking out to Leith Street, they followed their noses until they found food stalls.

Sitting on low stools, a plate of chicken and beef satay between them, they dipped the long sticks of meat into a tangy peanut sauce, then speared a chunk of cucumber to lessen the heat.

"Now may I have a Tiger?" Max asked, laughing.

"Sure. But I'll stick to water."

They ate in silence, taking in the bustle as Penang came out to eat in the cool evening air. Children played in the street, closed off to traffic once the sun went down. Scrawny cats slunk from behind carts and stalls, ever ready to dart in and snatch a fallen piece of meat. Indian, Malay and Chinese lyrics leaked from coffee houses to mingle in the street. It was a colorful, good-natured scene.

Licking her fingers, Jessica looked at Max. "This is fun but what happens now?"

"What do you mean?"

"Well, have you thought about next week? Does Simon shoot through to Dorset, and DeeDee to Townsville? I mean, you saw their faces this afternoon. I can't bear the thought of them being apart again."

"I guess we have to leave it up to them."

Chapter 31

DISTRACTED A MOMENT, Simon saw Max stop and speak to the maître d'. "They're good kids, aren't they?"

"Yes. They are. But look at us," said Dee, with a smile. "We're good role models."

"Modest as ever," Simon said. He leaned over and touched the jade necklace. "You've still got it."

"Of course. Probably why my marriage failed." Dee laughed at Simon's quizzical look. "Shouldn't have worn it on my wedding day. Jade symbolizes purity and love. And gentleness. Which would've been fine if I'd been marrying you!"

Their laughter marooned them from the murmurs coming from others in the Planters Lounge. Simon signaled the hovering waiter for the bill, but was not surprised when told it had been taken care of.

"Are you okay to walk along the beach?" Dee asked, looking at Simon's cane. "Which wound is it that causes the pain?"

"The last one. Nerve damage. Wasn't too bad when I was young. A bugger now though, combined with the hip of a 93-year-old."

"A remarkably vigorous one. Didn't you ever consider a replacement? And when did the mustache appear?"

Simon leaned on his cane waiting for Dee to take off her pumps, which she tucked under a hibiscus hedge where grass gave way to sand.

"Years ago," he said, fingering his mustache, "and in answer to the first question, not really. I was too old by the time the hip got uncomfortable."

"Hmph. I would've made you."

"I'm sure you would." Simon smiled. "I am so glad you went to medical school. I bet you were a wonderful doctor."

"Yes, I was. Not brighter or better than anyone else. But I learned to listen for what was not being said."

Simon stumbled, and clutched Dee.

"Don't bloody fall, Simon."

"I won't. It was just an excuse to hold your hand."

"Idiot. Here, my darling. You can hold my hand forever."

They walked in silence, enjoying each other's touch. The brief dusk silhouetted their bodies against the rippling sea. They stopped to watch a game of *sepak takraw* in the sand. The small rattan ball kept in the air by the lads' feet, knees, and chests before being headed over an improvised net. They moved on, slowly, the boys wishing them *selamat malam* as lights began to blink on fishing sampans putting out to sea. Nets folded ready to be released. The serenity was disturbed by jet-skis racing to the shore. Two laughing young men jumped off and hauled them up the beach before joining in the ball game.

"If we sit on the sand, do you think we'll be able to get up?" Simon asked. "I think that's far enough for me."

"I don't really care if we don't, darling."

Dee helped Simon down, then sank next to him. Shoulder to shoulder, hip to hip, their legs stretched out, they watched the Malacca Straits lap the shoreline.

"Do you remember swimming out to the raft?" Simon asked.

"Of course. The body might be a bit creaky but, thank God, my mind isn't. Or yours. We are lucky, Simon."

"Yes. Tess's mind was beginning to go. We never tested for Alzheimer's but it was our biggest fear. Then the cancer got her. It was in some ways a blessing."

"Oh, darling, it must have been awful. Isn't it funny? But I am glad you have been happy. You and Tess. I think I always knew you'd marry her."

"I'm sorry you weren't," Simon said, stroking Dee's hand.

"But I have been happy, darling. Very. Just because my marriage didn't work, didn't mean I didn't love Tom. He was a wonderful man. And a wonderful father to Abigail. I just don't think I was marriage material."

"To anyone?"

"That is something we will never know." Dee's deep laugh washed around them. "The only time I wanted to give up was when Abby and James were killed. Drunk drivers mowed into them. But of course I couldn't. Mitch was almost seven and Jessica five."

"What about James' parents?"

"Useless. They loved the kids, but said they were too old to have young ones in the house again. There were times when I thought the same. About me. But they were good kids. Mitch is serious and plans everything to the nth degree. It's always driven Jessica mad. And me too, sometimes. Jessica is the spontaneous one. I worry sometimes it'll get her hurt."

"Do we ever stop worrying about our children, or their offspring?" Simon asked.

"I doubt it. Come on, let's go home."

"Home?"

"This hotel is as close to a home as we've ever had together. Wait a minute, I'll go first. This won't be elegant." Dee got to her hands and knees and pushed herself. "There, not graceful, but I'm up. You're next."

Laughter thrilled around them as Dee, tiny as she was, managed to help Simon to his feet using his cane for leverage.

"Would you like to change for dinner?" he asked, as the shimmering lights of the hotel beckoned them.

"I have a sandy bottom, so I think I'd better," she replied, bending to reclaim her shoes. They took the lift to the third floor and, slipping her keycard into the lock she said, "You can collect me on the way down. Give me an hour."

***

Simon looked at his body in the bathroom mirror. His torso, puckered with scars he had not thought about for years, looked ugly and wrinkled. He had always kept a constant weight but muscle tone was a thing of the long distant past. His neck looked craggy without a collar to hide it. Still, he bared his teeth and peered in his mouth, most of his own teeth, and an almost full head of hair. He dressed. Light wool trousers, a blue shirt, and a tie Max had given him at Christmas. His blazer lay over the back of one of the armchairs in the corner. He chewed some nicotine gum, then tipped the rest of the Dalwhinnie from his hip flask into a tumbler and, barefoot, took it out onto the small balcony to wait for the hour to be up.

Five minutes before the appointed time, he put on shoes and socks, slipped into his blazer, checked his pockets for the gum, his wallet and keycard and pulled the door shut behind him.

Five doors along the corridor he stopped. Dee's door inched open under his quiet rap.

"Come in, Simon. Just finishing up. Sorry, it takes rather longer these days." Her voice came from the bathroom. "There's a bottle of Taittinger in the bucket."

Simon's breath caught as he turned to see Dee emerge, like a sea sprite. A diaphanous caftan of swirling blues and greens made it appear as if she were floating towards him. She still wore the jade necklace.

"God, you are beautiful, my darling, darling Dee," he said drawing her to him, and kissing her hair.

"Thank you! Do you know, I'm pretty sure that is only the second time you've called me that. The first time, was the last time we were in this room. Sixty years ago."

"Then I'm a fool."

"No argument from me," she said, snuggling into his arms. "I'm sure neither of us need a large dinner—I don't eat much at night these days—so I ordered some tapas-like niblets. Is that okay?" She continued before Simon could answer. "But champagne is another story. It has been my choice of beverage ever since we came here." She laughed. "Even when I was a student again, I'd rather forego a drink and save for a bottle of bubbles. And, I'll have you know, I have been known to drink it alone."

"A dreadful waste if you hadn't," Simon said, catching frothing bubbles in a flute. "Let's have it on the balcony. It's a rather different view to the one I have in Dorset."

"Did you miss Malaya?"

"Not really. I think we were done with each other. I was tired of being shot. Things improved dramatically under Templer, as you know, and it became more of a mopping up process."

"Still took a few years," Dee said.

"Yes, it did. But my being involved was neither here nor there."

"Were you really thinking of coming to Australia?" asked Dee, for the first time hesitant.

"Yes," Simon said. "I was on the brink of telling Tess. I had already written a couple of attempts, but tore them up. Not because I was having second thoughts, but because I didn't know how to tell her without being utterly hurtful that I had met someone who took my breath away. But there is no kind way to break up with someone, especially when you care about them, just not in the all-consuming manner in which I loved you."

"And then you got my letter."

"And then I got your letter," Simon agreed. "And I was shot. Rather badly."

Their hands reached for each other in the silence.

"Robin Nancarrow tried hard. He wanted to write and tell you but I wouldn't let him. Didn't want a pity party. He got rather angry. Said I had no right to make a decision for you."

"He was right," Dee said.

"Not entirely. You had made your decision. One I understood. Your mother needed you."

"But Simon, you never tried. You never wrote again. You must have known Mum was dying."

"People can take a long time to die."

"You don't think I know that?" Dee's eyes blazed, then softened as she looked at him. "Oh, Simon. What is the point in this? It was such a long time ago. And, my God, look at us now."

"In Penang, where it all started."

"Not for me. I knew the moment I met you. In Kuala Lipis. I was trying hard to make you take notice, without being obvious."

"You succeeded. You danced the light fantastic with Robin all night. Up and down that bloody verandah. I couldn't take my eyes off you."

Their laughter was whisked away on the sea breeze. Dee stood to let the waiter in with their supper.

"Shall I fix you a plate, darling?" she called.

"Yes, please." Simon looked out to sea. Thoughts washing over him. Of what-ifs, and what-had-beens. He smiled at the image of Max and Jessica scurrying away earlier, and hoped they were having a pleasant evening. She seemed a nice young woman. About the age Dee had been when he met her. They had the same smile. And eyes. But there the similarities ended. Jessica was tall and dark-haired. He thought he'd spotted a touch of pink amongst the curls drifting down her back, but it could've been the light.

They were comfortable in each other's company. Rather like Max with his sisters. An easy, teasing manner. Simon smiled. He'd never had that ease with women. He'd always rather envied Max that. And whilst he'd liked Lisa, he'd never thought she was right for his favorite grandson. He chuckled. His only grandson. What an eighteen months it had been, having him living at Woodland Farm. And this. Simon smiled again as he heard Dee come up behind him.

"What are you smiling at?"

"I was just thinking about the past year. How furious I was with Max for finding you."

"Why?"

"Because I didn't think he had any right to disrupt two people's lives. And mine was disrupted from the minute he told me. Gone was my pleasant slither into decrepitude. I was roiled in emotions I hadn't tangled with for over half a century."

"I think we should both be grateful neither of our grandchildren are able to keep a secret," Dee said. "Unlike you, I felt like a young woman again. I couldn't wait to write." She smiled. "Then poor Jessica had to tone everything down, because you, my darling, were being stuffy! She didn't know if Max would be able to persuade you."

They laughed again. They picked at the plates Dee had prepared. Then sat, their fingers entwined as they finished the champagne.

"Can we lie together? Just lie," Dee asked.

"I would like nothing better. Well, maybe a few years ago, something better. But not now," Simon said.

He picked up his cane and, holding Dee's hand, lead her to the four-poster bed, soft mosquito netting tied to teak posts. He pulled the blue satin ribbons free. She undid his shoe laces, and drew off his socks, then climbed onto the mattress and patted the space beside her. They lay together, cocooned behind the gauze, their bodies touching, chatting quietly about their lives. Their hopes for their grandchildren.

"What do we do at the end of the week, my darling?" Dee asked, her voice sleepy.

"Let's worry about that tomorrow, darling, darling Dee. Tonight let's just be happy."

Chapter 32

THE PHONE SHATTERED Max's dream-filled sleep. His hand flailed in the semi-dark for the receiver. Dawn was the merest glimmer.

"Come now. DeeDee's room."

Startled by Jessica's voice, he tugged on yesterday's shirt and a pair of shorts and ran barefoot up the flight of stairs and along the corridor. Dee's door was ajar. There was a quiet. No voices. Just quiet. From the hall he could see Jessica, a silhouette on the balcony. It looked as if she was wearing a sarong and tank top. Her night clothes. She was slumped against the rail. Staring out.

Max glanced through the netting, a translucent blur around the couple on the bed, and he knew. Dee lay still, gripping Fa's hand. By her side was her mobile phone. Tears ran in a constant rivulet, following the contours of her face. There was no sound. Unable to look at his grandfather, unwilling to intrude on such naked pain, Max stood still.

Jessica turned and came into the bedroom. She held him close. Through his grief, he noticed she smelled of vanilla. His tears fell on her shoulder until, stepping away, he moved to the bed. He touched his grandfather's forehead. There was a hint of warmth, but he knew it would not last much longer. His clothes barely crumpled. Fa looked peaceful. As if sleep had just deepened.

He looked across at Dee, her tears forming a damp patch on the pillow.

"Come on, DeeDee," Jessica said, gently helping her sit. "Come out to the balcony. Or shall we go to my room? Max has to phone reception. People will be coming in and out."

"I'll stay here, thank you, sweetheart. I want to be near." Dee looked at Max, and held out her hand. "I am so very sorry, Max. He was a wonderful man. A man I have loved most of my life. Thank you."

"For what? For opening more pain?" Max asked, his voice sad.

"No. Never that. For allowing us one last night together. I think he knew." Dee was silent, looking down at his grandfather, gathering herself, her eyes puffy. "And now, I am going out to the balcony. No, no," she said to Jessica, "you stay here, and help Max. I'd like to be on my own. Just for a while. I'll be alright. I always am."

***

The busyness of death enveloped Max. There was no time to mourn. The British Honorary Consul came immediately, and the hotel offered Dee another room. An offer she refused.

Max waited until it was seven in the morning in London, knowing he'd catch his father at home before he made the hardest call—to his mother. The time difference had given Max a chance to gather some facts. Answers to questions he knew his parents would have.

His mother cycled through anger to guilt to sad resignation.

"I suppose it was fitting. Back in Malaya. With Dee." Max heard his mother sob, before she added, "Thank God you're there."

"Mum, it was so peaceful. He'd been drinking champagne a few hours before. He and Dee lying on the bed together. It was beautiful. If death can be described that way."

His father took the phone.

"Max, I hate to ask this, but does there have to be an autopsy?" Max heard his mother's sharp intake of breath.

"No, Dad. Because of his age. Because it was in the hotel, and they have a doctor on call; the process just has to play out. It sounds complicated but that's probably because I don't understand most of the terms. They're in Malay, of course. But people, and the police, are being very helpful."

His mother's voice came back on the line. "The police?"

"Yes, Mum. Because he's a foreigner and died in a hotel."

"Oh, I see." There was a pause, and Max had an image of waves waiting to roll. "I want him brought home, Max."

"No, Mum. That can't happen. The Honorary Consul here told me commercial planes are not allowed to carry coffins." He heard his mother gasp. Before she could go on, he added, "He wanted to be cremated anyway, Mum."

"How do you know?"

"Because we talked about it. His will, and papers are in his desk. The bottom drawer. The keys are on the key ring in his bedside table if you want to check. He had everything written down."

"No, of course not, darling. He just didn't tell me. I want to be there. For the cremation." Her voice broke on the word. Max heard his father comfort her.

"That would be nice, Mum. It will take at least a week to get all the documentation sorted. Fly straight to Penang, it'll be easier for you. I'll book you a room here."

"Book two. Susie and Giles will want to come," his father's voice broke in again. "Emma is out of contact for the next few weeks."

"Yeah, I know. Who'll look after the twins?" asked Max.

"Giles' mother, I should think."

A knock at the door broke his train of thought. "Okay. I've got to go now, Dad. Sorry about all this. Will Mum be okay?"

"Yes, of course. He was 93, Max. We all knew it was coming."

"Doesn't make it easier, Dad."

"No, I know, Max. I'm sorry. I just meant it isn't really a surprise. That came when he said he was going to Malaysia."

"Yeah. Bye, Dad. Give Mum a hug from me, and Susie. Let me know your flight details."

"Oh, Max?" His father hesitated. "What's she like? Dee?"

"She's wonderful, Dad. Wonderful!"

He clicked his phone shut. Heading out to the balcony, he heard another tap at the door.

"Hi, come in," he said, opening the door to Jessica and rubbing his eyes. "I've just spoken to my parents."

"I know. I wasn't eavesdropping. I just heard your voice through the door and thought I'd wait. They okay?"

"Yes. A bit stunned. But as Dad said, the big surprise came with Fa's decision to come here. How's Dee?"

"She's sleeping. She actually took the Valium I offered." Jessica was quiet, looking out at the sea. "It's strange, isn't it? I mean, I only met Simon once, but it feels like I'd known him years." Her eyes turned liquid, like jungle pools on a cloudy day. She blew her nose. "I spoke to Mitch. He's coming. I'm glad."

"What a strange way for our families to meet, Jess."

"I know. What did the police say?"

"They were nothing but courteous. I'm sure it helps we're staying here. And the British Honorary Consul was here too." Max turned from the view to lean against the balcony. He realized his feet were still bare. "They've taken Fa to Gleneagles Hospital. It's the closest private one. I can't remember all the names of the different bits of paper I've got to get, but Mr. Dawler said the funeral directors can do most of it, if I want that."

"Then I should let them," Jessica said, rubbing his arm.

"The police report will take seven days. Seems strange having to need one, but it's because he's not ..." Max corrected himself, "... he wasn't a Malay citizen."

***

As the week progressed and paperwork associated with death was slowly completed, with help from the undertakers, Max had time to feel. Criss crossing streets one night, before heading off down another, he walked miles, stopping only at a stall for a bowl of noodles, washed down with a Tiger, before going on. He got back to the hotel as a cockerel announced a new day. In the lobby, the night manager nodded toward one of the library chairs in which Jessica was curled. Her head resting on her hand, her hair a dark curtain.

"Hey, Jess?" Max hunkered down beside the chair. "Wake up. Come on, time for bed."

"Oh, hey." She blinked. "You okay? I was worried. I haven't seen you all day."

"I'm fine. I'm sorry. I should've told you. It's what I do, when I need to think. I walk."

"That's okay." She rubbed her eyes. "I thought you might want to talk. You've been so busy you haven't had time to cry."

"I'm fine. Come on," he repeated. "It'll be daylight soon. Time for some kip. How was Dee today? Yesterday," Max corrected.

"Sleeping a lot. Talks a bit, then sleeps again."

"It's nature's way of getting through the pain of each day," said Max, as they climbed the stairs together.

"For an English bloke, you can be quite perceptive."

"I'm not sure whether to be insulted by the 'English' or 'bloke.'"

"Neither, you galah. It's nice you care." Jessica looked at her watch. "Strewth, it is nearly morning. What time do your parents arrive? And Susie?"

"Three."

"Do you want me to come to the airport with you?"

"No, but thank you. Do you think Dee would like to join us for dinner? I don't want to hustle her into anything she doesn't want to do."

"I'm not sure, Max. Let's play it by ear. It might be better if she met your mum on her own. Without all of us around."

"Sure. Whatever she wants to do."

"It'll be strange for your mum, too. Meeting the woman who loved her dad all those years."

"The whole thing is a bit odd, isn't it? Look what we started. What I started."

Chapter 33

MAX WAVED AS THE airport doors slid open. Giles, pushing the trolley, nodded. Susie and his mother walked behind him, and his father brought up the rear. None of them looked as if they'd just got off a long flight, though his mother's face was pale.

"Hi." He shook Giles hand, then hugged his mother and sister. And, uncharacteristically, embraced his father. Or maybe his father reached for him first. Thinking about it later, Max couldn't remember. But surprise had accompanied the hug.

"Flight not too bad?" he asked. "Customs okay?"

"Yes, everything very easy. Amazing what a lie-down seat can do. Courtesy of Dad upgrading us," Susie said. "Thanks, Dad; it made a real difference."

"Not to mention good food and unlimited alcohol!" Giles said, adding his thanks.

"A pleasure," Michael said. He stopped, flustered. "Well, you know what I mean."

"Yes, Dad. I do. Just thanks."

"Come on then, the luxury continues. The E&O sent the Rolls for you. The staff have been nothing but amazing." Max helped his mother into the car and nodded to the driver. "It's about ten miles."

"You must be getting to know Penang well," his dad said, watching tropical scenery flash by to give way to the myriad streets of George Town.

"Parts of it. Others I could do without seeing again," said Max.

"Yes, of course, darling," his mother said. "You've been marvelous, Max. Sorting everything out."

"Well Fa wouldn't have been here if it hadn't been for my meddling."

"Don't be silly, Max. Fa died happy," said Susie, her eyes damp. "What a fabulous way to go."

"Yeah, I know. But it's been a bit intense. Jessica has been wonderful. And Dee, though Jess says she's much quieter than normal."

"Not surprising," said Sarah. "When do we meet her?"

"Soon, but do you think it might be better if you met her on her own, Mum?"

"Yes, I suppose so. It'll be strange." She twiddled her wedding rings.

"But easier for her, and you. Then we can all have dinner together if it's not too late."

"And Jessica?" asked Susie. She reached across and tapped his knee.

"She's great. It's been like having either you or Emma around."

***

"Thank God that's over," Dee said, taking off a black straw hat and shaking out her silver curls. Her simple black dress was a replica of the white shift she had worn only ten days earlier to meet Simon. Her only adornment was the jade necklace and a gold bangle. "I hate funerals."

"It's something to do with being doctors," Jessica said. "We feel we've failed."

"Bollocks," said Max from the jump seat of the funeral car. "An end of a life is just plain sad. But I'd rather a crematorium than seeing a box dumped into the ground. It was peaceful there, wasn't it?" he asked as they drove out the gates of Batu Gantung Crematorium.

"Yeah, it was," Jessica agreed. She held Dee's hand. The filigree gold band she always wore on the little finger of her right hand flashed in the sun, which had emerged as they left the chapel. He wondered what it signified. If Ian had given it to her.

Max hadn't noticed what Jessica was wearing until now. He didn't usually like seeing Western women wearing Eastern clothing but the black cheongsam suited her lithe body. She'd undone the top frog knot when she'd got into the car, but her hair was still piled up on her head, pink strands vivid against the dark brown. Jessica reminded him of his younger sister. Not in looks, but in manner. One minute mercurial, the next calm. He wished Emma could have been here. She had been distraught when they'd finally managed to speak.

Mitch sat on the other jump seat. He was a nice chap. Quiet. Capable. And Jessica obviously adored him, for all her calling him a dag, and teasing him unmercifully at times. The five of them—he, Susie and Giles, Jessica and Mitch—had gone out for satay at the Chulia Street hawker stalls a couple of nights before. They'd drunk too much Tiger but it had been a good evening. One, as Susie said, of which Fa would have approved.

Max broke the silence and with a catch in his voice said, "I haven't talked to Mum or Dad about this but, when I collect Fa's ashes, I'd like to take some to Pahang. I know Mum will want to take the rest to England. Would you be okay with that, Dee?"

"Max, darling boy, I don't have a say in any of this."

"Of course, you do. You loved him. He loved you."

Dee's eyes welled and, dabbing her cheeks, she leaned across to pat Max's hand. "Then yes, that would be a wonderful thing. Thank you."

"I want to go too," Jessica said, looking at Max. "Please?"

"I'm not going the luxury route, Jess. Train, bus and foot. Maybe boat."

"I'm good with that. Please, Max?"

"What about the hospital?" he asked. "I'm not sure how long it'll take. Not traveling to a timetable."

"I'll take compassionate leave."

"Okay. Then, sure."

"Sweetheart," Dee said, "that'll only give you a couple of weeks. Are you sure?"

"I'm sure, DeeDee," Jessica said. "I've been getting restless. Thinking it was time for a change. I had half thought I might head back to Townsville."

"Not because of me, I hope," said Dee. "I am quite capable of living alone. One death does not mean another is about to follow."

"DeeDee!" Jessica and Mitch spoke together.

"It would be great if you came along, Jess. But what about Dee?"

"Don't you 'what about Dee?' me, mate." Dee's voice was angry, her eyes bright. "I'm right here!"

"Sorry, Dee. I know," Max apologized.

Before he could continue, Mitch spoke. "DeeDee, why don't you come home with me? You're always saying you haven't been to Sydney for years. Come and stay a bit, then fly back to Townsville. When you're ready."

"I'm sad. I'm tired. I'm not making any decisions today."

"I'm sorry, DeeDee. No one's trying to browbeat you into anything," said Jessica, looking over at Max. "Max has had such a lot to sort out; he's just trying to do the right thing for everyone. Give him a break, alright?"

They swung into the drive followed by the car holding the rest of his family. It had been a natural split as Giles and Susie, and his parents had climbed in. His mother's eyes were red rimmed, and Max couldn't remember ever seeing her cry before. They would stay in Penang another three days, then fly back to London. Max knew Susie was getting anxious to see the girls. It was the first time she'd been away from them for so long.

"I'm glad we're having lunch in the Planters Lounge," said Jessica. "It's apt."

***

A streak of dim light stole between the curtains in Max's room. He'd had a disturbed night. Thoughts and images chasing each other. He liked Jessica but wasn't sure he wanted to travel with her, for who knew how long. Travel either brought the best or worst out in people. In Lisa's case it had been the latter. And what he wanted to do could not, by any stretch, be described as luxury, or even easy. This was about honoring Fa, and trying to absorb the jungle—the *ulu*. So he could write from the heart and maybe learn something about himself. His adventure.

He pulled on shorts and a tee shirt and made his way downstairs, barefoot, through the empty lobby and out to the beach. Stripping off his tee, Max lunged into the water, tepid even in the cool of early morning. He struck out to the raft and, lying on his back, watched dawn come awake in a mélange of orange and purples. He felt purple. Bruised. Fa had left a monumental hole in his life and the only way he knew to start filling it was to follow his footsteps as much as possible, sixty years later.

"Hi." Susie's voice came from the side of the raft. "Give me a hand, the bottom rung of the ladder is missing."

Max rolled over to see his sister's hair plastered back, her hazel eyes looking up at him. He knelt to help her clamber up.

"Hello. I thought I was the only one awake."

"No. I've been sitting on our balcony for hours. Then I saw you come out. You okay?'

"Not really."

"Conflicted?"

"Yup."

"You know, Max, if you don't want Jessica to travel with you, you've got to say." She finger-combed her bobbed hair, her eyes on his face. "You might never have this chance again. You know, to do this for you, and Fa."

"Yeah, I know. I've been back and forth about it all night."

"Do you fancy her?"

"Honestly, Suse, I haven't thought about it. I like her. I admire her. But there's been too much happening to think about anything else."

"Even sex?" Susie asked, with a little laugh.

"'Specially sex. You know, Suse, I keep thinking about seeing Fa. They'd spent the night together. He and Dee lying there on the bed, holding hands and talking. The very fact they were dressed in evening clothes made it so intimate. Then I think of how he leaned across the tea table and stroked Dee's cheek. As if no one else was in the room. Honestly, I don't think they really registered Jessica and me, they just looked at each other. It was as if sixty years were expunged. Do you think you and Giles would be like that?"

"Shit, I don't know, Max. You can't compare. They lost each other. I can't imagine my life without Giles, but would I still want only him if we had that kind of time apart? I don't know."

"If I can't have what Fa had with Dee, I don't want anything. I don't want second best."

"What about Fa and Nana? We thought that was the best."

"I know. Funny, isn't it?"

"Not really. But Max, if you decide you don't want to travel with Jessica, you have got to say. I'll tell her, if you want."

"Thanks, Susie. But if that's what I decide, I'll do it. I don't need my big sister bailing me out."

They swam back to shore and sat on the sand drying off and watched late sampans returning with their night-time catch, fish scales glistening the decks. A fisherman walked along the beach with a bucket and stopped to show the crabs he was taking to the hotel kitchens.

"They're so small, I couldn't be bothered fiddling around with them," Susie said, once the Malay was out of earshot.

"G'day!" Jessica called from the hibiscus path. "I'm not stalking you. But I do need a swim. See you in a bit." She dived into the shallows and powered out past the raft.

"She's a surfer," Max said, smiling. "She's pining for the waves."

"Max," Susie said, watching the Australian swim, "forget what I said before. It'd be better to travel with someone. I don't know that I want you traipsing around out here on your own, getting morose."

"I don't get morose."

"Yes, you do. Then you go walking for miles."

"Well, that was rather the plan. Walking. But in the jungle rather than around the streets of London." They watched Jessica come out of the sea, long and lean in a simple black one piece.

"That's better, I needed to clear my head," Jessica said, wringing out her hair. "Can I join you or are you having a private beach party? No problem if you are."

Susie smiled and stood, saying, "Nope. Had that. I'm going in to shower. See ya!"

"Max," Jessica said, drawing circles in the sand, "I've put you in a difficult position, and I'm sorry. You've been flat out getting everything sorted and I tend to leap in sometimes without thinking things through. I absolutely understand if you'd rather scatter Simon's ashes without an interloper around."

Max was quiet. She was too.

"I've been awake most of the night mulling things over. Back and forth. And until this very minute I didn't really know what I thought." Max smiled at the woman next to him. "It'd be great to travel together. But, what about work? Do you really want to throw away tenure, if that's the right word, at the hospital? And what about Ian? He wouldn't be too thrilled at the idea of you traipsing around the jungle with a strange man."

"Two or three questions in there," Jessica said, shading her eyes and looking out to sea. "I meant what I said to Dee, you know, in the car. I have been considering moving back to Townsville. The surf's crap but I love the city. And I do want to be nearer to DeeDee, though I wouldn't live with her."

Max was quiet. Waiting.

"And that pretty much answers the second, or was it the third question. The one about Ian. If I was thinking about relocating, I was obviously not thinking long term about him. He's a good guy but he's a bit sedentary for me. I told him before I left Brissie."

"What about the ring?" Max touched the delicate gold filigree.

"No pining beau. It was Mum's wedding ring." She laughed. "I also phoned the hospital and handed in my notice. Not so I'm free to travel, but they need to start looking for someone else because whatever happened about the here and now question, I am going home to Townsville."

They smiled at each other.

"Great," said Max. "That's settled."

Chapter 34

"WOULD YOU CARE FOR a glass of champagne before lunch, madam?" The flight attendant's voice drew her back to the cabin.

"Sure. I might as well celebrate being alive."

"DeeDee!" Mitch said, nodding his thanks to the young woman serving the first-class passengers. "I could get used to this. Here's to you, and Simon." They chinked glasses.

Dee, head leant against the bulwark, watched Penang disappear as the plane climbed higher. She could feel Mitch's gaze and reached across the armrest to pat his hand without taking her eyes off the ground dissolving into a blur of jungle green as they flew south.

"I'm fine, darling boy. Really." She sipped her champagne, then dabbed the corner of her mouth. "I've been thinking." Dee paused, "I'm not going to stay in Sydney. I need to get home, get back to my life. Which before all this," she waved her hand around, "was very pleasant."

"You don't regret going though, do you?" Mitch asked.

"Never. But, oh God, it hurts. Just like the first time. Even after all these years." She sniffed. "I'm a silly old fool."

"Of course you're not. Just very sad. I'm sorry I didn't get to meet Simon. Jessica really liked him." He watched silent tears trace down Dee's lined cheeks to land on the hand in her lap. The other twisted the champagne flute back and forth. "DeeDee, please stay with me, even for a week. Then I'll fly up to Townsville with you."

"I don't need babysitting, Mitch." Dee repeated the words spoken before to Jessica.

"I know you don't, but you haven't been to my new flat and you might as well get your time clock back in sync with me before you have to worry about the mundane things of life. Like groceries. Okay?"

Dee patted his hand again, her eyes crinkled in a tight smile. "Put like that, how can I refuse. But only a week, Mitch. I want to go home."

***

"Righto, Dr. Cunningham, you're home!" The cab driver carried her suitcase up the front steps. "You be right from here, or shall I carry it through?"

"You're a dear boy, thank you, Harry."

"Hardly a boy, Doc. I've got me own son now!"

"I know, Harry. But you're still a scrabbly-kneed kid to me! Thanks again. Bye now."

Dee dragged the case and left it inside the front door, then wandered through to the kitchen and opened the windows. Two galahs, their gray necks fluffed up, stopped their squabble over space on the verandah rail for a moment then ignored her. She smiled. Some things never changed.

She gulped down a glass of water, sent a quick text to Mitch to assure him all was well, then popped a stubbie of Castlemaine Bitter and took it out to her herb garden. She sank into one of the pink chairs and noted the Rangoon creeper needed trimming and that the bird bath needed a scrub. A flash of yellow and royal blue chest and neck alerted her to a sunbird peering through the leaves, his head cocked as if to ask where she'd been.

Her eyes were gritty and sore. The well empty. She felt shriveled, desiccated, the life sucked out of her. Exhausted from trying to keep up a façade. When, she wondered, does a parent or, in her case, grandparent ever stop trying to protect its young by pretending? She knew Mitch had been unhappy about her flying home alone, about arriving back to an empty house. A house left with such excitement and joy. But, as with Jessica, she managed to convince him she would be fine.

"But I'm not." Her ragged voice startled the sunbird. "I'm not bloody fine."

She swigged from the bottle, her chair rocking back and forth in time to her dry sobs as she tried to catch her breath, to calm herself. She rested her head back. She needed to sleep. To be able to shut her eyes and not see Simon. Young, old, and dead.

Apart from those first few days she had eschewed all drugs. Even a sleeping pill, but now she was home perhaps it would help. No one to see her disintegrate into a heap, to see her padding from her bed to her bower in the herb garden clad only in a sarong, her hair dirty and her skin gray from fatigue and sadness. She didn't have to pretend now.

"Oh God, I'm 87. How can this hurt so much?"

It was the questions that kept her awake. The if onlys. Such a waste of time and energy but hard to stop as they swirled in her open-eyed wakefulness. She looked at the empty bottle in her hand and recognized how easy it would be to become dependent on the quick release it could give. She shook her head. If she could say no to valium she could say no to booze. But tonight she would take melatonin. A solid sleep and the pain would become manageable. It had to.

***

An early sun filtered through the bottlebrush tree to trickle in the window like soft wisps. The curtains wafted in a gentle breeze and kookaburras cackled in the distance. She thought she heard the clink of glass as the milko delivered a bottle. Her neighbor, Annie Wright, must have realized she was back and told the milkman. Sometimes a nosy neighbor was a bonus.

Dee stretched and rubbed her eyes. They felt heavy but not so dry. Blessed oblivion, aided by melatonin and wine, had finally let her sleep. No dreams shuddered her awake. Just a dark, deep sleep. She threw back the bamboo sheet and padded, naked, to the bathroom. What was it Simon used to say? "A shit, a shower, and a shave and a man could face anything." She rubbed her legs. No shave necessary but the former two, and a cup of tea, would set her up for the day.

She smiled. It was good to be home. Something about this old house comforted her, as she knew it would. Her memories were tucked into every corner. Scrabbling with her brothers as children, every family decision made around the kitchen table. Her fears, her sadnesses all absorbed into the weatherboard walls to become part of the fabric of her life just as they paraded the triumphs and joys in photographs dotted around the rooms.

A cup of tea beside her on the kitchen table, she pulled her laptop nearer and saw an email had arrived from Jessica.

Selamat pagi, DeeDee, apa khabar?

You see, my Malay is coming along. Slowly, and not very surely but it's a start.

I imagine you're at the kitchen table reading this. Are you? And how are you? I have to ask in English so you don't respond in Malay, which I bet you could still do. I didn't hear you speak much whilst you were in Penang but I'm pretty certain you understood a lot.

We left Penang two days after you and, much as I liked the island, it was good to leave. Too many jangled emotions and, if I feel that way, I can only imagine how you feel. And much as I loved the luxury of the E&O it is nice to be back to my usual level of living, though the first hostel we stayed in—in Ipoh—was a bit extreme. We shared a dorm with four others—three blokes and a girl. It was not a restful couple of nights! We have agreed our budget will extend to two rooms in future.

Dee smiled. Two rooms, huh? "Subtle, Jess," she said to the single galah, once again two-stepping on the rail outside.

Anyway, we found the FMS Bar in Ipoh and honestly I don't think much has changed since Simon went there. Did you go? So many questions, DeeDee, the more we follow your footsteps. We got to Ipoh by train but decided to hire a car. More freedom to go where the mood takes us.

And it took us a couple of days ago to Gua Tempurung. Not somewhere Max remembered Simon talking about but a Tamil bloke we met at the hostel said we should go. I dug my heels in and refused to go on the "wet" tour which involved wading through underground waterways for four hours. I don't think so! What we saw was impressive enough. Over three miles of caverns and, I suppose not surprisingly, used during the Emergency by CTs. And in case anyone needed

272

proof, it came in the form of graffiti, done in the '50s that showed a car—looked awfully like a Rolls—in the jungle and is presumed to be a record of Sir Henry Gurney's murder. It was actually a bit chilling, DeeDee, to see real evidence of all the stories. It's not that I doubt them but to see it etched on a cave wall was quite something.

That's it for now. This will probably end up being my travel diary. I'm too knackered at night to keep a journal. We're heading to Raub tomorrow. Hope we find your old house.

Max sends his love, and I think he means it. He veers from sad to happy in a heartbeat. He really loved his Fa, so I guess that means he loves you too!

X Jess

P.S. Oh yeah, how'd it go in Sydney? Mitch told me his side. What's yours?

Dee went to the fridge to pour a glass of milk. An image of chastising Mitch for drinking from the bottle popped into view. She grinned and lifted the bottle to her lips and slurped. If she couldn't break the rules at nearly 90 when could she? Wiping her mouth with the back of her hand, then on her sarong, she sat back down at the table.

My darling Jess,

Mitch's new flat is lovely. The views across the harbor are fabulous, which you already know. You were both right, it was good to recalibrate there for a few days but I'm happy to be home. You know me, pottering in the garden. Talking to the bloody galahs!

I must remember to thank Mitch for arranging for Harry Whatshisname to collect me from the airport. It was nice to have a friendly face waiting. I know Annie would've been happy to pick me up but I couldn't handle the interrogation. I'll have to face that tomorrow. But not today. Today I'm going to slip out to the shops and get some fresh supplies then make it very obvious I am not open to visitors. I'll pull the blinds down at the front of the house. Though then she might think I've died! Hell. I know, I'll text and invite her for coffee in the morning, then at least I can gird myself. Or maybe it should be a sundowner, so I can have liquid courage. And what do I say to her? That my heart is broken. Again. I should never have told her why I was going to Penang in the first place.

I am in a muddle, Jess. Not memory-wise so shut the Alzheimer's theory down right away. No, I'm in a muddle over the last month. Happy beyond measure, and now sad beyond measure. Simon loved me all those years. As I did him. I don't know, perhaps it was best. What would we have done? I'm buggered if I'd live in England and he probably felt the same way about Australia. Right back where we started. Anyway that's what I keep telling my heart.

Sorry, darling, but I've got to vent for a while. I'll be back to normal soon. Kind of funny really. Boots on other foots sort of thing, isn't it? I'm the teenager. Not sure I like it.

Righto, got to make myself reasonably presentable and get to the shops. Hope the car starts.

Have a wonderful adventure. And Jess, I'm so very glad you're taking Simon's ashes to the ulu.

All love, darling,

DeeDee

P.S. You know it's cheaper to share a room!

She hit send with a grin. Her good intentions deserted her, the thought of facing both the car and shops too daunting. Instead she roamed the garden, glad to have a tall hedge between her and Annie. She would have to see her tomorrow but today, her first day home, was hers.

***

It was a few days before she found the energy to shop. Thankfully the car started straight away and, waving to Annie deadheading roses in her front garden, Dee drove to the deli she favored for paté, cheese, salami and fresh fruit and vegetables. She'd live on salad until she felt like cooking. She walked along the wine aisle on her way to the till and paused. To hell with it. She reached for a bottle of Taittinger.

"Celebrating something, dear?" The check-out girl grinned.

Dee gritted her teeth at the "dear" and handed over her credit card. "When you get to my age, dear, you don't need an excuse to drink champagne."

She fumed at the impertinence as she waited at the lights, but as the house came into view she smiled. If she was in danger of becoming a cantankerous old woman, she might as well enjoy it. She must remember to tell Jessica next time she emailed. It would make her laugh.

The groceries unpacked, Dee felt an overwhelming weariness and, rather than fight it, she curled up on the daybed and slept. Again she awoke to birdsong, this time the sweet screeches of galahs lining the back verandah as the sun slid westward. She glanced at her watch. She'd never sleep tonight.

So what? She'd prepare a salad, open the Taittinger and toast love, and if she drank it all, what the hell? There was no one to see her drunk. The ground rules with Annie had been reestablished over a glass of wine. No checking on her unless the front room blind was down and the newspaper was still on the doorstep at noon.

But first she'd check her email. It had been a few days since she'd heard from Jess.

Oh my God, DeeDee, you are something. I can't think of anyone's else grandmother encouraging a granddaughter to share a bed with a virtual stranger. Hah. Actually he was a virtual stranger when we were emailing about you and Simon. Now he's just a great pal. Very nice, and a bit hunky, but I'm not going to muddy the waters with sex.

We had a bit of a detour on the way to Raub and went up to the Cameron Highlands. It was nice to breathe some cooler

275

air. And the black and white houses are still fabulous. Had a couple of amazing hikes. No tigers but lots of birds. I could imagine you and Simon sitting in front of the fire after a gentle stroll.

We're in KL now—Kuala Lipis rather than the other KL. From what you told me, you'd be so disappointed in Raub. I was. We couldn't find your bungalow, and the padang has gone. We also tried to find Samsuari's place but the kampong was gone too, and when we asked about Aminah, Ishraaq and Deen a nearby shopkeeper told us they'd gone to the city years ago. He didn't know where. We didn't bother to stay but pushed on to KL, which is a bit the same. Flashes of old grandeur and the Clifford School and the Pahang Club are well kept. Bet you can't guess where we're staying? The Residency known in your day as the British Residence. Isn't that cool? When Max told me that's where you and Simon met I came out in goosebumps. It's a bit jaded but quaint and there's a small museum about the gold mine. But you know what there is very little about? Yup, you guessed it. The Emergency. It's as if it has been expunged from memories. I suppose a civil war will always do that.

Max also told me you and Simon and the other blokes all danced along the verandah—you really are the most terrible flirt, DeeDee—anyway, I made Max dance with me. He's not very good but we had fun.

We're going to stay around here for a few more days then head to Jerantut.

X Jess

Dee popped the cork and poured a glass. She sat back down at the computer and watched bubbles fizz to the top of the flute but her mind was full of KL and dancing and Simon. Even that first night she'd known. She sighed and raised her glass to the only man she had ever loved.

Darling Jess,

How sad about Raub and KL. And Samsuari's kids. Still it's about twenty years since I heard from anyone. I suppose progress inevitably means new buildings, very few of which inspire the awe of the old. Oh God, Jessica, I am getting crabby. I snapped at that poor young girl in the deli—I can't remember her name—for calling me "dear." But it is a bloody cheek. I used to look down her tonsils!

All okay here. I've just raised a glass to Simon, and now I'll raise one to you and Max. I'm sure I'll be able to think of a few more people as I work my way down the bottle. I'm kidding, Jess, I'm kidding.

Enjoy this time, my darling girl. It is a liminal space you might never have again.

All love,

DeeDee

Chapter 35

"To HELL WITH IT," Max said over a supper of *nasi goreng*, "Let's buy a bloody boat. Then sell it at the other end."

"Are you nuts?"

"People do it with cars all the time. Why not with boats?" Max replied. The idea took root after two fruitless days in Jerantut, looking for someone willing to take them on the long trip to the estuary that emptied Sungai Pahang into the South China Sea.

Jessica looked at him, took a swig of Tiger and asked, "How good are you on boats?"

"Reasonable. I've done a bit of sailing."

"Is that a classic British understatement? You're really an Olympian."

Max laughed. "Not quite. But I've sailed in Greece and Croatia. And in the Solent, of course. How about you?"

"I grew up in Townsville. I'm okay."

With renewed energy next morning they took the bus to Kuala Tembeling, where most boat tours started, and put word out that they wanted to purchase a boat, but hope faded with each shake of the head. Dejected, they watched the last tour boat bump into the low wooden jetty and Max caught the line tossed by the elderly boatman, who clambered out after the last camera-clad tourist. He thanked Max with a toothless grin before ambling over to the shanty bar. Max watched the men relax, laughing about their day and the people they had ferried.

"Come on." He pulled Jess to her feet. "Let's buy him a drink."

Conversation ceased as they eased their way to the shaky counter, and with much grinning the men listened to Max's ragged Malay as he spoke to the boatman. His name was Panjang, and he lived in a houseboat on the other side of the river. And yes, he had a boat. An old *bot-bot sungai*—a traditional river boat he had been hoping to restore. The old man shook his head sadly and told them none of his sons wanted anything to do with the river and had moved to the big town, Kuala Lipis. So yes, he would sell it.

"Should have thought of this before," Jess muttered, as Panjang assured them the engine was reliable.

Good-natured haggling ended with Max and Jessica the proud owners of a *bot-bot sungai*. The purchase and repairs would delay them a week or so, but the delighted Panjang promised to help with the requisite permits and to mark known trouble spots along the river. Max grinned at Jessica and indicated to the sarong-clad woman in charge of the ice chest that she should open Tigers or Coca-Colas for them all. Bottles were raised in their direction, and the men drifted back to their own conversations before heading home.

"You go soon, before rains come or," Panjang chuckled, "before river dries."

"Either way we're stuffed," Max said, shaking hands with the grinning old man clad in a sarong and a tee shirt, extolling the joie de vivre gained from the bubbles in Coca Cola. "*Terima kasih*," he said to Panjang. As they walked away he said under his breath, "I'm sure we paid too much. No wonder he's grinning."

"Of course we did," Jessica said, laughter welling up, "but who cares?"

"Says the well-paid doctor." Max's smile removed any sting from his words.

"You have two publishers bidding for your book, Max. It's going to sell. Come on, or we'll miss the last bus back to Jerantut."

***

Whenever he didn't have tourists to ferry to Taman Negara, Panjang worked beside them as they sanded and caulked the old boat. Max told the Malay the reason for their journey and their story had, in turn, been related to others who congregated at the ramshackle bar at the end of each day, when the last visitor cars and buses pulled out of the potholed parking lot, eager to rush home to tell people what they'd seen. But for the boat people Max and Jessica's mission had been taken to heart.

They gazed at their purchase the night before their departure. She looked sturdy enough, tied up to the small jetty. The *attap* and tin roof would provide a little shade, and hopefully some protection if the heavens opened. Two of the three rows of bench seats had been removed to give space to spread out sleeping bags if they couldn't find somewhere to stop as the sun set. Between Max and Panjang a small hold cum deck had been fashioned at the prow. The engine started with a quick pull. Surprisingly it had power tilt which, should they run out of water, would make life a little easier for the shallow draft boat, and them. And two small sand anchors. They'd toyed with the idea of painting her, but decided against it, not wanting to stand out.

The map showed kampongs along most of the river but there was an element of uncertainty as to how much fuel the little boat would need.

"I suppose it won't take long to figure out how much fuel *Munah* guzzles?"

"Who?" Max asked.

"*Munah*. That's her name. It means 'one favored by destiny.' I asked the girl in the internet café. She said it was perfect. Do you think she said that because she thinks we're crazy?"

"Quite possibly. So, no discussion about a lifelong decision?"

"No. *Munah* is perfect."

"I thought changing the name of a boat was bad luck," Max said.

"Not when the previous name was *TN32*!"

And with that, the discussion was indeed over.

Animated chatter from the audience gathered on the jetty accompanied their stowing of rucksacks, a small camping stove, six gallons of water, two five-gallon emergency fuel tanks, a couple of boxes of basic supplies, and an extended medical kit. Max couldn't decide whether the rapid-fire Malay sounded positive or pitying. Either way, it was accompanied with many smiles from the courteous people who had helped them.

Panjang come across from his riverboat one last time and, with a proprietary air, gave last minute instructions in lisping English. They posed for a photograph with him in front of *Munah* before stepping down into the boat. He grinned, his gums a pink slash relieved by two stubby teeth on the bottom. A respectful silence fell as, after final checks, Jessica leaned over to loosen the mooring rope. She was motioned back by a brawny young man. Some of the gathering moved closer to shake hands with Max, and smile at Jessica.

"*Perjalanan selamat,*" was called as they were wished safe travels as they eased into the river.

"You okay?" Max asked Jessica.

"Yeah, I'm good. A bit overwhelmed. They have all been so kind. I think Panjang has adopted us. You?"

He nodded. The engine puttered quietly as they took turns getting a feel for *Munah*. A sense of peace slipped over Max and he glanced at his day sack where Fa was tucked in his metal canister. This felt right. They were silent as the majesty of the muddy Sungai Pahang flowed beneath them, and the *ulu* loomed on either side.

Max navigated the first snake bend in the river and Jessica opened her guide book.

"Did you know ...?" she started.

"Probably not," said Max. He smiled at her irritated glance. "Sorry, carry on."

"Did you know," she glared at Max daring him to interrupt again, "that the banks of the Pahang, according to the Malay Annals, were settled back in the 1400s. By seafarers from all around South East Asia. It was the main porterage route inland. Then settlers came and planted rubber and coconut palms."

"What are the Malay Annals?"

"They're a romanticized history of the Malacca Sultanate, written between the 15th and 16th centuries. Wow," Jessica said, reading on. "In 2001 they were listed on UNESCO's Memory of the World Programme. Cool, huh?"

"Yeah, that is. I read somewhere there are seven bridges over the river now. I bet Fa could have done with one. He told me of one horrendous crossing. Hand over hand, with weapons and radio, knowing they were sitting ducks for any CTs around."

"He was a tough nut, your Fa."

"They all were. And the bond between them, no matter what race, was tight."

"I guess it would be, if you were depending on each other for your life." Jessica looked ahead. "Pity the road keeps coming into view. There are more estates than I expected. Rubber and coconut right to the banks."

"It's deforestation that accounts for flooding each monsoon season. Panjang said it gets worse every year. And to be careful of any rains. Flash floods can, well, flash."

"As long as there aren't any crocs. They scare the hell out of me."

"Me too. I guess we'd find out who can run faster," Max said, laughing. "Once we make the turn east at Kampong Mengkarak we won't see another road until about the last thirty miles." He looked around, then at Jessica. "Is this not the coolest thing you've ever done, Jess? It is for me."

"Yeah, it is."

"You know, old Panjang was a softy. I think that's why he sold us *Munah*. He liked that we weren't in a hurry. Wanted to see his country. Tried to speak Malay, even if we mangled what little we know. And Fa, of course."

"I wonder if he was alive during the Emergency?" Jess mused.

"Hard to say. Maybe as a kid. But he would've grown up with stories. Especially around here."

***

Jessica broke their silence, although the banks were alive with jungle sounds audible over the puttering of *Munah's* engine. Panjang had told them river traffic was sparse south of Tembeling but they stuck, as much as possible, to the center of the river, hoping to avoid snags.

"I hate to say this, Max, but I need the dunny. Can we pull in?"

"Oh, okay." Max, embarrassed, looked at the map. "It'd be easier to find a sand bank first time we stop."

"Righto." Jess paused. "You're getting quite good at 'Strayan!"

"What can I say, I'm a linguist."

Max steered closer to the shore, studying the bank and river for logs. Jessica stood at the prow doing the same. She jumped into the shallows and waded to the narrow strip of muddy sand, unravelling a rope as she went. Tying off around a tree, she disappeared into the jungle. Hidden in a moment. Max rustled around in the 'hold' and found the flask of coffee. A shout jerked his attention to the tree line where he saw Jessica run and splash straight into the water, thrashing her leg around.

"What is it? Ants?"

"No, a leech. Revolting thing."

"Well doing that won't get rid of it. Here, give me your hand." Max hauled her aboard and stopped her pulling at the slug. "You know not to do that," he said.

"I know, I know, but it's disgusting. Hurry up. Get the stuff. It's in my daypack."

Max squeezed a couple of drops of eucalyptus oil on the writhing black body and watched it drop off to squirm a few seconds before dying.

"Lesson learned. For us both. Footwear, even for the quickest pee." Max started to laugh as he told Jessica the story of Frank Hobbs's leeches and the condoms, knowing she'd laugh too.

They sipped lukewarm coffee. "I don't think we should go far today. It's been a busy week, and this," Max waved at the river, "is all new to us. Do you want to stop at a kampong tonight?"

"No, let's get more practice before we have to tie up with an audience."

"Okay. Look, the road drifts inland after Kampong Kepala Pulau. That might work."

"Every name starts with either '*kuala*' or '*kampong*,'" Jess said.

"Not surprising. We're in the jungle with converging rivers and scattered villages."

Fishing in the river they had been promised teemed with delicious *jelawat* and *patin*, failed to produce anything more appetizing than footwear reeled in by Jessica from the back of *Munah*.

"Strewth, a thong!" Her comment made Max laugh from his position at the prow.

"A thong? Here? What happened to conservative Malaysia?"

"What are you on about? It's a bloody thong."

Max turned and, seeing what she was unhooking, laughed harder. "That's a flip-flop, Jess."

"It's a thong."

"In English," he explained between chuckles, "a thong is a skimpy pair of underpants."

"You mean 'knickers'?" She asked, a grin showing the slightly twisted eye tooth, the imperfection making her no less attractive. "Yeah, yeah, I know, a common language ...!" Despite a small fire on the narrow strip of land between the water and the jungle, sandflies pestered them before mosquitoes took over. Neither of them had bothered to put on long trousers or long-sleeved shirts. Between slapping bugs Jess opened two tins of sardines which she dunked in with the boiling rice. A tepid Tiger completed their supper. Boiling a billy—a purchase insisted on by Jess—they finished with a mug of tea.

"You do know this is just a small saucepan, don't you?" Max asked.

"It's as close to a billy can as I could get, so it's a billy!"

"Whatever you say, Jess. Go on, you get in. I'll hand everything back up."

Sitting on the prow they drank tea, their legs dangling above the sluggish water as they listened to the jungle sounds change as night fell. Wriggling into sleeping bags laid out either side of the hull, they settled down for the night. Max looked up at early stars glimmering in the narrow strip of sky visible along the river.

Their first night aboard was a lesson in what to do.

"Shit. We need a mossie net," Jess said. "I thought we'd be okay on the water."

The slap and flap of hands swatting mosquitoes, and muttered curses, accompanied frogs croaking and crickets and cicadas creating a forest symphony.

"Tomorrow," muttered Max from deep in his sleeping bag. "Burrow down. You'll be fine."

"Then I can't breathe." Jess's voice grumbled back.

***

Dew dampened their sleeping bags and they laid them on the prow to dry as early morning sunbeams sent shafts that turned the muddy water a shimmering ochre. Max grinned as he saw Jess disappear into the jungle, her sarong and tee shirt incongruously paired with hiking boots. He boiled the billy on the little stove and made coffee for the flask.

Digging his thumbnail into a mangosteen, he peeled the thick reddish purple skin back to reveal a cluster of glistening white kidney-shaped pods. The juice trickled down his stubbled chin.

"Did you know," Jessica's voice came from the shore, "They are known as Queen of Fruits?"

Max wiped his chin. "No, I did not know, but I'm sure you are going to tell me."

"There is no elegant way to climb into a boat. A set of steps would've been handy." She tumbled in, leech free. "Yeah, just think, if you'd managed to get a mangosteen to Queen Victoria you'd have been knighted!"

"I can see a couple of issues with that statement, but I'll let them go. Was anyone so honored?"

"Nope. They all rotted before they could get to England. The fruit. Not the men."

Max looked at Jess, a bundle of sarong and boots struggling to sit up. She and Emma together would be fun to watch, or listen to. Random pieces of information a constant entertainment.

"Here, have some," Max peeled another. "Careful, the skin stains. We don't want *Munah* marred! We also have on offer this morning, papaya, though it looks a bit green."

"Let's save that. I'll make a green papaya curry when we get a chook. I'll just have some bread and Vegemite."

"You're on your own." Max watched as Jessica spread a layer of the black paste on a thin slice of white bread, all they could find. "That truly is disgusting."

"You won't say that when you see how useful it is for cooking." She took a bite. "Yum!"

Max drank his coffee, and looked at the map.

"There's a stream of kampongs coming up. How about we go south of Kuala Krau? To somewhere more remote?"

"I'm good with wherever you want, Max."

Jessica steered *Munah*, and Max sat at the small foredeck, his toes forming their own wake.

"Let's tie up here," he called back, pointing to the left bank. This time he waded ashore and flung the rope around a trunk being strangled by a ficus whose grip would eventually kill the host. But for Max's purpose, perfect. Splashing back to *Munah*, he held his hand out for his daypack and boots then returned to shore. "Come on," he said, wading back again, "I'll take yours."

"I'm not coming. You should do this alone."

Max looked up at her in surprise and shook his head. "No, Jess. The whole point was to do this together, for them both. Come on."

Jessica searched his face then bent to collect her pack before sliding into the river.

Sitting on a log they dried their feet and tugged on socks and boots. Jessica handed over the tea-tree oil she used as an insect repellent. Checking the rope one last time, they set off. Sweat trickled down Max's face to tremble in droplets on his fast-growing beard. He slashed a path through the *ulu* with a parang he had bought at the market in Jerantut.

"Christ, this is hard. We're not going far." Max's breath came in short bursts.

"Imagine doing it whilst lugging Bren guns, radio and a full kit with CTs lurking," Jess said.

"They were better men than me!"

At the base of a massive tree, its buttresses taller than Max, he stopped.

"Fa talked about these." He patted the trunk, careful to avoid the huge thorns. "It's a ceiba or kapok. When it's bearing it sheds its foliage and the fruit hang like giant bats. The floss is like silk and they used it to stuff pillows and mattresses. Even, way back, life jackets. And the bark is used to help kids breathe. I guess they boil it up."

"A sort of inhalation," Jess said. "I'd like to study herbal remedies. There's a lot to be said for them. I picked up a book in Penang, but have only glanced through it." She looked at Max. "Why here?"

He smiled. "Fa liked luxury. What better than to be in the *ulu* surrounded by silk!"

Their quiet laughter melted through the lianas and ferns and dissolved into the jungle. Max took out the canister and holding it, looked down. Tears trembled on his eyelashes as he unscrewed the lid. He glanced at Jessica and taking her hand he upended the canister around the trunk of the ceiba. Fa's ashes fell in granules to the *ulu* floor to be cushioned by moss and leaves.

"For you, Fa. And for Dee. Back where it all started," he said, his voice a croaked whisper. "I love you."

They sat together under the kapok tree until a chittering and squeaking reverberated down the trunk, twigs and leaves falling around them. Macaques, flashes of browny-gray fur danced and swung their way through the canopy. Jessica laughed and reached, too late, for her camera.

"Come on," she said. "We'll grow roots too if we stay much longer."

They made good time as they thrashed their way back to *Munah*. Jessica climbed aboard and pulled a plastic bag tied to the side of the boat from the water and produced a bottle of Taittinger. "Not exactly iced, but it will have to do."

"Oh my God." Max grinned. "Perfect. I can almost hear Fa laughing. Where on earth did you find that?"

"Penang."

Chapter 36

THEY CHUGGED ALONG the Sungai Pahang, immersed in the country whose memories brought them together. Entertainment came from the river banks—one morning by a bulbul, its harsh song like a whistle from a builder high up a scaffold.

"It's like a lot of women." said Jessica, looking through the binoculars, "the bits taken apart are quite ordinary but put together are beautiful."

When supplies ran low they stopped at kampongs, but otherwise were happy tying up to trees. The mosquitoes had almost been beaten after they bought a large net, strung it between four of *Munah's* roof struts, and then tucked it around their sleeping bags well before dusk. An exercise which made preparations for bed time tricky, but one they were perfecting.

"I had romantic notions of slinging my hammock and sleeping in the jungle, but you can sod that," Max said, one night as they lay looking at the stars. "It must have been awful, most of the time."

"Yup, we're spoiled," Jessica said. "G'night, Max."

***

"Wake up, lazy bones." Max peered through the netting. "The billy's on."

Jessica groaned and, easing her hands out from under the sheet, flexed her fingers. Her gold ring looked tight. She stretched her neck. Her face creased in pain and she rolled over again.

"What's up?"

"I feel like shit. Let me sleep a bit longer, then I'll be right."

Max nodded, took his coffee to the foredeck and opened his notebook. His observations would be useful when it came to edits. He'd got the jungle wrong sometimes. Max wished he'd given the manuscript to Fa. Not been so precious. Stupid.

Soft moans interrupted Jess's restless sleep. Max frowned, snapped the book shut and boiled the billy. She didn't like sugar in her tea, but perhaps a hit would help. Crawling under the net, he touched her shoulder. It was hot.

"Jess, Jessica," he said softly, "come on, have a drink."

She whimpered. Her face was pale, and hair stuck in streaks across her cheek. Her eyes, when she forced them open, were bleary.

"Max, I'm crook."

"Here," he eased her up. "You've got to drink. It's sugared but it might help." Her face screwed up but there was no smile. She shuffled around to lean against *Munah's* hull. "Do you think you've got malaria?" he asked.

"No." She licked her dry lips. "I've taken the Malarone. I think this might be dengue."

"Malarone doesn't stop that?"

"Not really. My eyes hurt."

Max rootled around in her daypack and handed her the sunglasses. "Have we got something for it?"

"Acetaminophen. There's nothing else." Jessica stopped, tears leaking down her cheeks. She brushed them away wearily. "Sorry, Max. Feeling feeble."

"Don't be silly. You can't help it. Here," he said, finding the tablets. "How many can you take?"

"Give me four." She swallowed them with the rest of the tea then lay back down.

"We should get to a clinic," Max said. He pulled the map out, looking for a kampong with the distinctive red crescent marked. Dee's efforts on behalf of the Red Cross flashed through his mind.

"No. I'll be fine. Just stay put today."

Max looked around. It was isolated but sheltered from the sun on one side. There was a slight breeze. They'd stocked up on supplies the day before. They had water. He took in Jess' face bubbling with sweat. Her sunglasses slipped as she lay down with a moan.

Max unrolled his hammock, as yet unused, and unhooking part of the mossie net, clipped the cords to *Munah's* struts. He clambered into it, testing his weight against the uprights and watching the roof to make sure nothing gave.

"Jess?" he said, slipping back under the net before reclipping it. "Come on, I've rigged the hammock. It'll be gentler on your joints, and cooler."

"I'm okay," she muttered. "Don't want to move."

"No, come on." He eased her out of the sleeping sheet and, staggering a little as *Munah* lurched with their uneven weight, helped Jessica into the swaying hammock. She groaned again. Tears on her cheeks. He wet one of his tee shirts and wiped her face. Then held water to her lips. A rash appeared the next morning confirming Jessica's self-diagnosis. She swung in the hammock for three days, taking acetaminophen regularly and drinking as much as Max could coax into her. She'd cried when he had to help her pee over the side of the boat. He kept the mossie net rigged over her day and night. When he crawled under at sundown he spent the nights in his sleeping bag propped against the hull, dozing. Waking to wash and help her drink.

The third night he watched her delirious sleep and vowed the next day, despite what she wanted, they were moving on. He was out of his depth and had to find a clinic. With the decision made, Max finally slept. He woke to the trill of a songbird, one he had been watching each morning. He rubbed his eyes and looked up to find Jess peering over the edge of the hammock.

"Hey," she said, her voice croaky.

"Hey, yourself. How'd you feel?" He got to his feet and handed her water.

"Better. Weak, but definitely better. I'm sorry, Max. What a pain I've been."

"Don't be silly, Jess. You've had a rough few days. You had me worried."

"Thanks for not fussing."

With enough food for another day, and Jessica feeling better, Max changed his mind. They would stay one more day at what he called *Munah's Rest,* and continue on to the coast tomorrow. Taking it slowly. He helped Jess cool off in the river, her sarong swirling around her as she lay back in the water. Then he washed her hair with fresh water from their supply, the scent of vanilla shampoo mingling with the jungle smells, before cutting up fruit and giving her a breakfast of crackers and Vegemite. She spent the day dozing on the prow as he tidied *Munah*, washing the hammock and their sleeping bag sheets, and a couple of Jess's sarongs and tees.

After a sardine and cracker lunch, Jess dozed and Max picked up his notebook. He flicked back through his notes and grunted. A short story would need more work. His description of birds whose names he didn't know were vivid.

Black back, yellow tipping the wings and under its tail. A rosy colored chest with a white collar and yellow eyes. And topping off all that a brilliant blue beak. Can one call another bird's beak peacock blue, I wonder?

He had also described a sort of elongated but truncated cat that he thought might be a binturong. And the barking deer that came down to drink each evening, though he didn't hear them bark. Those he described as, *Pretty browny-red coats. Skittish.*

***

The expected battle to see a doctor rumbled as they edged closer to Kuala Pahang. It was a battle he doubted he'd win. Jessica stroked *Munah's* hull, tears in her eyes, before Max put her and her ruck-sack in a taxi to Kuantan, suggesting she find the nicest hotel and promising to join her as soon as *Munah* was sorted. Probably in a couple of days. They had been able to charge their phones at the customs post and so could stay in contact.

Panjang had been right. *Munah* was easily sold, though naturally for less than they had paid. Max patted her roof, as he handed over registration papers. Who knew if they were in order. He didn't care. *Munah* had been perfect for their journey. Jessica had named her well. He dropped Fa's canister in a dumpster on the way to the taxi rank.

"*Bawa saya ke Hyatt Regency, sila,*" he asked the driver.

Chapter 37

Hi Jess,

How's it going? Can you believe it's a year today since we flew out of Kuala Lumpur? Seems longer. Sorry I haven't written for a while. A lot going on.

I got through my 'bleah' patch as you called it. And, much as I hate to admit it, you were also right, it was a reaction to the excitement of getting home and seeing all the rellies—you will note I have retained my linguistic abilities and am still fluent in 'Strayan. It felt odd being back at Woodland Farm without Fa. At least Bacchus was here, currently curled around my feet in Fa's study. I still can't get used to calling it mine.

We sorted out Fa's will. Neither Susie nor Emma wanted the house so I have bought them out. Not fully paid for, but I'll get there one day. They, naturally, retain full rights to instant accommodation! Amazing. So much to thank that wonderful man for. The book is selling well—the benefit of going with a smaller publisher is that manuscripts get to the public faster—Sherry, my agent, made the right call on that one. Glad I left it up to her. I probably would've been greedy and gone for the money, even though I said I wouldn't.

How is Dee? And how is it being back in the house? It sounds fantastic. I like the idea of verandahs all the way around. Funny how things work out, isn't it? I ended up being with Fa as he got older and Dee finally decided she did want, not need of course, some company. So glad.

You said in your last email you were locumming—is that a word?—at the main hospital. Anything permanent yet?

That, Jess, is a loaded question.

What would you say to another trek? No dengue this time though, please. I'm sure that's why I have gone prematurely gray. My publicist—sounds grand but isn't as I still do all the work—wants me to do a book tour to Singapore and Malaysia. Says there's real interest in books about the Emergency, still. They'll set it up. Oh yes, and they think the Malaysian Tourism Board might be interested in me giving some talks about our trip down the Pahang. I should get old Panjang along.

Anyway, how about meeting me in KL, after all the yabbering is over?

More anon,

Max

G'day Max,

Congratulations. Delighted the book is doing well. And thank you for the autographed copies. Dee is thrilled, as am I. And Mitch, of course. I tell everyone I know a famous author. A trip sounds great but not possible. I'm getting my feet in the door at the hospital and don't want to blow that chance.

Max pushed back from the desk, his hands behind his neck. "Bugger," he said to Bacchus, then leaned forward to keep reading.

Dee's good. Feisty as ever. I love being back in the house. It felt strange living in Townsville and not being there. Glad I only rented. I'm sorry to report that I have taken a little off the verandah to build my own bathroom. Two women and one bathroom is not a good mix. Dee says it reminds her of her old lean-to bathroom in Raub. I love it. It has full length windows that open onto the garden. Enclosed, in case you were wondering. And I have a Shanghai jar! But instead of using it to slosh water over me, there's a bloody great plant in it.

I'm on nights, so must get some sleep. Sorry about the trip. Just not good timing.

Hoo roo,

Jess

Hi Jess,

No problem. It was just a thought. All good here. Great having Emma and Christopher down the road, not of course that I am spoiling my new niece. No one ever listens to me. I distinctly remember ordering a nephew. Don't know how long they'll stay put. The call of the wild, etc. The twins are gorgeous and driving their pregnant mother mad. Perhaps I'll be lucky this time. Susie doesn't want to know what she's having, so I am in a state of suspended anticipation. Mum and Dad are fine. Socializing madly as usual, though Mum is taking on less commissions these days, they seem to be getting grander. I have to say she has great taste. Don't think I could dress someone else's home up and make it seem theirs. And of course there's always a restaurant or hotel she's working on somewhere. Last stop was Minorca. Nice gig if you can get it.

Hope the nights on aren't too gruesome.

Max

***

Max looked around Emma's kitchen. A chaotic mix of paints, canvases, cameras and baby paraphernalia. His beard was grabbed by chubby fingers. He freed himself from Rose's grasp and lifted her in the air. Both Emma and Rose laughed.

"You should have a baby," Emma said, clearing a space out of Rose's reach for Max's coffee. "You're good with them. Of course you'd need to sleep with a woman first."

"Sod off!"

"Hey, not in front of the baby." Emma ducked the thrown napkin. "Really, Max. You've been a bloody monk, as far as I can figure out, since Lisa. That's over three years."

"Not entirely," Max said.

"Julia doesn't count. That was a fling with an old flame. They never count because they never go anywhere."

"Where's Christopher today?" Max asked.

"Don't dodge the issue. Go to sodding Australia. Sleep with Jessica. It will either be perfect or it will be a disaster. Either way, you'll know and can move on. This is ridiculous. Susie and I are running out of options to throw in your path."

"There's nothing there, Emma. I've told you before. We're good mates. That's it."

"Then why are you mooching around like a hang dog. You've had success with your first book. You've another almost finished. You should be floating on the moon, or at least sleeping with some of the women who keep throwing themselves at you. Get a life, Max."

"Have you finished?"

"For now," Emma said, giving him a hug. "Can you keep an eye on Rose? I want to nip into the village and pick up a few things. I still can't believe how long it takes to go anywhere with her."

"Sure. Where's Christopher?" Max asked, again.

"London. But he'll be back tonight. Meetings about a big show. I mean big."

"Where?"

"Not allowed to say. And I promised I wouldn't, even to you or Susie."

"Okay."

"Well, you could try a little harder." She said, grabbing keys, kissing Rose's curls and heading out the door. "You are staying for lunch aren't you?"

"Thanks. Can I have a look around the studio? I promise not to let the munchkin touch anything."

***

Lunch was a smorgasbord of meats and cheeses Emma picked up from the local deli, washed down with bottle of rosé. Rose was having a nap.

"Another good reason for weaning," Emma said looking at her glass.

"Thanks, Em, that was lovely. So, I do have a bit of news."

"What?"

"I'm going back to Malaysia. On a book tour. Just for a couple of weeks."

"Oh, Max, that's fantastic. Congratulations! Wow, you really are famous."

"No, just trying to get as much publicity as possible. To sell as many books as possible. So I can pay you and Susie off."

"Idiot. We are paid off." Emma said, cocking her head towards the hall, listening for her daughter. "Nope, not her."

"Well, so I can pay the bank off," Max continued. "Can you take Bacchus? He really isn't happy with Mrs. B. despite the treats she bribes him with. And when he stays with Joe Tine, he spends the whole time running home."

"'Course we will. When are you going?"

"In a month."

Hey Jess,

Well, I'm all set. Head off to Singapore next week. And end up in, of all places, Penang. I hadn't realized what a large expatriate population there is in Malaysia. I suppose we rather skirted the hotspots.

Hope your feet are becoming firmly entrenched. They'll be lucky to have you.

More anon,

Max

***

Old world charm of the Goodwood Park Hotel in Singapore greeted Max as he stepped out of the taxi. A buff envelope with the name of the agent in the corner was handed to him at reception. He tossed it, unopened, on the bed, sure it was an itinerary. Today was his.

After a nap then a swim, he dressed and ambled down to the bar with the envelope in hand. He ordered a Tiger then read the rules for his life for the next five days. A tour of Singapore. A radio interview. Back to the hotel in time to rest before a book signing and reading. Another at Kinokuniya Bookstore the next day. He was scheduled to speak to students after that.

Max grimaced and dabbed at droplets of condensation on the printed sheet. He felt a fraud. How could he talk to kids about "the writing process"? He barely had one. Yet. He'd talk about the power of raw information. Far more useful. Everyone had to find their own process.

Then, he continued to read, he'd be passed over to the publicist in each of the other towns in which he was booked to speak. Determined to see a little of the country between the two cities, he'd insisted he travel by train to Malacca and not fly. He'd upset the planners further when he said he'd drive, alone, from Malacca up the coast to Port Dickson then into KL. From there he was happy to fly to Penang.

It was a strange feeling, being fêted. One with which he wasn't entirely comfortable but, as he entered his room after his drink, admitted that at times it was rather nice. A bottle of Dom Perignon awaited him with compliments of the Goodwood Park Hotel. Along with a cheese and fruit platter. This, he grinned as the cork popped, was one of those times.

The alarm went off at 7:00 and Max awoke with a start and a fuzzy head. Idiot. Drinking the entire bottle when he knew he had to be up and sensible in the morning. On top of jet lag. He brushed his teeth, then, instead of stepping into a steaming shower, he went back down to the pool. A few lengths might help. At least the interview wasn't until after lunch.

***

The E&O Rolls Royce met Max at Penang airport, and the same manager welcomed him warmly, delightedly saying he would be staying in the same room on the second floor. He found walking into the Planters Lounge in the early evening difficult. Max shook hands and chatted with the British Honorary Consul, his host for the reception then, as the first guests entered, excused himself, knowing Mr. Dawler understood the scudding of conflicting emotions.

From the terrace Max watched clouds drift in somnolent curls across the tangerine glow suffusing the sky as the sun began its dip below the horizon across the Malacca Straits. The expectation of seeing Fa, with his silver-topped cane and wearing an immaculate summer suit with, of course, his Malay Regimental tie, stroll towards him added to the surreality. Straightening his shoulders, his grandfather's voice in his head, Max adjusted his tie in the mirror above an ornately carved teak sideboard and moved into the Planters Lounge with a smile. After being introduced he began to read:

> *The ulu swallowed the Iban tracker, then Razik carrying the Bren five paces behind him. Tom Richardson, carbine at the ready, was next. He never failed to be awed by the sinister majesty of the Malay jungle. Kapoks supported by giant buttresses. Lianas draped like colorful swags on a Christmas mantel. The omnipresent buzz of mosquitoes. And the constant need for vigilance. Sometimes the only warning of a CT ambush the chittering of a troop of macaques startled from their home in the canopy. A nod to Brian behind him and Tom hefted his pack ...*

Max glanced up to gauge the audience. He always found it difficult to know which passage to read. His eyes were drawn to the back of the lounge as a waiter bearing glasses of Taittinger opened one of the doors.

A young woman slipped in. She nodded, a glimpse of imperfection in her smile. Hair escaped the loose bun on top of her head, and curled in brown and pink streaks down her neck. She wore a dress of emerald green silk that shimmered against her long legs as she moved toward a cocktail table.

A gold ring glinted on the little finger of her right hand as she touched the jade necklace at her neck.

Glossary

amah a house servant
apa kabar? how are you? Response usually, *kabar baik* I'm fine/
   all good
attap thatch made from palm fronds

baik good
basha temporary jungle shelter
beca trishaw
belukar secondary jungle
binti daughter of
bot bot sungai river boat

CEP Captured Enemy Personnel
cepat hurry
char tea
cheongsam a tight-fitting dress often worn by Chinese women
chichak small house lizard
Chindits special operations units of the British and Indian armies
   who saw action during the Burma Campaign of World War II
CTs Communist Terrorists (initially known as bandits)

duffy patrol
dunny Australian slang for toilet

FMS Federated Malay States (Perak, Selangor, Negeri Sembilan
   and Pahang from 1910–1957)
FUBAR Fucked/Fouled Up Beyond All Recognition/Repair

Gujarati a native of Gujarat in India
Gurkhas a British Army unit made up of Nepalese soldiers,
   historically tough men

Hokkien a dialect of Chinese

Iban a native of Sarawak
ikan bilis dried anchovies
iya yes

jururawat nurse

kampong village
kris a twisted dagger

kedai makan/kedai kopi coffee shop
kongsi Chinese name for a group of workers/clan, also a group of shops
kukri curved knife used by Gurkhas

mata-mata a spy, literally meaning eyes
MCP Malayan Communist Party, also active in the resistance against the Japanese in WWII
merdeka independence
Min Yuen The People's Movement, the civilian branch of the MCP
minta maaf I'm sorry, an apology
MMR Measles, Mumps and Rubella vaccine

padang a field used for sports/parades
Paludrine antimalarial medication
parang machete

samfu blouse worn by Chinese women
SAS Special Air Service, an elite British Army unit
sampan a flat bottomed boat
SB Special Branch of the Criminal Investigation Department
sekarang now
selamat peace
selamat datang welcome
selamat jalan goodbye/safe travels
selamat malam goodnight
selamat pagi good morning
selamat petang, tuan good evening, sir
selamat tengah hari good afternoon
SEP Surrendered Enemy Personnel
sepoy a police constable
SF Special Forces
siap ready
SNAFU army slang for Situation Normal All Fucked Up
stengah literally one half, but used by the British to mean half whisky, half soda water
songkok hat worn by Malay men
sungai river

termia kasih thank you
tidak no
tidak baik not good
tiada masakah no problem
tidapa no matter?
Tommy cooker a compact portable stove

Acknowledgements

Some of the stories in this book belong to my parents with details tweaked to suit my narrative. Some research material came from my father's papers—he, for example, was credited with finding in 1953 the ancient printing press that produced the CT newspaper, *Battle News,* but the incident in the novel is fictitious. There are many wonderful books written by men, both military and police, who served in Malaya during this volatile time—the most well-known is probably *The War of the Running Dogs* by Noel Barber. *Our Man in Malaya* by Margaret Shennan about John Davis CBE, DSO and, remarkably, with a foreword by Chin Peng, is another worth reading from a long list of books I read whilst researching *Have You Eaten Rice Today?* Many of the characters are real—Bob Thompson, Bill Stafford, Lau Yew, General Sir Gerald Templer, and Irene Lee, for example.

My warmest thanks and love to Jeff St Aubyn, son of Jack, one of the two men to whom this book is dedicated in memoriam, the other is my father. Jeff lent me many of his father's books—two in particular are worth mentioning: *The Conduct of Anti-Terrorist Operations in Malaya* which covers everything from patrolling to ambushing to intelligence gathering—in essence everything to do with jungle warfare; the other is a collection of pamphlets about the Malay Regiment, detailing everything a British soldier would need to know about the country he would call home for a number of years. Jeff also showed me many of Jack's photos and papers.

My thanks also to my uncle, Robert Dick-Read, who was one of the last conscripts sent out to Malaya. The story about the Suez Canal is his!

My tried and true first readers, Kay Chapman, Sandy Lease and Val Miller, again have my eternal thanks. It doesn't seem to matter we all live in different parts of the world—their constant encouragement and support sees me through the days of "what am I doing?" I also thank Mary Cadell—we shared a dorm at NEGS, our boarding school many years ago—for her eagle eye for detail, particularly with regard to Australia. My thanks to Jo Parfitt who, over a long lunch in London, came up with the title. Thanks closer to home go to Emy Thomas whose love of Scrabble equals mine, and who is a tough grammarian and another wonderful first reader.

I am also supported by The St Croix Writers' Circle, who have listened to and commented on many parts of this book. Their understanding and acceptance of my somewhat idiosyncratic writing process, and the procrastination I am able to conjure, has kept me going.

To Vine Leaves Press and all who inhabit its space, staff and authors alike, an enormous thank you for the support, edits and encouragement. Melanie Faith, my brilliant editor, nudged me with pertinent suggestions to help take you, the reader, to these wonderful places—then and now, Malaysia, Australia and Dorset, England—thank you! My thanks to Jessica Bell for the evocative cover, and to Amie McCracken for the patient shepherding of the book to completion.

There is not much point writing books if booksellers won't sell them, so a huge thank you to Kobie Nichols, chatelaine of Undercover Books on St Croix in the US Virgin Islands for always being my first commercial supporter.

And lastly, to John. Without whose support, limitless love and encouragement I could never have started on this writing venture. Thank you!

Other Books by this Author

Crucian Fusion
Transfer
Fireburn
Expat Life Slice by Slice

Vine Leaves Press

Enjoyed this book?
Go to *vineleavespress.com* to find more.
Subscribe to our newsletter: